CAPEL BOAKE

(1899–1945) was the pen-name for the little-known Australian novelist and poet Doris Boake Kerr. The niece of the poet Barcroft Boake, she was born in Sydney, but as a child moved to Melbourne with her parents and remained there for the rest of her life. She worked as a book-keeper, was active in local literary circles and was one of the few writers of her generation to fictionalise the environment she lived in and knew so well. She wrote four novels, *Painted Clay* (1917), *The Romany Mark* (1923), *The Dark Thread* (1936) and *The Twig is Bent* (1946). She also contributed poems to a composite volume, *The Little Track, and Other Verses* (1922) and collaborated, with the poet Bernard Cronin, in *Kangaroo Rhymes* (1922) under the pseudonym Stephen Gray. A collection of her poetry was published posthumously in 1949.

VIRAGO
MODERN
CLASSIC

NUMBER

231

PAINTED CLAY

CAPEL BOAKE

WITH A NEW INTRODUCTION BY
CHRISTINE DOWNER

Virago

To Margot

Shall we weep for our Idols of painted clay,
   Salt dews of sorrow the sere blooms wetting?
Gods of the desert of dreadful day,
   Give us the gift of a great forgetting.

—Marie Pitt.

Published by VIRAGO PRESS Limited 1986
41 William IV Street, London WC2N 4DB

First published by Australasian Authors Agency, Melbourne 1917
Virago edition offset from Australasian Authors Agency 1917 edition

Copyright © Capel Boake 1917
Introduction Copyright © Christine Downer 1986

British Cataloguing in Publication Data

Boake, Capel
Painted clay.—(Virago modern classics)
Rn: Doris Boake Kerr I. Title
823[F]   PR9619.3.B/

ISBN 0-86068-766-X

Printed in Great Britain by
Anchor Brendon, Tiptree, Essex

CONTENTS.

PART I.

PART II.

PART III.

INTRODUCTION

Capel Boake is one of those women writers forgotten by compilers of Australian literary histories. Yet she was highly regarded by her fellow writers and well reviewed by contemporary critics. Her literary output was small —four novels, two volumes of collected verse, and a number of uncollected short stories. Writing was a part-time activity fitted in between working in an office or a shop and looking after her parents.

Capel Boake was born Doris Boake Kerr in 1899, the elder daughter of Gregory Augustine Kerr and Adelaide Eva Boake at Croydon, a suburb of Sydney. The family was Anglo-Irish. Her grandfather, Barcroft Capel Boake, was born in Dublin in 1838 and emigrated to New South Wales in the 1850s, where he set up as a photographer. Barcroft Capel Boake was an avowed agnostic with a very strong interest in education which he saw as the civilising influence necessary for survival in a distant colony whose new riches were founded on speculation and gold.

Following his marriage in 1865, nine children were born, only five of whom survived. Boake's agnosticism did not however extend to a belief in the state educational system and the children, including Capel Boake's mother Adelaide, were educated privately. The only boy, Barcroft, was sent to a church school to finish his education.

Capel Boake's interest in literature probably stems from her uncle Barcroft's poetry. Although trained as a surveyor, Barcroft Boake spent his formative years as a drover and boundary rider in the backblocks of Queensland and New South Wales. These experiences, and the admiration he felt for the "poet of the bush" Adam Lindsay Gordon, inspired his first attempts at verse. "For there is a romance though a grim one—a story of drought and flood, fever and famine, murder and suicide, courage and endurance", he wrote in one of his letters. These sentiments were expressed in one of the most famous of Australian bush poems, "Where the Dead Men Lie", published in the *Bulletin* in 1891, a few months before his death. Barcroft's suicide was dramatic and in this too he was influenced by Adam Lindsay Gordon. Prone to fits of depression all his life, he walked out of the house one day in May 1892, and eight days later was found hanging by his stockwhip from the branch of a tree at Long Bay.

In a memoir by A. G. Stephen who edited Barcroft's collected verse in 1897, Barcroft's father wrote 'His grandma was invalided and confined to her bed and his eldest sister (Capel Boake's mother) had found marriage a failure and was domiciled with me her husband being a hopeless creature was dismissed from the Railway Dept.' Barcroft's family was in fact dependent upon his savings of £50 for household expenses, the family fortune having disappeared in the crash of 1891.

Capel Boake's birth was recorded by her uncle Barcroft in a letter to his father. "I got a letter from Addie telling me about her little girl Doris. It is a pretty name. Fancy these two girls married and mothers! It will be right enough as long as they stop at one; but I have seen too many when I was in the Survey with big families and small salaries. Better to keep single than to drag your wife down to the level of a household drudge as many do."

Doris Kerr's family left Sydney in 1893. Writing in

the 1930s in response to a request from the noted
Melbourne collector and bibliophile John Kinimont
Moir, she mentioned her early life very briefly: "I was
born in Sydney, but came to Victoria at an early age"—
when she was four, according to her death certificate.
Her mother, faced with the necessity of supporting her
family, and having been trained by her father, worked
for a commercial photographer in the suburbs. One of
her photographs shows Doris, a beautiful child with
long yellow hair and a garland of ivy around her
shoulders.

It is not clear why, coming from a family with such a
strong belief in the benefits of education, Doris Kerr
went straight from school to work. Neither of her
sister's children is able to give a reason, apart from the
obvious one that her earnings helped to support the
family. Although badly off, the small house in the
Melbourne suburb of Caulfield belonged to them. Her
father, who may possibly have been an alcoholic, was
confined to a wheelchair because of a club foot and a
later amputation. He does not appear to have had
regular employment, although he was the draughts
correspondent for *Age* newspaper. Doris's sister, who
was two years younger, was sent to train as a teacher,
and her salary probably helped support them as well.

Doris Kerr's first work, a short story, appeared in a
Melbourne weekly newspaper, the *Australasian*, in
January 1916. She later described its publication as a
"great thrill", as her fellow writers in the same paper
included Vance Palmer, Katharine Susannah Prichard
and the poets Dorothea McKellar and Myra Morris.
When *Painted Clay* appeared in 1917, it was described
as being "in every sense an Australian book" and one
which "contrasts strikingly with the cheerful superficial-
ity and shallowness of the potboilers of some highly
popular Australian authoresses". That the novel was

not then highly regarded as a literary form is reinforced by an analysis of the published literary output between 1910 and 1917—poetry and short stories outnumbered novels by two to one.

The theme of *Painted Clay* is the isolation of the central character, Helen Somerset, and her attempts to make friends and a life for herself as an independent woman in Melbourne. She is a friendless only child living with her bitter and unstable father who has removed her from the corrupting influence of her actress mother. She grows up a lonely, old-fashioned figure in a seaside suburb made hideous by the wave of property development which followed the spread of the rail and tramway system. When her father dies, Helen is left to rely on the family next door, with whom she has struck up a casual friendship. Taken in by Mrs Hunter, the head of this ramshackle household, Helen is given her own room and made to feel as welcome as the difference between their backgrounds and characters allows. However, the opportunity of working as a shop assistant which had so appealed to her as a way of escape from an impossible life with her father gradually becomes "a passionate resentment against the monotony and uselessness of her life". The sisters Irene and Belle in her adopted family only reinforce the choices available to women of the period—"nothing to look forward to except a life spent in a shop, drawing a few shillings a week, or else marriage".

Much of the novel is based upon Doris Kerr's own experiences of work as a shop assistant and a typist. *Painted Clay* is dedicated to Margot, described by her niece as an honorary aunt who worked in the famous old Melbourne department store, Buckley and Nunn. The portrayal of the drudgery of shop assistants' and office workers' daily lives shows just how difficult it was for a single woman without family financial support to achieve independence or satisfaction. In the early years of the century, pay was low and marriage far from a universal option. Even before the terrible casualties of the First World War, the numerical imbalance between men and women meant that many women would remain single.

Helen Somerset, however, is convinced that the "gods held something wonderful in store for her". The attraction which she feels towards George Angliss, nephew of Mrs Hunter, is held in check by her determination to widen her experiences. With a group of new friends, including men, the hatred and bitterness which she felt towards her father, and the misery of her mother's abandonment, become less intense. Introduced to the artistic world by her new friend Ann Wilson, a country girl whose parents allow her an income to study at an art school, Helen insists that she be accorded the same freedom as men in forming relationships. Whilst believing that marriage is not the necessary foundation of a sexual relationship, Helen's resolve is insecure, for her desire for experience is undercut by the nagging doubt that as her mother "was only painted clay" perhaps she is also. She develops a relationship with the artist Alick Russell, but as it intensifies, Helen's feelings towards her unmarried state fluctuate and she questions her "goodness" in not only accepting such a relationship but also in resisting the bonds of marriage. Helen's adolescent belief that she is "one of the favoured children of fortune" is a naïve one. She is seeking an ideal which is baseless because it is not founded in experience. Her goal is happiness and it is only when Helen has experienced the unhappiness which is the reverse of her ideal that she can come to a fuller and more mature understanding of herself and develop a more mature relationship with a man.

Doris Kerr was twenty-eight when *Painted Clay* was published. The title is taken from a poem by Marie Pitt, a familiar figure in feminist and socialist circles. Although adopting a masculine sounding pseudonym as many women had done before her, Doris Kerr let it be known that this was for family remembrance rather than disguise. Those who read the Melbourne weekly, *Table Talk*, in July 1917 would have seen her photograph, taken in the front garden of the house in Keeron Street, Caulfield, and known from the caption that Capel Boake and Doris Kerr were the same person.

Painted Clay is not easy to place in the history of the Australian novel of the period, having little in common with them in subject matter or setting. In a foreword to a posthumous collection of Doris Kerr's poetry in 1949, her friend Myra Morris wrote that her work was distinguished by its closeness to everyday life. Despite its rather theatrical overtones, the novel succeeds in presenting a convincing picture of the working life of women who had only their own wits and energy to rely upon. Its pictures of urban life stand out in a period when both writers and artists considered that the essence of Australia was to be found in chronicles of bush life and interpretations of the landscape. Doris Kerr wrote three other novels, the last published posthumously. *The Romany Mark* she described as "only a thriller" when it was published in 1922. *The Dark Thread* (1936) is considered by many to be her best work. It too is a novel of urban life in Melbourne whose central character, Solomon Burton, marries a girl whom he knows to be pregnant with another man's child. "The dark thread" is their children's Jewish blood which draws them to the Zionist movement. Her last work, *The Twig is Bent* (1946), was written with the assistance of a grant and was probably inspired by the celebrations of the state of Victoria's centenary in 1934. Like many projects inspired by such events, it is lacking in interest and substance. An historical novel based on Victoria's founding, the characters are wooden and the events described, though

INTRODUCTION

historically accurate, are dull. Doris Kerr collapsed and
died suddenly in the front garden of the house where
she lived with her mother in 1944. Her personal pos-
sessions were few—a collection of books and a black
opal ring.

Painted Clay is a minor novel which deserves a new
generation of readers. Doris Kerr and her work form
part of a wide female culture which has largely been
neglected, possibly because the majority of creative
women in the period 1901 to 1917 were middle class
with private incomes or other means of family support.
Many of these women were unmarried. They, like
Doris Kerr, tended to form intensely close female
friendships which lasted a lifetime. Their lives were
bound up not only with their friends, but with their
fathers' occupations, and their mothers' charitable and
social work. Doris Kerr, having worked all her life
because it was financially necessary, did not have the
leisure which many of these women used so productively
in their chosen fields. It is a testament to the obscurity
of her life that so little is known about her and so little
can be discovered. A study of the contribution women
made to the creative life of Australia in the early years
of the twentieth century will help place Doris Kerr in
context, and accord her the position she deserves in
Australian literature.

Christine Downer, Melbourne, 1986

PAINTED CLAY

CHAPTER I.

THE HOUSE IN CHARLES ROAD.

Years ago the suburb of Packington had been a stretch of green, hilly land, covered with gum trees, overlooking Port Phillip Bay, and Melbourne. The advent of building speculators, trams and trains had changed all that, however, and now it was a popular, middle-class suburb, proud of its huge shops, State School, Public Gardens and Library. Through the main streets thundered the electric trams on their way to the city, and hundreds of people thronged the busy streets all hours of the day. Packington had rapidly become the busiest suburb outside Melbourne.

The sea had faded into the blue distance and now the only view to be had was that of the tall chimneys of the factories and the red roofs of the thousands of little villas that had sprung up, mushroom-fashion, all over the surrounding district. The curious visitor, looking casually as he passed by at one or two of the older houses would wonder why they were named, so inappropriately, "Bay View," and "Sea View." He did not realise that he was looking at a link with the past.

Charles Road was a typical suburban street, narrow and dusty. All the houses were semi-detached villas, each with a little piece of garden in front. With the love of the average Australian for flowers, each garden was carefully tended and bright with geraniums and nasturtiums. Some of the more ambitious houses had neat little lawns with a few rose trees and borders of many colored pansies. White lace blinds concealed the life that went on within, and each household was an enigma to the other.

At the end of the street stood a house of a slightly different appearance. It looked more careless and more haphazard, and the blinds and the window curtains showed no evidence, as the others did, of a careful housewife. Someone had evidently made an effort to make a garden, and then, tiring of it suddenly, left off. For the ground in front was half dug up and a few plants put in, and then left to grow carelessly among the thick, rank weeds that now overgrew all the plots. A few lilies bloomed spasmodically, and in the spring one side of the house was a riot of wistaria blossom and banksia roses.

The women of the street, on their way to the market, looked askance at this house. The unknown always excites suspicion, and the house was looked upon as a disgrace to the street. Several women had watched carefully and had made sure that the curtains had not been down for months. They always took their curtains down, washed them, and put them up again, every four weeks. The end house did not do this. Therefore there must be something very wrong with the occupants of the end house.

In this dull suburban street and in this attitude of suspicion and distrust, Helen Somerset had lived for the last ten years. Dimly, as in a dream, she remembered a life somewhere else—a life which ended abruptly—and a mother who cried, kissed her, and then disappeared. There was a gap in her memory here, and the next she remembered was being brought by her father and a strange woman to this house, and being told that this was now her home. She had wept and demanded her mother, and her father, with an abrupt gesture, had motioned to the woman to take her away. She had been gathered up in ruthless arms and put to bed, where she cried herself to sleep, sobbing for her mother.   Later on, when she was older, she learnt never to speak of her.   Asking her father to tell her about her mother, he had silenced her with a look, and the sensitive child shrank away from him, trembling.

Her father was a morose, melancholy man, much given to fits of brooding.   He would sit for hours, with his head sunk on his breast, and nothing could rouse him.   Helen would look at him with fear in her eyes, for his awful silence alarmed her.   She would speak to him timidly, and he would raise his heavy eyes, look at her without speaking, and turn away.   Then she would rush outside, biting her lips and clenching her hands, and when safely out of hearing, burst into tears, and mutter:—

"I can't bear it.   I can't bear it.   Oh God! save me from this life."

Arthur Somerset had not always been like this. He was a cultivated man, with literary instincts and artistic tastes.   He refused to send his daughter to school, and educated her himself.   The child had thrilled and responded, like a sensitive plant, to her father's teaching.   The ordinary education of an average child had been almost entirely neglected, but he taught her to love history, not only the history of her own race, but that of other races, and she loved poetry with a passion that equalled his own. The only luxury they had in the house was the library.   This room was lined with books and all were open to her, for her father placed no restrictions on her reading.   At the age of fifteen she had read Tolstoy's "Resurrection," and Zola's "Paris" and "Rome."

When she was thirteen years of age, the woman who had looked after them for so long left to be married, and no one had taken her place.   Arthur Somerset said that now Helen was old enough to be left by herself, and he did not like strangers in the house.   He went into town three days a week, where he had some pupils whom he coached for the University examinations. Helen was content to be left alone, and quite unconsciously came to look forward to the days when her father was out. She took on the household duties as a matter of course, and the women in the street had often smiled at the quaint little figure, basket in hand, who regularly every Saturday morning did her modest shopping. At first a few of them had good naturedly offered to help, and on one or two occasions had asked the child to their homes. But Helen was shy and her father sternly forbade her to visit anyone in the street, so the women soon got tired of asking her and left her severely alone. She had longed to respond to their motherly advances, but her father refused to allow it and, though she had wept bitterly, she had obeyed him. Now when she went out people looked at her curiously, but made no attempt to speak. Sometimes the children would shout out at her, but she only held her head down and hurried on. The State School was just round the corner from her home, and if she ever had occasion to pass when the children were coming out or were in the playground, she would run by on the other side, followed by their jeers and laughter.

At the age of sixteen she was a tall, slight, undeveloped girl, with a mass of reddish brown hair, and dark, thoughtful eyes. More often the curious glances which followed her in the street, which she took for scorn and contempt, were of half-wondering admiration, for the girl gave promise of quite unusual good looks and had a natural grace and distinction of carriage. She was less at ease with people now than she had been when she was twelve, even though for the last two years she had met a few girls of her own age.

Her father never spoke to her of religious matters, but he gave her a Bible when she was old enough, and told her to read it. She spent many hours over it, studying it gravely, and Arthur Somerset often smiled queerly when he saw the childish head bent so seriously over the book.   Later on he taught her the principles of evolution, and gave her "The Descent of Man," which she absorbed with avidity. From these readings she emerged with a muddled idea of a God who was apt to be very angry, and would severely punish any disobedience to any of His commandments.   She always said her prayers at night, and begged for a blessing on her father, quite convinced that if she omitted this simple precaution, some awful calamity would befall them.

Mr. Robinson, t, e minister of the church close by, shocked at the thought of the girl growing up without any religious instruction, administered in the correct manner, called on them and, giving Arthur Somerset up as hopeless, begged that at least the girl might be allowed to go to Church and Sunday School. With a shrug of his shoulders, Somerset consented, and Helen was sent, miserable and unhappy, to the Sunday School.   The first few weeks were a time of absolute terror to her, and during the whole two years she spent at the Sunday School, she barely spoke or was spoken to by any of the girls.   They knew who she was; that she came from the strange house round the corner, with the broken blinds and shabby window curtains, and she shrank from their sidelong glances and whispered words.   She longed for their companionship though, and after the class was over, she would walk away alone, looking enviously, and with a little catch in her breath, at the others, who walked off together arm in arm, laughing and talking.

She loved madly, for a time, the woman who taught her in the school, for the girl's long repressed affections were crying for an outlet.   She held long imaginary conversations with her, and created a drama in which she played the leading part, and Mrs. Roberts was a sympathetic audience.   Mrs.

Roberts was quite unconscious of Helen's feelings towards her, for she had made some tentative advances at first, but Helen's aloof and almost haughty manner repelled her, and she had desisted. The woman herself was a dark-eyed, austere creature, with a certain sardonic humor at times.

"Paste your daily texts on your mirrors, girls," she told her giggling class, "then you will be sure to see them."

Once, and only once, did Helen have a private conversation with her teacher, and this destroyed for ever any hope she might have cherished that they would eventually become friends.

Helen's reply to a question asked during the class had shocked and horrified her teacher. She told Helen, looking at her severely over the top of her glasses, to stay behind when the others had gone. Trembling slightly, and with her heart beating strangely, Helen did so. She watched, almost with a feeling of panic, the other girls leaving the room. For once she was impervious to their whispers and half-jeering smiles. Her teeth chattered slightly, but she clenched them together with an effort. More than the terror of the interview itself was the terror of betraying to the other the fear she felt.

Mrs. Roberts saw all the other girls out of the room, and then came back and drew a chair up close to Helen. She was unconscious herself of her terrible sombreness and impressiveness, but the sensitive girl was quivering to it and keying herself up to meet the onslaught. She felt that she had said or done something wrong, but had not the slightest idea what it was.

Mrs. Roberts looked at her gravely, and Helen met her eyes. The woman did not know the effort it cost the girl to do this, and could not appreciate her courage. As it was she thought it an impertinence, for she would have preferred the girl to hang her head and blush, and display a proper feeling for the enormity of her offence. As Helen appeared quite unconcerned, she was prejudiced against her from the beginning.

She picked up a Bible lying on the table, and tapped it impressively with two fingers.

"Helen," she said, "you amazed me during class. I have taught many girls, but never have I have heard one say such blasphemous words as you did to-day."

Helen's lips trembled, but she steadied them again. Her eyes looked a little brighter with the unshed tears that she was too proud to let fall.

"I don't remember what words you mean," she said.

"Don't remember?" repeated Mrs. Roberts. "Why, that is worse than I thought. What do you mean by saying that the world was not made in seven days?"

"But," stammered Helen, "I don't believe it was."

"Child! Child!" said Mrs. Roberts gravely. "Do you want to go to everlasting damnation?"

Helen could not reply. She was suffering from a revulsion of feeling. Her nervousness had forsaken her, and also her transitory affection for this unsympathetic woman, who looked at her with such a hard and cold expression.

"I can't believe that the earth was made in seven days, when my father has taught me that it was not," she said at last. "My father says that Darwin ——"

Mrs. Roberts interrupted her angrily.

"How dare you mention that name in this room?" she asked.

Helen said nothing, for there seemed nothing to say. She only wondered to herself how she could ever have felt any affection for this woman.

"Mr. Robinson must speak to you," she continued. "I feel that I cannot deal with you. This is too awful."

She really was shocked and horrified, for she was almost a fanatic in her religious beliefs.

Helen rose. "Can I go now?" she asked. "It is late and my father will be getting impatient for his tea."

"Yes," replied Mrs. Roberts. "You can go now, but I cannot have you in my class again, until you apologize to me."

"Apologize to you?" asked Helen, with a wicked little devil springing up in her heart. "It is not you I have offended against, is it? You didn't say you made the earth in seven days, did you?"

Mrs. Roberts flushed crimson with anger and mortification.

"You are extremely rude," she said coldly, "but that remark is only what I should have expected from anyone holding the beliefs you do. Go and apologize to your God."

Helen turned to leave the room, and then horrified at her behaviour, she made an attempt to apologize.

"Please forgive me," she muttered. "I didn't mean to be rude. I can't imagine what came over me."

Mrs. Roberts motioned her away.

"I'll forgive you," she said, "only when you come to me and tell me you believe."

Helen looked at her quietly for a moment with her disconcertingly clear eyes, and then walked slowly away. She was taking her mental farewell of the room and of the woman with whom she had been so unhappy for two long years.

When she had gone, the woman drew a long breath and sighed as if from relief.

"The girl is impossible," she thought. "I must send Mr. Robinson to her. Perhaps he will be able to turn her mind to God."

She picked up the Bibles and hymn-books that were lying about the room, and went in search of the minister. Not often had she to take such a bombshell to him.

Helen walked home slowly and deep in thought.
So that was over.   She knew that she could never
go back to the school again.   Two years she had
spent there and she left as friendless as when she
started.

After tea her father settled himself in his library
to read.   She came in softly and stood hesitatingly
by the table.

"Father," she said, after a moment's thought.
"Need I go to Sunday School any more?"

He put his fingers between the pages of the book
he was reading and looked up.

"Why?" he asked.   "Tired of it?"

"It's not that," she replied, "but I don't think
they will want me to come back."

"What has happened?" he asked.

"We were having a lesson about the origin of the
world and I said I did not believe it was made in
seven days.   I was rude to the teacher about it too."

Arthur Somerset threw back his head and laughed,
and Helen realised that it was the first time she had
heard her father laugh.   The sound seemed strange
to her.

"So they didn't like it, and they kicked you out?"
he said.

"They say I can't go back until I do believe it."

He looked at her curiously.

"What are you going to do?" he asked.   "Are
you going back?"

She shook her head.   "No, I don't believe it," she
replied.

"Um! well—there's no necessity for you to go
back.   You are old enough to leave."

He opened his book again and resumed his reading.

Helen never went back again.   The minister called a
few days later and saw her father, and there was an
interview during which Arthur Somerset looked
merely bored, and the minister flushed and angry.
He left the house abruptly, registering a mental vow

never to darken its doors again, and Somerset watched
him go, and smiled inscrutably.

The two years spent at the school had left their
impression on Helen's mind.   Mentally she was
keenly and vividly alive.   Her mind teemed with a
thousand questions as to life, and there was no one
to answer them for her.   She was beginning to think
and wonder too about her own life.   She had heard
the girls speaking of their future, for all of them
would eventually have to work for their living; indeed some of them were already apprenticed to dress-
makers and milliners in the district, and Helen envied
them their fancied independence.

What was to become of her, she wondered?
Surely all her life wasn't to be spent alone with
her father?   She shuddered at the idea, for she was
beginning to feel her father's manner more and more
oppressive.   She wanted to suggest to him that she
should be taught something so that she might be able
to earn her own living—but she dared not.   When
she was away from him, she felt brave and capable
of anything, but when she tried to speak to him,
her courage ebbed away.

For the last few days he had been in one of his
most forbidding moods; never speaking, not even
reading, just sitting at his writing-table staring aimlessly before him.   These moods wrought Helen up
almost to a pitch of desperation, for her nerves were
beginning to feel the strain.   She looked forward
with joy and longing to the day when he had to go
into town.

At last it came.   He had been locked up in his
library all the morning, and after lunch, to Helen's
inexpressible joy, she saw him take up his stick
and hat.   He left the room, and she listened,
trembling with fear lest she should have been mistaken.   Then she heard the door open and slam—
he was gone.   At last she was alone!   She danced
round the table joyfully.   He was gone, and she was

free from him for the whole afternoon.   The terrible weight of oppression that had been hanging over her lifted.   She finished her work hastily, put on her hat and went out.

Next door two girls were hanging over the gate. They both went to business at one of the large shops in Packington, and this was evidently their half-holiday.   They looked at Helen curiously as she passed, and she glanced at them with a faint smile, half-wistful and longing, if they had only had the understanding to read it aright.   But they merely thought of her as proud, and what they designated to themselves as ''stuck-up.''

She spent most of the afternoon in the large public gardens, and then as the shadows began to lengthen, she hurried off, stopping in the Main Street to buy something for her father, whose appetite was capricious.   She was standing outside a fruit shop and looking in the window thoughtfully, when she heard a voice say:

''Look, Sue, what a glorious scheme!   The sun gleaming on that girl's hair and on that heap of oranges.   By Jove!   I'd like to paint it.''

''Hush Jack, she'll hear you,'' said another voice, but in a lower tone, then as Helen turned round, wondering of whom they were speaking—''Why, what a pretty girl.''

Crimson with embarrassment, Helen realised that they were speaking of her.   Without waiting to hear any more she fled like a startled fawn down the street.   When she had gone some distance she looked back.   They were still looking after her, and laughing.

''Everyone seems to laugh at me,'' she thought bitterly.

But the words remained in her mind.   She had never thought about her looks before.   As no one seemed to like her, she had taken it for granted that she was plain and uninteresting.   This chance conversation, overheard in the street, therefore altered the whole outlook of her life.

"Am I really pretty?" she thought to herself, her cheeks flushing with pleasure. Then she became despondent again, for she was afraid to believe it.

Her father was unusually late that evening, and she wondered idly what was keeping him. A sudden thought struck her, and she went outside and looked down the street to see if he was coming. No, it was all right, there was no sign of him. She went inside into her own room and brought out the little mirror she had, the only one in the house. She stood at the window and examined her features attentively and gravely. So immersed was she in what she was doing that she did not hear the door open, and her father come in. He stood at the door watching her, and a spasm of anger crossed his face.

"So!" he said.

She turned quickly round, startled and ashamed.

"Be careful, my girl," he said coldly. "Be careful! You come of a bad stock."

For a moment Helen stared at him, meeting his cold, hard eyes; then with a cry she flung the mirror on the floor, and ran into her own room.

He bent down and picked up carefully the broken pieces.

"Yes," he muttered. "A bad stock. A bad stock."

Then he sat down at the table and began his meal.

CHAPTER II.

Helen, angry and ashamed, locked herself in her own room.

"He doesn't care about me," she thought bitterly. "I could die, and it wouldn't matter to him. Why is he so unkind to me?"

She leant out of the window, and the night air cooled her flushed cheek. The wistaria was all in bloom, and its perfume scented the air. She plucked a cluster and pressed it to her lips. Its delicate perfume made her feel inexpressibly sad.

Next door she could hear the people moving about, the chink of china and the low hum of conversation. A spasm of envy cut through her heart—they seemed to be so gay and happy, how different to her dull, gloomy home. She could hear a girlish voice speaking, and then laughter. No one ever laughed when she spoke, or even listened. If her mother had been alive it might have been different, or if she had had brothers and sisters to laugh and play with as others did.

She looked up at the little piece of sky she could see between the two houses, and a sudden sense of its calm aloofness soothed her troubled mind. Then across the night came the sound of a piano and someone singing in a clear, sweet voice. She listened intently, leaning further out. It was only a trivial ballad from a comic opera, but it held a curious soothing charm for the lonely girl. It seemed to bring her closer to the people in there.

She had forgotten her father and her angry thoughts, listening in a sort of half-dreamy content, when she heard his door slam loudly. That brought her back to reality with a start, and her ready anger flew back. Evidently the music did not please him,

(19)

and with flushed cheeks and eyes still bright with the tears she had shed, she fiercely wished they would continue.

"Anything to annoy him," she whispered. "I don't care."

As she thought of him an immense passion welled up in her heart.

"I hate him!"

She said it at first very low, as though almost afraid of hearing herself speak. Then, gaining courage, she repeated it louder.

"I hate him! I hate my father!"

She looked round triumphantly. She had deliberately disobeyed one of the commandments and nothing had happened to her. She whispered the commandment to herself:—"Honor thy father and thy mother." Then said again, loudly and clearly:—

"I hate my father."

She sighed with relief, and a tremendous weight rolled from her heart. You could disobey the commandments with impunity then? That being so, there was no need to be frightened of her father any more.

She opened the door and went out into the hall. There was a light shining from under the library door, so probably he was reading. She opened the door softly, but he heard her come in, and looked up with a heavy frown, for he was not used to being disturbed in his library at night. For a moment her courage faltered, but only for a moment. She remembered she had defied a greater than her father; she had defied God—and nothing had happened! She met his eyes with a glance so reckless and defiant that he was roused to momentary interest in her.

"Why, what's the matter?" he asked, half-rising from his chair.

"It's all right, Father," returned the girl, looking at him coldly. "Nothing has happened, only I want to have a talk with you."

He passed his hand over his forehead. For the moment he felt dazed, as she had taken him entirely by surprise.

"How like she is growing," he muttered. "How like—how like!"

"I can't hear what you're saying, Father," said Helen, in a clear, hard voice. "Please speak up."

Arthur Somerset, however, had now recovered his composure. He leant back in his chair, fingering the paper knife, and smiled quietly.

"My dear Helen, would you mind telling me what has happened to you to-day? First of all, I come home and find you studying yourself in the glass. By-the-bye, I hope the sight afforded you pleasure. Did it?"

He looked at her keenly, and smiled slightly as he saw her flush.

"What! no answer? Well, I hope that it did, for there is nothing that will take you women through the world so well as a steadfast belief in your own charms. Keep that belief, my dear girl, even if you throw everything else away."

She looked at him contemptuously, with her fine lip curling a little.

"Oh, you can sneer," she said, "but you can't make me angry." She paused, and then continued, "I am glad sometimes, when I look at you and think how you treat me, that my mother is dead."

He shrank visibly, and Helen smiled as she saw how her shaft had struck home.

"You did not think I would mention my mother's name, did you? You thought you had trained me too carefully for that."

She drew a chair up to the table, and sat down, facing him.

"Well, you see, you have made a mistake. I have been afraid of you all my life, but now—now—I am free!" She smiled exultingly. "I am not afraid of you any longer."

He rose to his feet, his face almost livid with anger.

"Go to your room," he shouted.

She shook her head.

"No, I won't go, and there is no use shouting at me. Do you know what I said when I was in my room? I said 'I hate my father,' and now I feel that you will never have any power to hurt me or frighten me again. All that has gone. But now there are a lot of things I want to ask you, and a lot of things I want to know."

His anger cooled suddenly, and he looked at his daughter with a half-unconscious admiration, for he liked her spirit. He saw that it had come to a duel between them, and she had won the first round, got in the first shot.

"Well," he said quietly. "What is it you want to know?"

Helen hesitated. What was there she did not want to know? Now that she had won, her spirit almost failed her; she suddenly felt tired and depressed. If her father had only loved her, how she would have loved him. Was it too late? She looked at him half in doubt. Yes, too late. There was no sign of affection in his face. He looked cold and hard, and all her antagonism flew back to her aid.

"First of all," she said slowly. "I want to know why you said I came of a bad stock."

Her father leant across the table with a smile so hateful that almost involuntarily she drew back.

"Do you?" he said. "Do you?" And he smiled again. "I suppose you have read your Bible well?" he asked.

Helen nodded, wondering what that had to do with it.

"Have you ever come across the word 'adulteress'?" he asked.

"Yes," she replied, looking at him steadily, though her eyes had clouded with a little shadow of thought.

"Do you know what it means?"

She did not reply, but dimly through her mind ran hideous things she had read, but did not understand.

"No, I see that you don't.   Well, keep the word in your mind, and when you learn what it means, think to yourself—'My mother was an adulteress.'"

Helen sprang to her feet, and stood looking down at him, her face pale, and her lips curved in a scornful line.

"Whatever you tell me," she said, almost in a whisper, "you cannot make me hate my mother.   I know whatever she did, that it was your fault."

That shook him, for he winced under the blow.

"My fault!" he half groaned.   "You don't know what you are saying.   I tell you she was bad—rotten to the core."

"I don't believe it," cried Helen.

"You don't believe it?"   He looked at her sombrely.   "You don't believe it?   And what do you know about it?"

He fell to pacing up and down the room, muttering to himself, and it seemed as if he had forgotten her.   She watched him curiously, listening intently to what he was saying.

"What can anyone know of my suffering and despair, when I lost her—when I lost her?"   He was silent for a moment, with his head sunk on his breast. "But I made her suffer," he cried in a louder voice. "I had my revenge."

She watched him with a puzzled frown.   What was he talking about, and what did it all mean. What was that he said?   His revenge!

"Father!" her voice cut sharp as a knife across his mutterings.   "Father! tell me—what do you mean by revenge?"

"Ah! my revenge!"   He paused in his restless walk, and came closer to her.   "You would like to know?   Well, you shall.   I struck at her through the thing she loved best.   I struck at her through you."

"Through me?"

"Yes, through you. Listen, this is how it happened." He spoke quickly, as if he were laboring under intense excitement. "When she left me, she took you with her. She thought she had covered up her tracks well, but I followed and found her. She had given you into the charge of a woman close to where she was living. I went there and took you away. You cried, I remember, and struggled with me, for you didn't want to come. Then I went to her and told her what I had done. She begged me, begged me on her knees to let her have you. I laughed at her. Then she offered to return"—he paused, and his face worked strangely—"offered to return. I could hardly keep my hands from her throat."

Helen listened to him, her face drained of every vestige of color.

"But—but—I don't understand," she faltered. "Is my mother still alive?"

"Alive?" He laughed harshly. "Oh, yes, she's still alive."

"Then where is she?"

"I don't know."

"All these years, then," said Helen slowly, "I've had a mother, and you never told me. You stole me from her. You've cheated me."

"Cheated you, have I? And of what has your mother cheated me? She betrayed and deceived me. You were my child, and I claimed you."

"I am more her child than yours," cried Helen, "I know it. I know it!"

He was silent, and his hand shook violently, he clenched it on the table to steady it.

"Why did you take me from her?" she asked. "Not because you loved me, but because you—hated her."

"You're right," he answered. "I hated her. I tore you from her heart, and left her with her—lover."

She recoiled, for his brutal words and manner shocked and horrified her. She felt too tired to speak, for all her energy seemed drained out of her. She leant her head on her hand and thought of what he had told her. How horrible it all was! Who was this man her mother was with? She raised her head, half inclined to ask the question, but changed her mind. After all, what was the use? Her mother had loved someone else better than she had loved her own child. That was enough to know.

"She ought not to have left me alone with you," she muttered at last. "She might have tried to find me. Though I suppose," she added bitterly, "she has forgotten all about me by this time."

He shrugged his shoulders, and sat down at the table again, taking up his pen, his emotions well in hand now. He held up his hand, watching it curiously. Yes, it was quite steady again.

He seemed almost inhuman to Helen.

"Father!" she cried passionately. "How can you sit there as if nothing had happened. Tell me, why is it we are like this? Why have you never loved me?"

He looked up impatiently.

"Now, my dear Helen, haven't we had enough of this for one night? There is nothing more I have to say."

"I won't let you chill me," she said, "you must hear what I have to say. How can we go on like this, day after day, as we have been doing? I can't bear it. Father, let me go away."

"Where can you go?"

She was silent for a time. Where could she go? Whom did she know who would welcome her and take her in?

"I must do something," she said at last. "I can't live this life for ever. I might as well be dead as live alone with you here. I have no friends, and don't seem able to make any. Everyone in the street shuns us. I don't mind that very much, but I wish I had some friends, even one friend would make me happy," she added wistfully.

"Friends!" said her father. "You're better without friends."

"I want friends," said Helen, not heeding him. "I want people to love me, and I want to be happy. I want to go out into the world and learn things. I don't know anything of life, except what these books have taught me," she swept a contemptuous arm around the room, "and I'm tired of books. Father! let me try and see if I can get work to do."

"Nonsense," he said, "it's impossible. No one would take you."

"I don't care what it is," said Helen. "Anything would be better than living here in stagnation." She rose to her feet. "Well, I've made up my mind, Father, I'm going to try."

He did not reply, and she walked slowly out of the room, closing the door very gently behind her, restraining a sudden desire to slam it. When she had gone, he threw down his pen and took a faded pocketbook out of his desk. Opening this, he drew out a photograph of a woman which, with frowning eyes and close set lips, he looked at for a long time. Then he put it back again and relapsed into one of his fits of melancholy brooding.

Helen's resolve to try and get out of the groove she was in, only hardened as she thought the position over. She would do it if she had to walk into every shop in Packington and ask for employment. The two girls who lived next door went to business somewhere in the suburb. She knew that, for she had often watched them going off in the morning, and envied them. They were not very much older than she, and surely if they could get employment, she could. She wondered if they would help her? Perhaps they would give her some advice, and tell her what to do. She shrank inwardly at the thought of approaching strangers, but the more she thought of it, the more she was inclined to do it.

During the next few days her father barely spoke to her, and she did not open the subject again with him. She was content that he should ignore it. Even his fits of melancholy abstraction left her unmoved, for her mind was busily engaged on the problem of how to strike up an acquaintance with one or other of the girls next door. She made one or two ineffectual efforts, but at the last moment could not do it. At last, however, just as she was beginning to despair, fate threw the opportunity in her way.

One evening she had hurried out at about six o'clock to buy something she had forgotten, when, coming home, she noticed in front of her the elder of the two girls. Now was her opportunity if she could take it. Could she? She was hesitating, when she noticed that the girl had dropped something. Hurrying forward, she picked it up. It was a letter. She ran on, and gave the letter to the girl, who took it with a word of thanks, and a half smile of recognition.

"You live next to us, don't you?" she asked. Helen shyly admitted that she did.

"It was lucky for me that you were coming after me. I wouldn't have lost this letter for anything." Helen murmured that she was glad she had been of use.

"I assure you," continued the girl, who was a voluble young person, with bright, blue eyes, and an open, engaging manner, "I don't know what I should have done. You know," dropping her voice to a confidential undertone, "you don't like to lose your love-letters, do you? Not that I mean that there is anything special in this, but still you don't like to lose them. But you are too young to know anything about that sort of thing yet, I suppose?"

"I don't know anyone who would like to write me love-letters," said Helen.

The girl gave a sudden, loud laugh, and looked at Helen quizzically.

"Don't you worry about that, heaps of men will, if you only give them half a chance."

But Helen was not interested in the least, either in men or love-letters. She wanted desperately to ask this girl's advice, and here they were almost at home, and she had not even attempted to open the subject. True, she had not had much opportunity, as the girl had done all the talking.

The girl paused at her own gate.

"Well, here we are," she said, "and you really are an awfully decent little sort, after all. The next time you pass us, don't go by with your head in the air, as if we were dirt."

Helen flushed in painful confusion. "Really I never, never did that. I always longed to speak to you, but I did not think you wanted me."

"Well, we always thought you a proud little minx, you know. Never mind, girlie," she added kindly, seeing Helen's embarrassment, "we'll know better next time. Come in and see us one night, will you?" She rattled on without waiting for Helen's answer. "Don't forget, I'll expect you. Good-bye!" and she turned to go.

"Please would you wait a moment?" asked Helen diffidently. "I want to ask you something."

The girl looked rather surprised.

"Yes, of course," she said. "What is it?"

"I want to know how I could get something to do," Helen said, rather hesitatingly. "You work in a shop, don't you? Do you think I could possibly get a position anywhere?"

"You? But what do you want to work for?"

"I want to be able to earn my own living. I can't expect my father to keep me all my life."

"Well, there's no reason why you shouldn't earn your own living, but you won't get much money at first, and you won't like the work, I'm sure."

"Oh I will, I will," said Helen passionately. "I don't care how hard I have to work, or what I do."

"Well," said the girl thoughtfully, "I think I might be able to help you. Look here, can you come in and see me to-night? I have an idea that my sister Irene said that one of the girls in the shop where she works, was going to leave in a couple of days. That might suit you all right, if you care about it. Come in about eight o'clock."

"Thank you," said Helen gratefully. "How kind it is of you to bother about it like this."

"Nonsense," said the girl good naturedly. "Why, that's nothing at all, and in any case we'll be glad to see you."

She waved her hand gaily and disappeared.

Helen walked home with a light heart, for she had taken the first step at last and the future beckoned alluringly before her. She waited on her father at the table, singing softly to herself.

"You seem happy!" he said, with a slight sneer.

"I am," she answered.

He said nothing further and bent over his meal in silence. Shortly after he rose from the table and shut himself in his library.

She watched the hands of the clock with a sense of the keenest anticipation. At last!—eight o'clock —now a little past eight. It was time to go and, with a feeling of adventure stirring in her blood, she stole quietly from the house.

CHAPTER III.

The house next door was brightly lit up, and through the open windows came the pleasant sound of voices and laughter. The garden was neatly kept with narrow little asphalte paths, and the imitation-copper decorations on the door shone with constant polishings.

Helen lifted the knocker, which was carved into the head of a lion, and used it gently. Her first timid knock had no effect, and after waiting a couple of minutes with fast-beating heart, she knocked again—but louder this time. She heard hasty footsteps along the passage, the door was flung open, and two hands caught hers and pulled her inside.

"Here you are at last! I've been waiting for you. It's all right. Irene thinks she will be able to fix it up for you. Irene! Come here, I want you."

"Coming!" cried another voice, and the younger sister came out into the passage.

"This is the girl I was speaking about, Irene. What's your name again? Oh yes, Helen Somerset."

Irene smiled at her. "I know you by sight, anyway. Come along into the bedroom, and let's have a talk. It's no use going in there," pointing to the front room, "we wouldn't be able to hear each other speak."

She led the way along the passage to the back of the house and opened the door of a room.

"There you are," she said, standing aside to let Helen go in. "That's our room—Belle's and mine." She pointed to her sister, who smiled happily and pirouetted gaily about the room.

Helen looked around her with a feeling of bewilderment. So this was how other girls lived! It was a small room, and seemed to be densely packed with furniture. Over the two beds hung pictures, evidently taken from some Christmas annual, of chubby little girls, caressing equally chubby little dogs. The rest of the walls were covered with photographs—photographs of young men, simpering girls, brides and bridal groups, and babies. On one side of the dressing-table stood a photograph of a favorite beauty actor, striking an impressive attitude, and on the other a photograph of a complacent-looking young man with carefully oiled hair.

"What a lot of friends you must have," said Helen as she looked at them.

"Friends?" said Belle, sitting down on the edge of the bed. "Why, the place swarms with them! Most of those boys there though"—she nodded to some of the pictures—"are cast-off flames of Irene's. She's a terror!"

"Do be quiet, Belle," said Irene, crossly. "You do nothing but talk, talk, talk."

Belle jumped up again, took Helen by the arm and led her across the room to the dressing-table. She took up the photograph of the young man with the carefully oiled hair.

"He's mine," she said in a half-whisper. "That letter, you know,"—she nodded mysteriously—"from him!"

"Oh!" said Helen. She looked at the photograph, and then handed it back. She could not feel any enthusiasm, but Belle did not seem to notice her lack of it. She gazed at the picture fondly and put it back again.

"And this one?" said Helen innocently, taking up the photograph of the actor. "I suppose he is your sister's?"

Irene looked confused, while Belle shrieked with laughter.

"Oh, you *are* a card!" she said between gasps. "Don't you know who he is? Why, he's an actor,

and you want to know if he is Irene's young man!
She would like him to be, though," she added, look
ing at her sister mischievously. "Why, she goes to
every matinee and just sits and adores him. Mother
wants to know how she spends her money, and Irene
won't tell her. I know though. She spends it all
on photographs and matinees," and she laughed
again.

Helen felt embarrassed, but Irene seemed to take
her sister's chaff in good part.

"You can laugh at me as much as you like, Belle,"
she said, "but I would rather be in love with him
than with Bert. There's no romance about Bert, and
there is about *him*. What do you think of him?"
she asked abruptly, looking at Helen.

"I think he is beautiful," said Helen simply.

Both girls laughed, and Irene put the picture back
gently, straightening out the mat on which it had
been standing.

"Now," she said, turning to Helen. "Let's sit
down, and have a talk."

They made Helen sit on the only chair in the room,
while they sat side by side on the bed. The girls
were rather alike and, though neither of them was
very good looking, there was something very attractive in their bright, youthful coloring and sparkling
eyes. Their frank manner made the lonely girl feel
at ease with them, and she responded to their friendly
advances.

The family had discussed Helen thoroughly at
dinner, for they had always been curious about her,
and when Belle had come in that evening and said she
had spoken to her they were anxious to hear all
about it.

"She's a poor, lonely child," said the mother, who
was a kindhearted woman, "and you must be kind
to her, Belle."

Belle had replied that she was quite willing to be
so, if she got the opportunity, as she had rather liked
the girl.

"She would be very good-looking if she dressed better," she said. "Have you ever noticed her, George?"

Her cousin, George Angliss, looked up. He had been listening to the conversation, and a close observer might have seen that he was intensely interested though he had taken no part in it.

"Yes," he answered. "I've seen her."

"What do you think of her?"

"Not bad," he answered shortly.

"You won't get anything out of George, he's as close as an oyster," said Irene. "But I caught him staring out of the window at her when she passed by the other day."

They all laughed, and George flushed deeply but did not reply. He was a tall, athletic boy of twenty-one, with bronzed face, dark blue eyes, and black hair. He had lived with his aunt since he was a baby, his mother dying when he was born, and his father soon after. His aunt loved him, if possible, more than her own children, his tiny helplessness having won her soft, motherly heart. His father had brought him to her and, though she had never liked the man, she opened her arms to her sister's child. It was a secret grief to her that the boy grew up resembling his father, in appearance at least, for he was like none of her family.

The boy had had to leave school early, and a position was found for him in an office. He hated the work, but stuck to it, as he was anxious to earn money and repay his aunt, as much as possible, for all she had done for him. His heart was set on becoming a mining engineer, and at night he had gone to technical schools, gradually winning his way to the University, where he was now taking a course. His cousins laughed at him for his studious ways, but he smiled at them quite unperturbed. He was happy and satisfied, for the way was opening out before him; therefore let them laugh!

He had seen Helen often and watched her surreptitiously, thinking that his interest was unnoticed. That Irene had seen him disconcerted him for a moment, for his cousin was an incorrigible tease. However, she said nothing further, and he inwardly sighed with relief, not knowing that Irene had registered a mental resolve to keep her eye on him in future.

She was thinking of this to-night as she sat looking at Helen. Both girls were interested in her, and secretly too they admired her, for her air of distinction impressed them, and they were quite ready to make much of her. Helen felt the subtle flattery expressed, and responded to it.

They asked her many questions, to which she replied more or less. Then they asked her about her mother.

"She's dead, I suppose?" said Belle.

Helen hesitated for an imperceptible moment before she replied.

"Yes," she replied, but in her heart she cried, "Mother, mother, it is best to say that."

"We thought so," said Belle, wisely. "We never saw anyone about. Has she been dead long?"

"I hardly remember her," said Helen slowly.

"You will find our mother will be wanting to adopt you," said Irene. "Mother is like that. If she thinks anyone wants looking after, she simply can't help herself."

"I hope she will like me," said Helen wistfully.

"Mother likes everyone, or nearly everyone," laughed Irene. "Doesn't she, Belle? But now, what about you? Do you really want to go to business?"

"Yes, yes," said Helen, leaning forward eagerly.

"Well, curious taste," remarked Irene carelessly. "We go to work because we have to, not because we like it, and we hope to get out of it before we are much older."

"I want to earn my own living," said Helen, "and be independent.'

"You won't be very independent with the money you get at first," said Irene, "but as you live at home that won't matter very much. At the shop where I am working—a rotten place, by the way—they will want another girl in a couple of weeks, and if you like to come along, I will put in a word for you."

"Do you think," said Helen, in a hushed voice, as if the prospect were too wonderful even to contemplate, "that I will have a chance?"

Irene looked at her critically. "You'll have a very good chance, I think," she said. "But you mustn't run away with the idea that there is anything wonderful in it. I tell you plainly there's not. Why, you look as pleased at the idea of going there as I would at the thought of leaving."

"It is a start," said Helen. "You don't know what it means to me, or what my life has been."

"I sometimes think that any kind of life would be better than mine," said Irene discontentedly. "Going to that wretched shop every morning—I'm sick of it. I'll take the first chance I can of getting out of it."

"How can you?" asked Helen.

"Get married, of course," said Irene, "and you'll be glad to do the same after you've been there a little while."

"Oh no," said Helen decidedly, "I don't want ever to get married."

"Oh yes, you will. We all have to, sooner or later. Don't we, Belle?"

"That's what life is for, at least a woman's life," said Belle, who was standing in front of the looking-glass, examining critically a small spot on her cheek.

Helen thought of her father and her mother, and what marriage had meant to them. She wondered what these girls would say if she told them the story.

"We must go inside now," continued Belle. "I

think I heard Bert come in a little while ago. Come along!"

"Not to-night," begged Helen, for the prospect filled her with alarm. "I must go home now. Let me come another time."

"Nonsense," they declared. "You must come in. Mother would be annoyed if we let you go off without seeing her."

Very reluctantly, but not liking to protest further, she followed them in. She had an instant impression of people who rose when she entered the room, shook hands with her, muttered "Pleased to meet you," and then sat down again, scraping their chairs along the floor.

This room had the same profusion of furniture as the other. The chairs were all upholstered in green plush, thickly studded with brass nails. On the floor was a green carpet to match the suite, with pink roses sprawling over it. The corners of the room were filled with little tables, and on those and also on the mantelpiece were displayed the same prodigality of photographs that she had seen in the girls' room. Some hideous German colored oleographs hung on the wall. The piano was open, the songs and dance music littered about.

A young man was seated on the music stool, strumming on the piano with one hand, patiently picking out an air. He swung round, when the girls entered the room, and bestowed a wink that was half a leer on Belle. It was the young man of the photograph, and his hair was flattened carefully down on his head. He grinned sheepishly at Helen as he shook hands with her. His hand was damp and unpleasant to the touch, and she carefully wiped her own as he turned back to the piano. Belle hailed him delightedly as "Bert," and to sit near him carried a chair over to the piano. He made no attempt to help her, though the chairs were great, heavy things.

There were two small boys in the room, who had

shaken hands awkwardly with Helen and gone back to their lesson books, over which they lolled, sighing and groaning.

Helen smiled at them all as they gazed at her and, with her color coming and going, she looked very diffident and charming.

"Sit by me, dear," said the fat, comfortable looking mother, patting the sofa on which she was sitting.

"Where's George?" asked Irene, looking round.

"He went outside just now," returned one of the boys.

"Go and tell him I want him, Joe," said Irene, and the boy went off, giggling.

"George is awfully shy of girls," she continued, turning to Helen. "Whenever we have any friends here, he always goes outside."

"Don't you be teasing the boy now," said the mother, in her fat, comfortable voice.

"Don't ask him to come in on my account," implored Helen.

Irene laughed. "Don't worry. I'm getting him in on my own account. I've made up my mind to cure him of his shyness."

Helen felt uncomfortable and nervous, but said nothing further, for she was aware that Irene was determined to have her own way, and also that Mrs. Hunter was claiming her attention.

"Don't you take any notice of my girls," she said. "I'm ashamed of them sometimes, I am."

Helen smiled, for she could see, beneath the assumed disapproval, the mother's warm pride.

"How lucky they are to have you for a mother," she said softly.

The mother smiled. "Now that's a nice thing to say," she said, patting Helen's hand.

Irene also smiled, well pleased, for she saw her mother had taken a warm fancy to the newcomer, and she herself was immensely attracted by her. There was something unusual and romantic about Helen.

which made people interested in her, and to-night she showed to advantage. Among these people who showed so plainly that they liked her she threw off a great deal of her unnatural reserve of manner.

Mrs. Hunter embarked on a long story of her children, and how she had brought them up. She also told Helen all about her husband's death, which had taken place a few years previously. Helen listened in a sort of half-dreamy abstraction, for she soon discovered that there was no need to give Mrs. Hunter all her attention. If she threw in an occasional word now and then, Mrs. Hunter was quite happy and needed no further encouragement to go on. She was half-way through an account of the birth of her eldest child, when Irene interrupted her.

"Here he is at last," she said. "Helen, this is my cousin, George Angliss."

Helen looked up, and met the gaze of a pair of blue eyes, which looked at her searchingly. Did some premonition of the future strike him as he stood there, looking at her? His grave, fixed regard embarrassed her, and she turned her eyes away, flushing slightly.

He came forward then and took her hand, and she noticed his long, sensitive fingers and the firm, cool clasp of his hand.

"I am sorry, Irene," he said, turning to her, and Helen noticed that his voice was low and more cultivated than his cousins, "that you should have had to send for me. I was just finishing some work I had to do outside."

"You needn't stay, George," said his cousin, looking at him with a wicked twinkle in her eye.

"No, Georgie, dear," said his aunt, "don't you stay here if you would rather be outside with your work."

He smiled, a sudden, charming smile that lit up his face.

"I want to stay, Auntie," he said.

"Belle," called Irene, suddenly. "George wants to stay in here with us to-night."

Belle laughed. "I wonder why?" she said, looking at him. "I wonder why?"

Both girls laughed at him, and Bert also joined in. George said nothing, but lowered his eyes, trying to conceal his irritation, while Helen wondered what they were all laughing at. She never for one moment connected George's desire to stay in the room with her presence there. He could see that she did not, and was glad of it. He sat silent by her side, trying to think of something brilliant and witty to say; something that would rouse her interest in him, but everything he said was utterly commonplace, and he was bitterly conscious of it.

"Why, that fellow Bert is a better man than I am," he thought. "He can do something, even if it is only make a noise."

Bert had gathered the two girls with him round the piano, and they were now all singing together. His voice was harsh, with a thick nasal drawl, horrible to hear, but Belle's voice was sweet and clear, and rose high above the others.

Irene had asked Helen to come and sing with them, but she shook her head, preferring to remain where she was and watch them all. She had taken a dislike to Bert, the back of whose round, bullet-shaped head she could just see, and when every now and again he laid his hand on Belle's shoulder, who was sitting at the piano, she felt a little shiver of distaste creep over her, for she remembered the damp, unpleasant touch of his hand. Belle seemed to be fond of him, for she leant back and looked up at him, with her pretty eyes shining. It was obvious to everyone that he was the only one in her world, and he took it as a matter of course.

Helen felt a pang of jealous anger as she looked at them, for Belle was the one she liked best, her pretty, bright manners winning her heart. She hated to see her affection for this man.

George, too, looked at them with his eyes darkening. He was fond of his cousins, and was filled with an instinctive desire to protect them, and he knew too much about Bert to trust him. He had tried, awkwardly and tactlessly, to warn Belle, but she had merely laughed at him and said he was jealous of Bert. Since then he had said nothing further to Belle, for his pride could not bear the suspicion that he might be jealous.

Helen stole a glance at George, and noticed his frowning eyes fixed on his cousin and her companion. "He doesn't like him, either," she thought. She too would have liked to make some brilliant and witty remark that would rivet attention to herself. She knew that if she were alone she could have carried on a most brilliant conversation with everybody, but now she seemed to have nothing to say.

The two small boys had been sent to bed, grumbling and protesting, and Helen began to think rather remorsefully of her father. He didn't know where she was, and perhaps he might miss her and be anxious. She immediately got up and said she must go. The girls protested, but she insisted. They went outside with her, and she hurried off, followed by their warm entreaties to come soon again and a demand from Irene to be sure and come in and see about the position.

When she got in, she saw a light was still burning in her father's room and heard him walking up and down. She felt his loneliness the greater in contrast with the friendship and geniality of the people she had just left. How terrible to live alone, as he had done, utterly friendless. She ought to try and make his life happier, but even as she thought it she knew that it was impossible. "He will never forgive my mother," she thought, "and I must remind him of her."

Helen's own feelings towards her mother had changed. From a child she had loved the idea of the beautiful mother whom she dimly remembered. That dim mother, she knew, had loved her, but now this strange woman had risen before her, filling her thoughts and torturing her mind. She could understand her father's bitterness, for she too felt bitter. Her mother should have found her somehow and taken her away, she declared passionately to herself, or else never have left her. She hated to think of her now. What her father had called her did not matter, but what did matter was the fact that her mother could not have loved her very much—that thought hurt her cruelly.

With the feeling of bitterness and anger against her was mixed an equally intense feeling of curiosity to see her mother. If she could see her—if she could only see her, she would be able to understand better why her mother had left her alone with her father. She vaguely felt that both of them had wronged her.

She listened to-night at her father's door with a feeling of compassion towards him. Now that there seemed some hope for her in life, now that she had made some friends who were interested in her, she felt kinder towards him.

"Father," she said, knocking softly at the door. "Is there anything you want? Can I get you anything?"

She hear his footsteps stop for a moment as though he were surprised, then he resumed his restless walk, but did not reply.

She waited a moment, and as he did not seem inclined to take any notice of her, she stole quietly away.

CHAPTER IV.

THE PATH OPENS OUT.

Arthur Somerset's moodiness and listlessness had increased, and he seemed to be sinking deeper into a slough of despondency. Helen made several attempts to rouse him, for she instinctively felt that his present mood was dangerous, though she could not have given a reason for her feeling. She watched him stealthily, wondering what was hidden behind his impenetrable reserve. Though she had caught a glimpse of what lay behind, she could now hardly believe she had done so. It seemed almost impossible to believe that this wall of reserve had broken down, that she had torn it down. He too appeared to have forgotten it, for he had not referred to the subject again. If he remembered it, or if it had made any permanent impression on him, she had no means of knowing. She was curious to know. She realised that her father was different from other men, and her interest in him had awakened since his passionate outburst. Unconsciously her manner had softened towards him, for she could understand and sympathise with his bitterness against her mother, and she could see how it must have changed his whole life.

She hovered near him as he was getting ready to go into town, though he raised his eyebrows with exaggerated surprise, when at last he noticed her solicitude.

"Do you want anything?" he asked at last.

"No, Father," she replied, with a sob in her voice, for she was glad that at last he had spoken to her. "I only want to say I am sorry if I said anything to hurt you the other night."

He smiled grimly.

"You must learn to stand by anything you say."

"Even if I do not mean it at the time, Father?" she asked wistfully.

"Never say anything you don't mean."

"But, Father, you can say a thing you don't mean when you are angry. I didn't really mean that I hated you. I didn't really mean that. Oh Father! forgive me!"

He looked at her angrily, and his brows met in a heavy frown. It was becoming now a constant pain to him to see his daughter. She seemed to have got older lately, and changed in some subtle way that he could not understand. Her mother looked at him out of her eyes.

"We both said things that night which we can never forget. I quite recognise that I have given you every cause to hate me. Now I wish for silence on the subject."

Again the chill which she always felt in his presence, and which she was not proof against, crept over her.

"It's no use," she thought. "He really doesn't care what I think, so what's the good of bothering about it?"

She heard the door slam and listened to his footsteps outside, with a feeling of desolation, wondering if this was how he used to make her mother feel. Then he was gone and his shadow lifted from her, and she became young and happy again.

She made herself look as much like Irene as possible, and brushed her shining hair as smooth as she could. She had no black dress to put on, which bothered her a little, but she had a dark blue serge which a dressmaker had made for her. Helen had insisted that it should be plainly made, though the dressmaker's ideas were quite different. She was glad now that she had not allowed the woman to sway her.

About three o'clock she set off with a light heart on her adventure. Such a lot of things had happened lately that she was becoming less nervous and more used to meeting people, for with the Hunter family it was impossible for anyone to be shy.

She knew the shop well, a big fancy goods shop, with cheap pictures, chinaware and stationery in the windows. It was in the Main Street in Packington, and on Friday nights—the late night when all suburban shops were open until ten o'clock—the shop was always crowded.

She stood for a moment outside, looking in the window. The afternoon sun streamed in on the china and silver ware, and dazzled her eyes. The trams thundered past, sounding in the distance like the roll of the surf on an ocean beach. She walked past the doorway, glancing in as she did so. Two or three times she went past, pretending to look in the windows, but really trying to summon up courage to go in. At last she heard the Town Hall clock boom the half-hour. That decided her—she must go in. She entered quickly in case her courage should evaporate, and was conscious of three or four girls standing about. She saw Irene in the distance and made for her. Irene threw down a feather-duster with which she had been pretending to work, and came forward to meet her.

She spoke hurriedly and in a low voice, and Helen wondered at the different girl she was now from what she was at home, when away from all restrictions.

"I've spoken to Miss Read about you. She's the manageress, you know? She thinks she's ill to-day. and we've all had to sympathise with her. Come along, I'll take you in and introduce you."

She knocked gently at a door with a glass partition, leading from the shop into a back room, and marked "Private." On being told to enter, she opened the door softly and motioned to Helen to follow her, giving a little "moue" of disgust as she did so.

Helen saw a middle-aged woman, with bright golden hair, obviously dyed, and a faded lined face, with a thin-lipped, discontented mouth and eyes which might once have been blue, but which were now a dull, greeny-grey color. She looked as if all the good red blood had dried up and withered in her veins, leaving only the mere envelope and semblance of a woman. She was sitting in a big easy chair, and when the girls came in threw aside the illustrated society paper she had been looking at, and leant her head on her hand.

"This is the girl I was recommending to you, Miss Read," said Irene.

"Very well, Irene," she answered in a faint voice. "You can go now, and leave me alone with her."

"Is your head any better?" asked Irene, with an appearance of sympathy.

"No," answered Miss Read with a stifled groan.

"I'm sorry," said Irene, and as she went out she winked solemnly and wickedly at Helen.

"Sit down," said Miss Read, pointing to a chair.

Helen did so and waited for her to speak. The silence was profound and Helen, not liking to speak before she was spoken to, looked round. It was a dingy room, with a sofa and a couple of chairs, and on the table lay the remnants of a meal. Still the silence was unbroken, and as Miss Read sat with her head resting on her hand, Helen became uneasy. The poor woman must be very ill, she thought.

"I am afraid your head must be very bad," she ventured at last. "Perhaps you had better not bother with me to-day, I can quite easily come another time."

This was what the woman had been waiting for. She uncovered her eyes and looked at Helen.

"No," she said. "I must fix up the matter to-day, even though my head is so bad. Mr. Gibson expects me to do my duty, and when he is away, I must do my utmost to fill his place. Pass me those smelling-salts."

Helen started and looked round eagerly, anxious to be of use, but could not see them.

"Dear, dear," Miss Read sighed resignedly. "There they are," and she pointed to the mantelpiece.

Helen handed them to her, and she held them to her nose and sniffed loudly, and then appeared to revive somewhat. She looked at Helen languidly.

"What is your name again?"

Helen told her, and she considered it for a moment with half-shut eyes.

"You've never been anywhere else before?"

"No," answered Helen, her heart beating excitedly, for it really looked now as if she stood a good chance.

"Then you can't expect very much money to start with. Quite inexperienced girls are not much use and they have to be taught the business."

Helen agreed, for she was quite ready to agree with anything. She felt that this woman held her fate in her hands; those hands with the short, thick fingers and assiduously manicured finger-nails.

"How much would I be worth?" she asked, flushing a little nervously, for it all seemed too good to be true.

"Well," returned Miss Read, "at present you're not worth anything at all, but we are willing to give you 7/6 a week to start."

"7/6!" Helen's eyes danced with delight. Why, that was enormous. What couldn't she do with such a sum every week?

"Well, if you're satisfied," the voice became fainter, and she had recourse to the smelling-salts again, "you can start next Monday week. Irene Hunter assures me you are quite respectable, and I'll take her word for it. You'll want a black dress, and please put your hair up. I can't have you going about the place with your hair all over your face. That's all!" She leant back in her chair and closed her eyes to intimate that the interview was ended.

Helen rose to go. "I can start on Monday week next?" she asked.

Her companion nodded condescendingly, but did not trouble to open her eyes.

"I'll do my best to please you," Helen continued, with something suspiciously like a lump in her throat. "It is very good of you to take me."

Miss Read waved her hand loftily towards the door, and Helen tip-toed softly out.

"It's all settled," she told Irene in an excited whisper. "I'm to start in about a fortnight."

"Hurrah!" said Irene, "that's good."

"Can I come in and see you to-night?" asked Helen. "She says I must have a black dress and put my hair up, and I don't know how to do it."

"Of course. Come in whenever you like. What a pity though to have to put your pretty hair up out of sight! I suppose the old cat is jealous of it."

"Oh, no," said Helen. "Why should she be? I'll be glad to have it up, for I'll feel quite grown up then."

"How much is she going to give you?"

"7/6! Isn't that a lot of money?"

"A fine lot!" said Irene contemptuously. "You won't find it so after a while, I can tell you. It amuses me; she says the girls must be respectable, and then she pays them 7/6 and 10/- a week. You had better get along now, for she'll be dodging out directly and making herself disagreeable. If she sees you and me talking together she will think we are discussing her, and she won't like it."

Helen hurried home, hardly able to believe in her good fortune as she conceived it. How glorious it would be to have some definite work to do! Her imagination painted the future in rosy colors, this was only the beginning, but—here her thoughts received a check. She still had to tell her father what she had done, and he might be angry and refuse to let her go. She bit her lip as she thought of this, and for a moment looked curiously like her father. Well! she would do it in spite of him. She had fought him before, and she would again.

To her dismay he was already home when she arrived. He was sitting in the dining room, which was unusual, and what was more extraordinary, staring fixedly at an illustrated paper he held clenched in his hand. She set about getting his tea, wishing he would go away, for his immobility irritated her. She tried to think that he was not there, going about her work and not looking in his direction, but across her consciousness loomed the silent heaviness of her father. At last she gave up the pretence. He was there and there was no good thinking he was not. She looked at him, and in a dim sort of way was aware of the fine outline of his features and the sweep of his iron grey hair back from his forehead.

Her sense of irritation gradually left her, but an intense curiosity awoke in its place. What was it he was staring at in that paper he held? Something had stirred him, for he looked as he did that night in the library. She felt that she must see what it was, and walked softly across the room. He did not move as she came closer to him, and emboldened by this, she looked over his shoulder. A picture of a woman caught her attention, and something vaguely familiar in the face awoke her interest. She bent lower to examine it, when a hand was laid across the pictured face, and she met her father's eyes looking into hers. She drew back quickly, startled but unafraid.

"Father!" she said, in a curious whispering voice. "Who—who is that?"

For answer he thrust the paper into the fire which was burning brightly, and the hungry flames seized eagerly on it. She gave a low cry as she saw what he had done, and tried to pluck it out again. He waved her back peremptorily, and she had to stand aside and watch it burn. The paper crumbled up

almost like a live thing, and for a moment the face
she had seen smiled out at her, and then disappeared.
She turned to her father, who was standing with his
arms folded and his eyes fixed on the fire. The
weary, despondent look on his face went to her heart.

"Father," she said softly, laying her hand gently
on his arm. "That picture looked—like—me!"

He shook off her hand with a muttered exclamation.

"Won't you tell me who it was?" she pleaded.
"Father, tell me."

"No," he said hoarsely. "It was nothing—
nothing that could interest you."

She recognised the finality in his voice and ceased
pleading with him. She knitted her brows trying to
remember if she had seen the name of the paper, but
she could not. She had an idea that it was an
English paper, and that was all.

They sat down to their meal in silence, and though
Helen opened her lips once or twice to tell him what
she had done, she shut them again without speaking,
mentally resolving that she would tell him on the
morrow. She was not aware that her father's glances
dwelt on her with a sort of tragic foreboding. When
he rose from the table suddenly and left her to herself, she sighed with relief.

Arthur Somerset had gone to his room, for the
sight of his daughter was more than he could bear.
To-night the past had risen up before him with redoubled force, for it was a picture of his wife he
had thrown in the fire. He had come across it while
waiting for a pupil, turning over idly the pages of
an illustrated paper which someone had left behind.
Suddenly she had smiled up at him, as young and
happy as she was in the days when he had just married her. All trace of trouble and regret seemed to
have vanished from that smiling face. Without waiting for his pupil he had taken the paper and gone
home, his thoughts in a turmoil. He strove to get
at the mind behind that smile, but it baffled him.

She kept her secret well. Whatever she may have felt of suffering and remorse was hidden from his eyes. He too had seen her smile as the flame caught the paper, and he had restrained a passionate desire to pull it out, but it was too late.

He groaned aloud as he thought of it, for he was mad with jealousy again. All these years of bitterness had been in vain, for he realised now that he loved her still and more passionately than ever before. So she had gone on the stage! That was another torture to him. Others could see her, but he was denied. How many men had loved her since he had lost her? He clenched his hands at the thought. He knew her emotional nature and utter dependence on love too well. It was that which had destroyed their life together, for he had not been able to restrain his temperamental moods of melancholy and reserve, even though he realised he was alienating his wife.

All the emotions and mad regrets of that troubled time crowded back. He had lived for over ten years in a haze of bitter hatred against one person. Now he could not contemplate another ten years of life, trying to forget her and racked with jealousy and vain desire. He could not do it. His troubled thoughts went round and round in a circle. How tired he was of it all! How drab and grey and uninteresting his life was, drained of all color and inspiration!

> From too much love of living,
>   From hope and fear set free,
> We thank with brief thanksgiving
>   Whatever gods may be,
> That no life lives for ever;
> That dead men rise up never;
> That even the weariest river
>   Winds somewhere safe to sea.

That was what he wanted, sleep and rest and utter forgetfulness. How easy to attain it. Utter forgetfulness! Why not? Why not? The idea fascinated him. Others had taken that way, why not he? There was nothing he could possibly regret leaving behind. There was the girl, of course, but he could make arrangements for her, and she would be better without him. Hastily picking up his pen he began to write.

Helen was too excited and restless to worry about her father for long, her own life was becoming too interesting for that. She slipped quietly outside, pausing to look for a moment, through a parting in the blind of her father's room. She could see him sitting at his table, and he seemed to be writing quickly. Quite easy in her mind, she went on.

It was getting very dark, a stormy wind had risen and there was a hint of rain in the air. The bright light from the Hunters' house streamed out across the verandah, and gave an air of cheerfulness and friendliness to the place. She hurried in, and met George Angliss waiting by the door. She looked at him shyly as she responded to his greeting, and he too seemed embarrassed, for his boyish face was rather flushed and he spoke in hesitating tones.

"They told me," he jerked his head towards the house, "that you were coming in to-night." He looked at her anxiously, "I hope you won't think I've got a beastly cheek, but do you really have to go to work in that rotten shop of Irene's?"

"Why?" asked Helen, looking at him with surprise.

"Oh, I don't know." He rubbed one boot against the other awkwardly. "You look different, that's all."

"Is that all?" She laughed gaily. "Indeed I'm not different, except that I'm not so clever as Irene."

"Irene is not clever."

"Oh, I am sure she is," returned Helen earnestly. "She knows such a lot more than I do."

"And I'll bet you know more about real things, things that matter, than Irene knows or ever will know."

"How can you tell? You don't know anything about me."

"Don't I, though! I've seen you often. I don't suppose you ever noticed me?" he asked wistfully.

Helen shook her head. "No, never," she said decidedly.

He sighed. "No, I didn't suppose so. You always passed by a fellow as if he didn't exist."

She flushed faintly. "Well, I really didn't see you."

He held out his hand. "Good-bye, I've got just about time to catch my train. I've got to go to some beastly University lecture to-night."

"Why don't you go during the day?" Helen asked.

"Got to earn my living," he returned. "I work in an office during the day."

He raised his hat again, and swung off down the street. Helen watched him for a moment before going inside, and Belle, who had been looking at them through the window, came out laughing.

"The shy George has come out of his shell," she said. "I suspected something when I saw him waiting about on the verandah. We always used to tease George and tell him he never thought about anything but books, and now he is going the way of all male flesh."

"How?" asked the bewildered Helen. "What do you mean?"

"Don't you know? Can't you guess?" She went off into peals of laughter again. "You'll find out in time, and it would be a pity to spoil it for him." She tucked her arm through Helen's. "Come along in now, the mother wants to see you."

The two girls went in and Mrs. Hunter greeted Helen with a motherly kiss, which she returned with warmth. She already felt an affection for this kind woman who had taken her right into her heart without question or hesitation. Irene, who had been reading, threw down her book as Helen came in, and took her off into the bedroom, followed by Belle. Here they experimented with Helen's hair, till at last they got the effect they desired.

"There you are," said Irene, holding the glass up in front of her. "What do you think of yourself now?"

Helen looked and laughed with an excited flush of color in her cheek. "Why, is that really me?" she asked. "How different I look!"

"Yes, don't you? It suits you beautifully. What do you think, Belle?"

"Yes, it does," said Belle rather absentmindedly. She looked at her watch and seemed to be listening intently. There was the faintest shadow in her eyes. Helen glanced at her, wondering what was the matter, but did not like to ask her, and Irene did not seem to notice. Suddenly they heard the rain come down, a perfect torrent beating on the roof, and Belle's face lightened and her eyes smiled again.

"Of course it is the rain that is keeping him," she said.

"Keeping who?" asked Irene. "Oh, Bert? Yes, I suppose so."

"Of course it is," said Belle, now quite happy again. "He'll be round to-morrow night. Helen, you look lovely."

Helen said nothing, but her evening was spoilt for her. She hated to see the power that young man had over Belle. It worried her to think that she could even like him. Shortly afterwards, as the rain slackened a bit, she went home, shivering a little as the cold, rain-wet wind swept across her cheek. Coming from the warmth and brightness of the Hunters' house, the darkness and chill of her own home struck her ominously. Why were all the lights out? Surely he couldn't have gone to bed so early. She listened at his door and then knocked gently. She could feel her heart beating in her throat, and in the silent house the persistent ticking of the clock sounded loud and clear. She counted mechanically. One—two—three—when she had counted sixty she would go in. Four—five—six——

She opened the door slowly and paused on the threshold, staring before her. When her eyes got accustomed to the darkness, she could see something lying on the floor. With a deadly fear clutching at her heart she went forward, and bent down. It was her father!

CHAPTER V.

Helen never forgot the horror of that moment; for years after the thought of it had power to bring a shadow across her happiest moments.

"He must have fainted," she muttered to herself. "He is dead," something whispered to her. "No, no," she said aloud, "he is not. He is not dead," she whispered to herself, trying to silence that other voice, which still cried in her heart. She fumbled about the dark room, trying to find matches, and stumbled and fell over something. She gave a low cry of horror and then a gasp of relief as she saw what it was. It was only a chair, but in that dim light, and with that silent figure on the floor, everything looked mysterious and terrifying.

At last she found the matches, and with trembling fingers lit the lamp. She knelt down and took his hand in hers. How cold it was! The contact with her warm flesh made her shiver.

"Father!" she whispered, and then louder. "Father," and shook him gently by the shoulder. The heavy, inert body sank back into its former position as she let it go. This couldn't be her father—it was something—something she had never seen before. Her eyes distended with fear, and a blind, unreasoning terror of that silent thing on the floor overcame her. She shrank back, holding out her hands as if to ward something off, and then, once free of the room, ran out into the night, stumbling and gasping for breath as she ran. Her mind was a blank; all she knew was that she must get away from that horror. As in a dream she heard brisk footsteps coming down the street and groped blindly towards them. She put out her hand and touched the passerby on the arm.

"What is it?" said a voice she knew.   "Why!
it's you!" and the voice rang high in surprise and
alarm.   "Good God! what are you doing out in the
rain.   What's the matter?"

She spoke with difficulty, the words coming slowly
and hoarsely.

"My father! in there—oh—horrible!"

George gave one startled glance at her, and then
ran quickly into the house.   She followed him, for
she could not bear to be alone, and stood at the door
with averted eyes and clenched hands, while he examined the body.   Two or three moments told him
that all was over, and he gently crossed the dead
man's hands on his breast.

"Poor fellow!" he muttered.

"You see," said Helen, her pale face turned away
from him.   "He is—dead.   I tried to believe he
was not, but—he is dead.   He was like that when I
came in.   I had been enjoying myself while he was
lying there—in the dark—alone."

She covered her face with her hands and burst into
loud and passionate sobs.   The boy looked at her,
his face working with distress.

"Don't!" he muttered.   "Don't cry like that!"
and held out a restraining hand, as she knelt down by
the body of her father.

She brushed him away.   "Please leave me alone,"
she said in a low voice, and George stood aside.

She looked for a long time at the quiet face and
gently touched the hair, a thing she had never dared
to do in life.   All her fear and terror had left her
and she felt nothing but grief and remorse.

"I asked you to forgive me—only to-day I asked
you that—and now you will never speak again.   It
is too late—too late!"

She took his hand in hers and rubbed it gently
as if trying to restore circulation, and then touched
the cold face with her warm lips.   "Father," she
breathed, "Father, can't you hear me?"

She listened a moment and then burst into wild sobs again, which almost seemed to tear her in pieces. George watched her in an agony, not knowing what to do. The girl's sobs hurt him strangely, and through the silent house they seemed to echo and re-echo. He bit his lip, and the sweat broke out on his brow. At last he could bear it no longer, and approached her where she lay with her head on her father's breast.

"You must come away," he said hoarsely, and attempted to lift her up. She repulsed him, motioning him away with her hand, but he persisted. She struggled with him fiercely, but he was the stronger, and at last managed to raise her to her feet.

"Leave me alone with him," she cried.

"You can't stay here," he said with quiet authority.

"I must," she said. "I can't leave him here alone. Can't you see that? He has been lonely all his life, and I will not leave him alone now that he is—dead."

She broke away from him again, and threw herself across the silent figure which seemed to mock with its immobility the futile passion of the living. She kissed him again, trying to warm his lips with hers, and George could hardly restrain an exclamation of horror.

"Don't do that!" he cried sharply, and lifted her up again, using his strength ruthlessly. She looked up at him, and he noticed how her eyes seemed to burn in her pale face.

"Let me go," she panted.

"I am going to take you away," he said, between his teeth.

"How can I go away and leave him alone? Don't be so cruel," she pleaded. "I must stay."

"I will come back," said George. "He will not be left alone. Not yet," he added in a low voice.

She gave in then, and he felt her a dead weight in his arms. Setting his teeth, he exerted all his

strength and carried the sobbing, half-fainting girl
into his aunt's house.   Though it was late, a light
still shone in one of the rooms, and he knew his aunt
was up.   He laid Helen down gently on a sofa, and
went in and told his aunt what had happened.   She
listened horror-struck.

"Do you think it is suicide?" she asked in a voice
which shook a little.

"I'm afraid so, but don't say anything about it
to her.   She hasn't thought how it happened yet.
I'll have to get a doctor and try and fix things up a
bit there.   You'll look after her, Auntie, won't
you?"

"Yes, my boy, of course.   The poor motherless
child!   Where is she?"

Helen still lay where George had left her, with her
face hidden in the cushions and her slender body
shaken with her sobbing. She gave no thought as to
where she was, or what would happen to her, for all
her thoughts were with her father.   If she could
only recall the words she had flung at him in her
anger; if she had only been home to-night, it might
not have happened.   So she reproached herself use-
lessly.   If she had tried to understand him more and
helped to make his life happier!   But it was now
too late—too late—too late.

She became conscious then of two arms lifting her
up, and a soft voice whispering:

"There, there, little one.   You're my child now.
Hush!   Hush!" as Helen's painful sobs tore her
throat.

It was Mrs. Hunter, and Helen threw her arms
around her neck and buried her face on her bosom,
in a sudden passion of love.

Meanwhile George took matters into his own hands.
He aroused one of the boys, and sent him off for the
doctor, who soon arrived.   He shook his head gravely
after his examination, and took up a small bottle
standing on the table.

"It's an overdose of chloral," he said, "judging by this. He probably was in the habit of taking it for a sleeping draught, but whether he took this accidentally or deliberately, well—" he shrugged his shoulders, "it is hard to say. We'll have to notify the police, and there will be an inquest of course."

"There are a couple of letters on the table here, one of them addressed to his daughter," said George suddenly.

"Um! that looks rather suspicious. Where is she by the way?"

"I took her into my aunt," said George. "She seemed very upset, for it was a terrible shock to her. I wish you would go in and see her."

"Perhaps I had better do so," said the doctor. "I'll run in as I'm going. Just help me, my boy, will you, and we will put him on his bed?"

They lifted the body between them, and laid it gently down, while the doctor peered closely at the face.

"He's been rather a distinguished looking man. Who was he, do you know?"

"No, sir. He was always rather a mystery to us. I only know his name was Somerset."

"Well, he had a decent taste in literature," said the doctor, running an interested eye over the bookshelves. "I would like to buy some of these if they are put up for sale. Well," taking up his bag and putting on his hat, "there is nothing to be done here at present, so I will just go next door and see the girl."

George was glad to see him go, for he thought he was hard and callous. His ardent youth had never been brought into contact with death before, and he was filled with a sense of the stillness and aloofness of it. He did not know that to the doctor death had become as commonplace as life.

He was afraid to touch anything in the room until the police arrived, but he took up the letters lying on the table and resolved to give them to Helen in the morning. His young chivalrous spirit was burning with an eager desire to be of service to her, and he longed to take on his own shoulders as much of the responsibility as possible. He knew there were a lot of unpleasant things that would have to be done, and he wanted to save her from them. In the morning, however, he was unable to see her, for she was suffering from the after-consequences of the terrible shock she had received, and the doctor had absolutely forbidden anyone to see her or to discuss her father's death with her.

It was three days before he was able to see her, and then the inquest was over, and Arthur Somerset gone to his last resting place, his face more calm and peaceful than it had ever been during life.

Mrs. Hunter had turned the sitting room over to Helen's use, and it was there that he found her. She looked pale and tired, and her eyes were heavy-lidded, but still his heart leapt at the sight of her.

"I am glad you are better," he said, and then paused, wondering how to go on, for she had not yet been told that her father died by his own hand. He took the letter out of his pocket and handed it to Helen. Her hand shook when she saw the handwriting, and she looked at him questioningly.

"He left it for you," said George in answer to her look. "I found it on the table."

"Then—" she said, and stopped abruptly, for a sudden realization dawned on her. She had been too tired and ill to wonder how it had happened, but now she knew.

"There was another," said George. "But I posted it yesterday. It was marked 'Urgent.'"

He waited for her to speak, but she was silent, only staring at the letter she held in her hand, so he left her alone.

She opened the letter slowly. The first effects of the terrible shock had worn off, but she still felt

unnerved and shaken.   How strange and mysterious
life was!   A few days ago he was alive; now he
was gone, and the whole course of her life changed.
She spread out the letter before her, thinking as
she did so that presently she would awake and find
it was all a dream.

> "That the last act of a secluded life should be a
> matter of publicity is regrettable and unavoidable. You,
> my daughter, will realise that nothing could annoy me
> more.   However, I have come to the end of my desire
> for life, and seeing no reason why I should stay in it,
> I am going to step out into—into what?   I don't know
> —yet.   After the few first natural tears are shed, you
> will not miss me, indeed you will be better without
> me.   You are too like your mother to be happy with
> me.   Post the other letter I have left at once.   It is
> to my brother, and I have asked him to look after
> you.   Have no qualms about accepting his help, as
> he owes me more than he could possibly repay to you.
> There is a little money in the Bank, about £50 I
> believe, which, of course, belongs to you. If you would
> rather play a 'lone hand' than go to your uncle, do
> so.   You have spirit, and life ought to be kind to
> you.   One thing I would tell you.   Grasp every chance
> of happiness that offers, but do not pin your faith too
> closely on any human being.   Your mother I cannot
> write of.   She is not in Melbourne now, but you may
> be sure she will return."

The letter broke off abruptly, without any signature or farewell.   She folded it up carefully.   So
that was the end?   The end of his life and the beginning of hers.   A lone hand!   Yes, a lone hand would
be best.   She could feel again the faint stirring
in her blood at the thought of the wonderful adventure of life.   It was strange to think she had relations, but she felt no desire to go to them.   She
could please herself, and a faint flush of color stole
into her pale cheeks at the thought.

She wondered why the fact that he had killed himself did not horrify her.   It ought to have done so,
she knew, but she felt she would rather think that
he had gone out of life deliberately, of set purpose,

than have been struck down suddenly and died unwillingly.

She called to George, whom she could see standing outside on the verandah, and he came in, surprised at her composure. She asked him when he had posted the letter, and he told her.

"It was to my uncle," she said. "My father suggests that I should go to him."

George felt a sudden pang of jealousy and disappointment. He had heard his aunt say that Helen could stay with them if she liked and no friends turned up to claim her. Now it seemed that she was going to recede from his life after all.

"Are you going?" he muttered.

"I don't think so," said Helen listlessly. "Mrs. Hunter says I can stay here, and in any case, wherever I live, I am going to start work as I intended to do."

Very unwillingly, and only from a strong sense of duty, George said she ought to go with her uncle when he came, but Helen shook her head.

"There are a lot of private papers," he said. "They haven't been touched, but you ought to go through them."

"Private?" exclaimed Helen, starting to her feet eagerly. "Why, of course—there must be. I had forgotten about them. I must go and look through them at once."

She left the room hurriedly, calling out to Mrs. Hunter where she was going, and George followed her. He was very silent, but she did not notice him, for her thoughts were concentrated on what she had to do. He was acutely conscious of her presence, and fiercely resented having to take her bright young youth into the house of death.

She paused uncertainly by the door. How familiar, and yet how unfamiliar, the room looked! The furniture was all packed together neatly, the floor coverings up, and all the books taken from the shelves and packed away in a couple of large cases standing near the door. The only thing that was untouched was the writing-table, where she had so often seen her father sitting. This was still in the same position, and on its smooth surface lay a bunch of keys. George pointed to them, and without a word she picked them up. He hesitated a moment, and then quietly left the room.

It was some time before Helen could bring herself to open the locked drawers. Half-fearfully she stood, with the keys poised in her hand. It seemed too much like an intrusion on her father's privacy, and she was half inclined to let it alone, and yet a devouring curiosity drove her towards the task. What secrets of the past might not those unopened drawers contain? She might be able to find out something about her mother.

That thought decided her, and she bent swiftly down, and inserted the key in the lock. The first key she tried would not fit, and she tried another. The key turned easily, and she pulled the drawer open. It was full of papers, and she turned them over feverishly, and then put them aside with a sense of disappointment. There was nothing of interest among them, only papers and letters relating to his pupils.

She opened the next drawer, and lying at the back, on top of what looked like a bundle of old letters loosely tied together, was a faded morocco pocket-book. Her heart beat quickly, and she looked round with a sudden fear, almost expecting to see her father appear and confront her as she held the book in her hand. She tore off the worn-out elastic band which held the book together, and opened it with trembling fingers. She gave a low cry of joy as she saw what it contained. She knew the photograph could only be of one person—her mother.

She gazed at the fair, youthful face, looking even younger than her own. The sweet mouth smiled, but the dark eyes seemed touched with a shadow of coming misfortune. So that was her mother. She looked at the picture hungrily, but across her heart swept a feeling of bitterness. She had left her alone all these years. The tears gathered in her eyes, but she shook them away, looking searchingly at the picture again as a thought flashed across her mind. That other picture she had caught a glimpse of in the paper! Wasn't it the same face and expression? She knitted her brows, trying hard to remember. She believed it was, but, if so, what was her mother doing, and why was her picture in an illustrated paper? Then she forgot her questionings and smiled back again at the pictured face. This was her mother, and alive. She would not worry about anything else.

With gentle care she laid the photograph down, and opened the pile of letters. She flushed vividly as she read the first one, feeling as though she had intruded on some holy place. It was evidently written by her mother to her father before they were married.

"I love you—I love you—I love you," the letter almost sang. Helen put it down, overawed and breathless, as though she were in the presence of some passion she could not understand. She went through the others with reverent fingers. They were all in the same handwriting. Her father must have kept carefully all she had written to him. Helen wondered if he used to read them when he was alone at night, for they were worn and falling to pieces.

She did not read any more, for she felt they were not for her, but now and then a word leapt up from the written page—"My lover!" "I am yours for ever!"

Helen sat very still, looking at them as they lay before her. How had all that love been lost? How was it her father had forfeited it? "I am yours for ever!" And what was the end? A wasted life and a premature death for her father, and what for her mother? Had she managed to snatch some happiness from life? "Violent delights have violent ends!" She shivered slightly, and a premonition of the transitory nature of human passion and love swept over her. She gave a passionate gesture, for all her youth cried out against the thought.

She looked round her fearfully, and again she could see that quiet and passionless figure lying on the floor. It was to that—that nothingness—her mother had poured out her passionate avowals of never-ending love. She leant her head on her hand, and tried to remember that time, years ago, when their home had been broken up. But she could remember nothing, except her mother crying and kissing her. She could not blame her mother for going, but there was that other. Her eyes darkened at the thought. She hated him, not because he took her mother away, but because he had had her all these long years, while Helen herself had longed and hungered for love.

"I will find her one day," she thought, "and then, and then—."

In her mind she envisaged her as still young and beautiful, for she did not think of the changing hand of Time. Another wave of sadness swept over her, and she wondered if life meant nothing but change and tragedy. There were her new friends, and they seemed contented and happy enough. No unhappiness weighed them down. There was George, of course, but he was different—she sighed and gave up the problem.

Finishing her task at last, she gathered her mother's letters together, and tied them up again. Then she called to George, who came in gladly for he had been nervous and wretched waiting about outside.

"George," she said, fixing her lovely eyes upon him. "It is only since I have been here that I realise all you have done for me. What could I have done without you?"

"Oh, that's nothing," he muttered awkwardly, with a boyish dislike of being thanked.

She smiled at him, and he thought her smile was the sweetest thing he had ever seen.

"You've done everything for me, I can see that. But I don't understand how you had the time."

"I got a couple of days off,"_ and then, changing the subject abruptly, "Have you finished going through the papers?"

"Yes," she answered, "but there was nothing of importance, just some old private letters," she held them tightly to her breast, "and some business papers."

"Well, we can get the furniture moved away," he said. "Don't you think we had better sell it?"

"Sell it? Oh yes, I won't want it."

"What about the books? Will you sell them?"

"Oh no," she said quickly. "I couldn't sell them, they are too much a part of him."

"I'm glad you don't want to sell them," said George. "I didn't think you would, so I had them all packed up. I'm afraid you won't get much money for the furniture though."

"No," said Helen rather vaguely. "I don't suppose I will. Well, it doesn't matter." She took out the photograph from the bundle of letters and looked at it in a hesitating manner, while he wondered what it was, though with great delicacy, he averted his eyes lest he should appear to be trying to see it.

At last she said, handing it to him:—

"There was something else in the desk. I found this—a picture of my mother."

He took it as carefully as if it were something precious that might fall and smash into a thousand pieces.

"Your mother?" he said, almost in a whisper. "Why! I should have thought it was you!"

She flushed with delight.

"George—really!" She came and stood by him, and both heads bent over the picture. "I would love to be like her, but do you really think I am?"

"I never saw two people so alike," he declared, handing it back, and then added, flushing slightly under his tan skin, "Thank you for showing it to me."

She slipped the photograph into the bosom of her dress, and they looked at each other shyly.

"You—you have been so good to me," she said simply, "that I had to show it to you. It is the most precious thing I have."

His boyish soul did not know how to deal with the situation. Dimly he felt that she was admitting him into her inner confidence. Searching desperately for something to say in reply to her gracious words, he of course hit on the wrong thing.

"She died when you were a child, didn't she?"

The light went out of her eyes and the color from her cheeks. She hated telling him a lie, but she could not tell him the truth.

"Yes," she answered slowly.

He was miserably conscious that he had said the wrong thing, and cursed himself for a fool. He imagined that speaking of her mother's death had recalled her father too vividly to her mind. A strange feeling of desolation and inertia had fallen over Helen. She stood, with one hand holding the letters clutched to her breast, and her dark eyes troubled with gloomy thought. George broke the sudden silence that had fallen over them.

"We had better go home now," he said. "Auntie will be getting anxious if you are too long away."

She roused herself with a start, suddenly realising that she was drifting into one of her father's habits.

"I must not get like my father," she said to herself in desperate resolution.

CHAPTER VI.

"MONNA LISA."

Mrs. Hunter hurried out to find Helen, in a state of great excitement. She found her on her knees going through her father's books which had been brought in.

"Dearie!" Mrs. Hunter exclaimed, in a loud, hoarse whisper, "There's a lady and gentleman to see you."

"It's not the clergyman again, is it?" asked Helen, who had had an exceedingly painful interview with him. She did not understand in the least why he had gone hastily away when she tried to tell him how she felt about her father's death. She was afraid he might have returned accompanied by the woman who used to teach in the Sunday School.

"No," answered Mrs. Hunter. "It's not him. It's a real gentleman, and the lady"—she turned up her eyes in astonishment, "she's that haughty, you'd think I was the dirt under her feet. Hurry up, dearie, and go in and see them. They seem to be in a hurry."

"It must be my uncle," said Helen, getting up from her knees.

"Your uncle, is it? Well, he's a regular toff to look at. Put on that black silk dress Belle brought home for you—hurry now."

She glanced quickly at the door, as if she expected to see a wrathful and impatient uncle loom in sight, angrily demanding his niece.

Helen changed her dress as quickly as possible. An unexplainable feeling made her want to appear to advantage before these strangers. Her father's brother must not be ashamed of her father's daughter.

"Will I do?" she asked anxiously.

"Yes," answered Mrs. Hunter, kissing her and

looking at her proudly. "You'll do beautifully.
Run along now, and don't let them take you away
from us."

Helen waited quietly for a moment before she ventured to open the door of the sitting room. It was
strange to think that at last she was going to meet
someone belonging to her own family. She turned
the handle very gently and went in. There was a
woman sitting on the sofa, tapping her foot impatiently on the floor. She was a tall, thin woman,
beautifully dressed, but with an intolerant expression and close-set, thin lips. Helen saw in one
swift glance that her uncle was not in the least like
her father; he was a short, stout man, with rather
a jovial expression, tempered with fear of his wife
when he remembered her. He was standing near
the window, whistling softly through his teeth, and
when he heard Helen enter he turned swiftly round,
giving an exclamation of astonishment as he did
so.

She stood for a moment at the door, looking at
them both and trying to conquer her feeling of disappointment; then came nearer, going to the man
first, for his face had the kinder, softer expression.

"I am Helen," she said.

He took her by the hand, and turned her head so
that the light fell strongly on her features; as he
looked his face went a little pale. He turned to
his wife.

"Arthur's daughter," he said. "But you can see
who she is like."

"I can see," answered his wife coldly, "and she
has no reason to be proud of that."

Helen felt immediately the latent hostility of the
woman. "She doesn't like me," she thought. "I
wonder why?"

Her uncle, however, fussed about, making her sit
down, and drawing up a chair opposite, he sat down
and took her hand again, holding it gently in his,
until recalled by his wife's sharp voice.

"James!" she said sharply, and he dropped Helen's hand at once, and turned towards his wife.

"Yes, my dear?"

"Don't forget you have an important appointment in a little while. Hadn't you better put your proposition before your niece?"

"Certainly, my dear, certainly. That was just what I was going to do." He coughed importantly, and Helen stole a glance at her aunt, who was looking about her with a contemptuous sneer.

"Now Helen, my dear child," insensibly his voice took on a softer tone in addressing her, "I want you to come away with us and we will give you a home. Your father—" he cleared his throat, and to her astonishment Helen saw that his eyes had dimmed with tears—" your father asked me to do this, the only thing that he ever asked me to do."

Helen looked at her aunt, and caught the hard and bitter expression in the woman's eyes. It was quite obvious the idea was unwelcome to her. She hesitated before speaking.

"Do you really want me to come, Uncle?" she asked him softly.

"Want you!" he cried. "Of course —" and then his voice died away in his throat as he saw the basilisk gleam in his wife's eyes. "Certainly," he murmured, and though his voice had become less enthusiastic, his eyes beseeched Helen, "Certainly we do."

"And does my —" she paused over the word, and could not say it—"does this lady want me also?"

"Of course she does," said her uncle, replying for his wife.

But Helen looked at her aunt, smiling faintly as she waited. She had already made up her mind not to go, but she was curious as to what the woman would say. There was silence for a little while, and then the woman said coldly:—

"You have heard my husband's offer. If you care to come my home is open to you. If not—well—the rest is your own affair."

"Thank you," said Helen. "I thought that."

They looked at each other, both antagonistic, while the poor man blew and perspired, wishing he could have persuaded his wife to stay at home. At last Helen said, turning away from her aunt with the same faint smile with which she had looked at her:

"I am very sorry, Uncle, but I can't go with you." She really was sorry for him, and her voice took on a soft and musical note as she spoke to him.

"What?" cried her uncle. "Nonsense; you must."

Helen shook her head. "I want to stay here with these people," she said. "They have been very kind to me and they say I can live with them. I am going to earn my own living."

"I can't allow that," he insisted. "You must come with us. Your father asked me to take you."

"He gave me a choice," said Helen. "I could either go with you, or I could play a lone hand. I want to play a lone hand."

"You are like your father in some ways," he said. "He wanted to play a lone hand, and look where it brought him. I can't let you do the same. You must come away with us. I can't have Arthur's daughter knocking round the world. Why, it would be on my conscience."

"If she prefers to stay here, James," broke in his wife, looking round the room contemptuously, "you can judge what her taste must be and need not worry about her. She will find her own level."

Helen smiled, knowing inwardly that her smile infuriated her aunt. But her uncle looked miserable.

"I tell you I can't leave her here, Emily," he muttered. "It would be on my conscience. I can't do it."

"But you must, Uncle," said Helen firmly. "Really, I will be quite all right. Father left me a little money, and I have already got a position."

"A position where? What kind of a position?" he asked.

"In a shop."

"A shop!"

Her aunt rose and moved towards the door. "That is enough, James. If she prefers to work in a shop and live here, rather than come with us, there is no more to be said. But I trust she understands that this subject will never be re-opened."

For a moment he stood uncertainly, but his wife eyed him ruthlessly, and Helen shook her head, smiling. Then with a muttered "Good-bye, my dear," he took up his hat and stick and went off with his wife, his shoulders stooping a little as though he were weary or depressed. Helen watched them through the window, and saw her uncle hand his wife into the taxi which was standing near; then he hurried back.

He came in breathless. "Pretended I forgot my gloves," he said, with a hasty glance out of the window, and then putting his hand in his pocket, he pulled out a handful of notes. "Take this money," he whispered urgently. "I won't be happy unless you take it."

She protested that she did not need it.

"Take it," he said, "quick—take it. You never know when you will want some money. I would have liked you to come with me, little girl, but as you won't, promise me if you ever want help you will come to me. Promise me that, and I shall feel easier."

Helen promised, and a load seemed to roll off his mind. His round, chubby face beamed, and he chuckled with delight. "Good idea about the gloves, wasn't it?" Then, taking out a card he handed it to her. "Perhaps it would be better if you came to my office in town when you want me."

She took the card and promised to do so, and he caught her round the waist and lifted her face to his.

"By God!" he said hoarsely, "you are like your mother, child."

"Uncle!" She looked at him eagerly. "Uncle, did you know her?"

"Know her?" He looked away and his face had changed. "I knew her. There never was such a woman."

"Uncle," she whispered. "Do you know where she is?"

He shook his head. "No," he answered. "I never heard. She just went—away. It broke poor Arthur up." He looked at her again, searching her face with eager eyes. "There is nothing I wouldn't do for your mother, child, and for you too, if ever you want it. Don't forget."

He kissed her on the lips, and hurried out, waving his hand as he vanished.

She stood where he had left her with the money clasped in her hand. So that was over and done with. She was now really alone in the world, for she could never look for a home with her aunt. Any life would be better than to live upon forced and unwilling charity, for she knew, despite her father's assurance, that would have been her portion. She would see her uncle sometimes, for there were many things she wanted to know that perhaps he could tell her, but she would not ask for his help. She would show them that life could not defeat her.

She was interrupted by Mrs. Hunter, who had heard the door close, and came in, devoured with curiosity. Helen told her simply that she had refused to go with them.

"I want to stay with you," she said.

She had already come to an arrangement that she should pay 5/- a week out of her salary to Mrs. Hunter. She had protested that this was too little, but her objections were waved aside.

"When you earn more money, we will see then."

Helen had pointed out that she had some money, but Mrs. Hunter held up her hands in horror.

"Touch that money!" she exclaimed. "Never!

That will just do for your trousseau." Now that she heard Helen was really going to stay with them her kind eyes beamed with pleasure. "We must try and fix up a room for you," she said, "One that will be your own."

There was a small room outside, opening off the verandah which she proposed giving to Helen. It was only small, but it was bright and airy, having a big window opening out on to the garden at the back of the house. She showed this room to Helen. "It's not much to look at, dear," she said apologetically, "but it's the best we can do at present."

"I like it," said Helen, walking across to the window and leaning out. "I would rather have this than any other."

She could just see above the dividing fence between the two houses, the top of the window of the room which used to be her own. She thought how she had leant out angrily, hating her father, and then how the scent of wisteria had soothed her. The wisteria was still in bloom, but he was gone. For one awful moment a sense of the terror of death overwhelmed her, and her mind became a blank horror. She had now no comforting beliefs in Heaven; she could not believe that she would ever see him again. All she could realise was that her father was gone for ever, the man her mother had so passionately loved lay insensible to everything—but the wisteria still bloomed. She knew that nothing could touch him now, for it had been that strange silence that had so terrified her. "Even mother's love couldn't move him," she thought.

She remembered how they had come to her whispering, their minds troubled, with news that affected her not at all. "They will not bury him in consecrated ground." The hushed fearful whisper had broken into her apathy, and she had smiled and thought secretly. "What does that matter to him now. He is dead—he can't feel anything."

She was recalled from these thoughts by the calm voice of Mrs. Hunter, who had been clearing the room, for it had formerly been used as a lumber-room.

"Now if we get your things brought in here, we will have it fixed up ready for you to-night."

Helen had picked out a few things that she thought she might want before the furniture had gone to the auction rooms. She had taken her father's writing table, a bed, and a couple of chairs; also a picture, her father's favourite, which had hung facing him when he sat at his table. Indeed it was the only picture in his room, except the photograph which he kept hidden in his desk where Helen had found it after his death.

She helped Mrs. Hunter bring these things in now, and they arranged the room together, Helen placing the bed under the window.

"I like to feel the night-air stirring on my face," she explained to Mrs. Hunter, who had grave doubts as to the wisdom of the proceeding, for she had a horror of draughts. However, Helen was insistent on this point, and at last she allowed her to have her own way.

They had fixed the room to their satisfaction, and Mrs. Hunter was gazing round proudly at the results of their labours, when a sudden thought struck her and she vanished from the room. Helen had just taken the picture to hang up, when Mrs. Hunter appeared again, holding in her hand a large framed, coloured copy of "Bubbles."

Helen felt a sudden sensation of dismay. "Bubbles!" She knew it too well, and had always hated it. Surely Mrs. Hunter was not going to suggest that it should be hung up in her room? Her misgivings were too well founded, for that was just what she intended doing.

"Look! This is for you," she said, holding it up so that Helen could appreciate to the full its awful banality. "I've taken it out of George's room."

"Oh, you must not rob George for me," said Helen, with relief in her voice.

"Don't you worry about that. I won't be robbing George. He always said that it got on his nerves, and I have been threatening to take it away from him. It will look lovely up there," and she pointed to the wall, facing the bed.

"You're very kind," murmured Helen, "but I don't really need it, for I have a picture I want to hang up there." She pointed to the engraving of "Monna Lisa."

Mrs. Hunter examined it closely, pursing her mouth to a line of disapproval as she did so. "I don't like it," she said, in a decided voice. "She looks—I don't know—" she wrinkled her brow in a puzzled fashion —"there's something wrong about her."

"She's mysterious," said Helen, in a hushed voice. "She changes, she has her moods just like a human being. I wish I knew what her smile really meant."

She had forgotten Mrs. Hunter, and was looking at the picture intently. It had always fascinated her—always, ever since the time when as a small child she had stolen into her father's room when he was out, and that faint enigmatic smile had caught her eye. Often she had been afraid of it, for that smile seemed to hover round her, ceaselessly questioning. Later, when she was older, she had read Walter Pater's essay, and woven his fancy into her own. The picture had smiled at her when she was a child, and it still smiled at her now that she had put off childish things, but now that smile was charged with a quality of subtle understanding. Perhaps, Helen thought, when she knew more, she would understand that smile fully.

Mrs. Hunter had no misconceptions as to her opinion of the picture. She thought the woman looked evil, and her strange smile disturbed her matronly respectability. She had no fine distinctions as to women; to her mind a woman was either good or bad. The good women married and had children, not otherwise; or if they had not the fortune to get married, they lived in regret. The other kind got into what she called "trouble," and that was the end of them. This woman in the picture struck her as one who would be very likely to get into "trouble," and Helen's absorption in it made her vaguely uneasy. She thought it strange that a young girl should like it.

"Put it away, dearie," she said persuasively, "and we will hang 'Bubbles' up instead."

Helen's hand tightened on the picture, for a moment she felt a sudden passionate instinct to defend it from Mrs. Hunter's irreproachable respectability, but with an effort she controlled herself, for she knew that nothing she could say would make Mrs. Hunter understand. She was, however, determined that "Bubbles" should not be hung where her eyes would rest on it as soon as she opened them in the morning, so she employed diplomacy.

"I must hang 'Monna Lisa' up there," she said. "This was my father's favourite picture, you see."

"Oh!" Mrs. Hunter's face fell—of course that was a different matter. If it was her father's favourite, she must like it, but she wanted her to have the other, too.

Helen was already standing on a chair, hanging up her picture, and as she looked down, the sight of Mrs. Hunter's disconsolate face smote her with a strange feeling of remorse.

"We'll hang that up wherever you like," she said, and Mrs. Hunter's face immediately lightened. She carefully hung it up on the opposite wall, and "Monna Lisa" looked at "Bubbles" with her inscrutable smile, rather pained, Helen thought, to find herself in such company.

Mrs. Hunter was so obviously delighted and so satisfied in her own mind that Helen was pleased that she had not the heart to say anything further. Mrs.

Hunter never knew that "Bubbles" was not appreciated, indeed she fancied it was Helen's favourite, and was astonished when George made a strange sound when she was proudly showing them all Helen's room that night.

"What's the matter?" she asked anxiously, for she feared that after all he might have been hurt by the summary way she had commandeered the picture.

"Nothing much, Auntie," he replied, "I only thought you gave that picture to me."

"My boy," she said gravely, "You never liked it, so I gave it to someone who will!"

His eyes twinkled and he looked at Helen, who smiled and motioned to him to be quiet.

When they went into the dining-room they found that Bert had arrived unexpectedly, and Belle flew up to him, murmuring soft words. He had a bad cold, and made the most of it, accepting Belle's attentions with a lordly air. He sat opposite Helen and smiled across at her whenever he thought the others were not looking, but she kept her eyes away from him. She hated him. He had a horrible habit of sucking his teeth which made her shiver and grow cold all over. It was painful for her to sit at the same table with him, for he had disgusting manners, eating his meals with gusto, and drinking in audible gulps. None of the others seemed to mind it, except George, who glared across the table at him savagely. George, too, was the only one who noticed the way Bert looked at Helen, and he went pale with rage. The only comfort he had was that Helen seemed quite unconscious of it.

Helen, however, was quite conscious of what was going on, and she knew the reason why Bert was stealing those glances at her. The last time he came to the house she had been sitting alone, tired and depressed after all she had been through, when Bert came into the room. He had been looking for Belle, but was by no means averse to finding Helen in her place. She did not hear him as he came in, and he tiptoed across the room, bent over the back of her chair and kissed her on the cheek before she was even aware of his presence. She sprang to her feet with a low cry and stood facing him, in utter amazement. The touch of his moustache against her cheek gave her a feeling of nausea.

"How dared you do that?" she demanded in a whisper. "How dared you?"

As he looked at her flashing eyes, he almost wondered himself how he had dared.

"It's all right, miss," he whispered, looking quickly round. "It's only a joke, you know. No need to tell Belle anything."

"I thought you were in love with Belle," she said, looking at him with contempt.

"Love?" he seemed rather shy of the word, and said it awkwardly. "I don't know about love. I like her all right."

She ignored that. "If you love her, how is it you could do what you did to me?"

He moved his feet awkwardly. "Oh, well, you know, a fellow might like one girl pretty well, and yet want to kiss another."

"Oh!" She looked at him thoughtfully, and then turned on her heel and left him.

When she had gone he sank down into a chair and wiped his face, which was flushed and perspiring.

"By Jove, she's a queer one. I never struck anyone like her before. A beauty, too, especially when she looked angry. Anyway I've kissed her," he added with satisfaction, "and I guess that's her first."

As he thought about it, this kiss assumed enormous proportions in his mind. He was filled with a desire to do it again, and he looked at her secretly but covetously.　His eyes gleamed triumphantly when he thought how he shared a secret with her, for he knew that Helen would not tell Belle.　He amused himself with dropping hints, trying to make the warm blood flame into Helen's cheeks, as he had seen it before, but he was not able to move her from her attitude of proud aloofness, and she avoided being left alone with him.

CHAPTER VII.

THE NEW LIFE BEGINS.

On Monday morning Helen awoke with a start. Something was going to happen to-day; what was it? She got up hastily, for she remembered that she was going to start work. She heard Irene go past into the bathroom, and Belle coming back, singing some popular air.

"Good-bye, my Blue Bell, farewell to you,
One last, fond look into your eyes of blue,
'Mid camp fires gleaming, 'mid shot and shell,
I shall be dreaming of my own Blue Bell."

Helen wondered where Belle learnt all her songs, for she seemed to have an inexhaustible supply of them, and she and Bert loved to sing them together. She banged at Helen's door as she passed.

"Get up," she cried. "Work, work to-day. It's Monday morning—Monday morning—" and her voice got fainter and fainter, then died away altogether, as she went into the house and shut herself in her room.

Breakfast was always a hurried, go-as-you-please meal at the Hunters' house. Mrs. Hunter bustled about, cutting lunches, pouring out tea, making toast, and quite happy in looking after her numerous brood. She gave Helen her lunch, and sent her off with a parting kiss.

"Good luck, dear," she said.

"I need it," thought Helen, and then said aloud, "Will it be very dreadful, Irene?"

Irene stifled a yawn. "Are you getting nervous already?" she asked. "Don't worry; you'll be all right."

F   (81)

When they reached the door of the shop the big Town Hall clock was just striking the quarter to nine. Helen hung back, almost deciding to run away and not come again.

"Come along," called Irene. "You have to go through with it now."

They passed through the deserted shop, and a youth who was cleaning the windows, grinned at Irene as she passed him, followed by Helen.

"Up to time this morning, I see," he said. "What's happened? I say," jerking a grimy thumb at Helen, "a new girl?"

Irene nodded rather impatiently, and stepped over his bucket and broom. "I wish you would move your things out of the way," she said. "Is Miss Read in yet?"

"Just come in a minute ago, looking as sour as a gooseberry."

"We had better go into her first," said Irene. "She will want to see you."

They went into the same room that Helen had been in on her previous visit. Miss Read, who had just taken off her hat, was standing at the looking-glass arranging her hair. She looked up as the girls entered but did not give them any greeting. In the strong morning light she looked more faded than before. The sun shone through the window and fell across her hair, but awakened no responsive gleam in it. It shone on Helen too, but her hair sparkled and gleamed like ruddy gold. The sun seemed to caress it, to laugh and delight in its beauty. Helen was unconscious of the difference but perhaps the woman noticed it, for she turned abruptly from the glass and moved out of reach of the sun's beams, and her eyes had a hint of dislike in them as they rested on Helen. It was a fading woman's instinctive jealousy of the opening flower of a girl's youth and beauty. Helen aggravated her offence by standing where the sun fell full upon her. She seemed lit up by an inner fire, her cheeks glowed and her eyes shone. She was in perfect health, and in a state of intense excitement. Unconsciously she threw her beauty like a challenge at the older woman, who had passed through life without living it, fading a little more as each day followed another.

Miss Read ordered Irene abruptly to take Helen outside and show her round, and she would be out in a little while. They passed out of this room into a smaller one behind, which Irene told Helen they used as a luncheon room.

"Hurry up and get your hat off," she whispered. "She'll be out in a moment, and she is already in a bad temper."

Helen did as she was told, while Irene, with a few parting words of advice, hurried up the side passage into the shop. She had no sooner gone when the door opened and Miss Read appeared.

"I have some work for you to do out in the store," she said. "You can't go into the shop yet, you are too inexperienced."

Helen was perfectly willing to do whatever she was told, though she did feel a slight sinking at the heart when she saw what it really was. Huge piles of dishes, plates, cups and saucers were ranged round the store, all of them covered in dust and some caked with mud. She was told they all had to be washed and dried, ready to be brought inside.

"Be very careful in handling them," said Miss Read. "All breakages will be deducted from your salary."

This counsel made Helen nervous to begin with, but she rolled up her sleeves and tackled the work. There was a large trough, which she filled up with dishes, and then turned the tap on. Miss Read watched her until she had started, and then went away, and Helen saw no more of her for the rest of the morning.

Next door was a cheap restaurant where meals were

served at sixpence.   Breakfast was still on, for she
could hear a continuous clatter of plates, knives and
forks, the waitresses calling out the orders, and the
voice of the cook grumbling as she received them.
A few days after Helen was tempted to peep through
the fence where she could see right into the kitchen.
Afterwards her companions could never understand
why she always refused to accompany them next door,
where they occasionally had dinner on Friday nights.

She worked with a will, though her back soon got
tired with the unaccustomed stooping, and her arms
ached with lifting the heavy stacks of dishes.   However it was pleasant enough, for through the large
open door she could see the up-stairs windows of
the neighbouring shop, and during the morning different faces would suddenly appear at one of these
windows, stare at her for a moment, and then smile
and wave a hand in greeting.   Helen smiled and
waved back, for she felt a wave of friendliness and
comradeship for the unknown people who smiled
down at her.   They were wage-earners, and so was
she.

She discovered a little later that her companions
in the shop thought they were superior to the girls
who served in the sixpenny restaurant, and they never
acknowledged them in any way.   Helen aroused much
indignation when she refused to stop exchanging
greetings with the girls, but as she soon created her
own clearly defined position in the shop her movements were never questioned.

The girls in the shop had slipped out to have a
look at her during the morning, glad of the chance to
escape for a moment or two.   They exchanged a few
words with her, and then scurried back to the shop.
The youth who had been cleaning the windows also
came out.   He sat down on an empty packing-case
near by, and watched her as she worked.   She soon
discovered that his name was Ernest and that he
fully intended to call her "Helen."

He was an undersized youth, with a pimply face, snub nose, and small and shifty eyes; and he talked to Helen mostly about horses and horse-racing. He could give her a good tip for the Caulfield Cup, which was to be run in a week or two. His brother knew a man who knew one of the jockeys riding in the Cup race; he had got a splendid tip from him, and if she liked to give him a couple of shillings he would put them on for her. He had got as far as this when he thought he heard footsteps along the side passage, and hurried upstairs. Shortly after he came down again, a basket in his hand full of goods which he was taking into the shop. Seeing Helen alone, he immediately put it down, took his seat, and resumed his interrupted conversation. Helen had not been able to convince him that she did not want to put two shillings on a horse, when he got another fright, and hurried off again.

At lunch time she was very tired and glad to be able just to sit down. Irene was very indignant when she saw all she had done, and advised her not to work too hard. The girls talked together in whispers, for they were afraid of Miss Read overhearing them, as they suspected her of listening at the doors. Helen was too tired to take the slightest interest in what they were saying, and at six o'clock she was absolutely exhausted and could hardly walk home. Directly she had finished her tea she went to bed, and fell at once into a heavy, dreamless sleep.

In this way started her life at the shop, which was destined to last two years—two long, wasted years, as she was to think of them afterwards when she had left that life behind her. Irene's prediction that she would not like the work and would soon want to leave was quickly fulfilled. Her first enthusiasm rapidly evaporated, for she saw that she was deliberately picked out for all the most trying and dirty work. She could not understand why this should be so, but the others knew well enough and laughed among themselves.

When they were very busy in the shop she was brought in to help, and she always came in on Friday nights.   There were a few people who got to know her by sight and looked forward to seeing the sweet-faced girl with the bright hair, and asked to be served by her.   She liked being in the shop, for the constant movement and life was exciting, and she was interested in the people she saw.   She took pains to please them, and was always polite and obliging in her manner, even to the poorest person who might come in to buy a two-penny cup.

However these interludes were merely occasional breaks in her monotonous life of washing dishes and dusting, and very soon she was looking round for a way of escape; but she seemed to have got into a coil from which she was unable to extricate herself.   At last she began to feel that nothing mattered very much, that the principal thing in life was to get through the day in the best and easiest way for herself, and she soon slipped into the habits of the others, and did no more work than she was absolutely forced to do.

Sometimes—though she smothered it as soon as felt—she was conscious of a sense of bitter disappointment that her life should have petered out like this —it seemed so futile, so unnecessary.   A machine could have done her work as well as she did, or even better; it was so purely mechanical.   She had got out of one groove only to fall into another. She found it difficult to rouse herself, and only lived from day to day, making resolutions to learn something, but the easy monotony of her life repressed these secret ambitions, and she still went on in the same way. The picture of "Monna Lisa" questioned her with her secret smile, but Helen shut her heart against her questionings.

She had become a great favourite with her companions.   They were all older than she, and they found her pliable clay to work with.   They rejoiced in making her blush, and soon effectually destroyed her innocence. When Irene was there things were not so bad, for she checked them, but soon afterwards Irene secured a position in a shop in town, and Helen was left alone. She soon became used to their whispered stories and insidious conversation, and though she never joined them, she listened to what they told her and laughed when she saw she was expected to do so. She was eager for them to like her, and it was this eagerness to stand well in their eyes that made her listen and laugh at things which she afterwards remembered with a queer little sense of shame.

By the end of the first year she had changed from the girl she had been. Her eyes had lost their look of appealing childishness and diffidence, and her manner had become more assured. It was only her intense love of reading that saved her from sinking to the level of her companions. All her spare time was spent in the Public Library, and she drugged her mind with books, forcing herself not to think of the future.

Though she was filled with a passionate resentment against the monotony and uselessness of her life, it never occurred to her to regret that she had not accepted her uncle's offer. He had been to see her twice since her father's death, when she assured him she was well and happy. She had implored him to tell her all he knew about her mother, but he could give her no information. He told her of her father though—how he had thrown up his profession (the two brothers were solicitors), and gone away, deliberately cutting himself off from all his friends. Helen listened, again realising how the action of her mother had ruined her father's life. "No wonder he was so bitter," she thought.

She would not complain to her uncle that she did not like her life, though she knew he would have taken her out of it, even though it meant providing for her

away from his wife; but she was too proud to think
of this, and she let him go away quite content, thinking that she was perfectly happy.

She made no friends among the girls at the shop,
though now and again she would go out with one of
them, perhaps to a theatre or a picnic.   At one time
a mania seized the girls for fortune-telling, and they
all went secretly to an Indian they had heard about.
For a long time Helen refused to go, but at last one
of the girls persuaded her to accompany her one
night.   Outwardly Helen poured contemptuous scorn
on the idea, but inwardly she was rather curious, and
allowed herself to be persuaded, though apparently
very reluctantly, and with a great show of going only
because she wanted to oblige her companion.

The house of the fortune-teller was in a little back
street and they soon found it.   The door was wide
open, and a flood of light streamed across the pavement.   Helen's companion was seized with fear immediately they got there, and begged her to come
away, but Helen laughed contemptuously.   Now that
she was there she would not go away until she had
seen everything.

"Nonsense!" she said.   "What are you frightened of?"

The other girl started nervously as a voice called
through the open window:—

"Come along, ladies.   Don't be frightened."

They entered, Helen leading the way, and a tall
man, with dark impassive features and glossy black
hair met them, bowing.

"Don't be frightened," he said again.

"We're not frightened," said Helen, with a curl
of her lip.

"No," he answered.   "I see you're not."

He bowed them into a small inner room where several women were waiting, and then beckoned to one
of them to follow him, which she did, giggling nervously.   The two girls sat down to await their turn

and Helen looked round, feeling at first a slight sensation of disgust and shame at the company into which her curiosity had lead her. She felt impatient at the credulous women and still more impatient with herself, for she realised that she was quite ready to be credulous too.

Most of the women were of the obvious servant-girl type, and they were clustered together in a corner, whispering and casting avid glances at the door, for they were all eager to hear their fortunes. All of them had been to other fortune-tellers, and they were comparing their experiences. There was one, however, who was an exception to the others—she was a small, slim girl, dressed in black, with a white, desperate face, and she sat by herself, nervously clasping and unclasping her hands. Helen realised that she was doing this to try and still their trembling. Now and again one of the other women would look across at her and smile knowingly at her companions. The girl was quite unconscious of the attention she was exciting. She was oblivious to everything except her own secret trouble. She fastened on Helen's imagination and haunted her. She longed to go across and say gentle words to her, anything to wipe away the hunted look from the staring eyes. But she was so aloof, so absolutely alone in her world of suffering, that Helen felt it would be an intrusion to speak to her. Shortly afterwards it was her turn to go, and when she got up Helen saw how violently her hands trembled. She could not forget that girl, and though she never saw her again, she stood in the background of her memory, clear cut as a cameo, and she never knew the meaning of the silent tragedy of her face.

The room kept filling up, more and more women arriving, for as fast as one woman left another would take her place. Helen was beginning to get tired of waiting, when the Indian silently appeared and beckoned to her to follow him. He took her into a small room, quite dark, except for a bright light which streamed on to a table covered with red velvet, which stood in the centre of the room. He motioned to Helen to sit in one of the chairs, then took her hand and laid it, palm upwards, on the table. He then turned the light so that it fell across her face and hand, leaving his own face in the shadow. Helen felt her heart beating quickly as he touched her hand, but her face was as impassive as his, for she had all the pride of the white race and the sense of the unfitness of showing any sort of emotion to a member of a coloured race. He looked at her for a moment or two in silence, and she was conscious of his dark eyes resting on her face, then he examined her hand.

"Are you not afraid of what I might tell you?" he asked at last.

She shook her head, smiling a little. Her smile seemed to anger him, for his grasp on her hand tightened, and he thrust his face closer to hers.

"What I tell you is true," he said. "True! You understand?"

"I understand," said Helen coldly. "But you haven't told me anything yet."

He drew his breath, with a hissing sound, through his teeth.

"No! not yet. I have nothing much to tell you, but yet that nothing is everything." He paused, and looked at her keenly. "Young lady, when you give yourself, be sure you are giving your heart also."

Helen drew her hand away as if he had stung her, and then with a sudden laugh put it back again.

"I thought you were going to tell me my fortune and my future?"

"That is your fortune and your future," he answered. "I will tell you no more, unless—" his eyes gleamed with a sudden cunning light, "unless you give me half a crown. I will tell you all I see for that."

Helen opened her purse, and threw a shilling down

on the table. "And I suppose you would tell me more for five shillings?" she asked. "No thank you, a shilling is enough to waste."

He followed her to the door as she went out.

"Don't forget! what I say is true. Young lady," his voice died away to a soft, insinuating whisper, "you be very careful."

She walked quickly up and down the little street, waiting for her friend. The man's words stuck in her mind and worried her. She tried to dismiss them, but they came back with their wealth of subtle meaning which she could not quite grasp. She was glad when her companion came out and she was able to get away from the place. The girl took Helen's arm affectionately.

"I'm glad we went, aren't you? He told me a lovely fortune, I'm to be married in about eighteen months to a dark man. What did he tell you?"

"Nothing much," said Helen.

"Didn't he tell you that you were going to be married?"

"No."

The girl looked pleased, it would have hurt her if she thought that Helen's future was to be better than her own.

"Poor old girl, you can't be going to be married then?"

"Probably not," answered Helen.

She told nobody at home where she had been, except George, and she did not tell even him what the man had said to her. He laughed heartily at her, for he had all the male's contempt for fortune telling. His frank contempt made her feel better, and she laughed with him at herself.

He tried to tell her one day, in his clumsy boyish way, how she had changed, how infinitely more desirable and attractive she had become, when she surprised him by bursting into tears. He had not seen her cry since her father's death, and he was puzzled and anxious. He touched her gently on the arm, but she shook his hand off impatiently.

"Why did you tell me I am changed?" she asked, wiping her eyes, and looking at him angrily. "Don't I know it well enough?"

"But I just meant," said George hesitatingly, "that you are better looking, more—" he waved his hand vaguely, "I don't know exactly what I mean. You look older of course, and well—" he added simply, "a man could fall in love with you."

Helen blushed, a blush that flooded her cheeks with vivid colour. A year ago she could have spoken of love without embarrassment, now she could not. She knew that she had changed in more ways than he realised, and she was beginning to have a sickening fear of the gradual deterioration of her mind. She knew if she could shake off the tentacles her companions had woven round her, and get away from the half lazy life she lead at the shop, she would be saved.

George watched her with a puzzled frown. He was making up his mind to suggest to her that she should go and live with her uncle.

"I say, Helen," he said at last, breaking into her thoughts. "You don't like the shop much, do you?"

She turned to him as one turns to an unexpected saviour, surprised into a sudden burst of frankness, for it almost seemed as if he had read her thoughts.

"I hate it," she said. "George, tell me what I can do—how I can get out of it."

"There is always your uncle to go to."

She looked at him angrily. "I told you before, and I tell you again, I will *not* go to him. I'm sorry I asked you, if you can't suggest anything better than that."

He knew something else he could suggest, but marriage on a few pounds a year, and with his future career still to be made, was impossible.

"What is it you want?" he asked.

"I don't know," replied Helen. "That's what I want you to tell me. I want to learn something useful. I'm sick of this work that doesn't need any brains or ability. I don't mind if I spend every penny of the money Father left me, as long as I learn something."

George considered deeply for a while, and then sprang to his feet.

"I've got it," he cried, "the very thing."

He had a sudden remembrance of a sight he was very familiar with—hundreds of girls pouring out of offices in town.

Helen's face changed; the half-moody, introspective look left it, and she became bright and eager.

"What is it?" she asked. "Tell me quickly."

"Why," he said, "learn shorthand and typing. What a fool I was not to think of it before."

"Why, of course," said Helen slowly, "that will do for me. I remember there was a girl in Uncle's office when I went in to see him."

At once her ambitions took a definite shape, and to get into an office became the whole desire of her life. She wanted to rush straight away and make arrangements to start at once, but George persuaded her to wait until he found the best college to go to. Shortly afterwards she became a night-pupil at a school near her home, and all her energies and faculties were concentrated on learning speedily and thoroughly. For a while she lived in a half-dream in which the "tap-tap" of the typewriter and the shape of the short-hand characters were the only real things. Every moment she could snatch during the day, when Miss Read was out of sight, she would take out her little book, prop it up in front of her, and while she was dusting and cleaning, steadily learn the rules, oblivious to everyone round her.

CHAPTER VIII.

THE AFTERNOON CALL.

Helen was still suffering from the secret advances of Bert. She dreaded to see him come in, for she knew that if he got the chance he would touch her hand, or press her foot and follow her about, trying to get her alone. She had to bear it in silence, too, for she could not have borne to cause any pain to Belle. He realised this and made use of it. The only way she could escape from his silent persecution was to shut herself up in her own room, making an excuse that she had work to do, and he never dared to come inside.

Mrs. Hunter had begun to get uneasy. She thought it quite time that an engagement had been announced between her daughter and Bert, and threatened to ask him what he intended doing. She was only restrained by Belle, who still believed and trusted him, and said he liked "to take his own time."

Only Helen, and she thought perhaps George also, seemed to be aware that it was Helen his eyes sought when he came and Helen he manœuvred to get alone. She thought that George noticed it, for, though they had never exchanged a word on the subject, he seemed unobtrusively to place himself in Bert's way when he was approaching Helen, and he always came down to the shop and met her when she was working late on Friday night.

One Friday night Helen was standing at the door of the shop, looking out on to the crowded street. The other girls were still serving, but as she was the youngest, she was never allowed to approach anyone unless all the others were engaged. She shivered a little as the cold winter's wind swept in, and moved away, looking carefully around to see that she was not observed. The few minutes she had at liberty were too precious to lose, and she took her shorthand book out of the pocket of her little apron, and started to study. She had forgotten the shop, the customers and everything else in the world, when she was startled by hearing a light laugh, and a white hand, heavily ringed, took the book from her. She looked up nervously, afraid for the moment that Miss Read had stolen upon her unawares and intended confiscating her book. Instead of the faded face and flat-chested figure of Miss Read, she saw a woman, who expressed more than anyone she had ever seen an absolute joy in life. She was wrapt in a heavy fur coat, and wore a little black fur cap. Her face was startingly pale against her black furs and her beautifully shaped lips, bright crimson. She saw the admiration in Helen's eyes and smiled again, as she handed her back the book.

"Shorthand, I see," she said. "Well, I suppose anything is better than this, eh?" and she looked round the shop.

"Yes," said Helen, in violent agreement.

The woman nodded her head slowly. "I thought so," she said. "I thought so the first time I saw you."

"Have you seen me before?" asked Helen in surprise.

"I saw you in the distance the last time I was in, but you were so intent on what you were doing that you did not notice me. The old dragon was serving me, so I did not have a chance of speaking to you." She drew Helen out of the range of Miss Read's eyes. "There is no need for her to see me speaking to you now."

Helen was puzzled, but agreed. She certainly did not want Miss Read to interrupt, for she was fascinated by the woman and her friendly manner.

"I am often in here," she continued, "you see I

have a—" she paused and looked at Helen, who was gazing at her with frank and open admiration. "I have a — house, and I shop here. My servants are careless and I have a lot of breakages."

She laughed as though something amused her, and Helen laughed too in sympathy. Most of the women she knew required condolences when their servants broke anything. This was the first woman she had met who laughed.

"I am sure you are sick of this place, and I might be able to help you," said the woman, giving a swift look round to see that no one was coming. "I want you to come and see me. What day are you off? Saturday! Well, come next week on Saturday afternoon and we will have tea and a talk together. That's my address—be sure you don't lose it, and don't tell any of the others I have asked you. Promise me that?"

Helen took the card and promised she would not say anything to the others, feeling rather sorry at the same time, for she was so pleased and flattered at the invitation that she wanted to boast about it. She put the card carefully between the pages of her book, and then in response to an urgent command from the woman, walked slowly down the opposite side of the shop, as Miss Read came towards them. Miss Read looked after Helen suspiciously, and when she had finished serving the woman, beckoned imperiously to her, and she came up very reluctantly.

"Did I see you speaking to that woman?" she asked sharply.

"She spoke to me," Helen said, rather sullenly.

"Another time don't stand near the door, that isn't your place. I notice you like to put yourself where you are sure to be seen."

Helen shrugged her shoulders as she watched her walk away. She was always having this kind of scene with Miss Read, and she had become so used to them now they hardly affected her at all.

When the shop closed, she hurried off, waving good-bye to the girls.   She did not expect George to meet her to-night, as he had told her he was working late at his office, but from mere force of habit she glanced at the two or three young men waiting by the door.   She uttered an exclamation of annoyance as one of them came forward.   She nodded carelessly to him, and hurried on without speaking, but he followed her.

"I heard George say he couldn't get down to-night, so I thought I would come instead."

"Why aren't you with Belle?" Helen asked, looking at him with a dislike she made no attempt to conceal.

"Oh, she's all right," he answered easily.   "Don't you worry about her.   I want to have a talk with you, for we never seem to get a moment alone together."

"I take good care we don't," she said.

"What?"   For a moment his self-complacency suffered a shock, then he laughed.   "You don't really mean that, I know."

"I do mean it, but still now you are here, I am glad of the opportunity of speaking to you."

"I thought so," he chuckled.

"I dislike you," she said slowly.   "I dislike you very much.   You are objectionable to me.   The first time I met you I disliked you, and it has grown and grown.   It is the greatest grief of my life that Belle likes you.   I am fond of Belle—I love Belle, but you—!"

She had struck at last through his armour of complacency; his masculine pride was bleeding.   Her words could leave no doubt as to her meaning, and the glimpse he could catch of her half-averted cheek, and the curve of her scornful mouth, tortured him.   At that moment he hated her; hated her the more that he knew his hatred was impotent—that his love or hate was nothing to her.

G

"I'll make you pay for this," he muttered. "One of these days I'll make you pay."

Helen stole a glance at him out of the corner of her eyes. She could see his face was livid and distorted, and his eyes bloodshot, and she laughed at him mockingly. She hated him for Belle's sake, and she was glad she had hurt him.

Her laughter stung him into sudden words. "You love Belle?" he said. "Well, we shall see. I'll hurt you yet."

"*You* can't hurt *me*," said Helen.

"I'll try," he said. "I'll hurt you through Belle. You'll come to me on your knees one of these days."

"What do you mean?" she asked sharply.

"You'll see," he said, and left her suddenly, stumbling now and then as he walked.

When she reached home, Belle had already arrived. She heard her in her bedroom, and went in.

"You didn't see anything of Bert, I suppose?" Belle asked her wistfully.

Helen hesitated before she replied.

"Yes, I did see him for a moment. I met him in the street. He seemed in a hurry and said he was sorry he could not meet you to-night."

She was glad she had told the lie, for Belle's eyes at once lost their anxious expression.

"I was afraid that something might have happened to him. ˙ I suppose he was working to-night."

"I suppose so," said Helen, and then on a sudden impulse, she flung herself down beside Belle.

"Belle," she whispered, "are you very fond of him?"

Belle looked at her dumbly, and Helen hid her face from the sudden light that flamed in her eyes.

"Give him up, dear," she whispered. "Try and give him up."

Belle shook her head, and rising, walked to the window, looking out on to the dark night.

"I can't," she said. "You don't understand,

Helen.　How could you?—you are too young.　Besides," she turned round again and laughed merrily, "how foolish we are to talk like this.　What should I give him up for?　I know he loves me too."

Helen felt depressed and a foreboding of trouble fell over her.　She could not say anything more and persuaded herself that his words were merely idle threats.　How could he possibly hurt her through Belle?

On Saturday she dressed with unusual care.　She had spent some of her money on clothes, and Belle had bought a couple of pretty dresses for her.　Belle had an unerring eye and artistic taste, and knew exactly what suited Helen.　She took a pride in dressing her.

She slipped out without telling anyone where she was going.　George wanted her to come out for a row on the river, as she often did on Saturday afternoons, but she refused.　Seeing his disappointed face she had half a mind to tell him where she was going, but some unknown feeling kept her silent.　She was afraid he might think there was something strange in it, and interfere, and Helen was already developing a faculty of always following to the end the alluring gleam of a possible adventure.

She soon found the house, a large mansion standing well back amongst tall pine trees.　As she opened the gate a man who was passing turned and stared.　She looked back when she was half-way up the drive, and found him still staring after her.　She imagined that he was surprised at such an ordinary looking girl as she going into such a beautiful house.　She did not wonder at his surprise, for she was surprised herself; and even to her inexperience it seemed an extraordinary thing that a wealthy woman should invite a young girl from a shop, who she had just seen casually, to visit her.

A rather grim-looking servant answered the door and looked at Helen curiously as she asked for Mrs. Forrester.

"She expects you," she said.   "Come this way, please."

She ushered Helen into a long narrow room, with French windows opening on to the verandah, and then closed the door behind her, pursing up her mouth as she did so.

"Another of 'em, I suppose," she said to herself. "Well, it's nothing to do with me, so long as I get paid.   But, thank God, I'm respectable."

Mrs. Forrester greeted Helen like a long lost and intimate friend.   She helped her take off her hat and smoothed back her hair.

"Pretty hair," she said.   She then put an arm across Helen's shoulders, letting it slip down to her waist and on to her hips.   Helen moved uneasily under the embrace, but she soon forgot her slight uneasiness, for Mrs. Forrester laid herself out to charm her and make her feel at home.

The room was luxuriously furnished, but after a little while Helen noticed that the air was heavy and oppressive; thick with some scent which either radiated from her new friend or else was scattered about the room.   She did not like it, for it made her feel drowsy and heavy-eyed, and she longed for the fresh air and a whiff of the sea breeze.

Mrs. Forrester rang the bell and the same grim-faced maid brought in tea.

"Just you two?" she asked, and Helen could not help looking at her in surprise, her manner was so obviously disrespectful.

"I find it so hard to get servants," said Mrs. Forrester half apologetically when the girl had gone, "that I have to be very easy with the ones I have."

She poured out the tea, talking lightly and easily. She was a perfect hostess, and an expert in character reading.   She knew exactly the right note to strike with Helen and flatttered her subtly, for she saw that Helen would quickly see through too obvious flattery.

Helen was in a maze of bewilderment. She had been given tea and cakes, petted, caressed, and flattered, but even in the midst of her natural delight she still had enough sense left to know that there must be some reason why she had been brought there.

However, when tea was finished she had not long to wait for enlightenment, for Mrs. Forrester saw that now she might safely unfold her plan.

"How old are you, dearie?" she asked.

"Nearly nineteen," answered Helen.

"Nineteen? that's a charming age. I thought you would be about that, but you never can tell with girls. Now, my dear, how would you like to come and live with me?"

"Live with you?" gasped Helen. "But why? Whatever for?"

The woman laughed. "You would soon find out why," she said, and laughed again. "Now listen, you want to leave that miserable shop, don't you?" Helen nodded. "You would like to live in a beautiful home, and have everything you could possibly desire. My dear, there is nothing you couldn't have if you came and lived with me."

A sudden light of understanding was beginning to dawn on Helen's mind.

"What would I have to do in exchange for all this?" she asked.

Mrs. Forrester thought Helen was almost won over, and smiled at her easy victory.

"Do?" she said airly. "Nothing that would hurt you in the least, my child. You would only have to be kind to any friends of mine who might call here. You understand, eh?"

"Yes," said Helen. "I see now." She knew why the man had stared at her when she was coming in, and the disrespect in the servant's voice. She tried to imagine that she felt a virtuous horror, but it was only an intense curiosity.

"Come, now," urged the woman. "Be sensible, and listen to reason."

Helen could not help smiling. "Listen to reason," indeed!

"I like you," continued the woman, "I like you. I really do. Of course I can get plenty of girls who would only be too glad to come here, but I want a girl who is good looking and a lady as well."

Helen shook her head. "No," she said. "I can't."

Her tone was final, and the woman recognised it, though she made a last effort to persuade her. "Why not?" she asked.

"I don't know why not," answered Helen. "It's not my way, that's all."

"Well, if you won't, you won't, and there's no more to be said, but I think you are very foolish. What is the good of a girl like you sticking in that shop all your life? You need pleasure and love."

"Do you think I could get that with you?" asked Helen.

The woman shrugged her shoulders indifferently. "All my girls are quite happy," she said.

"I wonder?" said Helen. "Well, anyway, I'm not going to make one of them."

"I'm sorry," she said regretfully, "that I cannot persuade you, but we've talked it over with perfect good breeding on both sides, haven't we?"

"Oh, perfect!" laughed Helen, and she rose to go.

Mrs. Forrester rang the bell, and the servant appeared, muttering under her breath. Mrs. Forrester told her to wait, and she whispered to Helen:

"You won't tell anyone that I asked you to come here? I might get into trouble if you did."

"No," promised Helen. "I won't say anything."

"Ah!" said Mrs. Forrester, with a sigh of relief, "I knew I could trust you."

Helen said good-bye, and followed the servant, who seemed surprised that she was going.

"Aren't you going to stay after all?" she asked, as she opened the door.

Helen shook her head, breathing in deeply the pure, fresh air. She walked briskly down the path, looking up and down the street in some trepidation, hoping that no one would see her. Fortunately the street was clear, and she slipped hastily out, feeling unaccountably guilty as she did so.

The clock was just striking five, and she swung off down the road which lead to the sea. She walked quickly, smiling to herself, and the exercise soon made her warm and brought the vivid colour to her cheeks. When she reached the long pier no one was about, for the afternoon had been chill and dull under a gray sky. She walked to the end of the pier, enjoying the mere physical sense of well being and health, and stood looking out across the slowly darkening waters. Across the bay the lights of Port Melbourne and Williamstown were beginning to twinkle one by one; she could almost see them being lit. She could just make out in the distance the dim outlines of the ships lying at the wharves or anchored in the bay. A line of verse passed through her mind:—

> Yonder the long horizon lies,
>   And there by night and day
> The old ships draw to home again,
>   The young ships sail away.

The magic and romance of the sea and the ships stirred her imagination. She remembered how she and George had gone out one summer night for a row. They took a boat and rowed far out to where a big ship was lying at anchor. Except for a single light gleaming redly at her mast-head, she showed no other signs of life. Silent and mysterious, she lay quietly at rest, undisturbed by even a ripple of the water, whose anger she had fought so often. Helen remembered the strange sense of fear that shook her as they neared her. It seemed to her that the ship knew all the secrets of the sea, and their mystery still hung about her. On the off-side a shadow lay across the water, turning it almost black. George had said they would row right under her and try and touch the sides. Helen said nothing, though she was curiously reluctant to row across that dark patch of water, for to her it looked almost sinister. She had let him take the oars, while she leant over the side of the boat, gazing at the dark, gloomy water, and letting her imagination run riot. She thought she could see a pale face gleaming, and hear the chant of a far away song. Fascinated, and yet afraid, she had leant lower over the side, and put out her hand to touch the water. She had drawn it quickly back, as Undine's fate flashed through her mind, and it was with relief that she had heard George's cheerful, matter-of-fact voice, telling her to look up at the ship.

She had looked up, almost with awe, at the huge sides of the ship towering so high above them. The utter silence of the great, inanimate creature was strange and terrifying. But George had no fear. He had stood up in the boat and laid his hand gently on the side of the ship.

"Dear old thing," he had said affectionately. "A man could love a ship almost as much as he could love a woman."

She thought of his words now as she stood on the pier and, strangely enough, she could understand what he meant. That ship had gone and was probably ploughing its way through strange waters, to strange and unknown lands, at least unknown to her. She shivered a little as a cold wind swept over the sea, waking the waters to restless motion again. Suddenly realising that it was late and she had a long way to go, she turned and hurried home.

When she arrived she found the others were already sitting down to tea. She hesitated a moment outside the dining room, for she could hear Bert's voice. So he was coming to the house as though nothing had happened? Well, she could play that part too. She entered, fresh and glowing, bringing in a breath of cold air with her. Bert looked at her gloomily as she came in, hardly returning her greeting, and then averted his eyes. She stole a hasty glance at him as she sat down, but he had turned to Belle and was whispering to her. Belle's cheeks were flushed and her eyes bright. Under Bert's changed manner she looked happier than she had done for a long time.

All that evening Helen watched him in surprise, but he never looked at her, all his attention was devoted to Belle. A tremendous weight rolled off her heart. He had not really meant what he said. It had done him good the way she had spoken to him, and he had turned again to Belle. She ceased to worry and began to look forward to hearing their engagement announced; not that she wanted to see Belle married to him, but it was obviously what would make her happy.

CHAPTER IX.

THE PARTING WITH GEORGE.

The whole house was in consternation. George was going away; in two days he had to leave for Western Australia. He had a chance at last of getting a footing in his profession and he had to take it, for the opportunity might not occur again. Mrs. Hunter broke down and wept bitterly when she heard it, and Helen went quietly away to her own room and shut herself in. She felt stunned at first, and could hardly realise that he was really going away. She had always thought of George being near her so that she could turn to him when she wanted him, and now he was going away.

She choked back the sobs that rose to her throat, for she heard his footsteps outside. She waited in tense silence, and then heard him knock softly at the door. She opened it, and they stood facing each other in the half-light. He waited for her to speak, but she averted her eyes, for her heart was sore against him for wanting to go away from her. He looked round the room, mysterious in the dim twilight, and his heart contracted with a sudden pain. In a few days he would be far away, and he might never see that room again. The white face of "Monna Lisa" smiled down at him; she knew all about love and hate, sorrow and joy, and she knew they were all the same in the end.

"I like that picture," he said inconsequently.

Helen did not reply. He was going away, and all he could speak of was the picture. She would take it down and burn it. She walked away from him into the deeper gloom of the room, so that he should not see the tears in her eyes. If he did not care, neither did she.

"Nell," he said in an urgent whisper. "Why don't you speak to me? Say you're sorry I'm going."

He was the only one who called her Nell, and he only called her that when they were alone. Secretly she wiped her eyes; he should not see that she cared enough to cry—no, he should not see—but immediately the tears came again.

"You—you are glad to go," she said in a low voice.

He gave a bitter little laugh, "Glad to go? Why, Nell, you don't mean that. You are only saying it to hurt me."

He came closer to her, and laid a gentle hand on her shoulder. "Nell, turn round and look at me. Why, Nell, what's the matter?—you're crying."

He took her in his arms, and she broke down altogether, and wept against his shoulder, while he kept muttering to her not to cry.

"Don't go, George," she pleaded. "Don't go! I'll be so lonely without you."

"Don't make it so hard for me," he almost groaned. "I've got to go; this is the chance I've been looking for. I dare not miss it."

A sudden revulsion of feeling swept over her. "Oh, what a selfish creature I am," she cried contritely. "Of course you must go. Why! it's your whole future; but how long will you be away?"

"Two years!"

"Two years!" echoed Helen. "Anything may happen in two years."

"I know," he said. "I know, but I have to take my chance of that."

"Chance of what?"

"That you might meet some other fellow you will like better than me."

They could hear Mrs. Hunter in George's room, pulling out his boxes; she was already beginning to pack up for him.

"I must go and help her," he muttered. "You don't believe I'm glad to go? Answer me!"

"No," she whispered.

With a half-smothered exclamation, he bent his head and kissed her on the lips. The next moment he was gone and she could hear him talking to his aunt.

She went down to see him off the day he sailed for the West. She was the only one there, for Mrs. Hunter was too upset to come, and neither of the other girls could get off. Helen only managed to get a couple of hours off by forfeiting some of her salary. The ship was to sail from one of the river wharves, and she and George stood together, very silent, watching the cargo being loaded into the hold. The scream of the winch as its burdens rose in the air, and the shouts of the wharf-labourers seemed to mesmerise her. She felt if she did not think of these things she would remember that George was going away and break down. His face was very white and strained, and he too seemed to find the cargo the most interesting thing to look at.

At last he pulled out his watch and looked at it.

"I'll have to be getting on board shortly," he said, in a low voice. "Well, Nell, it's good-bye to Melbourne for me. I've often wanted to get out of it, but I will be glad to get back. I will always return to Melbourne."

A sudden remembrance flashed through Helen's mind. There was someone else who was sure to return to Melbourne. Who was it? Why, her mother, of course; was she forgetting her? She had never told George the truth. He, like the others, thought she was dead. Ought she to tell him? She looked at him half-doubtfully, and a sudden lassitude overcame her. Oh, what was the use? It didn't matter after all.

A bell sounded shrilly from the steamer and she started violently.

"I've got to get on board, Nell," George said hoarsely. "Good-bye—don't forget I love you."

She watched him run up the gangway and push his way through the crowd to the side of the ship where he could look down at her. A lump rose in his throat at the sight of the lonely, forlorn figure; but he was a man, and a man was not supposed to cry. He stared hard in front of him for a moment or two, until the lump was gone and his eyes were clear again.

She stood looking up at him, and then, unable to bear the strain of waiting any longer, made a gesture of farewell with her hand, and turned and hurried away down the long length of the wharves, hardly able to see where she was going. Once she looked back; the ship had moved off from her moorings and was steaming slowly down the river. She could distinguish nothing except a sea of white faces, waving hands and handkerchiefs. It wasn't a dream then—he had really gone.

She missed him horribly for a time, but gradually the first sharp sense of separation wore off, and she settled down to her studies again. He wrote to her very often, long letters, but rather stiff and formal, for he had not the gift of expression, and she laid them down with a feeling of disappointment, vaguely missing something in them, though she knew not what. At last he got to seem very far away from her, as though he were a part of her life which would never, never return.

Her anxiety about Belle had returned with redoubled force. After a period of unremitting attention to Belle, during which he had scarcely spoken to Helen, Bert had suddenly ceased from coming, and had now not been near the house for weeks. Belle's vivacity and gaiety had deserted her, and she looked drawn and almost haggard. All her time, when she was at home, she spent looking out of the window of the front room, watching for him. It made Helen's heart ache to see her, but she dared not speak to her, for Belle seemed to shrink into herself if any of them approached her. Belle had always been very fond of her mother, but now she seemed to have developed a horror of being left alone with her. Now and again she would make a pretence of being her own bright self again, but it was a ghastly farce and deceived no one.

It seemed to Helen that though Irene and her mother sympathised with Belle, they were inclined to blame her to a certain extent. They implied, rather than said, that Belle had only herself to thank if she had been jilted. Mrs. Hunter's unexpressed opinion was that no woman should let a men see she loved him until she was safely married.

Helen did not discuss Belle with them, for she felt more uneasy than she cared to admit, even to herself. It seemed to her that Belle's stony calm was unnatural, for she was a facile nature, and given to easy emotion.

She was sitting one night at the writing-table in her room, the table at which her father had so often sat. She imagined sometimes she could see him still sitting there with his head bent over his writing. She sat there trying to study, but unable to do so. She could not set her mind to it, for she could not help thinking of Belle looking out through the window, as the night got darker and darker, waiting and watching for someone who did not come.

She was so occupied with her thoughts that she did not hear a gentle tap at her door. It was repeated, and as she did not answer, the door opened slowly and Helen suddenly saw in the mirror in front of her, the reflection of Belle's pale face. She sat staring at it for a moment without moving, for it came so apt on her thoughts that she imagined it was a creature of her imagination. Then as Belle came into the room she sprang up to welcome her.

Belle waved her outstretched hand away, and groped her way to a chair.

"He hasn't come again to-night, Helen," she said.

A spasm of pain crossed Helen's face, and her whole soul rose up in rebellion against the awful thraldom of pain one person can impose on another. A phrase in her father's letter to her came back into her mind. "Do not pin your faith on any human being."

"I gave him until to-night," Belle said, in the same dull, toneless voice; "after to-night I knew I could not hope any longer."

Helen was in despair. She felt so impotent, so powerless to comfort the stricken girl, and it would have only taken a word or a smile from Bert to make the white face brighten and the dull eyes shine again.

"It would be better if she could cry," she thought. She sat on the arm of Belle's chair, gently touching her hair. It saddened her inexpressibly to see her like this—pretty, bright Belle; she did not seem made for tragedy.

Suddenly Belle seemed to awake to life. She began to speak, quickly, breathlessly, in a low, hushed whisper, as though she were afraid of being overheard.

"You are the only one I dare come to, Helen. You are young, but you are different from the others; you will not hate me too much." She looked up with her pathetic eyes. "Helen, I am a wicked woman."

"Are you, dear?" said Helen, still touching her hair with gentle fingers. "Why?"

"Oh, Helen, I loved him too much, and now I have to pay for it. I'm one of those women you read about—wicked women who everyone hates."

Helen understood at once, and the shock was great. Her hand still kept mechanically stroking Belle's hair, but her mind was in a fierce flame of anger. To make him suffer—to be revenged on him, if she only could! She almost forgot Belle's distress in the rush of anger that shook her. It was only with an effort that she could keep her attention on what Belle was saying.

"Helen, tell me what to do. I dare not let Mother know. I would kill myself first."

"Let me think," said Helen slowly. "Does he know?"

"Yes, he knows," and then she added in an ashamed whisper. "I had to ask him to marry me, and he—refused."

"Marry him!" cried Helen. "Surely you are not thinking of marrying him."

"Helen," she whispered. "I must! I must! That's where you can help me. He said he might consider it if you asked him."

"Oh God!" cried Helen to herself. "This is too much." Her futile anger almost choked her. She saw now what he had meant—she would go down on her knees to him one of these days.

"Anything would be better than to marry him," she said. "Listen! you could go away. I would think of some good excuse to tell your mother, and you could go into the country for a time. I've got about £40 left, and I could get more. I'll look after you, I swear I will, and no one will ever know. Only don't marry him."

"I must, I must," repeated Belle. She suddenly fell on her knees beside Helen and caught her hands in hers. "Helen, help me. You can, I know you can. He would listen to you."

Helen felt suddenly very tired. She saw it was no good saying any more and a sense of fatality swept over her. "What must be, shall be." She would go to him.

"I'll ask him," she said at last, and immediately Belle caught her breath with a gasp of relief. "Write and tell him to some and see me. You had better make it one night when your mother is out. Say Wednesday, for I know she is going to that church meeting."

"You'll plead with him," whispered Belle. "I'm desperate, Helen. If he won't marry me, I'll—"

"Hush! don't speak like that. I give you my word he will marry you, if I have to go on my knees and beg him. I mean it, Belle, he shall marry you."

She knew that Bert was covetous, for he had shown it in a hundred different little ways, and his meanness had always been a joke amongst them.   She intended to offer him money, and she knew she could probably buy him, though she was sure at the same time that he would humiliate her as much as possible.

Belle clung to her like a child.   Now that she had confided in Helen she could not bear to let her go, she seemed to draw comfort and vitality from her.   She looked deadly tired, and Helen made her lie down on the bed, taking off her shoes, and covering her up with a rug.   She lay with half-shut eyes, and Helen thought how young she looked and how pretty.

"Too young and too pretty for him," she thought.

Belle went off into a doze, and then woke again with a sudden start, imploring Helen not to think her wicked and not to tell her mother.   Helen soothed her as well as she could, and gradually her limbs relaxed and she fell into a deep sleep.

Helen settled herself in the arm chair, prepared to spend the night there.   She looked up at "Monna Lisa" before she put the light out—the smile seemed different to-night, sadder, and so very, very wise.

"What do you think of life?" asked Helen. "You who know everything!   Is it worth while in the end?"

But "Monna Lisa" kept the answer to that question to herself.

CHAPTER X.

THE MARRIAGE.

Helen was waiting in the sitting-room for Bert. She had just managed to get Mrs. Hunter off to the church meeting, though with some difficulty. At first she had seemed disinclined to go, remarking that it could get on quite well without her, but by dint of judicious handling Helen had at length persuaded her. She had not been gone ten minutes when the gate creaked on its hinges as it was opened, and then slammed loudly. Helen lifted a corner of the blind and peeped out to make sure it was Bert. Her heart was beating a little nervously, but otherwise she was quite calm and self-possessed. She opened the door for him quietly, for she did not want him to knock in case Irene should hear it and come out to see who it was. He did not speak as he followed her into the room, but looked at her with an unpleasant smile, though Helen could see he was obviously trying to keep his courage up. He stood awkwardly by the table, fumbling with his hat in his hand.

"Won't you sit down?" said Helen politely. "It will be just as well to be as comfortable as possible under the circumstances."

He obeyed her, and she took his hat out of his hand, and placed it on the table; then she drew a chair up and sat down opposite him. During these preparations he stared at her, open-mouthed. This was not at all what he had expected. Since he had got Belle's letter he had rehearsed the interview a dozen times. He had pictured himself storming in, carrying everything before him, and Helen pale and trembling, pleading with him. He made an effort to make the real interview coincide with his conception of it.

(114)

"Well," he said roughly. "What do you want me for?"

"You know very well," said Helen, smiling.

He cleared his throat noisely, and spat on the floor. "You'll have to tell me why you sent for me," he said.

Helen raised her eyes, and a faint expression of disdain crossed her face.

"I have no objection to telling you since you choose to be so explicit. I sent for you to ask you to marry Belle."

He laughed jeeringly. "You ask me to marry Belle? What's it got to do with you? Why should I marry her because you want me to?"

"Don't make any mistake about that," Helen replied. "I don't want you to marry her. I begged her not to. I told her anything would be better than to marry you."

"Oh, you did, did you?" he said, a dull flush spreading over his face. "Belle wouldn't agree with that, I'll guarantee."

"No, she wouldn't," Helen answered tranquilly. "It is foolish of her, but still she wants to marry you."

"If she can get me," he sneered.

"Ah, yes, of course! How much are you worth do you think?"

"How—how do you mean?" he stammered, taken by surprise.

"I mean would you sell yourself to Belle for £45?"

A covetous gleam came into his eyes. Money! That put a different complexion on the whole matter. He had intended to marry Belle all along, and had just wanted to have the satisfaction of hearing Helen plead with him. Certainly she had not been very humble so far, but if she was willing to pay out money, he would be a fool not to take it. Forty-five pounds would buy him a share in a cycle shop that he had had his eye on for some time. Forty-five pounds!   He rubbed his chin thoughtfully as he looked at her.

Helen saw that she had got him, and she hid a smile.   He was very easy sport after all; his vapid boastings of humiliating her were so much "hot air."   She despised him utterly; he had the chance in his hands, and he was going to let it slip for £45. This was all the money she had left, but she did not give that a thought.   If £45 could give Belle what she wanted, it was cheaply bought.

"I wish you would hurry up," she said at last. "Mrs. Hunter will be coming home shortly, and she will want to see her future son-in-law."

"Um!"   He bit his lip, and then sprang to his feet suddenly.   "I'll take it."

"I thought so," said Helen.

He sat down on the table, swinging his legs and looking down at her.

"Yes, I'll take it—but there is something else I want, too."

She involuntarily clenched her hands.   It wasn't finished then?   There was something else he wanted.

She got up slowly, indolently stretching herself.

"It's no use asking for any more money, for I simply haven't got it."

"It's not money," he said slowly.   "You remember I kissed you once—on the cheek.   I want to kiss you again, not on the cheek this time, but on the mouth."

Helen stood very still for a moment, and then threw back her head with a light laugh.

"Bah!" she said contemptuously, "Why not? What are your kisses to me?"

He frowned heavily as he looked at her, and she noticed vaguely a pulse beating quickly in his cheek. She wondered why she had never seen it before.

"You agree then?" he asked hoarsely.

"Yes!"

"Well, first give me the money!"

She laughed mockingly. "The money first? I'll give you the money the day you are married to Belle, and—after the ceremony."

"I'm to trust you then, but you won't trust me?"

"That's it," she replied carelessly. "You know quite well that you can trust me, but I can't trust you."

"All right," he said thickly, "and now for the other payment."

She had turned very pale, striving to make herself believe that she did not really mind it—that it could not possibly affect her, but in spite of her reasonings all her senses revolted against him. She could smell the highly-scented oil he put on his hair. She never came across that scent afterwards, but a vivid picture of the scene rose up before her. She shivered slightly as she saw his moist hands, the finger-nails broken and dirty. She sometimes thought she hated him most for his hands, for she had a love of beautiful hands.

She closed her eyes as he approached her, and then forced them open again, while her lips curved in a scornful line. It was the expression that roused him to fury, and he seized her roughly and pressed his lips to hers. A horrified thought passed through her mind. "How could Belle—" and then she tore herself away, pushing him violently from her.

"You've been paid now," she said.

He leant against the table, panting heavily. He did not seem to have disturbed her calm serenity. He could have cursed himself and her too, himself for his impotent desire, and she for her coldness and scorn.

"Haven't you got any feelings?" he muttered at last.

"Not for you," she replied. "Here—," she pushed a chair towards him. "Sit down, and try and compose yourself. I'm going to bring Belle in."

He sat down, and leant his head against his hand.

His rage was subsiding, and he was beginning to think of Belle—she at least had feelings—she loved him, and he consoled his hurt vanity with that.

"Listen," said Helen. "We may as well finish the subject now, for I don't want to speak to you about it again. If I find out that you don't treat her well after you are married, I'll write to George and tell him everything."

"I'll treat her all right," he answered sulkily. "What about the money?"

"I'll give that into your hands directly you are married. Now I'll send Belle in." She paused and looked back at him, as she opened the door. "Be sure you don't tell her anything about the money."

"Am I likely to?"

He seemed to have quite recovered himself, and was carefully curling the ends of his moustache. Helen smiled as she saw what he was doing, and then went out to find Belle.

Belle was waiting in Helen's room, divided between hope and fear. One look at Helen's face was enough; she saw that she had been saved. It needed no words from Helen to tell her that. Without speaking she ran out of the room, passing Irene at the door, without seeing her.

"What's up, Helen?" Irene asked casually, coming in.

"Bert is inside."

"Oh," said Irene in astonishment. "He's come round again, has he? Belle ought to show him the door pretty quick."

"Perhaps she ought to, but she won't. Belle told me they are going to be married. He has come round to-night to fix it up, I believe."

"Really?" said Irene. "Well, that's good news. Mother will be pleased. She is beginning to think it is quite time that some of us got married."

Helen longed to be able to get away from them all; she dreaded seeing Bert again, but she knew she would have to be there to take part in the congratulations and rejoicing that would follow the news of the engagement. She heard Mrs. Hunter come in, down the side passage and go past her room, walking very heavily and slowly as though she were tired. Helen went out to meet her, and give her, as she thought, news that would please her, and she was surprised when Mrs. Hunter burst into tears.

"Isn't that what you wanted, then?" she asked rather impatiently.

"Oh, my dear, it's what I have prayed for night and day. You don't know how I felt the disgrace of my daughter being jilted."

Helen wondered grimly how she would feel if she knew the real truth.

"Well, we won't say any more about Belle being jilted, for after all she was not. You know Belle always said that Bert liked to take his own time."

"So she did—so she did," said Mrs. Hunter, wiping her eyes and becoming cheerful again. "Now we must have a special supper for the occasion. Send one of the boys down the street for some cakes and fruit, will you, dear?"

Helen sent a protesting small boy off on the message, and then helped Mrs. Hunter lay the table for supper.

"Heard the news, Mum?" asked Irene, who had just strolled in as they finished the work.

"Yes," answered her mother. "Put the kettle on will you?"

Irene did as she was told, grumbling under her breath, and then, though they expected it, they all started when they heard the sitting-room door open and footsteps coming down the hall. Belle burst into the room, flushed and happy, followed by Bert, who looked rather sheepish and as if he wished himself out of it.

"Mother!" said Belle, with a sob in her voice. "Mother!"

She flung her arms round her mother's neck, and they clung together for a moment. Then Mrs. Hunter took Belle's hand, giving it to Bert, and laid her own hand on his shoulder as she did so. She had never looked so dignified as in that moment when she administered the only rebuke she ever made to him.

"Bert," she said, "you have taken your own time about it, but now that you have made up your mind we welcome you into the family. Be good to her, Bert."

He moved uneasily, and then said with an apparent effort. "It's all right, Mother, don't you worry."

Belle flushed with pleasure as he spoke, and hung on to his arm, smiling up at him. He looked down at her, flattered and pleased by her humble adoration. This was a seemly attitude in a woman, and he glanced quickly at Helen, glad that she was there to see it. Helen could not help a feeling of wonderment at how quickly Belle had recovered herself. It was as if all the terror and anxiety of the last few weeks had been wiped away from her remembrance.

"When are you going to be married?" she asked abruptly, striking a jarring note in the general sense of deference towards Bert.

"Plenty of time for that," said Mrs. Hunter easily.

"Oh, no," said Bert. "We want to be married as soon as possible. We'll have the banns put up next Sunday."

"Impossible!" gasped Mrs. Hunter. "That's far too soon."

"That is what we have arranged, Mother, Belle has agreed that there is no use waiting. Besides—" a flicker of a smile passed over his face—"I have had a little windfall lately, and I am investing it in that cycle shop I had my eye on. Belle and I can live behind the shop."

Helen breathed an imperceptible sigh of relief as she heard this. Everything was fixed up, and he was going through with it without any trouble. He was behaving very well, too, much better than she had expected. She was so relieved at this that the anxious, rather strained expression of her face died away, and she was able to join in the laughter and talk at the supper-table. They toasted the future bride and groom in coffee, and rallied them cheerfully.

"Who will be the next, I wonder?" said Mrs. Hunter, leaning back in her chair when they had finished supper. "Irene or Helen?"

"Not I," answered Irene. "I am happy enough as I am, thank you—for the present at least. But you, Helen—you needn't look so innocent. What about—you know who?" and she nodded her head wisely.

Helen's eyes narrowed a little, though she pretended to laugh.

"You are always romancing, Irene," she said.

"Am I?" answered Irene. "Well, Time will tell."

Bert rose to go, and Belle accompanied him to the door to say good-bye. She was not away long, and came back just as Helen was leaving the room. The others were in the kitchen and the two girls could hear them talking together loudly. Belle hesitated a moment as she saw Helen—it seemed as though she were ashamed to meet Helen's eyes. Helen herself felt nervous and embarrassed. She had hoped that Belle would not open up the subject again, but evidently Belle was determined to do so.

"What is it, Belle?" she asked at last, seeing that she found it difficult to begin.

"I just want to say, Helen," said Belle in a low voice, "that it was good of you to do what you did for me; but I think after all he—he would have asked me himself, don't you?"

She looked at Helen imploringly. Her pride had awakened and she wanted to save some self-respect from the wreck.

"I am sure he would," Helen answered gravely.

Belle's face cleared, and Helen thought how easy it was to re-assure her, and also how easy it was to deceive her. She was turning away when Belle called her back again.

"Do you think I am very wicked?" she asked wistfully.

"No, no, no!" cried Helen passionately. "Of course not—don't dream of such a thing. And, Belle, after to-night we will never speak of the subject again—we will forget it."

There was a moment of suspense, and both girls avoided each other's eyes, and then as Belle said nothing further, Helen left the room.

The wedding was an affair after Mrs. Hunter's own heart, for though she had only three weeks' notice, she yet managed to gather together an imposing array of relatives. Helen felt bewildered amongst them all, and yet aloof. The flood-tide of the Hunters' relatives seemed to have engulfed her and then flung her high up where she stood looking down on them. For the first time she felt glad that her own relatives were so few.

There was a Hunter uncle, a fat man, a very fat man, who followed Helen about, whispering mysteriously. There were also two spinster aunts who watched the uncle with sour and relentless eyes. They looked at Helen with suspicion, and she heard a whisper about "dyed hair." Numerous other aunts and cousins and several of Bert's people helped to swell the tide.

They all went off to the church where the marriage ceremony was to take place, and several of the women wept audibly, while the men fought for the first kiss from the bride, the fat uncle easily succeeding. Then he laughed richly, and winked at Helen.

"Smarter than any of the young fellows, my dear! It's the old bird that catches the worm, ha, ha, ha!"

Helen met Bert's eyes as he followed Belle out of the Church. That morning she had drawn all her money out of the Savings Bank ready to give to him. She had it in an envelope and handed it to him, as he pressed close to her. He took it and hastily slipped it in his pocket, and Helen was congratulating herself that it had been so neatly done that no one had noticed the transaction, when a hand smote her on the shoulder, and a rich, throaty voice exclaimed:

"Now, now! Passing notes to a married man! That won't do!"

Crimson with annoyance, she looked up—it was the fat uncle. Bert, with a muttered curse, hurried on with Belle, leaving Helen to deal with him.

"That's my little gift to them both," she said, glad that no one else was near.

"Well, well, well," he rolled as he spoke, "I'm glad it's no worse. And now for the breakfast. Ah!" He smacked his lips.

About twenty people had to be packed into the small dining-room at the Hunters' house. Helen was unfortunate enough to be seated next to the fat uncle, and opposite the spinster aunts. The uncle had thoughtfully provided the table with lager beer, of which he had a large share, and as it warmed his blood, he leered engagingly at Helen. Every time he did so, Helen met the unwavering stare of the spinster aunts fixed sternly upon her, and one made an audible remark to the other about "painted young hussies who can't even leave men alone who are old enough to be their grandfathers."

Everyone was uproariously happy; they clasped hands and sang "Auld Lang Syne," and told Bert in song that he was a "jolly good fellow," and he seemed to think he was.

At last the breakfast was over, and the festivities at an end. The presents had been viewed, the usual amount of tears shed, and the usual indelicate jokes made; and the bride and bridegroom at last were allowed to depart for their own home.

They all went out to see them drive off in a hansom

that Mrs. Hunter had ordered as being more fashion-
able than a cab.   The unhappy pair were smothered
with confetti and hit in the face with the sharp grains
of rice, while the fat uncle, in a final burst of enthusiasm (and perhaps lager beer), purloined a shoe
and, throwing it wildly, struck the protesting driver
over the ear.   —

Helen stood with the others, though she did not
join in their laughter.   The fat uncle had enjoined
her several times to ''cheer up,'' but by a gradual,
almost imperceptible movement, she had managed to
lose him amongst the other guests.   She could catch
a glimpse of Belle's face through the window of the
hansom and thought she looked pale and tired.   During the breakfast Belle had looked at her often, when
she thought that Helen was not noticing; but Helen
was aware of it, and knew that Belle was looking at
her, in fear of what she might be thinking.   Belle
could not be natural with her, and Helen knew that
never again could they meet without self-conscious-
ness.   She was taking a mental farewell of Belle,
and just before the hansom drove off, as Mrs. Hunter
climbed up to kiss her daughter, Helen imagined that
Belle's eyes sought hers over her mother's head, and
her lips moved a little.   Then Mrs. Hunter got down,
the driver whipped up his horse, and they were off,
followed by cheers and waving of handkerchiefs.

Helen watched the hansom until it was out of sight,
and then went inside to help clear away the debris of
the wedding breakfast.

PAINTED CLAY

PART II.

CHAPTER I.

For months past Helen had been steadily answering advertisements she had seen in the papers for typistes, but without success. One morning, just as she was leaving the house the postman handed her a letter. The handwriting was strange to her, and she opened it with trembling fingers. It was short and curt, the writer evidently not believing in wasting words.

> Dear Madam,
> Call immediately on receipt of this, at above address.

The signature was indecipherable, but the letter was headed "Thomas & Co., Little Collins Street."

Call immediately! That meant to-day, or she might lose the chance. She would have to ask Miss Read to let her off for a couple of hours, and they were very busy stocktaking. What if she refused? Helen paled at the thought—but she must get off at whatever cost—she must.

Miss Read was late in arriving at the shop that morning, and Helen waited for her in a state of nervous irritation. At last she came, her arrival being heralded by one of the girls who was standing idly at the door looking out on to the sreet. She gave the alarm to the others, who immediately scurried back to their work. When Miss Read came in, they were all working industriously, and though she glanced suspiciously around, she found nothing to query. She nodded curtly to them, and went into her own room. After waiting a little while so as to give her time to settle down for the day, Helen knocked softly at the door and went in.

"What is it?" asked Miss Read snappishly. She was annoyed at being interrupted, for she was just going to make herself a private cup of tea.

"Could I possibly get off for a couple of hours this morning?" asked Helen, putting all the deference she could into her voice. "I want to go into town."

"What! Get off this morning! Don't you know how much there is to do? And I with a headache nearly blinding me!"

"I'm sorry," murmured Helen vaguely. "If you could arrange to let me go, I could quite easily be back by twelve and then, if I don't take my lunch hour, I will really only be losing an hour's work."

"What do you want to go into town for?" asked Miss Read, suddenly suspicious.

"On business," faltered Helen, who was unprepared for the question.

"On business!" retorted Miss Read. "Your business is here, and here you stay while I've got anything to do with it, at any rate."

"Then you won't let me off?" asked Helen, who had turned very pale.

"No!"

"Then I must go without your permission, that's all."

"What?" cried Miss Read, thunderstruck at being defied. "This is impertinence, miss."

"I don't mean to be impertinent," said Helen, "but I must get off for a couple of hours, and as you take the time off my salary I don't see that you lose anything by it, especially as I will have to work harder to make up for it."

Miss Read flushed angrily. She had always disliked Helen. If it had been one of the other girls she might have stretched a point and let her off, but not Helen.

"If you go this morning," she said, "you don't come back here again."

Helen hesitated in an agony of indecision. She

saw that Miss Read meant what she said, but she still had a chance to draw back. She could apologize and stay on. If she went in defiance of Miss Read, it would be forever. She was utterly dependent now upon her earnings, for all her money had gone and she had been unable to save anything. If she lost this position, and could not get another at once, she would have to accept the charity of the Hunters or her uncle. Neither of them would grudge it to her she knew, but the thought of accepting it was intolerable.

"Well?" asked Miss Read, brusquely breaking in on her thoughts. "What are you going to do? Hurry up now."

What was she going to do? Here was the opportunity she had been looking for and, through the antagonism of this woman, she was in danger of losing it. Yet even if she defied Miss Read and went into town, she might not get the position. But she might —she might. She would be a coward to let the chance go. Besides it was too alluring—too exciting. She could not resist it. She would take the risk.

"I am going," she said.

"Very well," answered Miss Read. She brushed rudely past Helen, motioning to her to follow her into the shop. Helen did so, conscious of a feeling of pure joy. It was all over now. She had taken the step that severed her forever from the life she hated. Everything would be all right, for the gods must be kind to her. The girls looked at her in wonderment. They knew that something unusual had happened, and yet Helen looked so happy that it could not have been anything unpleasant—at least for her. The look on Miss Read's face intimidated them, and they averted their eyes, only stealing side-long glances at Helen. They concluded that she was going to be married, and a sigh of envy stole through the lips of each girl. How gladly would any of them have changed places with Helen!

Miss Read pulled out the till roughly, the bell sounding sharp and clear in the silent shop.

"There's your week's wages," she said, almost throwing it at Helen. "You needn't come back here again."

Helen took the money and counted it slowly; for her two years' service she now received fifteen shillings a week.

"Thank you, that is quite right," she said, when she had finished counting it.

Miss Read opened her lips as if she were going to say something, but closed them again without speaking. Turning on her heel abruptly she walked to the other end of the shop, where she vented her spleen on a small girl who was trying vainly to make two dozen jugs stand on each other without breaking.

Helen went outside to gather up the few belongings she had there. She looked round their sordid little luncheon room for the last time. How often, when she had finished her lunch, had she sat at that table with her head propped up on her hands, and her eyes devouring a book. Well, she would never see this room again. How familiar it was to her, and how little she regretted leaving it. She walked quickly back into the shop. Miss Read was still scolding; her voice was shrill and high, and cracked alarmingly when she raised it above its normal pitch, as she always did when she was angry. What a "nagger" the woman was, Helen thought, as she heard her. She smiled as the thought crossed her mind that never again would she have the right to nag at her. She waved good-bye to the girls as she went through the shop, and then just as she reached the door, she caught a glimpse of Miss Read's face turned for an instant towards her. Helen paused, and a feeling of compunction overcame her as she looked at the faded woman. After all she could afford to be generous; she was sorry for everyone this morning who was not young and happy.

"Good-bye," she said softly. "Won't you forgive me?"

Miss Read stared at her without speaking. She was surprised at Helen's words, but not softened. Again Helen offended by her youth and something high and gallant in her bearing. She looked at Helen venomously.

"I've said all I have to say to you," she said harshly, "now I'm waiting for you to go."

Helen was not surprised at the rebuff and therefore it did not anger her. Neither could she cherish any bitter feeling in her heart; she could leave all that behind her. She felt sorry that she was leaving at such enmity with her, but she saw by the hard, bitter look on the woman's face that it was useless to say anything further. She must just go. She looked round again for an instant, checked a sudden impulse to say something to the girls, and then went out, her heart singing over and over again—"I'm free—I'm free."

Her sense of joy and exultation lasted until she arrived in town, but as she walked up Little Collins Street her spirits swung down to the opposite pole. The interview loomed in front of her now, unknown and terrifying. Might they not laugh at her claims and send her away? How had she been so foolish as to think they would not?

She passed the building, a dark, gloomy-looking place, with a big brass plate outside the door. This was the place she wanted! She was trembling a little with nervousness. This was dreadful—she must try and control herself. Without giving herself any further time for thought, she hurried in.

There was a long and narrow passage, leading into a large, barn-like room. Several men were working about, but they did not take any notice of her. She could hear the click of several typewriters being used at once, and above that the sound of machinery at work. On two sides of the room were several offices, and close to where she was standing was one marked in large black letters "Manager." She knocked softly at this, and an irritated voice cried out:

"What is it now? Oh, come in!"

This did not sound very promising, but she went in, and a man who was writing at a desk stared at her in astonishment.

"Why, hulloa!" he said, "I thought it was one of those fellows outside. They're always bothering me. But what can I do for you. This is a pleasant surprise, you know." He smiled pleasantly at her, showing a line of strong, white teeth.

For answer Helen took out the letter she had received, and handed it to him.

"Oh! I see," he said, looking at her keenly. "Sit down, will you, while I make some enquiries about it."

He vanished, closing the door behind him, and Helen had leisure to look about her. It was a comfortable office, with a carpet on the floor, and several easy chairs standing about. Some framed photographs of motor cars hung on the walls, and just behind the door, but hidden when it was open, hung a couple of French prints of ladies very scantily clothed. They gave Helen a distinct shock when she saw them, for they seemed so incongruous in the quiet, businesslike office.

"What queer taste people seem to have in pictures," she thought.

She looked away from them as the door opened, and he came in, humming lightly to himself.

"It's all right," he said. "They tell me they do want another typiste."

He sat down opposite her and, leaning back in his chair, regarded her thoughtfully. He was a good-looking man, with straight features, and a small well-cut mouth, almost like a woman's, of which he was inordinately proud; his age was difficult to place—he might have been anything from thirty to forty-five.

He was immaculately dressed, and his socks, as Helen noticed when he swung one leg over another, exactly matched his tie.   She waited for him to speak, wondering vaguely whether he bought his socks to match his tie, or his tie to match his socks.

He tipped his chair as far back as it would go, supporting himself with one foot on the edge of the desk.

"I bought these in France," he said, as Helen looked up at him.   "Don't you think them pretty?"

"What?" she asked in surprise.

"These," and he pointed to his socks.

"Oh!"   She blushed in confusion.   She did not know that she had been staring at them, but she must have been or he would not have said that. He laughed as he saw her confusion, which was exactly what he had been aiming at.   She had looked so demure sitting there waiting his pleasure, that he could not resist the impulse to embarrass her.

"Never mind," he said, letting his chair come back to its former position with a jerk, and sitting up straight at his desk.   "We'll get on to business now."

He would not listen to anything she said about her speed in shorthand and typing, and waved aside impatiently the testimonials her teacher had given her.

"No, no.   That's nothing.   I don't take much notice of those things—anyone can do them with a little practice.   But see here, I want someone with intelligence, someone who won't gape like a fool when they're asked to do anything.   Now you look intelligent."   He paused a moment, and then shot out abruptly, "Are you?"

"Yes," replied Helen quickly, before she had time to consider her answer.

He laughed.   "That's right," he said.   "I'll take your word for it.   Can you start to-morrow?"

She looked at him with shining eyes and parted lips.   "I could start now," she said eagerly.

"You're in a hurry to begin," he said.   "I hope you won't be in as great a hurry to stop.   Anyway it's no use starting to-day.   To-morrow morning at nine o'clock.   Now is there anything else?"

She looked at him shyly.   There was something else, but he had been so kind to her that she hardly liked to mention it.

"Come on, what is it?" he asked, smiling a little as he saw her hesitation.

"What—what about salary?" she faltered.

"Oh, of course, salary!" he laughed.   "Did you think I had forgotten it?   I was beginning to think that you had.   What do you say to a pound a week?"

Helen accepted it eagerly.   It meant riches to her, or at least she thought so.   She had not yet learnt that as her salary increased, her spending powers would also increase.   Glorious vistas opened out before her.   This was really her start in life, the other had only been a dream.

"By-the-bye," he said, "there's a—er—lady in charge of the typistes here.   If I'm not here in the morning when you come, tell her I engaged you."

She felt a slight sense of disappointment when she heard this.   She had been getting on so well with him; he had seemed so friendly and interested in her, but a woman, as she now knew, was a very uncertain factor.

"She's not in just now," he continued, "or I would introduce you.   However you had better come with me, and I'll show you round."

She went with him, eager to get into touch with her new surroundings.   He took her into the office next to his, from which came the clicking of the type-writers.   This office presented a startling contrast to the one she had just left.   It was indescribably dirty, waste papers and letters littered the floor. Advertisements for motor cars, bicycles, incubators, electric belts, face creams and massage rollers were plastered on all the walls.   A small, dirty window, thick with the dust of years, looked out on to a narrow side lane.   Five girls were seated at the tables, and they looked up from their work as Mr. Thomas came in, followed by Helen.   He beckoned to the eldest girl, who immediately got up and came over to them.

"Miss Hillyard," he said, "Miss Somerset starts here to-morrow.   Look after her—show her round, you know, and all that sort of thing."

The girl listened to what he said with a grave expression of forced attention.   When he mentioned Helen's name, she looked up at her swiftly and as swiftly looked away again.   She was a pale girl of neutral colouring, and as the two girls stood together, the man looked at each of them with a faint quizzical smile in his eyes.   Helen was smiling in an eager friendly way at Miss Hillyard, but Miss Hillyard did not look at Helen again.   She stood silent, with her eyes on the ground waiting for further instructions. When she did not get any she moved slowly away. He waited until she was seated again and then said in a curious, jerky sort of way :

"Er—Miss Hillyard—I will be out this afternoon. You might tell Miss Masters when she comes in about this young lady."

"Very well," said Miss Hillyard sedately.

Helen, who had been looking at her future companions, noticed the girls look quickly at each other, and exchange the faint ghost of a smile.   She glanced back as she was leaving the room, and caught two of the girls whispering excitedly together.   They saw her looking at them, and smiled and grimaced at the retreating back of Mr. Thomas.   Feeling rather puzzled, and wondering what they meant, she smiled faintly at them, and followed him.

"I keep everybody separate as far as I can," he said.   "See, the men down there, and the girls here. I don't want any time wasted. That is Miss Masters's room," and he pointed to an office opposite his own.

Helen had already noticed it, for the name was painted on the door. Her curiosity about this woman had been aroused and she longed to look into the room. Perhaps he read her thoughts, for he threw the door open, though as he did so he glanced down the passage leading into the street with a curious expression of fear. He looked as though he wanted to make quite sure that the owner of the room was not anywhere about.

Helen stood on the threshold and looked in. No superfluous papers here; everything was rigidly in order. The room had an austere, almost cloisterlike effect, except—and Helen noticed this with a queer little intake of her breath—on a small table, half concealed and yet horribly visible, stood a bottle. It had been opened, and was half empty. It contained a yellow coloured liquid, but she did not know what it was. She only knew that it looked strange and suspicious in the neat and orderly room. Evidently the man noticed it too, for she heard him draw a sharp breath, and mutter something to himself. He walked swiftly across the room, bent over the table with his back to her, and when he turned round the bottle was gone.

She tried to look as if nothing had happened, and though he glanced at her keenly he made no remark about it, for which she was thankful. He closed the door behind him, and called to one of the men who were engaged in taking a bicycle to pieces.

"Has anyone been in there this morning?" he asked, pointing to the office they had just left.

"No, sir."

"Who was working late last night?"

"I was, sir," answered the man. "Jones, and two of the typistes. Miss Hillyard and— "

"Wasn't Miss Masters here?" interrupted Mr. Thomas.

"Oh, yes, sir, of course."

"That's all right." He waved the man away.

"Wait a moment, though, who was the last to leave?"

"Miss Masters, sir. She was still working when we left."

"Um!" He turned away, pulling his under-lip thoughtfully, and Helen, who had heard the whole conversation, wondered what it meant. He stood lost in thought and seemed to have forgotten her, until she spoke to him timidly, when he roused himself.

"Want to go, do you?" he said, "What's the time?" He looked at his watch. "Nearly lunch time. What are you going to do now?"

Helen intended to have some lunch in town and then spend the rest of the day exploring the city. Now that everything had turned out so well she felt she could take a holiday. She told him shyly what she was going to do, at which he laughed a little.

"Explore the city, eh? You'll soon get to hate the sight of it. But I say, you'll have to eat somewhere first, won't you? Why not come —" He paused, and then muttered to himself, "No, no, better not."

She heard him at first with alarm, for it certainly seemed as though he were going to invite her out to lunch, and she certainly did not want to go. She felt too shy to be happy at the thought of undergoing such an ordeal, and was glad when he suddenly changed his mind, though she could not help wondering at the abrupt change in his manner. He seemed curt and almost gruff.

"Come sharp at nine o'clock to-morrow," he said.

She was glad to get away and almost danced up the narrow little passage into the street. She did not look back, so she was unaware that he had followed her softly, and was standing looking after her with a very curious expression in his eyes.

CHAPTER II.

Mrs. Hunter listened, with a very disapproving face, to Helen's account of what had happened during the day. The disapproval was so marked that Helen made one or two mental reservations in her story. Mrs. Hunter had an instinctive dislike of what she called "offices and those sort of places," and insisted with a mysterious air that "you never knew what went on inside them—it didn't seem natural for girls to be working there." She told Helen she would sooner she had remained quietly at the shop, and, when the right time came, marry and settle down.

However, she knew Helen well enough by this time not to waste words in trying to make her change her mind, for Helen had a soft, but yet unyielding obstinacy against which all argument beat in vain. On previous occasions Mrs. Hunter had come up against this in Helen, and it had ended by Mrs. Hunter having to give way herself.

The last time this had happened had been when Helen had steadfastly refused to visit Belle in her new home. She had no adequate reason for her refusal that Mrs. Hunter could see, and it seemed to her that Helen was unkind and unreasonable. She brought Irene into the battle, but Helen still stood firm. She merely shook her head, smiled sweetly at them, and said that she had not the time to pay calls. As Mrs. Hunter pointed out to Irene, this could not possibly be true, as she found the time to spend hours over her books. At last, after a great deal of fruitless argument, Mrs. Hunter came to the conclusion that, despite appearances to the contrary,

Helen had really liked Bert and now was a little jealous. Irene had laughed at first at her mother's idea, but Mrs. Hunter had insisted on it, saying that she remembered at the time of the engagement that Helen seemed strange and not herself. This belief on her part went far to reconcile her to Helen's refusal to visit her daughter. When Helen heard of it she smiled and let it go at that.

Irene had told her: she had almost come to believe what her mother said for, now she thought of it, she remembered how strange Helen had looked that night. She mentally constructed the scene and everything fitted in so well. Belle, too, had seemed to avoid Helen, so she must have suspected or known something. Irene told Helen what she thought, just to see how she would take it, and had been rather disappointed in the result, for Helen was very calm and unconcerned. She had merely shrugged her shoulders and smiled.

"Do you really think so, Irene? Well, perhaps I did like him."

But Irene, after staring at her for a moment or two, had shaken her head, and told her mother that after all she thought she was mistaken. Mrs. Hunter clung to her own idea. She told Belle what she thought, and, being a woman without any fine perceptions, the strained smile on Belle's face had not struck her as curious. Belle knew well why Helen refused to come to her house. She knew that if she had given Helen even the slightest pretence at friendship and understanding, Helen would have forgotten everything and come, even though her own inclinations told her to stay away. But Belle could not forget what had happened, and it rankled in her mind. Against her will she cherished in her heart a feeling of bitterness towards Helen.

She had only seen Helen once since her marriage and that was at her mother's home. It had been an awkward meeting, and they were both glad when

Mrs. Hunter took her daughter into her own room to talk to her confidentially. Helen had immediately seized the opportunity and gone out, walking about the streets for an hour or so, for she felt she could not go home until Belle had gone. When she returned, Mrs. Hunter had something to tell her, which she imagined would come as a great surprise. Helen listened with grave attention and tried to show the proper feeling which Mrs. Hunter evidently expected of her.

"I'm glad," she said. "How pleased they both will be." And then, rather hesitatingly, "Don't you think Belle has changed?"

But Mrs. Hunter had laughed cheerfully. "Why, my dear, everyone changes after marriage. Wait until you are married yourself." She laughed again, her hands on her hips and her fat body moving with a gentle undulation.

Helen had shrunk away from that. Marriage! She hated the thought of it. All the sordid details of Belle's marriage were too fresh in her mind. She fiercely said that she would never get married—never. She fled from the thought of sex; it horrified her— but it came back and back. She tried to close her mind against it, but it came insistent and whispering, distorting her view of life. In despair she went to her books again. Those that told of love she threw aside as hateful, they reminded her too much of what she was trying to forget. She took a fierce joy in the turbulent scenes of the French Revolution, and for a long time lived in a world peopled only by the noble and majestic figures of Danton, Camille Des-mouslins, Charlotte Corday and Madame Roland.

Then one wonderful day she came across Nansen's "Farthest North," and the romance of the ice-fields seized on her imagination. Every book on Polar ex-ploration she read eagerly. Courage and endurance —the two grandest masculine virtues—she came to look upon as the only things that mattered. She followed her heroes in their struggles against Nature, their ships drifting with the ice packs, or driving their dogs on and on across the ice in a land that was cold and pure and hard—hard as the ice beneath their feet, and strong as the wind that froze their blood.

It was only by this kind of reading that she could counteract the poisonous talk of her companions, and the effect of the scene she had had with Bert, which seemed to have left an indelible impression on her mind. When she was at the shop all her time was spent doing work with her hands, and her mind was unoccupied. She looked forward to her new life, for she knew her mind would be occupied, and she would not always have to be guarding her thoughts. She felt as though she were a slave escaping into freedom. The badge of her servitude—her black dress—she tore off.

"I will never put another black dress on," she said to Irene that evening when she came home. She had been eagerly awaiting Irene to tell her the great news, but Irene had an air of subdued excitement about her, and did not seem at all impressed.

Both girls were sitting in Irene's bedroom, which, since Belle had gone, was shorn of many of its former glories. Bert's photograph was gone, though every time Helen looked at the dressing-table, she thought she could see his smug face with the complacent expression that irritated her so. The photograph of Irene's favourite actor still stood in its former place, for Irene had never swerved from her allegiance though it had become a standing joke in the family.

Irene looked round the room with a meditative air, and then took up the photograph and sighing deeply handed it to Helen.

"I'm going to give this to you," she said.

Helen laughed, thinking she was joking.

"I mean it," said Irene sadly. "It has to go."

"Whatever's the matter?" asked Helen in surprise. "Have you met him and found that you don't love him any more?"

Irene shook her head. "No, it's not that. I am going to be married, and if I keep this I will always be making comparisons."

"Married! You?" cried Helen in astonishment. "Why, I never dreamt of such a thing—at least not for a long time yet."

"Oh, I used to say that," admitted Irene, "but I never meant it. You see there isn't much chance of me getting married. I know I'm not much to look at. Belle was ever so much prettier than I am, and she didn't make much of a match."

"Do you—love him?" asked Helen in a low voice.

"I like him well enough," said Irene indifferently, "but I can't afford to pick and choose. I've got to grab the first one I can get."

"But that seems so—so— "

"Oh, it's all very well for you to talk," interrupted Irene angrily. "You can take your time—it's not necessary for you to marry the first man who asks you."

"I don't intend to get married at all," retorted Helen.

"We all say that," sneered Irene, "but none of us really mean it."

Helen closed her lips firmly to prevent an outburst of anger. She knew she meant what she said, but she was not going to argue with anyone about it. She meant to live alone, free and untramelled in the world. Even George, whom she had a dim sort of idea she might marry some day, she had thrust out of her mind.

She could hear Irene muttering angrily to herself. Suddenly a sympathy and understanding of Irene's point of view came over her. Why shouldn't she take what she could get? She had nothing to look forward to except a life spent in a shop, drawing a few shillings a week, or else marriage. Why shouldn't

Irene take the latter if she could get it? She pictured Irene, droning her life away, gradually growing old and faded like Miss Read. Even marriage could not be worse than that. As for love—she scoffed at the thought of it. She didn't know what it was and she did not want to know. With a sudden leap of the heart she remembered her mother's letters. Was that love? She threw it off with a laugh. If that was love, it would have been better if her father and mother had not loved each other. Life would not have been so disastrous to one of them at any rate.

Let Irene marry if she liked then, and for whatever reason. She would congratulate her, or make a pretence at congratulating her. As for herself, she would not take that way out. She would marry no one, even though she grew old and faded and worn out with hard work. She had a few unhappy moments trying to see herself old and worn out, struggling alone in the world, but she could not really imagine it at all. Her unconscious egotism came to her aid. Other people might grow old and faded with a monotonous life, but not she. In her heart she cherished a dream that the gods held something wonderful in store for her. The present was only the waiting time to be got through somehow before the grand reality happened. It beckoned her onwards, this dream of the unknown future, mysterious and alluring. It placed her among brilliant crowds of people of whom she was always the central figure, admired and loved by all. It took her to strange and beautiful countries in a single instant of thought. Sometimes she sang to admiring multitudes; sometimes danced. They strewed flowers in her path, and she gave them in return gracious smiles. Yes! others might have a hum-drum life, but she—she was one of the favoured children of fortune. One day all would open out before her, and she would find this wonderful life. Others might grow old and faded in uncongenial occupations, but not she—ah, no! not she. She would believe in her fate.

It was because of this unacknowledged dream and belief in her own future, that she could sympathise with Irene. How dreadful to have nothing to look forward to—Oh! how dreadful! The tears came into her eyes at the thought of it.

"I'm sorry, Irene," she heard herself saying. "I'm a horrid little prig sometimes, I'm afraid, but I didn't like the idea of you getting married and leaving us so soon after Belle's marriage."

Irene had soon got over her momentary annoyance at the way in which Helen had received her announcement. She was an easy going girl, and moreover she looked upon Helen as very young in knowledge of the world, and also thought she was too romantic. Helen was not aware of Irene's opinion of her, and her mental attitude towards Irene was one of pity—pity for the queer blindness in Irene that closed her mind against all beautiful things, so that she could only see the obvious and commonplace. But Helen did not realise the fact that Irene was happier than she, because the ordinary things of life contented her. She did not ask much, and therefore would not be likely to suffer keen disappointment. Buoyed up with her secret dreams, Helen only felt sympathy and pity for Irene.

"Are you going to be married soon?" she asked.

"Not for a long time," replied Irene. "A year at least!"

"I'm so glad," Helen sighed with relief. Anything might happen in a year, and anyway it would give her time to get used to the idea of meeting all the relatives again.

"Why?" asked Irene, rather flattered. "Will you miss me so much?"

"Yes, of course I will," smiled Helen. "And— oh Irene! you have never told me who he is."

"No. neither I have," said Irene awkwardly. "He's

one of the men in the shop—in the Manchester department."

"Really! that's rather nice," she said vaguely. "Why! what are you doing, Irene?"

Irene was fumbling with the silver frame which held the photograph of the actor. She took it out and laid it carefully down. She then took a photograph which she had wrapped up in tissue paper, and put it in the frame instead.

"There he is," she said, handing it to Helen.

Helen looked at it. Her first distressed thought was—"Oh, why hasn't he got a chin, and why does he look so much like what he is?"

Then she saw with relief that, though his chin was weak, yet he had nice eyes and looked immeasurably superior to Bert. He had not the smug complacency of Bert, and there was something very boyish and wistful in the expression of his mouth. His hair was not brushed back in a greasy wave, but was short and inclined to curl.

Irene watched her with an anxiety she tried to hide. Though she scoffed at Helen's youth, and said she knew nothing of the world, yet she unconsciously valued Helen's opinion, though she would not have acknowledged it.

"I like him," said Helen at last, and Irene breathed a little sigh of relief. "I really do. He looks—nice. He could not be a bully."

The thoughts of both girls had flown to Bert and Irene's lips set in rather a grim line. She had seen Bert at home with his wife, and Helen had not. Irene knew!

"I would not have promised to marry him if I thought he was a bully," she said aloud, "even though it meant that I never got another chance."

Helen handed the picture back. "No, he could never be a bully," she said. "He looks too gentle."

"Yes, he's not a bad sort of boy," said Irene, her eyes growing softer as they looked at the pictured face. A swift thought ran through Helen's mind that it was a pity Irene did not love him. She stifled it almost as soon as born, for had she not convinced herself that she did not believe in love? Therefore, why pity her?

"Do you really want me to take this?" she asked, picking up the photograph of the actor, which lay face downwards on the bed.

"Yes," replied Irene, sighing. "Take it out of my sight."

"I do believe he is your only weakness," said Helen, laughing. "Well, I'll do what you want, and take it away."

"Let me have one last look at it," Irene begged.

Helen handed it to her, and watched Irene's face. To her surprise she saw that her eyes were full of tears. She looked at the picture in silence for a moment, and then gave it back to Helen and turned away hurriedly.

"I wonder," thought Helen to herself, as she went out into the kitchen and threw the photograph on the fire. "I wonder if this was Irene's secret dream? She might have thought that one day she would meet him, and now she must give the dream up—who can tell?"

A long tongue of flame shot suddenly up into the air, and as suddenly died away again, and Irene's dream, if indeed it was her dream, became ashes.

CHAPTER III.

If Helen wished for excitement and occupation, she got them both during the next few months. Her first day spent at the office was a series of blurred impressions, from which she could not disentangle one incident from another. At the end of the week, owing principally to the gossip of the girls, she had gained a very clear idea as to the character of all the people surrounding her.

Mr. Thomas was the one they were most interested in. They spoke of him in whispers, and with a self-conscious air, giving hurried glances at the door by which he might come in unexpectedly upon them. Each girl had something she wanted to confide to Helen, and when she had received all their confidences, she found they all amounted to the same thing. Mr. Thomas seemed to have a predilection for kissing. He appeared to have kissed each of the girls at some time or other and, looking at them, Helen could not help wondering at his taste. They warned her in exaggerated terms to be careful of him, which made her, for the first couple of days, rather stiff and shy in her manner towards him. This soon wore off, for his manner to her was a subtle compliment. He treated her with a deference he never extended to the others. He loved to see the sensitive colour come into her cheeks, and how easily he could bring it there! She would listen, with downcast eyes, to what he said, trying to look severely businesslike, but at last would have to look up and smile. That would satisfy him—for the time being. He arranged, but very deftly, so that it was hardly noticed at first, that Helen should do all his work.   In private he called her his secretary, and asked her how she liked the title.

But Helen was rather uneasy with things as they were.   She would rather have been left alone to work with the other girls, for she realised that unconsciously she had roused their antagonism.   They were all very friendly to her when she was with them; some of them almost effusive in their friendliness, but she was aware of their sudden silence when she appeared.   At first they had talked freely to her of Miss Masters and Mr. Thomas, but gradually they had stopped, though she knew their conversations went on just the same when she was not there.

"Do they think I would tell him what they say about him?" she thought contemptuously.

Miss Hillyard, the head of the room, who had treated her with unnatural reserve for the first few weeks, suddenly thawed and seemed to seek Helen's society.   She hovered round Helen, trying to draw her out, but Helen refused to be drawn.   At last she asked Helen to come out to lunch with her, and was so persistent that Helen was unable to refuse. She had gone very unwillingly, for she did not like Miss Hillyard.   She guessed that Miss Hillyard had some ulterior motive in taking her out, though she did not know what it was.   She knew that none of the girls liked her, saying that she spied on them and reported to Miss Masters.   She smiled a little as she thought of this.   If Miss Hillyard thought that Helen would make a confidant of her, she was greatly mistaken.   As she was going out at lunch-time one of the girls whispered, with a friendly smile that made Helen's heart go out to her:

"Be careful!   She's been as thick as thieves with Miss Masters all this week.   Don't tell her anything."

Helen did not think it necessary to explain that there was nothing to tell, but she was grateful for the girl's warning, and pressed her hand impulsively as she thanked her.

Miss Hillyard was very friendly during lunch, but very undiplomatic in her methods. She so obviously wanted to find out Helen's attitude towards Mr. Thomas that Helen saw through her at once. She answered in monosyllables, and they walked back to the office together, Miss Hillyard completely baffled.

There was a message for Helen that Mr. Thomas wanted to see her. She took off her hat in silence, and then as she was going out, turned to Miss Hillyard.

"You won't have much information to give to Miss Masters, will you? I hope she won't be very angry with you."

As she softly closed the door behind her, she heard a gurgle of laughter from the girls. They were evidently pleased at the shaft which had struck one of their enemies.

The other enemy was Miss Masters. They both hated and feared her. Helen had been over a week at the office before she saw her, but she had become familiar with her name. The girls spoke of her with awe and trepidation, telling Helen terrible stories of her sudden outbursts of rage. She goes purple in the face, they declared, when she is in one of her passions. Life became a weariness and terror for everyone when she was about. They had heard she was ill, but they were expecting her to appear any day. One of the girls pursed her lips significantly when she spoke of her illness.

"She does a little of this, you know," she said, raising her arm as though she were drinking.

A sudden remembrance of what she had seen on the first day flashed through Helen's mind, but she kept her own counsel.

"She's a devil," said another girl. "It's an awful thing to say, but you can't call her anything but that."

They all agreed with that. She was—she was—

they declared passionately. Oh, how they hated her!
Everyone was afraid of her, even Mr. Thomas, but
then she had a hold over him. Helen asked what
it was, but none of them seemed inclined to put it
into words. They contented themselves with nodding
mysteriously, and said she would soon find out for
herself.

Miss Masters came back unexpectedly. It was late
in the afternoon and everyone had given her up for
that day. As Mr. Thomas was out they had relaxed
somewhat, and no one was working very hard. They
were talking in a desultory way, when a sibilant
whisper hissed through the room.

"Hush!   She's coming!"

There was a moment of tense silence, and Helen
heard light footsteps hurrying along the passage.
Then the girls started to work, and the noise of the
typewriters rose high, drowning every other sound.
The pale Miss Hillyard was bustling about, en-
deavouring to hurry up the already frantically hurrying girls. Helen thought how futile she looked,
with her little pretence of work and authority. She
kept looking nervously towards the door, and when
a sharp voice summoned her by name, she almost ran
out.

She was back within two or three minutes, her pale
face a little flushed.

"Miss Masters wants to see you, Miss Somerset,"
she said, looking anywhere but at Helen.

The others looked at Helen with a pitying air,
but she went out with a smile, and carrying her head
high. She was not going to let them see that she
was afraid, though she seemed to have gone suddenly
weak in the knees and could hardly walk.

The door of the office was wide open, so she went
in without knocking, her footsteps sounding clear
and distinct on the varnished floor. Miss Masters
was sitting at her desk, looking through a large pile
of letters. She did not look round as Helen entered
and seemed to be unconscious of her presence.

Helen stood waiting, rather at a loss. She did not know what to do. It was too banal to cough, and she certainly had not the courage to touch Miss Masters on the shoulder, or to speak. She was considering whether she should walk out on tiptoe and knock loudly at the door, when Miss Masters suddenly swung round on her chair.

"Well!" she said.

Helen stared at her, at first too astonished to speak. Was this the coarse, red-faced, violent woman she had been expecting to see? The face was almost delicate in its refinement. The skin pale, but clear, and smooth as ivory, the forehead low and broad. Her eyes were a beautiful gray, rather long and narrow in shape. They darkened to black when she was excited or angry. They were almost black now as she looked at Helen. Her mouth was the only feature that betrayed her. It was loose-lipped and sensual looking, and the under lip sagged open. Her dress was masculine in its severity, and her dark hair dragged tightly back from her forehead, in a very unbecoming fashion. When she spoke, she had a nervous habit of biting her under-lip. She did this now as she looked at Helen.

"Well!" she said again. "Have you quite finished staring at me? If so, tell me what you want."

Helen flushed deeply, conscious that she had perhaps staring rather rudely.

"They told me you wanted to see me," she said timidly.

"See you!" repeated Miss Masters, coldly. "Why should I want to see you?"

She drummed with her fingers on the table and tapped her foot impatiently on the floor.

Helen did not reply, though she thought to herself that it seemed as though Miss Masters wanted to see her, for she was subjecting her to the closest scrutiny. Helen bore it as well as she could, trying to seem at ease, though her heart was beating a little faster than usual.

"When were you engaged?" Miss Masters asked harshly, frowning at her.

Helen told her.

"Um! No experience, I suppose? No! I thought not. This idea of employing inexperienced girls is more than I can bear. I don't suppose you can even spell?"

"Spell?" repeated Helen, rather puzzled. "Oh, yes, I can spell."

"They all say that," said Miss Masters with a sneer. She fumbled about her desk, and then handed Helen a typed letter. "Look at that. Pretty, isn't it? That girl swore she could spell."

Helen smiled faintly as she looked at it. "I think I can do better than that," she said.

"You'd better—you'd better—or—." She did not finish her threat, but Helen knew what she meant to imply, and she made a mental resolve that never would she give Miss Masters cause to find fault with her.

In spite of herself, however, she could not carry out this resolve. Miss Masters was always looking for an opportunity to criticise her work. This worried Helen at first, but she soon got used to Miss Masters's violent abuse, and met it with an imperturbable coolness. She noticed this seemed to disconcert Miss Masters, and that if she met her attacks by feigning absolute indifference, she was soon silenced. The others looked on at the battle, their sympathies were with Helen, but they dared not emulate her.

Helen did not realise that the admiration and flattery of Mr. Thomas had much to do with her new poise. She was absolutely sure of herself. She knew that if she chose to complain of Miss Masters, he would make it his business to see that she did not suffer again. He had often made tentative remarks, trying to see how she felt about her, but Helen was always very reserved. She knew she was capable of fighting her own battles, and she would have despised herself if she had drawn Mr. Thomas in on her side. Slowly and surely she was silencing Miss Masters. Each day she became more inclined to leave Helen severely alone, and confine her energies to the other members of the staff. Soon everyone in the office noticed that Miss Masters never spoke to Helen if she could avoid it. They also began to whisper among themselves, for they had noticed something else—that Mr. Thomas was in love with Helen.

Helen was quite unconscious of what they were saying. She never asked herself whether he was in love with her or not. She never thought about it. She liked him, and found his delicate compliments pleasant to hear, but that was all. She knew that Miss Masters was jealous of her, and was aware of her sullen, suspicious eyes which always seemed to be watching her. She smiled scornfully to herself.

"Does she think I am going to enter into competition with her?" she thought.

The envious looks of the other girls, the obvious jealousy of Miss Masters, and the open admiration of the men, had taught her more than she was aware of. Unconsciously she absorbed the lesson—that good looks go a long way, and are a valuable asset. She also learnt that men will do things for a pretty woman that they would not be bothered doing for a plain one. She was beginning to realise her own attractiveness and what it meant. If she had liked she could have lived a very easy life. Her employer was only too anxious that she should not overwork herself. She disdained to take advantage of her good looks, preferring to work on an equality with the others, and refusing to take any concessions in which they did not share.

Once, however, she came into collision with Miss Masters, and she consciously exercised all her charm over Mr. Thomas to gain her point. One of the correspondence clerks, who only made spasmodic appearances at the office, was the object of much comment among the girls. He was known to have "seen better days," and Helen had heard it said that he had been a University professor. Now he was content to earn a miserable pittance, dictating letters to giggling and hostile girls, who openly sneered at him. It was quite allowable to laugh at poor Vaughan, indeed it was one way of gaining favour with Miss Masters. For some reason she seemed to hate him, and actually encouraged the girls to be rude to him.

About once every three months, after living in strict sobriety for that time, Vaughan would be overcome with a mad craving for drink, and disappear. A month or so would elapse, and he would reappear again, trembling slightly with downcast eyes, and shaking hands, thoroughly ashamed of himself. Helen had dreaded meeting him at first, for she had a horror of drunkenness, but when she saw the gentle-faced old man, with his humble, appealing eyes, which seemed to plead for sympathy and understanding, all her aversion left her. A tender, protective feeling grew up in her heart for him, and she tried to shield him from the cruel and sarcastic jeers of the others.

Helen and the old man had long conversations together. He would tell her of all he had seen in the world, and she loved to listen to him. He would often look at her wistfully, wondering why she was so sweet to him. Then he would sigh, and give it up, content only to know that she was. He had great plans in his mind for Helen. To him it was a dreadful thing that she should have to work there. He would look after her with anxious eyes when she went into Mr. Thomas's office, and shake his head sadly.

"You must leave here," he would say to her. "Once I had influence. You wait and see. I will do something for you."

Helen would think pitifully it was not likely he

could do anything for her when he could do nothing
for himself. She would thank him, however, with
the tender smile she seemed to keep especially for
him, and he would be quite happy, building castles in
the air.

Unfortunately, Miss Masters soon got to know of
Helen's friendship with the old man, and with a
devilish ingenuity laid herself out to insult him. She
guessed that in this way she could hurt Helen most.
Vaughan never complained, only it seemed to Helen
that his pale cheeks grew thinner and paler, and he
trembled at the sound of Miss Masters's voice. Helen
writhed under this persecution, but could do nothing.
He was under Miss Masters's authority, and she had
absolute power over him. On two occasions, with a
spark of the old fire of his manhood rising in him,
he turned on her. There were terrible scenes when
he did this, and each time he was beaten. The woman
flew into one of her passionate rages, and screamed
foul abuse at him. The old man seemed to crumple
and wither up under the onslaught.

They were beginning to whisper about it in the
office.

"He'll be off again, you see," they said. One
girl, with quite unconscious cruelty, said to Helen:—

"It's all your fault. She's taking it out of him
because she hates you. She's afraid to tackle you
direct."

Helen shrank under the words, but she knew the
truth of them. How gladly she would have drawn
the whole storm on her own head, if she had been
able. She put herself in Miss Masters's way purposely, speaking insolently to her. But Miss Masters avoided an encounter with her, only glanced at
her obliquely out of her long, narrow eyes.

One morning Vaughan did not appear, and everyone laughed, so correctly had they foretold this.
When Miss Masters came in, she took in the situation at a glance. She called Helen to her.

"So your friend isn't here?" she said.

"No," replied Helen, her eyes on the ground. For some reason she felt that his shame was her own.

"Do you know where he is to be found?" Miss Masters continued. Helen shook her head mechanically, but did not reply. She had a mental vision of her friend, with his fine face discoloured—and horrible. She shivered slightly.

"You'll probably find him in the hotel down the street," Miss Masters went on. "There's a barmaid there he used to be very fond of. You'll see them drinking together."

Helen flushed painfully, and Miss Masters laughed. Helen raised her eyes and looked at her, and a sudden feeling of disgust for the woman overcame her. The mouth looked hideous, for the under-lip had sagged open and showed a long row of uneven teeth. She seemed to read Helen's thoughts, for she bit it with her teeth. A wild desire to insult her came over Helen. If she could only make her suffer for the insults she had heaped on the old man.

"I would rather see him drinking openly in the hotel than secretly in the office," she said, with a significant look at Miss Masters's desk.

Immediately she said it she was sorry, for the woman looked as though she had received a death thrust. She sank back in her chair, staring at Helen. She seemed suddenly to have grown old and shrivelled. Like the ostrich with its head in the sand, she had thought that she was so safe. She never dreamt that anyone suspected her secret. No one could suspect, she told herself, and now it seemed she was exposed for all the world to see. She had thought she was so safe. She thought she had made doubly sure by her treatment of Vaughan. That was the reason she had laughed and jeered at him. She imagined that if she openly showed her contempt for his weakness, no one would suspect her of a similar failing herself. Now this girl, whom she had hated

from the first moment she had seen her, had discovered her secret.

But only for a few moments her composure deserted her. She persuaded herself that she must
be mistaken—the girl could not know anything, it
was merely a chance remark. She pulled herself
together, and dismissed Helen with a curt word.

It was during the morning that Miss Masters
made a discovery—a discovery which made her forget
her fear of Helen, and turned her for a few moments
into a shrieking, foul-mouthed virago. Vaughan,
before he left, had robbed her private cash box.
There was no doubt about it, for they found the box
in his office, broken open. In a moment the news
was all over the place. Miss Masters shouted it
out with violent denunciations and threats of revenge. Awestruck, the girls heard her rush into
Mr. Thomas's office and slam the door.

"How much did he take?" Helen, white-lipped and
trembling, asked one of the men.

"There wouldn't be more than 30/- in the box
altogether, though she's making such a song about
it," said the man scornfully. "Poor devil! no wonder he stole. They paid him barely enough to keep
him in food, and when she got the chance she'd dock
him of some of his money. I'll bet that's at the
bottom of it. She's been up to her old tricks again,
and he took the money when he was half-mad for
drink."

He looked at Helen's white face and horror-struck
eyes. "Don't worry about him," he said kindly.

"I liked him so much, and I'm afraid of what
they might do to him," said Helen dully, turning
away.

In the typistes' room the girls were burning with
excitement. It seemed they always knew something
like this would happen. One girl declared that
she knew he was a thief the first day she saw him.

"I wonder what do you think an honest man looks

like, then?'' Helen demanded, turning fiercely on
her.

That was the signal for them all to fall on Helen.
She ought to be ashamed of herself. He was a
proved thief and a confirmed drunkard. They had
known from the beginning what he was, and took
care not to become friendly with him. They had
too much respect for themselves, but of course Helen
was different—everybody knew—. The girl who
was speaking stopped suddenly, as Helen looked at
her.

''Everybody knows what?'' asked Helen.

''Oh! nothing,'' returned the girl, pursing up her
lips, and looking as though she could say a great
deal more if she had the least encouragement.

''It doesn't matter,'' said Helen wearily. ''I don't
care.''

The girl looked disappointed at Helen's lack of interest, and was going to enlarge on the subject, when
a look from Miss Hillyard stopped her. They heard
Miss Masters come out, and looked at each other in
astonishment, for she was singing! The girls watched
her covertly, and when she slammed her door, they
began to discuss the situation in eager whispers.
Something was going to happen. They felt as though
they were living in the midst of big events.

But Helen was in an agony of apprehension. The
fact that Miss Masters was so pleased struck ominously upon her consciousness. She must find out
what was going to be done. She glanced anxiously
round, knowing that if Miss Hillyard saw her leaving
the room, she would demand where she was going,
and probably inform Miss Masters. She was thankful to see that no one was looking at her, and she
slipped out very quietly. She passed Miss Masters's room on tip-toe, and knocked very softly at
Mr. Thomas's door. She felt if she could only get
a few minutes alone with him, she could save the
old man from the horrible thing that threatened him.

She did not wait for him to tell her to enter, but went in at once. He looked up with surprise, and then with pleasure, as he saw who it was. He saw that something was the matter, and rose from his seat and came close to her. Something in the sight of her distress; the sensitive lips trembling, and the eyes shining through a mist of tears, moved him profoundly.

"What is the matter?" he asked in a low voice. "Don't cry—I don't like to see it."

She smiled up at him with unsteady lips.

"Come, that's better," he said, and for a moment his fingers trembled near her cheek. She shrank from the proffered caress, and he noticed it, and immediately drew away.

"What is it?" he asked quietly.

She nervously locked and unlocked her fingers.

"It's about Mr. Vaughan," she said. "What are you going to do?"

His face changed at once. It became hard and grim, and the mouth took on a sullen line.

"Give him in charge," he said harshly.

"Does that mean—prison?"

"That's so," he said briskly. "I'll have no stealing here. Prison is the place for a man who steals, and to prison he will go."

Her heart seemed to hammer in her throat, and a rush of blood drummed in her ears.

"You wouldn't be so cruel," she heard herself saying.

"My dear girl," he said impatiently, "don't you see that if I let this pass, they might all be doing it? I've got to make an example of him."

She must stop it—she must. She felt she would die if he went to prison. What could she do? She must do something! In her despair she wrung her hands. Then her intuition came to her aid and told her what to do. She leant closer to the man and her voice took on a softer, lower note.

"You wouldn't be so cruel," she said again. "Don't do it. Please—." She faltered a moment. "For my sake."

He stared at her, his eyes suddenly alight, and he took her hand in an iron grip. She winced, but let him have it.

"Do you really care so much about it?" he asked.

She nodded. "I do care—tremendously."

They were startled by a knock at the door, and he dropped her hand quickly, and turned away. Miss Hillyard came in, carrying a pile of letters. Her face was perfectly expressionless, but Helen thought there was a glint of malice in her eyes. She did not speak, but laid the letters on the table and then left the room quietly.

Helen knew that there was not a moment to be lost. Already Miss Hillyard would be with Miss Masters telling her what she had seen.

"You will let him off," she implored. "You will promise me that?"

"You really want it?" he said hastily. "Well, for your sake I'll let him off, but he can't come back here again."

With a whispered word of thanks and gratitude Helen hurried away. She wished to avoid an encounter with Miss Masters if possible. Just as she got to her room, she heard Miss Masters come out. The girls looked at each other enquiringly, for Miss Masters seemed very angry. They could hear her voice raised in angry expostulation, but could not distinguish what she was saying. They sighed, for if she was angry that meant bad times for them. They looked at Helen reproachfully, for they knew she was the cause of the outburst. She sat with her fingers flying over her typewriter, apparently engrossed in her work, but there was a vivid flush on her cheeks, and her heart felt ridiculously light. She had won—he had done what she wanted. Oh! it was good to be young—young and—she hesitated, and then admitted it to herself—young and pretty.

CHAPTER IV.

THE APPEAL TO HELEN.

It was shortly after this that Helen began to realise the best thing she could do would be to go away. Miss Masters never spoke to her at all now. If she had anything for Helen to do, she sent her orders through Miss Hillyard. Helen did not mind her silence, it was the expression of the eyes that worried her. There was a curious wistfulness in their depths, very different from the hostile expression with which she had been wont to regard her.

"I'm not harming her," the girl thought angrily. "Why does she look at me like that?"

She had a guilty feeling when she was with Mr. Thomas. Even in his office, with the door closed, she seemed to be able to see Miss Masters's eyes, with that new, strange expression in them. The sense of being ceaselessly watched, made her restless and uneasy. Her manner changed towards him, and became cold and reserved. He was beginning to annoy her also. One day he had caught hold of her as she was leaving the office, and held her tightly in his arms for a moment or two, with his face very close to hers. She had been furiously angry, and shown it, and he had let her go abruptly, realising that he had made a mistake. Even in the midst of her anger, Helen had noticed, with a shock, the network of tiny wrinkles on his face. Also that his eyes were bloodshot. She had always thought of him as young. If he had ever had any attraction for her, he lost it in that moment.

He hardly knew himself what were her intentions with regard to the girl. He told himself that he meant no harm to her, and yet he was unable to keep

away from her.   Her elusiveness enraged him, and
yet added to her charm.   He had already made
several advances to her, asking her to come to the
theatre, or for a drive in his motor.   She had refused, but he put that down as shyness.   He told
himself that it was only a matter of time before she
would fall into his hands—if he wanted her.   That
was the trouble.   He did want her, but he was also
afraid of her.   He firmly believed that all women
were the same.   That every woman had her price,
only the price of some was higher.   Still, even with
this fixed belief, there was a faint doubt in his mind
about Helen.   Not as to his ultimate success in winning her, but as to the price he might have to pay.
He brooded over her—she became an obsession on his
mind.   The thought of her worried him, and he
became nervous and irritable.   He would have asked
her to marry him, to save trouble, only he was already
married.   He was living apart from his wife, a
cynical woman who had taken up politics, and said
she preferred it to marriage.   He never thought
about her; she only existed as an inconvenient fact,
which he quite successfully ignored.

But Helen!   She was someone who had crept
into his heart and refused to be dislodged.   No
other woman had ever had the appeal for him that
she had.   It was her youth that charmed him.   His
own youth was past, and all the dreams of romance
he had cherished in his heart had come to nothing
and withered.   But she had revived them again.
She stood for all the beauty and eagerness of youth,
the spirit of romance—and she was a woman.

He was not a man who read much, but in secret
he had read some verses.   In secret, for his business
friends would have been looking for his name in the
Bankruptcy Court, if he had confessed to them.
Some lines he had read somewhere, he had even forgotten the name of the poet, sprang unbidden to his
mind, when he thought of Helen.

"With little hands all filled with bloom,
   The rose tree wakes from her long trance,
And from my heart as from a tomb
   Steals forth the ghost of dead romance.''

He felt that from his heart the ghost of dead romance had stolen out, and all its dreams and aspirations had centred round Helen.

He knew he could not take her without spoiling her, without blackening her in the eyes of the world. He told himself that he would be good to her, that his love would more than make up for all she would lose. Even as he assured himself of this, he knew that his reasoning was false. Then he would suffer from a reaction. He would leave her alone. He would be unselfish for once in his life. But he would see her again, and all his good resolutions would be gone in an instant. Miserable and undecided, he hesitated, and in the meantime, Fate took the decision out of his hands.

He had to go to the country for a week on business, and when he returned Helen had disappeared. No one could tell him where she had gone, or why. Though he suspected Miss Masters of knowing, he did not ask her, but accepted the news with a curious sort of fatalism. She wasn't for him, and there would be no romance in his life after all.

In the meantime, Helen was quite happy and contented. Two or three days after Mr. Thomas left for the country, she had received a telephone call from her uncle. He knew where she was and what she was doing, and for some time had been trying to make a place in his office for her. In consequence of something he had heard, he made enquiries about the place where she was working, and what he learnt had so alarmed him that he decided she must leave at once. He told her he wanted her to come into his office immediately, and was surprised and pleased at the eagerness of her acceptance.

Helen was only too glad to get away. She had had a painful interview with Miss Masters, and had promised her to leave as soon as she possibly could. Her uncle's offer therefore seemed to be sent by Providence.

She had been surprised to receive a message from Miss Masters, through Miss Hillyard as usual, asking her if she could come back to the office in the evening. Wondering very much what was the matter, Helen had replied she could. She had never been back at the office at night, and it was with a queer little thrill of nervous expectation that she entered. The place looked so different—it was so dark and still. She stumbled along the dark passage, feeling her way with her fingers along the wall. All the rooms were in darkness except Miss Masters's office, where a bright light streamed out through the half-open door.

"Do you want me in here?" asked Helen.

She could see Miss Masters seated at her desk, with her head bent. She seemed to be writing quickly. She paused as she heard Helen's voice, and put down her pen, but did not turn round.

"Yes, in here," she answered.

Helen came in quietly and sat down. The silence was profound. She glanced at Miss Masters and thought how strange it was that she should be sitting there with her. She could not see her face, for she sat with her head leaning on her hand. Helen wondered what she was thinking, and stirred rather uneasily, for the silence was beginning to get rather eerie. Suddenly, from the vaudeville theatre next door, a band began to play a monotonous air, accompanied by the steady thud of feet as the ballet girls danced to its strains.

Miss Masters threw her head up in the air, listening intently for a moment or two. Then turned abruptly round with a sudden swing of her chair.

"They play the same thing every night," she said passionately. "Every night—and I hear it in my dreams."

Her eyes were bloodshot, and her skin a curious, dull purple shade. She bit her lip nervously, and there was a tiny wound on it, where the teeth had closed too often in the tender skin.

"People like it, I suppose," murmured Helen, not knowing what else to say.

The woman ignored her remark. She fixed her eyes feverishly on Helen, and Helen felt herself flushing under the scrutiny.

"Tell me," she said at last, speaking with an evident effort, "did you mean anything when you spoke about drinking secretly in the office?"

"No," replied Helen uneasily. "I was just speaking generally."

"No, you weren't," said the woman. "Did you mean anything—do you know anything about—me?"

Helen hesitated. What could she say? She could not bear to tell her the truth—that it was common knowledge. She was silent, but the woman read her silence aright.

"You do know then?" she said at last in a whisper. "You do know?"

Helen looked away. It was dreadful to her to see the woman's agitation. Miss Masters had laid her head on the desk, and was sobbing unrestrainedly. All Helen could think was:—"How she will hate me for having seen her like this."

At last she could bear it no longer. She went over and touched the woman gently on the shoulder.

"Don't cry," she said with an effort. "I have told nobody what I know."

As though she had been waiting for the sound of Helen's voice to find her own, Miss Masters burst out into passionate words.

"I only did it because I was unhappy," she cried. "If I had been happy, and young and—and." She stumbled over the word "—good-looking like you, do you think I would need anything to make me forget? Listen, I will tell you why I am unhappy—why— "

"No! No!" cried Helen. "Don't tell me. Please don't tell me."

"I must," said the woman. "If you know why I am unhappy, you might help me—you can."

"Tell me," said Helen softly, after a pause, "I will help you if I can."

She did not want to hear. She resented the position in which she had been placed, but she had no choice.

"I am unhappy because I love—him—you know who I mean?"

Helen nodded. She knew quite well who she was referring to.

"Ever since you came here he has changed. Oh! I know it. I tried to fight against you at first, but it's no use. I'm beaten—I'm done. You're young —you've got everything in front of you. Surely you don't want him. Give him up—and he will come back to me."

Helen listened to the strains of the music. It seemed to be repeating over and over again—"I'm beaten—I'm done." How hopeless it sounded! "I'm beaten—I'm done."

"Aren't you listening to me?" she heard Miss Masters's voice saying. It seemed a long way off. She aroused herself, but still the music kept repeating the same thing.

"I'm listening," she said mechanically.

"Then what are you going to do? Will you give him up?"

"Give him up?" repeated Helen. She had not realised the word before. "Give him up? But why? He's nothing to do with me. He's only my employer."

She knew that she was not speaking quite the truth, but she persuaded herself that she meant what she said.

"He's not—he's not," cried the woman. "He can't mean much to you, and I have a claim on him. If you weren't here he would come back to me."

Helen had flushed scarlet. It was all so horrible. She wanted to get away—out into the fresh air. Away from the sound of the music with its maddening monotonous refrain, and away from the sight of the woman whose cheap emotions had made her the wreck she was.

"What do you want me to do?" she asked stiffly.

"I want you to leave," said the woman angrily.

"Very well. As soon as I have made my arrangements I will do so."

Miss Masters leant back in her chair. Already she looked changed. The curious colour left her face, and her eyes faded from black to gray again. She raised a hand that trembled slightly and straightened her hair, a lock of which had fallen grotesquely across her face.

Helen watched her for a moment in silence. Then with an abrupt "Good-night," she turned on her heel and left her alone.

As she walked down the narrow, dark street, she was a prey to conflicting emotions. She was angry and ashamed, and yet mixed with these feelings was one of pleasure. She walked slowly along, thinking over what had happened, and a man following close behind her thought she was an easy prey. He accosted her genially, but she turned on him in such a rage that he retired discomfited, pondering over the infinite complexities of women.

The next day was a very uncomfortable one. Miss Masters avoided Helen's eyes, and Helen was in a perfect panic lest chance should leave her alone with Miss Masters. When her uncle rang up and offered her the chance of escape, she thought that the gods were indeed good to her. She told Miss Masters she was going, and Miss Masters made no remark. Only Helen noticed that the blood flamed in her cheeks for a moment, and then faded away. They parted without even shaking hands, and with no reference to what had passed between them.

As Helen left the place she felt a queer, little sense of regret that she was going without saying good-bye to Mr. Thomas. He had been kind to her. He had made life more interesting to her, and made her conscious of herself. She paid him the tribute of a passing sigh, and then he faded out of her memory.

CHAPTER V.

Helen now felt that she was a wealthy woman of the world. She was getting £3 a week. The work was comparatively easy and the hours short. Her prospects had materially improved, and though she had grown right away from the Hunters, she felt she could not leave them. She had never forgotten the tremendous debt she owed them, and was bound to them by ties of honour and gratitude. As time went on Mrs. Hunter seemed to depend on her more and more. She took Belle's place in the house, for since Irene had become engaged, she had become quite inaccessible to the family. She was prosecuting her engagement with vigour. She lived in a whirl of excitement. Picture-shows, theatres, dances—something claimed her every night. She explained that she wanted to get as much enjoyment out of life before she was married; for she did not expect to get any afterwards.

Belle had quite faded out of their lives. After a year or so at the cycle shop, Bert had tired of it. He gave them to understand that farm-life had always been his ambition. If he could only get a piece of land he would be happy. Meanwhile he visited his thwarted ambitions on his wife. A man with a wife and child was ruined—he could do nothing. He painted glorious pictures of all he would do if he were only a single man. Belle bore it patiently, though sometimes she came weeping to her mother.

"I'm sure if we could only get into the country he'd be better," she would say. "I know plenty of people who have settled on the land. If we only had some influence!"

Helen heard this from Mrs. Hunter, who always told her everything. She wasted no time, and knowing her uncle was a man of some influence, she had appealed to him. He had promised to do what he could, and shortly afterwards Bert found himself in possession of a piece of land in one of the richest districts of Victoria. From that day he had been a changed man. He threw all his energy into it and worked strenuously. He seemed to have found his level at last, and was happy and contented. Belle wrote home glowing accounts of their new life. Helen liked to read these letters, for she seemed to find in them an echo of the care-free, light-hearted Belle she had once known.

Mrs. Hunter had grown more discursive and full of reminiscences as time went on. She had recounted to Helen at various times the history of her life and her whole family. Helen was quite familiar with all the incidents surrounding their births, christenings, marriages, and deaths. She was able at last, by long practice, to dissemble very successfully. She appeared to listen to the conversation, and at the same time could occupy herself with her own thoughts. All Mrs. Hunter required was an occasional remark thrown in to prove that she was listening. Helen became an expert at this, and Mrs. Hunter was grateful accordingly.

"My own daughters," she said plaintively, "never pay me the attention that Helen does."

As she grew older she seemed to desire to gather her relations around her. Much to the disgust of Irene (who made it a point to be out if possible) she said that every second Sunday was to be her day at home for all her relatives. As she was a good cook and made quite a festival of the day, it was very seldom that any of the relations omitted to come. Helen had to help with the entertaining, a task which she dreaded. It seemed to her to be a day of endless relays of food. She thought it must be a peculiarity of theirs to be always hungry, for they never seemed satisfied. Any mention of food was invariably greeted with brightening eyes and general sighs of relief. She often wondered if they starved themselves beforehand so as to be able to eat more. She found them singularly unpleasant, and her delicate lip curled with just the faintest shadow of disgust, as she watched them. She attended to their wants and joined in their conversation, but there was alway a mental reservation in her attitude towards them.

For their part, though they were not conscious of her distaste, they nevertheless resented Helen's presence among them—"just as if she were one of the family," they said among themselves. They were careful not to allow Mrs. Hunter to hear this, for they appreciated too much her hospitality to put it in jeopardy.

Helen was aware of their feelings towards her, and she managed to get a good deal of quiet amusement out of them. Only once had she been hurt, and that was by one of the spinster aunts, who had openly expressed the conviction that Helen's hair was dyed. One Sunday she had left in the sitting-room a book of hers that she had been reading. Some of the relatives had already arrived. One of the young men picked up the book and examined it idly.

"Arthur Somerset," he read out. Then turning to Helen. "This belonged to your father?"

Helen nodded, and held out her hand for it. "Give it to me," she said. "I must put it away."

The spinster aunt saw her opportunity and rushed to it.

"I should have thought you would have destroyed all mementos of your father, Helen."

"Why?"

"Why? My dear girl, can you ask why? Didn't your father commit suicide?"

"What has that got to do with it?" asked Helen calmly. Her eyes were disconcertingly clear as she looked at her opponent.

"Oh, nothing—but, thank God! we have no suicides in our family."

"Oh! I see. You don't think my father will occupy the same place in the afterworld as your family will? Well, I don't think father will mind. Excuse me for a moment."

She took her book and walked out of the room. The young cousin chuckled, enjoying the discomfiture of his aunt.

"Good for her! One in on you, Aunt Jane."

His aunt deigned no reply, but discovered that she had forgotten something which would call her home immediately. She took leave of the surprised Mrs. Hunter, who was unaware of what had happened. The aunt explained that Helen had been very rude to her. This Mrs. Hunter declined to believe and they parted with mutual coolness on both sides.

Helen wondered what George would think of these family gatherings. She could not imagine him among them all. He did not seem to fit in. She wrote to him describing the Sunday visits, and he replied, indignant with Irene that she should leave her to bear the brunt of them. She liked these angry letters of his, for they seemed to bring him closer and he became more real. Most of his letters were rather stiff and shy, giving no indication of what he was doing or what he was thinking. He wrote vaguely of staying out there another year or two, for there was so much for him to learn. She felt angry at first, when she read this, thinking bitterly that he could not care for her very much, but this feeling soon disappeared. When she wrote she forgot to mention it, she had already become so resigned to his absence. His picture hung in her room, and she looked at it sometimes, vaguely wishing that he would come home, but she was conscious of no deep desire to see him again. He seemed such a boy to her, while she herself was a woman. She did not realise that as she was growing up, George was also.

Irene was getting ready for her marriage. She was tired of work, she told Helen, and wanted someone else to keep her.

"We'll all be married before you, Helen," she said one day, looking at her intently. "It's funny you haven't got married yet. You must have met heaps of men too. I say"—as a sudden thought struck her—"are you waiting for George?"

Helen went crimson. "I'm waiting for no one," she said crossly.

"I wouldn't be surprised if you married old George in the end," said Irene, shaking her head wisely. But Helen would not listen to her, though the words disturbed her. Was she really waiting for George? She thrust the thought away with a quick little shake of the head.

It was shortly after Irene's marriage that Mrs. Hunter received a letter, which excited her very much. She conned it over to herself for a day or two and then took it to Helen.

"It's not that I want to leave you, dearie," she said as she gave it to her, "but you know I would love to see Belle again and the child."

Rather amazed at this preamble, and wondering what was the matter, Helen took the letter. As she read she felt a sense of freedom and joy sweep over her. It was from Belle, who suggested that her mother should come to live with them in the country, and bring the two boys. The boys could be taught farming, and perhaps later on they might secure a farm for themselves. The latter made no mention of Helen until the P.S., in which she said:—

"I don't think Helen will mind. She is getting on so well now, and she could easily come up here and see you during her holidays if she wished to. We would be glad to have her, for we know how much we owe her."

Helen flushed with pleasure as she read this. She had not expected nor wanted any thinks, still it was sweet to receive them all the same.

"What do you think about it?" asked Mrs. Hunter, who had been watching her anxiously.

"I think you ought to go," replied Helen, handing the letter back. "It is a good chance for the boys. They will do better in the country. See how it has improved Bert."

"Then you don't mind leaving me at all?" complained Mrs. Hunter.

"Darling! Of course I do!" replied Helen, kissing her fondly. "Still, if Belle wants you, she has first claim."

"I don't like leaving you alone," went on Mrs. Hunter, cheered by Helen's warmth, for she was not much given to demonstrations of affection.

"Don't you worry about me," laughed Helen. "I am quite a rich person now, you must remember, and perhaps I will go and live with my uncle later on."

She knew that there was not the least possibility that she would, but it relieved Mrs. Hunter's mind. Quite cheerfully she set about her preparations for leaving.

Helen was glad they were going. She never passed the house where she once lived, without a stab of remembrance. Even though bright light streamed out of the windows, she could always see the dark room where she had found her father's body. The house had quite changed now. Its garden was as trim as any other garden in the street and childish voices and laughter echoed through the rooms. But it had never changed for Helen. While she lived next to it she could never quite forgot the tragedy that had happened there. Sometimes, catching a glimpse of the wisteria which still bloomed by the window of what had once been her room, she could hardly believe that she was the same girl who had hidden away from her father, hating him and yet dreading him.

Yes, she would be glad to go. She would leave the suburban street behind—the little life that she hated and the people who peered at her as she went by. She was still remembered there as "the girl whose father committed suicide." Mrs. Hunter was considered to have done rather a risky thing in taking Helen into her house—"especially as she had that young fellow, George, living with her."

In the first excitement caused by the suicide of her father, they would have taken her to their hearts, in their desire to learn all about it. But the white-faced, wide-eyed, frightened child had eluded all their efforts and they had fallen back, unsatisfied, on Mrs. Hunter for information. They had never quite forgiven Helen for not satisfying their curiosity, and always spoke of her to strangers with a little hesitating pause. They seemed surprised too that nothing had happened to destroy Mrs. Hunter's confidence in the girl.

"I believe they would be only too glad to hear anything about me," Helen would say bitterly, and she would experience again the wonder she so often felt that Mrs. Hunter had risen so high above her suburban conventions and taken her in.

In her joy at the thought that she was really going away, she almost forgot that it would mean parting with Mrs. Hunter. But when the time came to say good-bye she found out how much she really loved her. Mrs. Hunter sobbed bitterly, beseeching her not to leave her, and Helen had to tear herself away. She knew that Mrs. Hunter would soon recover—she had wept bitterly when Belle left, and later on when Irene married and went away, but that did not make the parting any easier to bear.

Helen was going to a boarding-house for the time being, and as she stood in her narrow little room that night, she had never before felt so lonely and unhappy.

"I have no one who loves me now," she thought. "They all leave me."

The typical boarding-house room with its narrow bed, one chair, wardrobe and dressing-table of cheap yellow wood, increased her depression. She had taken out a few of her own things and put them about, but they only seemed to accentuate the unfriendliness of her present surroundings, and she put them away again.

She went to the window and looked out. It was the twilight hour just before the night descends, and in the misty distance the city looked soft and dreamlike. Already the lights were beginning to twinkle out. The tall buildings melted into the sky, looking as if at the merest breath they would dissolve quite away. On the opposite side of the street she saw a wide park with hundreds of trees, and resolved to explore it in the morning. She watched the color fade out of the sky, red and orange to pink—pale and paler. Then to a creamy yellow which disappeared slowly as the dark blue curtain was drawn over and the stars began to come out. Down in the street below two lovers walked, hand in hand. Their shoulders touched and their heads were bent together. She watched them for a moment or two, and then, with a sudden rush of tears, she pulled down the blind to shut out the sight. The room looked cold and uninviting, and she was very unhappy. She threw herself across the bed and went off into a kind of dreary dream.

Incidents of her life crossed her mind, but they had no sequence. She revelled in the luxury of being melancholy and would have been content to be there for hours. It was only the gong, beaten loudly by an infuriated maid who had just given notice, that brought her back with a start. She forgot her melancholy at once, and examined herself anxiously in the glass to see that no traces of tears could be seen on her face.

She had already met her landlady, who had introduced her to some of her fellow-boarders. The landlady was a majestic being with a manner calculated to strike awe into the heart of the man bold enough to approach her with the request that she should allow his board to run on for a week or two. She did not appear at meals, but made a dignified appearance in the drawing-room when coffee was served there after dinner. They very seldom saw her at other times, except on Friday, when everybody knew that she was to be found in the little room at the end of the passage, sitting majestically at her desk with a pile of receipts in front of her. Very few people omitted to visit her on this day. Two or three of the young men—brave, hardy souls —had conveniently forgotten. On Saturday morning early they were honored by a visit from their landlady and their souls were brave no longer. Alone and unprotected in their rooms they crumpled up at her first attack and meekly paid what was owing to her.

When she appeared in the drawing-room at night, she was always dressed in black silk, which rustled loudly as she walked. The bodice was rigidly boned at the back and shaped so as to display her bust to fullest advantage. She was inordinately proud of her figure, and the boarders wickedly called her amongst themselves "Venus de Milo." She had heard of this, but, thinking it was meant seriously, was pleased and gratified.

She moved among her "guests," as she called them, with dignity. With them and yet not of them. She stayed perhaps half an hour, while the conversation, which had been flowing merrily before she appeared, floundered miserably on. If asked she would sit at the piano and play to them. It was always the same thing, "The Siren's Song."

Sometimes on special occasions she would sing. Her voice was composed mainly of head notes, and she only seemed to know two songs, "Willy, we have missed you," and "The Gypsy's Warning," as an encore.

"Songs of my youth," she would explain graciously to her nervous guests. "Ah! there are no songs like the old songs," and she would sigh sentimentally.

She devoted herself to Helen the first night that she spent there. Helen's uncle had chosen the boarding-house and made all arrangements, and she had been much impressed by him. She asked Helen to invite him in any evening, explaining at the same time that she herself belonged to a "genteel" family and could appreciate a gentleman when she met one. Her liking and interest in him suddenly evaporated, when, in reply to a question, she found that he was married. She rose, and, with a bow that included everyone, swept out of the room.

When she had gone Helen picked up the evening paper and pretended to read it. Behind this barrier she was able to examine all the people without risk of being seen. There was an interesting-looking girl talking to a dark, ugly young man who, she thought, she would like to know. They had been sitting opposite her at dinner, and she had been conscious of their interest in her. They were looking across at her now, and she saw the girl whisper something to the young man, who nodded and went out of the room. Then, to her surprise, she saw the girl coming in her direction. Panic-stricken she began hurriedly to read the paper, but not seeing a word of it.

"You've got it upside down, you know," said a laughing voice. "Do you always read like that?"

Helen looked up, her cheeks a deep crimson. She felt embarrassed for the moment, but the friendly smile put her at her ease, and she laughed.

"How stupid of me!" she said, putting the paper down. "I had been staring at you and I was afraid you had found me out."

"Staring at me, were you?" asked the girl. "Well, I have been staring at you, so that about equalises matters."

Helen thought that she was worth staring at. She had brown hair with glints of gold in it, hazel eyes with flecks of gold, and straight regular little features. Her mouth was small, with full lips.

"I know your name," went on the girl. "I asked. You don't know mine though. You weren't interested enough to find out. No! I thought not. Well, I'll tell you. It's Ann Wilson!"

"Ann Wilson!" repeated Helen softly.

"Not much of a name, is it?" the girl rattled on. "But it will serve. 'Not so deep as a well nor so wide as a church door but 'twill serve.' Now don't look so astonished. I don't serve up quotations with every remark I make. Listen, I'll tell you a secret if you swear never to let it out. That's the only bit of Shakespeare I know, and I built up a reputation for cleverness here on the strength of it. S-sh! I wonder if anyone heard me telling you that." She looked round with exaggerated caution and then joined in Helen's laughter.

The drawing-room was quickly emptying. All the men had gone, and the only people left were two old ladies playing Patience and another group doing some intricate kind of needlework.

"What are you going to do to-night?" asked Miss Wilson. "Got anything special on?"

Helen shook her head. She had nothing to do, unless she joined the group of the old ladies and was taught to play Patience or instructed in the art of fancy needlework.

The girl clapped her hands. "I'm so glad," she said. "You can come with me then. Some artist friends of mine are giving a little evening at their studio to-night. They'd love to see you—they'll rave about you. Come along.''

"But——'' said Helen, half-protesting as the girl pulled her towards the door.

"It's no use making excuses. You've got to come. I want you to see my studio too. I've got a room in the same building. Oh, yes, I'm an artist, or at least I hope to be some time.''

Quite overwhelmed by the girl's energy, Helen allowed herself to be swept away. She ran upstairs to put her hat on, singing happily to herself. The room no longer made her feel miserable and depressed. She had already made a friend. Oh, it was good just to be alive!

CHAPTER VI.

THE ARTISTS' STUDIO.

Ann's friends had a long narrow room in a big building in Flinders Street looking over towards the river Yarra. The bottom floors were all merchants' warehouses, but the top floor was let entirely to artists. The light was good and the rent cheap. Two young artists shared one studio together, and between them they had managed to make a very attractive room of it. An oak table, which someone had presented to them, a few chairs and a cane lounge were the only articles of furniture in the room. The floor was covered by a beautiful Indian rug of scarlet and gold, which they had bought for a trifling sum in a second-hand shop.

Their best work hung on the walls, the rest were bundled unceremoniously into a corner. Some black and white illustrations cut out of the "Bulletin" (principally Norman Lindsay's) were pinned carelessly about. On the mantelpiece lay a plaster cast of the hand of Marie Antoinette, and the death mask of Napoleon.

Both artists were very young, very much in earnest and very poor. Their poverty did not cause them a second's uneasiness. "We're poor but honest," they consoled themselves laughingly. They worked hard, their whole heart in their work. If they were in funds they dined sumptuously at a restaurant. If not, they dined just as happily at home on tea and bread and butter.

Charlie Donaldson was the more commercial of the two. He had more of the money sense than Walter Trevor, who, as long as he had a paint brush in his hand, would not have bothered about anything else. Charlie looked after their combined finances and expended them to best advantage. After long experience and many heart-breaking failures Charlie had become quite a good housekeeper and an economical shopper. He knew a shop where sausages could be bought one half-penny cheaper than any other shop in town. He knew where he could get eggs "almost fresh" as advertised, and which tasted almost as good as really fresh eggs when fried.

He it was who swept the studio in the morning and made the two small camp beds in the little room where they slept. He was very methodical and had reduced his housework to a fine art. Half an hour sufficed to finish all the work, and even the most careful housewife could not have found fault with the neatness and cleanliness of the place.

He was much more energetic than Walter. He would be working with quick, nervous strokes, while Walter spent most of the morning dreaming over his canvas. But Walter's dreams were always worth while. Sometimes Charlie would get impatient at his friend's idleness, but when Walter seized his brush he worked indefatigably, and Charlie could only stand and admire the result. Walter's pictures had always a touch of genius in them, while Charlie's were never more than mediocre. Charlie knew this too well, and a feeling of discontent would seize him when he compared Walter's work with his. He was gradually giving up his attempts in color and turning more and more to black and white work. He had designed the covers for a couple of magazines on several occasions, and some of the weekly papers had printed his drawings. He was gradually finding a market for his stuff and this encouraged him.

Their studio was the happy hunting ground of several young artists, both men and girls. It had become a sort of informal club. No one ever came during the day—they were all too busy—but after eight every night quite a dozen young people were to be found there. They never came empty-handed. One would bring a tin of sardines, another some saveloys, another some butter or bread. Indeed there had been occasions when one or other of the artists had eaten nothing all day and had depended on the supper to fill up the void.

Ann explained this to Helen as they walked briskly down from East Melbourne. She carried a parcel which she said contained cold ham and gherkins.

"I'm all right," she said, "but all the others haven't twopence to jingle on a tombstone. I get an allowance from my people, who, by the way, don't approve of me in the least. Still they wouldn't like me to starve, and they know I can't live on art."

"What would you do if you hadn't any people to make you an allowance?" ventured Helen.

The girl shrugged her shoulders. "God knows! I don't. Pose as a model perhaps. I haven't bad shoulders."

As they approached the building they could see the studio was brightly lit up. All the windows were wide open and the light streamed through.

"Looks cheerful, doesn't it?" said Ann. "Now we've got about five hundred and sixty stairs to climb up. I hope you don't mind, but it can't be helped if you do. There's no other way of getting up."

They toiled up five flights of stairs and arrived at the top panting and out of breath. Ann knocked sharply at a door opposite the landing, and then leant heavily against it. The door opened from the inside and Ann staggered into the arms of a freckle-faced, snub-nosed, sandy-haired young man, who, without a word, leant her gently against the wall.

"Oh, it's you, is it, Sandy MacGregor," said Ann. "I was hoping it would be Walter."

"Walter's there all right," replied Sandy with a grin and speaking with a slight Scotch burr. "But are not my arms as good as Walter's?"

"No," said Ann. "Not nearly." Then in a lower voice. "Sandy, I've got a pleasant surprise in store for you all to-night. I've brought with me the loveliest girl I've ever seen. When you see her you'll go down on your knees and call me blessed."

"Produce her at once," said Sandy.

"Hush! not so loud. She'll hear you, and I fancy she's a little bit shy."

"She won't be shy of us," scoffed Sandy.

"You would be a little overpowering for anyone who wasn't used to you," said Ann. "Wait there and I'll bring her in."

She went out into the passage and called to Helen, who was examining the names on the other doors. They were written on envelopes and scraps of paper and pinned up. She turned as she heard Ann's voice and came towards her.

"Now, Mr. Sandy MacGregor," said Ann in a whisper. "We'll see."

She introduced them solemnly and in the most formal and dignified manner at her command. Sandy knew she was making fun of him, for he was always a scrupulous observer of the conventions at a first introduction. He bowed very low to Helen, who thought that his politeness and his humorous face went strangely together. But Sandy had been brought up by a careful mother. In his youth he had been taught to be polite to ladies, and he still clung to it—the only remnant of his old life.

"Come inside now and meet the others," said Ann, standing aside to let Helen go in first. Sandy followed them in and managed to whisper to Ann:

"For once you have not deceived me!"

Helen saw six or seven people clustered together at the end of the room. They seemed to be examining something and were talking excitedly.

"Hullo!" said Ann. "What's the matter? It must be something new of Walter's." Beckoning to Helen to follow her she hurried down the room towards them.

They looked up as she joined them.

"Hullo Ann!" said somebody. Then—"What do you think of this?"

"Something new of Walter's?"

Charlie Donaldson, who was holding up the picture, nodded. Ann did not speak; she looked at it for a long time in silence. Helen saw that Ann had forgotten her, so she peeped over her shoulder. Even her inexperienced eye could see the power of the work. It was only an old man's head. A rather bleary eyed and disreputable old man he was, but the artist had written his life's history in his face.

"He's our master," said Ann with a sigh. "Where's Walter? Oh, there you are! Walter— we're proud to know you."

Walter laughed nervously. He liked their praise but he never courted it. "It's not me. It's the model," he said. "I managed to get hold of a good man, that's all."

"Where did you get him from, Walter? He looks a regular old scoundrel."

"Yes, doesn't he? I was down at the wharf one morning and met him shuffling along. He had been stealing bananas, for I could see the tops of them sticking out of his pocket. I asked him if he would like to earn the price of a few beers by sitting for me. He thought at first that I was a detective but I persuaded him I was not. Now I can't keep him out of the place."

"No," said Charlie. "He comes here to breakfast sometimes."

They laughed. "Well, he's worth the price of a few beers and breakfasts," said one of the boys.

"He's a gay old scoundrel," said Ann. "I like the look of him—don't you?" she added turning to Helen.

"Yes," replied Helen. "He looks as if he had been wicked and had enjoyed it. That's the right way to be wicked, I think."

In the interest created by Walter's picture they had not noticed Helen. Now they turned and stared at her in amazement. Where had she come from? Charlie looked from the pictured face with all its evil suggestions, to the innocent face of the girl, and thought what a contrast they made. Ann awoke to her duties and introduced Helen round. There were four men and two girls, and Ann did not bother telling her their surnames.

"We all call each other by our Christian names," she said. "You'll soon get used to it."

Helen thought she would not, but she found that by the end of the evening she addressed them quite naturally by their nicknames. She liked their attitude towards her. They took her right into their circle and made her feel one of themselves. She did not understand half what they were saying at first, for they talked a sort of professional jargon, but she listened intently and soon found her feet.

Ann had opened up her parcel, disclosing the contents, at the sight of which there was a howl of joy.

"We'll have quite a decent lot of things tonight," said Charlie. "I bought some luxuries on the strength of two commissions for designing menu cards for a big dinner."

"What did you get?"

"I got some cigarettes, a bottle of claret, and a pound of China tea. Alick Russell's coming tonight and that's the only stuff he'll drink."

"Oh, is he coming to-night?" asked Ann, who

was getting out cups and saucers and placing them round the table.

"Yes, he's coming to have a look at that picture of Walter's. I met him and told him about it, and he said he would be along."

Helen, who was looking at Ann, wondered why her face had changed. The bright look had left it, and catching Helen's eye, she turned hastily away.

"He has not been here for a long time," she said after a pause, in an elaborately indifferent tone. "Where's he been?"

"I don't know, I'm sure," replied Charlie. "He didn't say."

"Russell, is it?" asked Sandy, who was sitting near Helen, admiring the gleam of her hair under the light. "He's been away. Up at that place of his at Warburton. You and he used to be great pals once upon a time, Ann. What happened? Did you quarrel?"

Ann flushed slightly. "Mind your own business, Sandy. We didn't quarrel."

"Well now, she's nice and polite, isn't she?" he demanded of Helen.

Helen stole a glance at Ann. She saw that Ann was annoyed, though she tried to hide it.

"You were rather rude, I think," she said seriously.

They all shouted with laughter. "Serves you right, Sandy."

"Well, perhaps it does," he muttered, rather discomfited.

Ann, quite restored to good humor, laughed with them at Helen's sally, though she had not meant it as a joke.

"Pass along those cigarettes, Charlie," she ordered. "Everything is ready except the China tea. I won't make that until His Highness arrives."

The cigarettes were passed to Helen quite as a matter of course. She took one, stealing sidelong glances to see what the other girls did. They tapped them in a business-like way on the table and then lit up, so she did the same. She did not like it in the least. She only seemed to get a nasty taste in the mouth while the others puffed away with apparent enjoyment. She would not have acknowledged for the world that she did not like it, though the smoke blew into her eyes and made them smart and she was afraid of burning the end of her nose.

They carefully diluted the claret with water so that there would be enough to go round. Helen was given hers in one of the three tumblers the studio possessed. She would rather have had tea, though it gave her a delightfully wicked feeling to be drinking wine. She gathered that the tea would not be made until the man they were expecting arrived. They seemed to think a lot of him, for she could catch his name several times, and the speakers were always enthusiastic—except Ann, who said crossly that he was conceited and spoilt.

Helen was leaning back in her chair, her half-smoked cigarette in her fingers, which, though she did not like it, nevertheless gave her great satisfaction. She told herself proudly that no one would have guessed that she had never smoked a cigarette before. She was listening idly to Sandy, who had already fallen violently in love with her and had warned all the others off. Though she was listening to him, she was not looking at him, so when the door opposite her opened quietly, she was the first to notice it. The others were so intent on their conversation that they were unaware that anyone had entered the room.

But Helen saw! She laid down the half-smoked cigarette and looked away from the infatuated Sandy to the man who stood at the door. For a moment their eyes met. Then, embarrassed by the stranger's gaze, she averted her eyes and drew

Sandy's attention to him. Sandy sprang to his feet with a shout.

"Here he is at last, boys."

Helen watched them as they greeted him. They had all left the table and clustered round him, except herself and Ann, who had taken the teapot and was quietly making the tea. He stood among them laughing and talking for a minute or two, then strode across to Ann.

"Well, Ann?" he said quietly.

Ann poured the water into the teapot before she turned round. When she did so her face was a little flushed, perhaps from stooping. But she held out her hand frankly.

"So your Highness has condescended to appear again? I, as usual, am attending to your wants. This, sir, is tea bought especially for you and made especially for you—no one else will drink it."

He laughed. "It's good to hear you chaffing me again, Ann."

"Oh, is it?" she replied. "Well, you will get plenty of it. But what will you do first? Have your tea, or look at Charlie's picture?"

"Look at Charlie's picture. But first of all——" he paused in front of Helen.

"Oh, yes," said Ann. "I had forgotten. What a nuisance you people are with your formal introductions."

"Are you also an artist?" he asked Helen.

"Oh, no," replied Helen hastily. "I'm nothing! I'm only an onlooker."

"You're nothing?" he repeated. "If you're nothing, what are we?"

Before Helen could reply, Sandy had taken his place again by her side, and Alick Russell turned away. She felt a little impatient with Sandy. He had hovered near her the whole evening, and she was beginning to get rather tired of him. But Sandy was impervious to even the broadest hints. It was the last thing he would believe that anyone could have too much of his society. Helen lent an inattentive ear to Sandy's conversation. Her attention was centred on Alick Russell. He stood under the gas-jet examining the picture, the light throwing his rugged features into strong relief. He wasn't good-looking, she thought. George was better-looking, and so was Mr. Thomas. Some of the boys in the room too had better features, but people would look at this man where they would not at the others. He looked about forty, and she wondered that she had ever thought forty old. It seemed to her now to be the ideal age for a man.

"Striking looking chap, isn't he?" asked Sandy, breaking in on her thoughts.

"Yes," she replied. "He seems to stand out somehow."

"Fine fellow, too," Sandy went on. "I don't suppose there's a chap here to-night who he hasn't helped at some time or other. They all know if they are in a hole Russell would help them out. He's not much of an artist, though. At least he could be if he tried. The trouble with him is that he can do too many things, and he's got too much money. Now if he had either to work or starve he would do something worth while."

"But if he's not a good artist, why are they so anxious for him to see Walter's picture?" objected Helen, who would rather have heard that he was a famous artist.

"Ah!" said Sandy. "Now, that's where you make the mistake. It doesn't follow that because he is not a good artist he can't criticise a picture. If he says a picture is good, you can bet what you like that it is good."

"I see," said Helen. She glanced again at the group gathered together at the lower end of the room. Russell had finished looking at the picture and Charlie was putting it away. He came back to the table, his hand on Walter's shoulder.

"Well, what do you think of it, Russell?" asked Sandy.

"I would give all I possess to be gifted with half the talent that Walter has," he replied curtly. "Where's that tea you were talking about, Ann?"

He sat down opposite to Helen and next to Ann, who seemed pleased at the arrangement. He did not speak to Helen again, and Helen, afraid lest he should do so and she would not know what to say to him, devoted herself to Sandy and listened with flattering attention to all he had to say.

When it was all over and she was standing near the door ready to go and waiting for Ann, Russell came to her.

"I believe you are staying at the same house as Ann," he said. "I live quite close, so I will have the pleasure of walking home with you."

"Oh!" replied Helen. Then, enraged with herself for her stupidity, she rushed into conversation. "I've never met people like these before. They are interesting, aren't they?"

He ignored her question. "Why did you say that you are nothing?"

"Oh, really, I did not mean anything by that remark," Helen assured him earnestly. "Here's Ann," she added, with a little sigh of relief.

They walked slowly home. Helen was very silent, but Ann had a lot to say. She kept up a running fire of question and banter. Helen was glad, for it relieved her of the necessity of talking when she did not want to. Now and again his hand touched hers and she drew it away quickly, ashamed that she liked the touch. They passed a shop brilliantly lit up, and she felt his eyes on her face. She did not look up, and they passed into the darkness again, but as they walked on her pulse beat a little quicker. He took them through a park along an avenue of trees. It was autumn and the leaves were falling. Their feet made a pleasant swishing sound among the leaves.

"Is this the park I can see from my window?" asked Helen.

"Yes," he replied. "The Fitzroy Gardens, they call it. It's just a little bit of England poked away here. When you go into town you must come through here. It's a short cut."

A policeman passed them, going towards the city. He looked at them stolidly. They were neither drunk nor disorderly, so they were no concern of his. He thought what fools they were to be wandering about the gardens on a cold night when they might be in their beds. But he was used to fools. He had become a disillusioned man since he had joined "the force."

"I've got my latch-key, fortunately," said Ann, as they neared the house. "I don't suppose she has given you one yet?" Helen shook her head. "I often forget mine, and I either have to hang about the doorstep waiting for someone to come in, or else ring the bell and rouse the whole house."

Russell left them at the gate, and they watched him striding away.

"Well, what do you think of him?" asked Ann as they went inside.

"I think he is—interesting," replied Helen.

"Most women do who know him," returned Ann rather bitterly.

"Now what did she mean by that," Helen pondered as she lay on her uncomfortable bed, tossing restlessly from side to side, unable to sleep.

CHAPTER VII.

THE PORTRAIT.

Helen's time was fully occupied. From nine until five o'clock she had to be at the office, while most of her evenings were spent at the studio. They loved to get her there and make her sing to them. Long ago Helen had discovered that she had a voice people liked to listen to. One of the young men had a flute upon which he performed very badly, but none of the circle minded very much as long as they knew what he was playing. Accompanied by this, Helen sang to them all the old-fashioned airs. She had never learnt any modern songs and dreaded the usual popular ballads. She had too vivid a remembrance of Belle and Bert singing them at the piano in their old home to wish to repeat the performance.

She had given up smoking altogether. On confiding to Sandy that she did not like it, he laughed at her and told her there was no necessity for her to smoke if she did not want to. If she refrained there would be all the more cigarettes for the others.

After a few weeks, she had left the boarding-house, but not without some remonstrances from her uncle. He had a strong sense of responsibility towards her, more so now than when she had been a child. She had grown up too "deucedly good-looking," as he phrased it to himself, to be quite safe alone in the world. He had suggested to his wife that his niece should come to them, but her reply was decisive and he did not repeat the suggestion. He had chosen the boarding-house as the lesser of two evils, and he was taken aback when he heard that she wanted to give it up and go and live in rooms. He shook his head decidedly when Helen first told him what she wanted to do. But he was not proof against her for long. He took her out to dinner so as to have an opportunity of pointing out why it was impossible that she should live in residential mansions, and ended by allowing her to have her own way.

Once he did give his permission he entered into her plans with enthusiasm. She took two small rooms, a bed-room and sitting-room, and he helped her to furnish them. When she had everything fixed up—her father's books unpacked and her mother's picture, which she had had framed, hanging on the wall, as well as her old favourite "Mona Lisa" and others she had collected, he looked round with pleasure and acknowledged that she was right. The room looked like her and expressed her own individuality, whereas the boarding-house had been merely a place where she slept and sometimes dined. He liked to come up and have tea with her sometimes, though she was always careful not to ask him when she had any of her other friends there, for she knew he would not approve of them.

Ann openly envied her. She still lived at the boarding-house, and though she hated it she was unable to leave. Her parents paid her board direct, and thus hoped to keep some control over her. They were simple country people who had not yet got used to the idea that their daughter wished to be an artist. It was only by making herself very unpleasant at home that they had allowed her to come down to town.

Helen had posed for Walter. He had painted a head of her with her hair hanging round her shoulders. The picture had been in his studio for a couple of weeks, hanging next to the head of the old man; then it disappeared. She asked what had become of it, and he told her the two of them were sold. She was curious as to who had bought them, but he seemed to evade the question. It was Sandy who enlightened her.

"It's supposed to be a secret," he said, "but I'll tell you. Russell bought them both."

"Mr. Russell?"

Sandy nodded. "Yes, that's so. Russell asked Walter to keep it dark, but of course we all guessed."

"If he wanted it kept a secret you had no right to tell me," Helen said sharply.

"Now, now," said Sandy soothingly. "Don't get cross. You would have heard sooner or later, so what's the odds? Look here, Helen, I'm an unselfish sort of chap, you know. I'm in love with you myself, but it will never come to anything. I'll never have enough money to get married; besides a wife comes between a man and his art. Now if you married someone else, I could love you just the same, and yet have the satisfaction of feeling that you were for ever out of my reach, so there would be no use worrying about you because I couldn't get you. It's my belief that Russell is falling in love with you. Why don't you go for him?"

"Don't be ridiculous, Sandy," said Helen turning away. "I think you are the most impossible boy I have ever met in all my life."

"Think it over," called Sandy after her. "I know what I am talking about."

There was no need to tell Helen to think it over. It was a subject that occupied a great deal of her thoughts lately. She saw more of Alick Russell than most of them were aware. He very seldom came to the studio, at least when she was there, but by some means or other, he soon found out her usual haunts.

Every day she had lunch at the Fitzroy Gardens. She loved to sit in the little Kiosk and watch the changing shadows cast by the trees on the grass. Though it was winter and the trees were bare of foliage, and to some people the place might have looked cold and bleak, yet it held a romantic charm for her. It was so still and silent, and yet so close to town. It seemed like a green dreamland hidden away in the heart of the city. Often, as she walked through the noble avenues of English trees she found herself repeating:

> "The green land's name that a charm encloses,
>   It never was writ on the traveller's chart,
> And sweet on its trees as the fruit that grows is
>   It never was sold in the merchant's mart.
> The swallows of dreams through its dim fields dart
>   And sleep's are the tunes on its tree-tops heard.
> No hound's note wakens the wild-wood hart
>   Only the song of a secret bird."

She often fancied she could hear the note of the secret bird, though she could never find the bird— it remained hidden and apart.

One day when she arrived for lunch she was surprised to find Russell. He gave no explanation of his presence there and she asked for none, content only that he should have come. It came to be an understood thing that they should lunch together always. Sometimes it happened, as the days got colder and darker, they would be the only two people lunching at the little tea house. These hours seemed all too short to Helen, and also to Russell. On Saturday afternoons she would find him waiting for her and they would go to their favourite spot. If it was fine they would get deck chairs and sit on the lawn in the sun. If it was too cold or wet they went to the Art Gallery instead, though it was seldom they looked at a picture. They were too interested in themselves.

She told him the whole story of her life. Of all the people she had known. Her mother and her father, all—except George. She hardly knew why she did not mention George to him, when she told him everything else. Things she had never spoken of to anyone before she told him quite naturally. He listened, his eyes on her face, watching the changing expression as she talked.

"How strange life is," he said. "While you were going through all that I was just sauntering along. Not very interested in anything or anybody. I felt that I had just about reached the end of my tether and I would have to go away—my life was so flat and unprofitable—when suddenly I met you and the whole face of the world is changed." He made a wide sweep of his arm.

She smiled at him. They were in the Gardens making the most of the wintry sun. She was lying back in a deck chair, while he leaned forward clasping his knees between his hands.

"You didn't say much to me that night I first met you. I didn't think you were very interested in me."

"No?" he said musingly. "And yet I was. While I was speaking to Ann I was conscious of you the whole time. You looked so childlike sitting there, talking so earnestly to that absurd Sandy."

"But I'm not young," protested Helen.

"Sometimes I think you are not sixteen, child; other times I try and persuade myself you are thirty."

He sighed and fell silent. Helen too was silent. He had spoken about Ann and revived a little doubt in her heart. Why was Ann so perturbed that night when he came unexpectedly? She tried to put the thought out of her mind, but it came back. Her face changed and he noticed it immediately.

"What is the matter?" he asked softly, touching her hand.

She drew it away quickly. "Nothing," she replied curtly.

"Have I displeased you in some way?" he asked. "I wouldn't hurt you for the world."

"Oh, no, you haven't. It is only——" She got up hastily. "Come and have some tea. I'm so thirsty and I'm getting cold too."

He got up slowly and followed her over to the Kiosk. A cloud seemed to have fallen over the brightness of the afternoon. She kept up a bright and animated conversation till the waitress retired, then she relapsed into silence.

"Shall I pour out?" he asked.

She nodded, and sat with her head resting on her hand watching.

"Tell me," she said, as she took her cup, and trying to speak in an indifferent tone, "do all women find you interesting?"

He seemed taken aback for a moment and then laughed. "I don't know, I'm sure; but I hope you do."

Helen waved that aside. "I suppose you have known a lot of women?"

He put down his cup. "What are you trying to get at?"

"Nothing at all," Helen prevaricated. "I just wanted to know."

"You can't get out of it that way. You brought up the subject. Now what have you got in your mind about me?" He spoke in a joking tone, but with an underlying note of seriousness.

"Why do you make such a fuss over it?" Helen asked crossly. "I'm sorry I said anything now. It's nothing that I really care about in the least, only someone told me that all women you knew were interested in you and I was rather curious to know."

"I've been too interested in them," he said in a low voice. "I've always been too fond of women."

"How horrible you are," cried Helen, springing to her feet. "I hate men who are too fond of women."

She turned and left him, and he made no attempt to detain her, but sat watching the slim figure hurrying away between the trees. When she was out of sight he gathered up the things she had left behind and followed her. He caught her up just as she had passed the Parliament House buildings and was turning into Collins Street. She knew when he joined her, but she refused to look at him. Her eyes were wet and she would not let him see she had been crying. He walked beside her in silence until they reached the buildings where she lived. She passed into the passage and up the stairs. When they reached the first flight she turned to him. Her eyes were dry now and she was furiously angry.

"How dare you follow me like this?" she demanded. "What do you want?"

"I want to speak to you."

"Well, what is it?"

"I can't speak to you here. You had better ask me to come in."

She already had the door open and entered herself. She half closed it as he spoke but he stopped her.

"It's no use. I'm coming in. You don't want people to see me waiting about outside, do you? That is what I shall do unless you let me come in now."

She yielded, but very ungraciously. "Very well, then, under that threat I will have to let you in."

The room was quite dark and she switched on the electric light. He laid down her gloves and the book she had left behind in her flight. Then he turned to Helen, who had lit the gas-heater and was sitting in an easy-chair with her back turned to him.

"Look to me," he commanded. To her surprise she found herself obeying.

"You're angry with me?" he said in a softer voice.

"No, why should I be? After all, it's nothing to me if—," she faltered a little, "—if you are fond of women."

"You quite mistook my meaning. Every man finds women interesting more or less. I admit the study of women has interested me, but no woman has made any great impression on my life—as yet."

Helen's cheeks flamed. There was a significant note in his voice as he added the last words, but she pretended not to notice it.

"I'm sorry I was so rude to you," she said at last. "But when you said that I remembered a man I used to know who was said to be fond of women and he did horrible things."

"We're brutes, I'm afraid," said Russell. "All of us. Some more so than others. I've never had the desire nor the energy to be as great a brute as I could be. As I could be—don't forget that, Helen. I'm not much of a man when all is said and done. There are women I have been—fond of, but I have never been any good to them. I'm an unsatisfactory sort of man. Helen, I warn you."

Helen rose to her feet, laughing a little.

"I don't think it matters to me, does it? Come and have a look at my pictures."

He seemed about to speak, then changed his mind and followed her obediently.

"That's my mother!" she said proudly.

He bent closer and examined the picture.

"She's lovely, isn't she?" asked Helen.

"Yes," he replied. "How alike you two are." He stared at it again. "Do you know I have seen that face somewhere."

"You say she is like me, perhaps that is why you think you have seen her?"

"No!" He frowned and snapped his fingers impatiently. "I've seen her somewhere—somewhere I can't remember; but it was not in this country, I'm sure."

He gave it up at last. "It's no use. Perhaps it will come to me one day. What a romantic history she has had. I wonder where she is now?"

"I am always wondering that," said Helen. "But I don't think I will ever see her again."

"I would like to see the two of you together," he said after a pause. "No wonder your father gave up life when he had to give her up. He must have been something like me. He made a failure of his life, and I've failed at most things." He turned away and picked up his hat. "Why! Who is this?" he asked with a sudden change of tone.

He was looking at George's picture, which Helen had stood on a little table near the door.

"That?" said Helen in an embarrassed voice. "That's George."

"Who is George?" he asked coldly.

"Just a friend of mine," replied Helen, feeling at the same time that the reply was very inert.

"A very great friend?"

"I am very fond of him," said Helen, smiling a little maliciously.

"I must go," he said quickly, his face flushing a little.

"Won't you stay? I will tell you a little more about George if you do."

"I am sorry," he said. "It would not interest me in the least."

"No?" said Helen, "and yet I thought you seemed very interested in him just now."

"You were mistaken," he said stiffly.

"Really? I am so sorry. Must you go? Good-bye."

She accompanied him to the door, secretly rather pleased, for she saw that he was angry. He looked sulky and she thought what a big boy he was. Her heart warmed to him.

"I am not so very fond of him," she whispered as he went out. His face lightened at once, the sulky expression leaving it. "Only as fond of him as you are of women," she added.

He gave an exclamation of annoyance and she laughed and closed the door. She waited to hear his footsteps along the passage, but he did not move. She wondered what he was doing, and looking down saw a note pushed under the door. She heard his footsteps receding down the corridor, then opened the note and read:

"I shall see you to-morrow."

She laughed again and put it carefully away. It was the first time she had seen his handwriting.

CHAPTER VIII.

"It's a joy just to get into this cosy little room of yours, Helen. I don't know what I should do without it. It's become quite a haven to me now. I've been at classes all day and feel as stupid as an owl."

Ann had just come in, tired and wet. It had been raining heavily all day, and the streets were glistening under the lamplights. Their smooth shining surface reflected back the green, red and yellow lights of the trams and the blazing advertisements of the theatres and picture palaces.

Helen had hurried down from the office, cold and shivering, glad to get inside. She had been going to the theatre with Alick Russell, but at the last moment rang him up and put him off. It was too wet to go out that night, she told him. He seemed annoyed, and told her it had not been his intention to walk her about the streets; they would be under shelter all the time. She had persisted in her refusal and rang off rather abruptly.

All that day she had been in a strange state of excitement. By the mail that had come in that morning from the West she had received a letter from George which had disturbed her. He spoke of coming home within a year, and in his delight at the thought of seeing her again he had overcome his natural disinclination to seeing his emotions set out on paper, and let himself go. For the first time since he went away he had written Helen a love-letter—and Helen was not prepared to receive it. She had flushed nervously when she read it, feeling almost as embarrassed as though a stranger had made a declaration of love to her. She felt that George was almost a stranger to her now, and she really was to him. He could only be in love with his idea of her, for she knew she had changed since he had known her. She wished vainly that he had not written it, for it forced her to think about him again, and this she did not want to do. She had almost persuaded herself that he had quite forgotten everything that had passed between them, and it was disconcerting to find that after all he remembered.

She read the letter through again when she reached home, very gravely and seriously. Then she put it away, thinking she would answer it directly, though she knew her reply could only be evasive and unsatisfactory to him.

She looked round the room. For the first time it struck her as cheerless and lonely. She felt she would be miserable there to-night if no one came in, and she wished that she had not put Russell off. There was a telephone downstairs. In two minutes she could ring him up and hear his voice, surprised and pleased when he learnt who was speaking. She played with the temptation for a moment and then shook her head decidedly. No! she wouldn't do it. She would stay at home and try and answer George's letter.

She put a match to the gas-heater and the room looked more cheerful at once. She had just put the kettle on and started to lay the table when Ann came in unexpectedly. Helen gave her a joyous welcome. Apart from her pleasure at seeing Ann she was glad, for it gave her an excuse to herself for not answering George's letter that evening. She knew this was merely procrastination, for it would have to be answered sometime and that very soon. She was only putting off the evil day.

Ann looked pale and dispirited. She had been wet through twice during the day, and had sat for over an hour in her wet things. She was chilled to the bone and crouched near the fire, shivering. Helen fussed over her, pleased at the opportunity, for Ann was usually so sturdily independent and hated to be waited on. Helen made her remove the wet dress and shoes and put on a warm dressing-gown and slippers. Then as the kettle had just started to boil she made her a cup of tea, which Ann sipped at first mechanically, then with obvious enjoyment.

"You're just in time for dinner," Helen said, laying an extra knife and fork for Ann, who gazed at her preparations with interest.

"Do you know," she said meditatively, "I believe I am hungry? I couldn't get out to have any lunch to-day, and during the afternoon I began to get so miserable. I couldn't think what was the matter with me. I must have been merely hungry, I suppose, though I thought I was getting spiritual leanings, I felt so unhappy."

"I notice that when I am most unhappy it is usually because I am hungry," replied Helen. "Come along and make yourself happy."

There was a marked improvement in Ann's spirits when she had finished her meal. She sat by the fire and drew out her cigarette case with a little sigh of content. She offered it to Helen, who shook her head. Both sat in silence for a time. They knew each other well enough not to try and make conversation when there was no need for it. Helen glanced at Ann once or twice, wondering if she were happy. She looked perfectly content as she sat there, her half-smoked cigarette between her fingers and her eyes on the fire, smiling a little at her thoughts. Again Helen assured herself that it was absurd to worry about her. She looked so strong and self-reliant as though life could not offer any problems to her.

The rain, which had died down, had sprung up

again, and burst with sudden fury against the window pane.

"Listen to that!" said Helen in a low voice.

"Well, what does it matter?" returned Ann, puffing at her cigarette. "We're inside, warm and comfortable, so we need not bother about it."

"No, it does not hurt us, but what about the poor creatures who are out in it? The blind beggars with their pitiful singing, and those women whose living depends on the street. Just think of it, Ann, A wet night may make all the difference to them as to whether they went hungry or not."

"My dear Helen," said Ann, petulantly throwing her cigarette away, "why do you think about such unpleasant things, or, if you must think about them, why tell your thoughts to me? We can't do anything—it's not our fault; so, for goodness' sake, do get it out of your mind."

"No, it's not our fault, I suppose," said Helen slowly, "and yet—I don't know. I read somewhere that Lecky called those women 'the Saviours of Society.' Do you think they are, Ann?"

"Oh, I don't know," replied Ann morosely. "What's the good of making ourselves miserable, when we were sitting here so happy and comfortable?"

"No good at all, I suppose." She sighed. "Well, we won't talk about it, Ann, as you don't want to."

She rose and went to the window, pulling aside the blind and peering out into the darkness.

"You can't go home to-night, Ann," she said, coming back to the fire again. "You will have to stay with me."

"I wish I could, but I dare not. If I did not come home to-night the guardian of my morals would immediately hope for the worst and write to my parents. Then it would be good-bye to hopes of future fame for me, and an ignominious return to my country home."

"I wish I could do something that would give me hopes of future fame," said Helen. "When I was young I used to have dreams of all I was going to do in the world, but they have come to nothing. Why, there is absolutely nothing that I can do!"

"Listen to Miss Hopeless talking!" cried Ann mockingly. "Anyone would think you were fifty two, instead of—what is it? Twenty-two! What about your voice, anyhow?. You've got a beautiful voice."

"Do you really think so?" asked Helen eagerly, and then growing despondent again. "But what good is it to me? I haven't got the money to get it trained, and even if I did, what would be the use? There are hundreds of people with nice voices, or good voices, and I would only be one of that crowd. I want to stand alone."

"Another Melba?" said Ann laughing. "You are certainly modest, Helen. Look at me! I haven't given up hope and I am older than you. There are hundreds of people who can paint quite nicely. At present I am only one of that crowd, but I don't sit down and cry about it. I'll just go on, and if I find out in the end that all I can do is to paint pictures quite nicely, I'll make the best of it and send them round to my friends for wedding presents. After all, what are friends for?"

"Don't send me one, Ann," said Helen laughing, then immediately wished she had not said it, for a sudden constraint seemed to fall upon them. She noticed Ann flushed a little at her words, as though she had thought of something unpleasant.

Ann looked quickly at Helen, and then averted her eyes. Helen noticed the glance, though she appeared unconscious of it, and her heart beat a little faster.

"We're friends, aren't we?" asked Ann.

"Yes," replied Helen. "Of course we are."

"And friends ought to be able to say anything to each other without fear of being misunderstood?"

"They ought to," replied Helen, though there was an undercurrent of doubt in her voice. She was aware that unnecessary frankness had been the grave of many friendships.

Ann moved uneasily. She seemed to find some difficulty in beginning. "It's about Alick Russell," she said at last. "I don't know how you feel about him. I can only guess." She paused interrogatively.

"I don't know myself," Helen thought, but she did not speak. Ann waited a moment and then went on.

"He is a man with an insatiable appetite for experiments—experiments with women. He likes to study us, to find out the motives that lie behind our actions and our words. He is a dilettante in everything—in art, in life, in love. He is no good to women —" she paused, frowning and seeking her words carefully. "You see it is like this. I know he has a rooted objection against marriage. A woman might very easily take him seriously and be disappointed. We don't sympathize with his experimental attitude. I hope you don't mind my speaking like this?" she asked anxiously.

"Oh no! Go on," said Helen, in a muffled voice.

"There is nothing else to say, except that I just want to warn you not to take him too seriously."

"Why? Do you think I am his latest experiment?" Helen asked coldly.

"Don't speak like that, Helen," cried Ann distressed. "I wish I hadn't said anything. You are angry with me now."

"No, I'm not, really." She forced back with an effort the feeling of anger and mortification that had threatened to overcome her. "But there is one thing I would like to know. Don't you—like him?"

"I suppose you think I told you that because I do not like him. I wouldn't do anything so mean. I do like him, but I don't want to see you unhappy."

"I won't be made unhappy. You need not worry about me," said Helen in a firm voice. "You do like him then?" She was not yet satisfied that Ann had told her everything.

Ann stared into the fire, and then looked at Helen and laughed. "I can laugh about it now," she said, "but a year ago I could not. That shows you how quickly one can forget. A year ago I though I was in love with him—to-day—" she shrugged her shoulders, "I can meet him just as a good friend. It was not his fault. He never made love to me. I don't think he even guessed how I felt. He never seemed to look on me as a woman at all, perhaps that is what hurt." She sighed, and taking another cigarette, lit it. "Well, that is all over. I'm glad, too. I feel free now and at peace with the world."

"If that is so, why were you so upset when he came to the studio that night you took me there?" asked Helen in a low voice.

"Did you notice that?" said Ann surprised. "How widely open you must have kept those large, bright eyes of yours. Of course I felt nervous at first. I was afraid that when I saw him it might all come back. But it did not, and now I'm free. I'm not going to fall in love again. Don't you either, Helen!"

Helen laughed. Her heart was light again, and she was happy. She had soon shaken off the effect of Ann's warning, for she realised that she knew him better than Ann did. What had disturbed her had been the thought that he might once have been in love with Ann. Now she found that fear was groundless, she could smile again.

"I don't want you to think that I don't feel friendly towards Alick, Helen," Ann continued. "I do—just as friendly as I can be towards him. I like talking to him. I don't know any man who is as interesting as he is. But he wants waking up—he's spoilt. Now that I have got that off my mind we won't speak of it again. Do what you like, I don't care. After all he may have met his fate in you. You may be the woman who will make him change his view of marriage."

"What nonsense," cried Helen, angry at this. "And what about my fate, and my views of marriage? You seem to think that he has only to beckon and I'll come running to him."

"That's the spirit for him," said Ann, rising and stretching herself lazily. "I see there is no need for me to lose any sleep about you."

She got dressed again slowly, and made ready to go home. The rain had stopped by this time, and Helen said she would walk a little way with her. She still shirked answering George's letter, and was afraid to be left in the same room with it.

They took the lift downstairs, and hurried into the street. Both girls shivered as the cold wind blew in their faces. They bent their heads to it and sought the shelter of the verandahs. It was Friday night and the streets were crowded with a restless throng that wandered aimlessly up and down, apparently with no object in view. The newsboys yelled out the contents of the evening paper—"Semi-final football—To-morrow's Winners—Suffragette riots."

The two girls picked their way through the crowd, following closely behind a burly policeman who was clearing the pavement with his mechanical "Move on there—move on there." They paused in front of one of the Picture Theatres to laugh at the glaring advertisements of the picture showing within, the latest product of the American producer's brain. It had evidently met the popular taste, for as fast as one lot of people came out satisfied, another lot who had been waiting in a long queue went in.

"I'm longing for some excitement," said Ann. "Do let's go in."

They got their tickets and joined the crowd moving slowly up the stairs. They reached the top and were blocked for five minutes or so by the strong arm of an energetic usher, who was waiting for the signal that more people had left the theatre. The crowd pushed restlessly behind them, throwing Helen against the man's arm.

"No shoving there," he cried harshly.

There were some mutterings from the crowd, but in the main they were goodnatured and waited patiently. Helen looked at them, and shivered slightly at their proximity. Under the glaring electric light the faces looked deathlike and the eyes bulged out strangely. She wondered if her face too, under that light, looked like those other faces. She had a moment's horror at the thought of Alick Russell seeing her in that company, then pulled herself up sharply. Why should she mind if he did see her there? She was free to do as she liked.

Close behind her stood a couple of Chinamen, who stared at her with their expressionless, yellow masks. She was afraid of touching them and feeling their breath on her cheek, and turned her face away. She was aware of Ann whispering to her:

"This is life at close quarters. How I would like to paint some of those faces staring up."

"I wish we could get in," muttered Helen. "I don't like life so close to me."

There was a sharp noise as she spoke, and the usher lowered his arm for a moment.

"Room for two only," he said sharply, and let Ann and Helen slip through. The crowd outside pressed against him and he threw his weight on them. They drew back muttering again.

Inside at last Ann and Helen stumbled to a seat, sitting down cautiously. It was a strange world they had wandered into. White, upturned faces stared intently at the flickering screen. Dim, shadowy forms moved slowly down the aisle. Helen thought vaguely that they had wandered into a dim underworld—the underworld that Proserpine moved through must have looked something like this—as strange, mysterious and uncertain. She looked at Ann, wondering what she was thinking, but Ann had all her attention fixed on the screen. She had come in to see the pictures, and she was not going to indulge in foolish thoughts about Proserpine and the underworld. Helen too looked at the screen. Her eyes had become accustomed to the light, and she could see quite plainly. All the strangeness and mystery had disappeared and she saw now only a rather sordid theatre, with scarlet and gold walls, and painted panels of stout water nymphs dancing. As she looked at the screen, she too became one of the crowd of staring, upturned faces.

It was the usual American travesty on real life, with impossible men, impossible women, cheap, tawdry sentiment and mawkish emotions. It pleased the audience, however, for they followed it with absorbed interest. The struggle of the heroine with the villain to preserve her honour was realistically portrayed, and the final mauling of the villain by the hero was enthusiastically applauded. An orchestra played suitable selections, or what they conceived to be suitable selections, in a tired, uninspired fashion. Even the heroine's plight did not awaken any fire in their hearts or their playing—they had seen it so often before.

They sat through the "American Star Drama of great heart interest," and the slightly improper Continental comedy that followed, and then, finding the air of the theatre rather thick, they left.

"Waste of time," said Ann, rather disgusted with

herself and everything else. Her enthusiasm for life at close quarters had rapidly evaporated, while in the meantime Helen had gained some.

"I don't know so much about that," said Helen. "It's rather interesting in a way. It's perfectly absurd, of course—the whole thing, I mean. Still, don't you think these pictures are rather a good thing on the whole? To all those people they must mean something of romance—of adventure—something they don't get in their own lives."

"Romance!" said Ann scoffingly. "People don't want romance in their lives. Romance is no good to them. What they want is work—hard work and plenty of it."

"You're too hard," said Helen laughing. "I wouldn't have any work in the world at all if I could help it."

They parted at the corner, and Helen walked home quickly. Already the thought of George was bothering her, and she decided she would answer his letter at once. When she had reached home she seized pen and paper and started to write. She tore up several sheets, but at last began to write rapidly. She finished five pages, read them through, and then hurriedly addressed the envelope and sealed it. She had written to him, but she had not really answered his letter. The whole five pages were filled with reflections on the romance of picture plays for people who had no romance in their lives. It was just at the end that she struck a personal note and added that she was glad he was coming back sooner than he had expected. Even as she wrote it she knew it was a lie. She did not want him to come back just now. She instinctively felt that he would complicate her life.

CHAPTER IX.

THE COMING OF SPRING.

Winter was almost over and already Spring could be felt in the air, the gentle, yet all-powerful Spring that would not be denied. Already the trees in St. Kilda Road, the Fitzroy Gardens and the Alexandra Avenue bordering the Yarra, were beginning to put forth shoots of tender green. The flower shops were bright with the golden wattle, and the scarlet and purple leaves of the young gum trees— the young gum tips that people were only just beginning to learn were such a perfect decoration for their homes. The air was sweet with the perfume of the wild boronia which was being sold at every street corner to the eager passer-by.

Helen seemed to walk on air. Life stretched before her full of infinite possibilities of joy and adventure. Her eyes had lost the rather brooding look they once possessed, and now smiled as though in answer to some secret joy within her. If anyone had asked her why she always smiled and sang she could hardly have answered. She did not know why she felt so exquisitely happy. She thought perhaps it was because the skies were so blue, the grass so green, the sun so warm and the air so fresh and invigorating. But she did not trouble to analyse her emotions to herself. She did not want to think now—she only wanted to feel.

Alick Russell too was happy. He was simply living from day to day, drifting aimlessly along on a sea of dreamy content. "Love well the hour and let it go." He did, and turned with half-closed eyes to grasp the next. He was barely awake yet. No tide of passion or feeling had ever swept him entirely off his feet. He had been an amateur at

(214)

everything and the circumstances of his life had conspired to keep him so. Anything he had wanted had fallen to his hand too easily. But he was not conscious of ever having wanted anything very deeply. He had a feeling of vague regret sometimes that life had yielded him so little after all. Tired and blase he had turned from one thing to another, dissatisfied with himself, conscious of his limitations, but with no motive strong enought to force him to work. But already, though he had not realised it yet, Helen was slowly awaking him. She laughed at him and teased him, laughed him out of his moods of depression and reproached him with his idleness. Under her tuition he was beginning to take life seriously—beginning to think it was not too late for him to make something out of it.

The Spring was beginning to move in his blood. He thought of his wanderings through the world, of all the strange lands he had lived in, and pictured Helen with him. He saw her against an Italian background. He imagined the delight of taking her where Byron, Shelley and Keats had lived. But that might be in the future, he told himself, for the present he was content with things as they were. Just now he wanted to take her up to the mountains, for she had told him she had never been outside Melbourne. He wanted to see the freshness of her delight in a new experience.

"In a little while, when it gets warmer, we must go up to my place at Warburton," he said to her. "We will take Ann with us, and go up one Sunday morning by the early train."

Helen caught her breath with delight at the prospect. She had heard of his home up there, for the artist boys often spoke of it. He had lent it to them on several occasions, and many happy times they had spent there. They had described its beauties to Helen and some of them had sketches of the mountains and the river, which they had brought back with them.

"When shall we go?" she asked.

"In a few weeks," he replied. "It's a bit cold up there as yet. I want you to see the wattle when it is in full bloom along the river. The Yarra runs through Warburton, you know, between the mountains and down to the city. You would not think it was any relation to the sluggish but useful old stream we see crawling through Melbourne. Up there it is so clear you can see the pebbles on the bottom. It dances along so merrily and quickly, singing all the time. Wherever you are in Warburton you can hear it singing to you. Many and many a night I've lain awake, listening to it."

He seemed to have forgotten her for the moment and was speaking abstractedly, staring in front of him. But Helen was all impatience to know when they were going.

"Don't look so far away," she said, touching him on the arm. "Tell me when you will take us up there. Next month?"

He looked at her again and smiled. "Let me see—this is August. Next month will be September. Yes, September!" he cried with sudden animation. "September is the month. September will sing for us as she did for Kendall. You remember—

> Sings the yellow-haired September
> With the face the gods remember.

His voice caressed the lovely lines. Helen had never heard them before and she thrilled to them.

"Say it all to me," she said.

He looked at her lovely, sensitive face with the wrapt expression in the eyes, and his own changed.

"Ah! Helen! What couldn't I say to you? You have a face the gods remember. The gods would love you, Helen, and I am only a poor mortal. Tell me, what do you think of me?"

But she was nervous and refused to answer. She did not want to think about love just yet. She was happy and life was very sweet—that was enough for the present. The blood raced through her veins and her cheeks glowed with health. Old men sighed for their vanished youth when they passed her in the street, and young men looked after her with a quickening of the pulses. But she was quite unconscious of them all. She looked through them and away. She could not understand how it was she had just begun to realise the beauty of the world. Had she been walking about all these years blindfolded? She felt she must have been, for it seemed as though a bandage had been suddenly torn from her eyes, letting in the light. She could not get too much of it. She was vividly alive to impressions of beauty.

The life of the streets held a never-ending fascination for her. She watched the huge lorries, laden with goods from the over-sea ships, driven through the streets, with the strange, terrifying noise they made. She loved the great, patient horses that pulled them, with their mighty limbs and straining muscles, and the grimy kindly-faced men who controlled them. She would watch them pulled up at the corners of the streets, stopped by the warning hand of a policeman, and wonder how easily it was done. At one moment they were grinding heavily along, seemingly a menace to everybody; the next they were standing, patiently waiting, until the surging crowd of people had hurried to the other side. Then they would resume their journey.

In Flinders Street railway construction was going on. A new line was being built over the Viaduct to Spencer Street Station. When she passed she looked up, wondering at the strength of the men. She could see their bare arms gleaming in the sunlight as they lifted huge weights. They whistled as they worked. Life seemed good to them too. Perhaps it was because they worked under a blue sky and the spring-tide moved in their veins. When a train thundered past they looked up, grinning at

the white-faced passengers who stared at them out
of the windows.

Beyond the railway lines the spars of the ships
stood out against the sky. Sailing ships and barques
lay up the river, with the cargo tramps and inter-
state steamers. The big mail steamers berthed at
Port Melbourne. They were the aristocrats of the
sea, and she liked the hardy plebeians best that came
up the river. Most of the ships flew the flags of
her own race, but among them were alien flags—
French, German, American, Danish, Norwegian—
they all came, stayed a little while, bringing with
them a breath of strange lands. Then they went
back again on their journey of mystery.

It amused her to wander about the wharves in
her spare time, though she never went alone. The
old man who had posed for Walter always accompanied her. He had been many things in the course
of his long life, though as a boy he had been brought
up to the sea. He had taken a fancy to Helen, and
told her many strange tales of the sea and his adventures in the South Sea Islands, where he had
spent many years. The boys said that most of his
stories were lies, but Helen believed him and listened
spell-bound. The old man, with a glance at her
wrapt face and sucking his pipe contemplatively,
would be moved to further efforts.

"I don't care," Helen cried passionately when
they tried to upset her faith in the old man and
point out how manifestly absurd some of his stories
were, "I don't care if they're not true. He has
the gift of imagination which is more than any of
us have. I like to listen to him and I'm going to
believe everything he tells me."

She found him in the studio sometimes when she
came in, a rather grotesque figure, sitting at the
window with his pipe in his mouth, staring over to the
buildings beyond which the sea lay a blue line on
the horizon. If Walter or Charlie were there they
would look up from their work and grin, then resume

it again and forget about them. They were used to seeing Helen and the old man in earnest conversation. Alick Russell did not like him, for once Helen had repeated to him a story the old man had told them one night. Russell had been angry and told her not to talk to him again. But the story had not offended Helen. It had interested her and she thought that Russell was making a fuss about nothing. After that she did not speak of the old man to him, or tell him any of the old man's stories.

He had told the story to them all one night when they were seated round the fire. Ann was there and Sandy, Walter and Charlie, and a couple of others. The old man had come in and joined the circle. He liked to be with them and often came in during the evening. They liked him to come, for he amused them. It also gave them pleasure to think that they were making someone happy, even though it were only a bleary-eyed, scoundrelly and not too clean old man. There was something of wistfulness in the old man's eyes when he looked at them. Something in the sight of the young faces stirred his old blood and moved him to a longing for "old, unhappy, far-off things." He would sigh and plunge into reminiscences of his stormy youth.

Helen was his favourite auditor. She encouraged him and he always addressed his stories to her.

"Ah those were the days!" he would say. "Why, my pipe is empty!"

They would pass him the tobacco jar where his favourite plug was kept, Helen saw that it was always full. She had evolved this plan, not liking to hurt his feelings by giving him tobacco herself, though she need not have worried on that score.

He filled his pipe slowly and then lit it, drawing a long breath of satisfaction.

"Ah! that's better. Now, what was I going to tell you? Ah, yes. About those days when I was a young fellow in Fiji. The first time I went there I was on a trading ship. I had occasion to be left behind.   There's no good of asking me why.   I had my reasons."

He solemnly winked one, wicked old eye.

"No, don't tell us your reason, Jerry," interposed Walter.   "Get on with your—er—story."

"I see you understand me," said the old man with a chuckle.   "Well, to go on with what I was telling you.   There was a young fellow working there—we'll call him Smith.   He had just come up from Sydney and was as innocent as you make 'em. Just been married too and brought his wife with him—a pretty thing she was, I remember."   He shook his old head and puffed for a moment at his pipe.   "Well, he was book-keeper at a big store there, run by a German—we'll call him Schmidt. For a time everything goes all right with the young man.   Then we begin to notice that the life was getting hold of him.   He began to go to pieces—drink and cards—they did for him."

He fell into a deep abstraction and was silent for such a long time that Helen got impatient.

"Well, what happened to him, Jerry?" she asked. "That isn't all the story, is it?"

He roused himself at that.   "No, missie, that isn't all.   The next we heard was a rumour that young Smith had stolen £300 from Schmidt and been caught red-handed.   We all expected he would be jailed, for Schmidt was a hard man."

"And wasn't he?" asked Helen.

"No, missie, he wasn't.   Schmidt let him off."

"So he really was a kind man after all?"

"Well, hardly that," replied the old man.   "You see it was like this.   After it happened we used to see old Schmidt walking up to young Smith's house. When Schmidt appeared, young Smith went out and left his pretty wife behind him."

"Well?" asked Helen, hardly understanding as yet.

"She paid his debts for him."

"Oh," gasped Helen.   "How horrible."

"Well, well, missie," sighed the old man. "That's life for you.   It's all mixed up, the good and the bad, and you don't know where you are."

"A bright, cheery customer you are to have in to supper," interrupted Sandy.   "Tell us something amusing now, for God's sake."

When Helen told the old man's story to Alick, he was angry.   He hated to think she should know anything of the sordid side of life.   As it was he did not like her going to the studio because of the free and easy way they discussed everything.

Helen was eager and avid to learn.   She took the keenest interest in everything.   Never before had she been so alive, so responsive to life as she was now.   She was like a tree sending out its roots in search of water.

Some of the Strauss operas were being played in Melbourne.   Russell took her to see them.   The dreamy, sensuous music affected her strangely. She flushed and paled, her heart beat quickly, while her body seemed to sway to the rhythm of the waltzes. One night they went to see "The Chocolate Soldier." The theatre was crowded and filled with murmurous sound.   They had good seats right in the front of the dress circle, and Helen seated herself with the happy feeling of adventure she always experienced when entering a theatre.   The people were still pouring into the circle and the stalls, though the gallery was already packed with a hilarious crowd.   It was Saturday night, the great pleasure night.   Everyone was in good humour and in a mood to be pleased with everything.

Helen stared at the people coming in, but she knew none of them, though her companion had several friends—mostly women, she noticed.   She thought with a little smile, that if any of her friends were in they would have to patronise the gallery where she herself had often been in the days when she went by herself and could only afford a shilling. Two of the boxes at the side were already occupied and she was watching idly to see who came into the others, when she suddenly gave an exclamation of astonishment and touched Russell on the arm.

"Look! there's my uncle!"

It was indeed her uncle. He had just entered one of the boxes accompanied by his wife and a girl of about twenty. It was evidently their daughter, for she bore an unfortunate resemblance to her mother. Helen stared at them. She knew that she had a cousin but she had never seen her before. She had always had a vague sort of idea that she was a schoolgirl. She was frankly interested in her, but the girl looked as though she could not be interested in anything. She stared straight before her with a bored expression. She was a plain girl and the look of boredom did not suit her, but she evidently conceived it to be the correct thing.

Helen looked at her uncle, trying to attract his attention, but she was unsuccessful at first. He had sat down, and made some remark to his wife. She seemed annoyed with him for speaking. She looked coldly at him and then turned her head away without answering, pointedly addressing her daughter instead. He did not attempt any further conversation, but sat with his arms folded, staring round the house. It was not long before he caught sight of Helen. He leant forward surprised and Helen waved her programme gaily at him. His wife noticed the movement, and turned round. She saw Helen, who smiled at her in a friendly way. She did not return Helen's smile but looked over her head, then bowed most elaborately to someone who was sittting just behind Helen. Helen flushed deeply, and then shrugged her shoulders, trying to believe that she did not mind the snub.

"I don't care," she said. "She has always disliked me."

"The old cat!" muttered Russell.

"She has only seen me once, too. It's not quite fair, is it? See—she won't let my cousin look at

me. I would love to know her too. We might
be friends!''

''It's not much loss to you,'' returned Russell.
''She looks too much like her mother for my taste.''

''But she can't be altogether like her mother,''
objected Helen. ''She must be like Uncle in some
way surely, and he has always been kind to me.''

''I don't like the way he is looking at me now.''

''No? Yes, he does look rather fierce, doesn't
he? He is rather jealous of me, you know. He
will ask me all sorts of questions about you on Monday. Are you afraid?'' she asked, rather mockingly.

''Afraid? No. He will have to know me one
day. I am going up to see him soon.''

''Whatever for?'' asked Helen surprised.

''On private business.''

''I see,'' said Helen, rather nettled. ''I don't
want to pry into your private business.''

''Silly child!'' he whispered.

But Helen did not like being called a child, and
she was annoyed. She looked away, across the sea
of faces to where her aunt sat so stiffly erect in her
box. Helen was terribly hurt at her attitude. She
felt that she was a pariah. Womanlike, too, she
was angry with her uncle. She felt that it was
all his fault. She thought he should have insisted
on his wife showing at least a semblance of friendship to her, and he should have introduced his
daughter to her long ago. Angry tears came into
her eyes. ''Evidently he thinks I am not good
enough to mix with his family,'' she thought bitterly, though till that moment she had never felt
bitterly against her uncle.

''What's the matter?'' said a voice in her ear.
''Are you still angry with me?''

''No,'' she replied. ''I had forgotten about you.
I am angry with those people over there.''

''Don't let them upset you,'' he said. ''Just
think how much more beautiful and sweet and

charming you are than any other woman in the theatre.''

''What's the use of thinking that?'' said Helen angrily. ''I know quite well it isn't true, and even if it were, the fact would still remain that I've been insulted and my uncle allowed it. After all he was my father's brother, and he had always pretended to me that he was fond of Mother.''

''Perhaps that's the reason,'' said Russell. ''Your aunt was probably jealous of your mother and she has simply transferred her jealousy to you.''

Helen pondered that for a moment or two.

''Perhaps that's it,'' she said at last. ''I would rather think that it was that than what I thought.''

''And what was that?'' he asked.

''I was thinking that perhaps she thought I might contaminate her daughter,'' Helen said in a low voice. ''You know what my mother did, and she may think that—that—well, that it runs in the family.''

''I forbid you to think like that,'' he said quickly.

''Well,'' said Helen, with a sigh, opening her programme and looking through it. ''I won't think about them any more. I won't even look at them. I refuse to allow them to spoil my evening.''

The orchestra had come in and were tuning up. A buzz of expectation ran through the house as the lights were lowered, the footlights flared up and the curtain rose on the first act.

The opening bars of the music made Helen forget all her unpleasant thoughts. She leant forward slightly, her eyes on the stage and her lips parted a little as she drank in the music. The man beside her knew the opera from beginning to end. He thought it rather cheap stuff, but the girl's enthusiasm delighted him. He did not look at the stage, but kept his eyes on her face which he could see silhouetted against the dim background. It was as he looked that a sudden memory came to him and he gave an involuntary exclamation. Angry

voices round him demanded silence, and Helen
glanced at him in surprise. He leant back in his
seat, wiping his brow. As he looked at Helen he
had a sudden vision of another face he had seen, a
face with Helen's profile and Helen's expression at
moment, and a face seen as he saw Helen's now,
against a dim background. He remembered it all
now. It must have been the music that brought it
back, and he wondered how he had forgotten. It
was in London he had heard the "Chocolate Soldier" last. Sitting in one of the boxes was a woman
who attracted his attention. He could see her face
standing out against the dim background and something in the purity of the outline fascinated him.
His friends told him she was a singer from the Coliseum Music Hall. She sat through half an act and
then went out. He went to the Coliseum to see
her afterwards and was bitterly disappointed. He
hardly knew what he had expected—something in
the Grecian style, a classic dance, full of dignity and
beauty. That was his ideal of her, but the reality
was somewhat different. She sang cheap cockney
songs and indulged in repartee with the gallery.
She was a popular idol. Alick Russell had been disgusted. It seemed to him to be a crime that a
woman with a profile of the true Grecian beauty—
should have prostituted herself like that. He had
listened to her for a few minutes and then gone. He
looked at Helen again. There was no doubt about
it. The two faces were identical.

"I can't tell her," he thought. "Why, that
woman was—rather notorious."

Helen was unconscious of him; for the time being
she had forgotten all about him. Her hand lay
temptingly near his. He laid his own gently over
it. Even in the midst of her exultation she felt
and responded to his touch. She turned to him
and smiled, then looked back to the stage again, but
she did not move her hand. It lay in his until the
lights flashed up again.

CHAPTER X.

RETROSPECT.

It was Saturday evening early in September and Alick Russell was pacing restlessly up and down his sitting-room. He had a flat of four rooms in a big residential building in the City. He had furnished the rooms himself and spent a lot of money over them, but they had never really pleased him. Somehow he never seemed able to get the effect he was aiming for. His moods were too changeable and his tastes too variable. To-night he felt a longing for Spartan simplicity and wide spaces, and the luxuriousness of his surroundings revolted him. He would have got more pleasure from a room in a bush hut, with a camp bed and bare floor, than in this room with its colour effects and soft tones. He looked with disgust at the pictures on the wall, at the ascetic yet sensuous faces of the women of Rossetti and Burne-Jones. He stared at them, wondering how he could ever have seen any beauty in them. They looked down at him, and he thought the faces had assumed a sardonic expression.

His hands, too, annoyed him. He looked at them with their delicate shape and long tapering fingers. Once he had been rather proud of them, but now he only felt a sick distaste. He would rather have seen them rough and discoloured.

"I wish to God I had been brought up to work with my hands," he thought moodily.

There was a ring on his little finger, a ring with a single diamond that caught the light and flashed with white fire as he moved his hand. He suddenly hated to see it there—it made his hand look too much like a woman's hand. He pulled the ring off and threw it into the grate. However, after a moment's thought he took it out again and put it carefully away. A woman who had once loved him had given it to him. It seemed cruel to throw it away, but he would not wear it again.

He wondered what Helen was doing now. To-morrow they were going into the country. Perhaps that was making him restless. He would have liked to have seen her that evening but she had been very decided about it. She could be very decided some-times, he reflected ruefully. He was interrupted by a knock at the door and his housekeeper entered silently.

"Is there anything else you want, sir, before I go?"

He shook his head. "How is the boy now?"

"Better, sir, thank you."

He nodded vaguely. "That's good! There's nothing else I want. You need not come in to-morrow. I shall be away all day."

"Very well, Sir. Good-night."

"Good-night, Lily."

Lily! The name never failed to awaken his grim amusement. The name and the woman were so absurdly incongruous. She was a tall, thin woman and bent a little at the waist. She was hopelessly, irretrievably plain. Her hair, skin and eyes were all of the same dull, drab colour. Her feeble little wisp of hair was drawn tightly back from her face and pinned in an uncompromising fashion on her neck. She never made any effort to adorn her person, no doubt recognizing the hopelessness of it. Alick Russell's friends smiled when they saw his housekeeper for the first time. Alick Russell, who had made a cult of beauty, who had always declaimed that he must have beauty about him! Alick Rus-sell, who had said that virtue was nothing in a woman if she did not have beauty! They laughed among themselves when they saw his housekeeper, for she was so plain that they judged she could not be any-thing else but virtuous. Alick Russell never ex-plained her presence, and at last they came to the conclusion that she must be a poor relation of his to whom he was giving employment.

She had been with him five years now. Five years! He realized with a sudden pang how quickly they had slipped away. He had been only a little over thirty-five then, and now he was close on to the border of middle age. Five years—five wasted years they seemed to him, looking back. What had he done with them? Nothing much! Travelled a little, painted a little, written a little, loved a little. There was only one decent thing he had done during that time, and that was more through the force of circumstances than through any innate kindliness and sympathy. How his friends would have smiled, he thought, if they could have seen him that night when he was forced to play the part of the good Samaritan much against his will.

It was all through Rodgers, he remembered. If Rodgers had not insisted on keeping him late, it would never have happened and Lily might possibly have been in the river instead of slaving for him. He had not wanted to stay late that night, but Rodgers was always a great talker and it was after twelve o'clock when he finally did manage to get away. It was raining slightly and all the trams had stopped. As there was no cab in sight he had decided to walk. He turned up the collar of his coat and, with his hands buried deep in his pockets and his head bent, he tramped steadily along. He turned into the wide Domain that separates the Botanical Gardens from the road, meaning to take the path that leads on to St. Kilda Road. The rain had commenced to fall heavily and the raindrops dripped unceasingly from the great overhanging branches of the Moreton Bay fig trees along the path. The ground was strewn with the fallen leaves and figs which the wind had blown down. He could not avoid treading on them and he hated the feel of them under his feet, for the figs were over-ripe and soft and squashy. He kicked them aside with an exclamation of disgust as he went along.

He was close to the gates when he noticed the figure first. He could quite easily have missed it, but something made him look aside and he saw the figure huddled up on one of the seats. He thought at first it was a man, probably drunk. He had gone closer to examine, and found to his amazement that it was a woman. He peered down to look at her, but she did not move or seem aware of his presence. A sudden fear took him that she might be dead, and he laid his hand on her shoulder. At his touch she moved slightly and looked up at him, her face glimmering whitely through the darkness. She had not even sought the shelter of the trees but sat where the rain streamed full on her. He noticed how the drops had settled on the brim of her hat and as she raised her head, poured off in a little cascade. He looked at her, at a loss what to do. The woman seemed to be in a sort of lethargy and after her first movement had sunk back into her previous position. For all the sign of life she gave she might have been dead.

"You can't stay here, you know," he said at last.

She did not answer, and he began to get impatient, for the rain was beating against his back and dribbling down his neck. He felt uncomfortable and irritable and wanted to be gone. He shook her by the shoulder.

"You can't stay here," he said rather gruffly. "You had better go home."

Without a word the woman rose and moved away. She walked in a hopeless, resigned sort of fashion, with her arms hanging nervelessly at her side. Her steps were slow and heavy. Russell stood looking after her, biting his lips nervously, for directly she had stood up he had seen her condition.

"Confound it all!" was his first thought. "Why the devil did I come through here?"

He followed her slowly, uncertain what to do and

cursing under his breath. He could tell by the aimless way in which she walked that she had nowhere to go.

"What a rotten predicament?" he thought irritably. "I can't leave her here. Oh, damn it all!"

He caught up with her. "Look here," he said, "haven't you anywhere to go?"

She shook her head and a tremor seemed to go through her.

"Nor money?"

"No."

She spoke for the first time. Her voice was hoarse and uncultivated. It grated on Russell's fastidious ear. He liked women with sweet and musical voices. This woman seemed to be everything he did not like. None of the women he knew would sit on a seat in the park at nearly one o'clock in the morning, nor would they be wandering about without any money. He put his hand in his pocket and pulled out some money. Then he hesitated. He instinctively felt that, even if he gave her money, she would only sink on another seat as soon as he was gone. He might just as well kill her straight out, as leave her alone. Again he cursed. What the devil could he do with her? He thought of the gaol, the hospital. No good! He did not fancy taking her to any of these institutions. He shrugged his shoulders and made up his mind to the inevitable.

"You had better come home with me," he told her.

She displayed no surprise or emotion and her acquiescence further annoyed him. He did not expect her to take it so much for granted. However, he gave her his arm, thinking he might just as well do the thing properly as he was about it. They turned out of the Domain and into St. Kilda Road. Under a flickering light he saw her face plainly for the first time, and smiled. No one could accuse him of any ulterior motive in taking this woman home. The streets were deserted except for a stray passer-by, who looked after them curiously, for they were such a strange and incongrous pair. Only once she spoke on their way home.

"I couldn't get work because I am like this," she said. Then she relapsed into silence again.

They reached the house at last and he fumbled with his latchkey, swearing softly to himself as the door creaked loudly when he opened it. He had no desire to meet any of the inmates of the house and run the gauntlet of their raised eyebrows and whispered jokes. He thought he would never get to the floor on which his rooms were situated and he was in an agony of apprehension lest the woman should stumble and awaken someone.

However, they reached his rooms without misadventure, and he switched on the electric light. The woman stood blinking in the strong glare. He wished she had more initiative. It annoyed him to see her just standing about. He threw open the door of his bedroom telling her to go in and take her wet dress off and put on a dressing-gown which he gave her. He then retired to his sitting-room to think things over quietly to himself. But this he was unable to do. The only thing his flustered mind could catch hold of was food. She must have something to eat. He went into the kitchen and made her a cup of cocoa. He had some brandy himself, for he felt in need of something to settle his nerves. He cut some bread and butter and discovered cold meat in the safe. He put all the things on a tray and took them into the other room. Then he called to her and she came out, a grotesque figure in his dressing-gown. He did not like to look at her, and turned his eyes away, motioning to her to sit down at the table and eat. She looked at him and then at the food, then without a word sat down and commenced to eat ravenously.

"Good God!" he thought, "the poor devil's hungry."

Somehow the fact of her hunger made him feel more kindly towards her. Also she was less offensive to him sitting down, and he felt he could look at her without his ideals of women receiving too great a shock. When she had finished she sat with her hands folded, waiting for him to speak. She seemed just as hopelessly lethargic as before, though he noticed a dull colour had crept into her cheeks.

He questioned her and by degrees heard her story. It was a sordid tale and he listened with a feeling of contemptuous pity. She did not seem to have any clear idea as to how it had happened. She had been in service in the country for a long time, then came down to town. She had no friends and she was lonely. One night she met a man on the beach; his Christian name was Tom, she said. That was all she knew about him—his name was Tom. They parted and she never saw him again, though he had promised to meet her on her next day out. Some time after that she had to leave her situation. She could not get another place and had no money and no one she could go to. She didn't know what to do. She thought she could stay in the park all night. She had been going to drown herself but the river looked so cold and it was such a wet night. She gave Russell to understand that she was going to wait for a fine day before she could do it.

When she had finished speaking she leant back in her chair and closed her eyes. She looked very, very tired. For the first time Russell felt a pang of pure pity, the pity he might have felt for his mother or his sister. He raised her very gently to her feet, telling her not to worry about anything as he would look after her. His kindness seemed to awaken a spark of life in her for, lifting her eyes to his, she burst into tears. Very much embarrassed, Russell hurriedly helped her into his room and closed the door.

He wiped his brow on which large beads of perspiration had gathered.

"By Jove!" he said aloud. "I'm in a nice fix. What have I done to deserve this?"

He spent a very restless and troubled night, and the next morning after a careful perusal of the papers, went to a nursing home and made arrangements with the matron for the woman to go in at once. He still remembered the amused and speculative way in which the nurses looked at him. He could see they were puzzled about him and could not think what connection existed between him and the woman he had brought in. He left them to their bewilderment and escaped as soon as he could.

When the child was born and the woman was better, he dismissed his charwoman, who came in every day, and put the other woman in her place. She served him with a dog-like devotion and he soon found that he could trust her absolutely. When he had gone to England he left her in charge of his flat and when he returned he found it just the same. Every penny of the money he had left with her was rigidly accounted for. It amused him to listen to her arguing with the tradespeople about their accounts. She kept a strict eye on them and regarded them all with the greatest suspicion.

The child had grown into a bright, intelligent boy and Russell was surprised to find how fond he had grown of him. He had made up his mind that he would give the boy a chance in life. He felt it would be interesting to see what the child of an unknown father and unwilling mother would become. Already he was more than ordinarily intelligent and Russell was staggered to find how little parenthood appeared to matter.

He wondered what he would have done if Lily had been a pretty or attractive woman. Could he have kept up his altruistic attitude towards her? Probably not. He presumed he would have made her his mistress. It had been Lily's extreme plainness that had safeguarded her, not any particular merit on his part. He felt almost grateful now

towards Lily for being so unattractive, though he
had often resented it.   It meant that his hands were
free and his life clear of any complications.   Now
that he had met Helen he wanted to be free. Helen!
The thought of her made him restless again.   If
to-morrow would only come!   How long the hours
seemed!   Why had she refused to see him to-night?
She had been so casual about it, too, simply said that
she had something else to do.   Her desire to see
him could not have been very strong.   Well, she
had promised to come with him to-morrow and that
was something to look forward to.   He only wished
he had not thought it necessary to invite Ann. Next
time they would go alone.   Quite suddenly he felt
surprisingly happy.   Life held a lot of promise for
him still, after all he was only forty and a man is
as young as he feels.   He lit a cigarette and stepped
out on to the little balcony outside his room.

It was a bright scene that met his eyes.   A scene
that in his present cheerful mood he liked to look at.
The sun had already set, but his lingering touch was
still in the Western sky. The days were lengthening
out, and there would be quite an hour of light before
the night finally fell.   From where Russell stood
he could see the river winding down to the Rich-
mond Bridge, the noble sweep of the Alexandra
Avenue, and the undulating hills of the Botanical
Gardens, their highest point crowned by the Temple
of the Winds which stood looking out towards the
City.

On the river the crews of the different boating
clubs and Public Schools practised vigorously. Their
young faces were sternly set, and the supple muscles rippled under the smooth skin.   They were
very much in earnest about what they were doing,
for in October the annual regatta was held.   Their
coaches tore along the bank on bicycles, shouting
instructions through the megaphone.   Sometimes,
heralded by the throb of the engine, a motor launch
cut through the water.   The pleasure boats were

creeping reluctantly back to the sheds. They came from places further up the river, from picnics at Heidelberg and Kew. These boats were filled with gay and careless people who alternately cheered and jeered the racing boats. They themselves had caught many crabs during the course of the afternoon, but it seriously annoyed them to see anyone else do the same thing. They had a keen eye for faults and signified their approval or disapproval vigorously as the boats shot past them.

Across Princes Bridge a laughing throng of people was moving out from the City. These were the pleasure-seekers who had come in from the outlying suburbs bent on enjoyment. All of them had money to spend, and no one was going to worry about the morrow. They passed and re-passed each other in an endless promenade. Most of them walked in couples, but sometimes a group of girls passed walking together, and after them a group of young men. They looked at each other shyly enough at first, but the young men, obviously screwing up their courage, made the necessary remarks, always prefaced either by a whistle or a cough. Some of the young women felt the seduction of these advances and responded. Others walked on with a haughty tilt of the head and a swing of the skirt. All the women were gaily and extravagantly dressed, though it is not the wealthy class which frequents the banks of the river on Saturday evening.

Some of the people walked sedately side by side, others more bold, walked hand in hand. As it grew darker many of them could be seen lying on the grass, clasped in each other's arms, heedless of the passing crowds. Far off across the water a band played some elusive tune. It floated across the slowly dying day with something infinitely sad in its sweetness. It seemed to Russell it was mourning another spring day which was passing, never to return.

Never to return! It was a terrible thought. He

realized that one must pluck all the sweetness from
life that it offered, for too soon the rose colour faded,
leaving only the dull, cold grey of age. He must
take hold of life with both hands before it was too
late. Live and feel! Live to the utmost and feel
—whether it was love, joy, sorrow or despair, it did
not matter so long as he could feel. Some lines of
Stevenson's flashed through his mind:—

> "Come ill or well, the cross, the crown,
>   The rainbow or the thunder,
> I fling my soul and body down
>   For God to plough them under."

Yes, he felt he could face the buffetings of fate.
With a thrill of exquisite joy that was almost pain
he realized that he loved at last, as a man should
love. Not as he had loved before, but with a poig-
nancy that seemed to eat into his very bones and
made his heart melt within him. He closed his
eyes and Helen's face came up before him. He
could see that turn of the head he loved and her sudden smile.

Inside on the landing the telephone bell rang
shrilly, but he did not hear it. It rang again louder
and continuously as the exchange girl got impatient.
At last it pierced through his dreams and he hurried
inside to answer it, thinking it might be Helen.

It was Helen. Across the telephone wires her
voice sounded thin and indistinct, like a fading
ghost of the voice he knew so well.

"Is that you?" she asked. He smiled as he
heard, for Helen had never yet been able to call him
by his Christian name. He refused to answer to
"Mister," but still she had not been able to use his
first name. A feeling of tenderness overwhelmed
him. He felt he loved her the more for her exquisite shyness.

But Helen was distressed. She had bad news
for him. Ann had just received a telegram from
home saying that her mother was ill and she had

to catch the train for Gippsland that left that night.

"What about to-morrow?" he asked, bitterly disappointed. "Everything will be ready for us. I wired yesterday to a woman up there who does the house out, to get in everything we wanted."

"What do you think?" she asked, after a pause, during which he shook the telephone violently, afraid that they had been cut off.

"There is no reason why you shouldn't come up alone," he said.

She seemed to hesitate a moment before speaking, and he was afraid she was going to refuse to come.

"I will be disappointed if I don't go," she said at last. "I've been looking forward to it."

"So have I. You will come then?"

"Yes." Her voice came quick and decided this time. "I'll meet you to-morrow as we arranged."

He heard the click of the receiver as she hung it up and he put his own receiver down very carefully, for his fingers were trembling.

She was coming with him, and he would have her to himself. He blessed the chance that had made Ann's mother ill.

CHAPTER XI.

A SEPTEMBER DAY.

In the meantime Helen was being very helpful to Ann. Her conscience was pricking her a little, for Ann had taken it for granted that, as she was unable to go to Warburton, Helen also would not go.

Helen had gone to the telephone with the intention of telling Russell this, not because she saw any reason why she should not go, but because Ann apparently did. But when she heard his voice over the telephone she realized how intensely she did want to go, and she knew she would not refuse him if he asked her. When she did arrange to go with him she made up her mind to tell Ann, but somehow when she faced Ann the task seemed extraordinarily difficult. She made one or two futile efforts and then gave it up, compromising with her conscience by being very attentive to Ann and helping her to pack up. She accompanied her to the station and saw her off, buying her magazines and at the last moment, a huge bunch of violets which she thrust through the window as the train moved off. She felt rather guilty as she went back to her rooms, for deep down in her heart she knew she was glad that Ann was unable to go with her.

Sunday dawned—a day sent straight from Heaven. It was such a day as the old gods sent to the earth. A day plucked from out the golden age of the world. No one could be sad on such a day. Even the broken-hearted would catch an echo of hope from its blue and golden pages. To the young and light-hearted it sang of all the pleasures, all the desires, and all the delights of the world. It only needed the first breath of the Spring morning on her cheek to banish all Helen's misgivings of the night before. Why had she bothered about Ann? She was foolish. Nothing in the world mattered except happiness. She wanted everything the world could give, and the greatest thing was happiness. She must take it where it offered itself.

She met Russell with a gay and joyous light in her eyes that he had never seen before. His heart leapt as he watched her cross the street to him. Her light, active steps, and the lithe swing of her young body delighted him. Her walk reminded him of the young poplar trees swaying in the breeze. He was oblivious to the pushing crowds as he took her hand and felt its warmth against his own and the sudden quiver as he pressed it. But Helen was acutely conscious of the crowd—the people who stared, who pushed past her impatiently. She drew her hand away quickly and, for the first time since she had known him, she felt shy.

They joined the moving crowds that poured on to the station, eagerly making for the mountain trains. Across the road the bells of the Cathedral pealed loudly, but to heedless ears. No one in this crowd was going to church. They were going to spend the day in a more perfect church than ever the hand of man invented—the country and the seaside awaited them.

The train was packed, but Russell managed to secure a seat for Helen next to the window. For himself he had to stand, but he was content to be where he could watch the changing shadows on her face. He did not want to have to talk to her in the railway carriage. He resented the presence of the other people. Even if he had been sitting close to her he could have spoken of nothing but trivial things, and trivial things would not satisfy him to-day.

Helen, seeing that it was impossible to try and talk to him, stared out of the window. They had left the suburbs behind and were running through the open country. Far away on the horizon lay a blue line of mountains looking as though they were etched against the sky. On either side of the railway line stretched hundreds of farms and orchards, the fruit trees a mass of bloom. From the little farm houses rosy-cheeked children rushed out to wave and shout as the train passed by. When she saw them Helen was overcome with a longing to live a simple country life. It seemed to her just then that all one wanted in life was the open air and the sunshine.

She was glad when they arrived at the little country station, for Alick had been standing the whole time and she was afraid that he must have been finding it rather dull. He certainly had towards the end of the journey, but as long as Helen was happy he was content. He had amused himself watching for the turn of her head and the quick little smile she would flash at him sometimes. He tried to read into that soft smile and glance all the interpretations his heart desired.

When the train drew up at the station he jumped out quickly and helped her out. Then she saw him throw up his head and stand as though he were listening for something.

"Ah! There it is," he said with a sigh of satisfaction, as the noisy little engine finished its shrieking and the passengers left the station. "Listen, you can hear it now. It always welcomes me back."

She listened and heard a faint and pleasant rippling sound. The air seemed alive with it. It was like the sweetest natural music. She looked at him questioningly.

"Yes," he said, in reply to the unuttered question, "it's the Yarra. You can't see it from here, but come along with me, and I'll show it to you."

She followed him outside and he pointed to a silver streak winding between the hills, dimly seen through the masses of wattle trees and gums which fringed the banks.

"That's the river," he said, "and see there, across the valley—up that road on the side of the hill— that little brown place—that's my home."

It clung to the side of the hill looking over the valley, with the mountains rising beyond it, and far off, higher than them all, the snow-crowned top of Mount Donna Buang. Snow-crowned still, for though the Spring had already conquered the valley and the lower ranges, it had not yet been able to brush away the mantle of Winter from the queen among them all.

They crossed the river and took the little path leading up to the house. It was past one o'clock and in the valley the sun was hot. In spite of the heat Helen shivered a little. She had suddenly felt a sense of gloom which clutched at her heart with cold fingers. Russell was quick to notice every change of her expressive face.

"What is it?" he asked anxiously.

She hastened to re-assure him. "It was nothing

really," she said, "only for a moment such a strange feeling came over me. I felt as though the mountains were closing in on us. They seem so close together and we are so low down."

"It had that effect on me when I first came here," he said, "but it soon wears off."

"It has gone already," said Helen with a laugh. "Still I am glad your house is built up high and not right down in the valley. But where is it? We seem to have lost sight of it."

"Wait a moment," he said, "just round the corner and there you are."

They turned the corner and she saw the house, standing high up, its gardens sloping down towards the river. He paused with his hand on the latch of the gate and looked back at her.

"Do you know what place this is?" he asked.

"Why, of course," she answered shyly.

"Are you sure?" he whispered. "You might not want to come in when I tell you. You have heard of it, I know. A man whom we both love told us about it. I've brought you to the 'Castle Perilous' beyond the dark, enchanted wood.' Now are you brave enough to come in with me? Who knows what giants and ogres might not be inside?"

She looked away and he could see the color mounting to her cheek.

"Are you brave enough?" he insisted.

But Helen edged away from the question. Again she felt shy but she quickly overcame it, laughing at him and talking in a quick haphazard way. He followed her lead at once and adopted the tone of gay badinage they used to each other sometimes. He saw that he had made her nervous and that was the last thing he wished to do. He opened the gate and they went up the path together between the gay spring flowers.

After dinner they went out for a walk, but soon came back, for the darkness comes on quickly in the Warburton valley. The woman who had cooked for them had left and gone to her own home, so they had the place to themselves. He took Helen out on to the verandah that ran the whole length of the house. They sat there for the rest of the afternoon, watching the shadows lengthen in the valley beneath and the lights in the little township flash out. A cold wind came down from the mountains, and Helen shivered a little. He rose and, going inside, brought out a coat, which he put over her shoulders. He did not go back to his seat then, but pulled a low chair closer to hers and sat where, looking up, he could see her face and her starry eyes. She looked down at him, and a sudden silence fell between them.

"What are you thing of?" he asked.

"Nothing," she replied musingly. "I am just— content."

"Are you happy here with me?"

She colored faintly in answer to his question and looked away.

"Don't turn away from me. Look at me. Let me see your eyes again. Helen, I think all the wisdom of the world is in those dear dark eyes of yours."

She sat leaning back in her chair, her hands clasped on her lap and a tender little smile just curving her lip. He leant forward and took her hand in his and began to speak in a low passionate voice. Down in the valley the lights of the station were flaring out and the train for town stood waiting for its passengers. Slowly the people who had come up in the morning were beginning to move back again to the station. They came down the mountain roads laden with ferns, wattle blossom and gum-leaves. But neither Helen nor Russell noticed them.

"Helen!" he whispered. "Look at me. I know I'm not much to look at, dear, but I want to see your eyes. Ah! that's better. Do you know you combine in the small body of yours all the spirit of beauty and romance there ever was in this dull old world? Helen, do you remember all that I remember, or have you forgotten? 'When I was a King in Babylon and you were a Christian slave!'

It's a long time ago now, Helen, but I still remember. Countless centuries have passed over our heads, but always I have known you. From the beginning of things, Helen. Do you remember, or has it all passed away? Always I have known you, Helen, but always you have eluded me. I loved you when you were Diana, but you were for no man then. As Daphne I desired you, but the laurel bush hid you from my eyes. You were a vestal virgin and I, one of the worshippers outside your temple, but I loved you in vain. You passed me by with your cold pure lips—lips that no man had ever kissed, and your eyes as clear and cold as the water in the spring—eyes that never looked at me, though you knew me, Helen, even then. You were a queen in Rome once, Helen. You loved me then, for I was the gladiator in the ring, and more than anything you loved strength. You looked down at me, exulting in my prowess. Your eyes told me if I won the fight you were mine. But still you eluded me, Helen, for I lost, and the last thing I saw were your cold indifferent eyes as I fell. Now, Helen, now I have found you again, but is it only to lose you? Tell me.''

He lifted her to her feet. His face was very close to hers, and she could see it in the half-light, very white and strained. As he held her close she could feel the violent beating of his heart.

"Tell me," he whispered. "Do you love me?"

He pressed his lips to hers and kissed her until her own lips warmed in passionate response.

"You do love me?"

She hesitated and hid her face on his shoulder. He held her gently, waiting for her answer. Did a memory of a warning, heard years ago, flash through her mind? What was it the Indian had said? "Be sure you love."

"Oh, I do—I do," she said aloud, trying to silence the warning voice that still cried in her heart.

But when he kissed her again she had no remembrance of anything else in the world. Everything was blotted out; she thought that she really started to live from that moment. Fate had its hand upon her and she was acquiescent.

Sharp across the night came the warning shriek of the engine. Russell started violently and rushed to the edge of the verandah. Too late! Already the train had started to move out from the platform, and he could see it, a long flash of light, disappearing between the hills.

He turned to Helen, dismay in his voice. "The train has gone."

"Gone!" she echoed.

"Careless brute that I am," he muttered. "I ought to be shot."

But Helen, distressed though she was, would not allow him to blame himself. She was of too generous a nature to reproach him with his carelessness. The want of reproach on her part cut him like a knife. He felt he could not forgive himself. He thought rapidly. There was the hotel across the river. Yes, that would do.

"I will take you to the hotel," he said aloud. "We must go at once."

He meant it. Every good instinct of his nature was calling out telling him to take her away, while he desired, passionately, to keep her with him. He went inside and lit the lamp, telling Helen to get her things on. She followed him in, not understanding his abrupt change of manner. She was terribly hurt, and the tears were very near the surface. Had it all been a dream then? After all he did not love her. She saw him standing near the window, staring at the floor, a heavy frown between his brows.

"Why are you angry with me?" she asked in a low voice.

He started and looked up and saw the wistful appeal in her eyes.

"Angry with you? Oh, my darling, how can you say such a thing?" he almost groaned.

All his good resolutions melted like mist before the sun. He could not bear to see her unhappy. The next moment she was in his arms.

PAINTED CLAY

PART III.

CHAPTER I.

"THE WALTZ DREAM."

Helen did not arrive home again until early on Monday afternoon. She had taken the early train, while Russell was coming down by the evening train. He had thought it better for them not to travel together. The last Helen had seen of him was his tall figure on the verandah as the train steamed out of the station. She had sunk back with a sigh of relief on the cushions of the carriage, suddenly realising how tired she was—too tired to feel or even think.

When she got home she found one of the office cards under the door, and knew that, as she had expected, someone had been round from the office enquiring for her. But she felt she was too tired to bother about them now. In the morning she would have to give some reason for her non-appearance, but in the meantime they could wait; she did not care. She had brought an armful of wattle blossom down with her, but, without waiting to put it in water, she threw it on to a chair and her hat and gloves on another. She then went into her bedroom and threw herself across the bed, and, with a half-formed wonder in her mind as to why she did not feel like a repentant Magdalen, she went off into a heavy sleep.

About three hours afterwards she was aroused by someone knocking loudly at the door of her sitting-room. She listened drowsily for a moment or two, hoping whoever it was would assume that she was not in, and go away. But it was evidently someone with a great deal of determination and who would not be denied, and at last she got up reluctantly and went to the door and opened it.

To her surprise and consternation she found it was her uncle. He was the last person she expected to see or wished to see in her present state of mind. He seemed distraught, and his ruddy face was paler than usual.

"Good God, girl!" he cried when he saw her. "Where have you been all day? I've been nearly distracted. I've had the clerks running round here all day, and at last I became so alarmed I had to come myself."

Helen wished irritably he were not so fond of her. She was tired and sleepy and in a bad mood. However, she dissembled as well as she was able, greeting him prettily and telling him not to worry as she could explain everything.

He came in, grumbling under his breath, and laid his hat very carefully down on the table. Then, standing with his back to the fireplace and his hands planted firmly in his pockets, he surveyed the room. Helen recognized his attitude with misgiving. He always stood like that when he was reprimanding one of his clerks.

"Now we shall have those explanations of yours," he said.

"Explanations! Oh, yes, of course, Uncle. But won't you sit down first? You look so uncomfortable standing there."

He ignored her remark. "You look as though you had been out of town," he said, glancing at the wattle lying on the chair.

"So I have, Uncle, but how did you know?" She followed his eyes. "Oh, by the wattle!" She gathered it up in her arms. "I had forgotten all about it. Now you must have a little bit." She broke off a small piece and put it in his buttonhole, standing with her head on one side to admire the effect. "There! That's pretty, isn't it? Why don't you thank me for it?"

He grunted, but mildly, for she was beginning to disarm him. "Pretty enough! But that doesn't explain, young lady, why you did not put in an appearance at the office to-day."

"Now, don't be cross with me, Uncle," she pleaded. "And do sit down. Take this nice easy chair and I'll tell you how it happened. Wait a moment though, until I put this wattle in water."

She put it, a glowing mass of color, into a bronze jardiniere, and stood it on the little table by the window. Her movements were deliberately slow, but her heart was beating madly. She would have to deceive him, but how she hated doing it.

"There!" she exclaimed, when at last she could spin it out no longer. "There's a color scheme for you." She drew aside the curtains and looked out of the window. "How dark it is getting. I think we had better have some light."

She crossed the room and switched on the electric light, stealing a glance at him as she did so. What would she do, she wondered, if he could know what had happened to her. It would be a terrible shock, but still, she thought, with a little touch of cynical bitterness, he must be inured to shocks by this time. However, he was not going to know anything if she could help it.

She sat down on the arm of his chair, where he could not see her face when she was speaking, and ruffled his hair with her hand.

"You're getting very bald, dear," she said.

"Perhaps I am," he answered, trying to be stern, "but if you don't mind we will talk about that another time. Just at present I want to know where you have been all day."

"Not all day, Uncle," she protested.

"Well, the greater part of the day, anyhow."

"You won't be cross when I tell you?"

"I'll make no promises," he answered guardedly.

She sighed. "You are being grumpy after all, and I did hope you wouldn't. Now be calm," she said as he showed signs of interrupting. "I am going to tell you now. It's really quite simple. You see, I went up the mountains with a friend on Sunday—just for the day, you know." Her voice was rather breathless, but he did not seem to notice anything wrong.

"You are not going to tell me you missed the train?" he asked.

Her heart gave a sudden leap to her throat and she felt it would suffocate her. She could feel it beating in her ears. How did he know? How could he know? Unless she had been seen! For one wild moment she thought that he himself had been at Warburton.

"Yes, Uncle," she faltered. "I did miss the train. How—how clever of you to guess."

"Not so very clever," he returned. "You see, it has happened before. Where did you stay the night? At an hotel?"

At an hotel? Oh! Why did he question her? Why didn't he take things for granted? It would have been so much simpler.

"Oh, no, Uncle," she said in a tone of assumed brightness, and wondering at the same time how she was able to speak without betraying herself. It was natural deceit she supposed, though she seemed to have developed the quality quite suddenly. "We did not stay at an hotel. My friend knew some people who lived there."

"Oh, indeed, that was very handy. No wonder you missed the train. By-the-by, where did you go to?"

"Lilydale." Her tongue refused to say Warburton, and she remembered they had passed a place called Lilydale on the way up.

"Who were you with? That harum-scarum girl I've met here, I suppose? What's her name—Ann! I don't remember her other name if I ever heard it. Your friends seem to think that only one name is necessary."

"Yes, Uncle. I was with her." How firmly she was able to say it. Another positive proof, if she needed it, that she was a natural liar and deceiver, though it was strange she had only just found it

out. She supposed she had inherited it from her
mother, and as she had never had any necessity to
lie before the faculty had laid dormant until it was
needed. In a sort of a dream she heard her Uncle's
voice meandering on, reproaching her for not having telegraphed or telephoned to him, leaving him
in suspense thinking that something had happened
to her.

"I will never do it again, Uncle," she declared,
when the voice stopped at last. "I promise you
that." .

"Another time I might not be so anxious, remem-
bering how you fooled me this time. However, we
will say no more about it. I am only too glad I
know that you are safe."

She threw her arms around his neck and kissed
him. She felt a sudden lightening of her heart and
a rush of gratitude towards him. The danger was
over, and she could breathe once more.

"Uncle, you are good to me," she murmured.

"Not as good as I should have been, child," he
sighed. "But you know I haven't been able to
follow my own inclinations all through."

"I know, Uncle, but that doesn't matter. You
have been kinder to me than ever my father was,"
she said rather bitterly.

"Don't speak harshly of your father, Helen.
Poor Arthur! Circumstances made him what he
was."

"I know." She rose and stood on the rug in
front of him looking down at him. Under the strain
of the last few minutes her face had gone very
pale. "I know that, Uncle. I suppose we are, all
of us, the victims of circumstances more or less.
But my father should not have treated me as he
did. I was not to blame for the circumstances
of his life. I was innocent of any wrong towards
him. If he had allowed me I would have
loved him and been happy. At it was he made me
hate him. He ruined my childhood. I can't remem-

ber being happy when I was a child except when I was reading. But I have forgiven him for that— he is dead, and somehow you don't seem able to hate the dead. But—there is my mother. I haven't forgiven her. Once I used to love the thought of her. Even when I knew what she had done I defended her against my father, but now—now I think I hate her. How dare she bring me into the world and leave me to fight my way through life alone? She must have known what my life with my father would be, yet she was content to leave me with him while she lived with her lover."

She spoke with a concentrated bitterness of feeling that shocked and amazed him.

"Helen! What's come over you?" he cried. "You must be mad. Remember you are speaking of your mother."

"It is because she is my mother that I speak like that. Of course you can't understand. You are caught in her toils. Tell me, what was there in this woman, Uncle, that made men love her? Why, to the end my father loved her. And you, Uncle? I believe you loved her too. What was there in her? Look at her—there——" she pointed to the picture. "What do you see?—a pretty face and that is all."

He lifted a helpless hand. "I don't understand you, Helen. Never before have I heard you speak like this." He sighed heavily. "God knows I can't blame you, but neither can I find it in my heart to blame her."

"No, because you loved her and you could see no fault in her."

"Yes, I loved her," he answered quietly. "And I love you too, Helen. I love you for yourself and for her sake—you are very like your mother, Helen."

"Yes," flashed Helen. "I have cause to know that."

He looked at her inquiringly, and she flushed suddenly and dropped her eyes.

"What do you mean?"

"Compare us," she said. "Every feature is alike, and as she was only painted clay perhaps I am also." She burst into passionate tears. "Oh, Uncle," she sobbed, "surely I've got more depth, more stability of feeling than my mother had?"

He soothed her gently. "You're tired, child, that's the matter with you. Come, come, don't cry. You mustn't spoil those pretty eyes with tears. Have you had anything to eat? I thought not. Come out with me and we'll have dinner together. Eh? What do you say to that?"

She raised a tear-stained flushed face to his and laughed as she saw his anxious eyes.

"You're right. I do believe I'm hungry. How unromantic!"

"I knew," he said. "I knew it! Women half-starve themselves and then they wonder why they get hysterical. Hurry up now. I'm hungry myself."

Helen disappeared into her room to get ready. She was still in the same half-wild, half-hysterical mood, and wanted the relief of bright lights and movement to keep her thoughts from turning on herself. The outburst against her mother had astonished her as much as it had astonished her uncle. She had not been conscious before that she had been feeling so bitter towards her, and now as she thought it over she realized that her bitterness was mainly jealous love. She knew too well that if the impossible happened and her mother came back again she would forget everything and fall at her feet.

"Where are you going to take me, Uncle?" she asked as they walked down the street together.

"I'll take you anywhere you like."

"Will you?" She slipped her arm through his. "I see you are going to be nice. Well, take me to the very wickedest place you know. Somewhere where there is plenty of people and lights and music and corks popping and all that sort of thing, you know."

"I'm afraid the first part of your order will be

rather hard to execute, but the others will be easy enough to find.''

''I don't care so long as there are not stodgy family parties seated round the tables with their eyes on their food and only speaking when they want to order something. Take me where the men and women talk and are interested in each other.''

As she spoke the City clock told the citizens of of Melbourne that it was half-past six. The streets were now almost deserted. The shops had closed and all the work people had left the city. Two mounted constables rode past slowly. The racing season had commenced, and they were returning from Flemington, where they had been on duty. They were stern-faced men with steady, level eyes. The beautiful creatures they rode picked their steps delicately and arched their necks proudly. It almost seemed as though they knew their own beauty.

The sky was a soft creamy yellow, and sharply outlined against it they could see the grey bulk of Parliament House with all its windows blazing, telling all who were interested that Parliament was sitting.

The enchantment of the City seen in the twilight caught Helen by the throat. ''I love it all, don't you, Uncle?'' she whispered.

''Love what?'' he asked, not understanding. His thoughts had been engrossed with the problem of a client that he had not yet worked out.

''All this ——'' She waved a hand. ''The soft, indefinite light, the stately, grey buildings, the noble sweep of Collins street up the hill to the Treasury Buildings, and see—those English trees against the Town Hall—the green and the grey. Could you imagine anything more beautiful. The man who planted those trees there must have had the soul of an artist.''

''Yes, very nice, very nice indeed!'' he said abstractedly.

''Nice!'' she repeated in disgust. ''Nice! What a—what a puerile word!''

"A very good word," he answered. "Very expressive. But here we are."

They entered the restaurant, the porter swinging back the heavy doors, and passed through the long room preceded by an obsequious waiter, who conducted them to an empty table. They sat down and Helen looked eagerly around. Her eyes sparkled and her cheeks flamed with vivid color. Yes, this was what she wanted. The room seemed to sparkle with a hundred colors. All of the women were handsome, and most of them laden with jewels. Their fingers were heavy with the weight of the rings they wore. The tables were bright with the different colored wines. The bright scarlet of Burgundy (almost like blood, Helen thought, as she saw one woman hold her glass up to the light and look through it)—the pale amber champagne and the brilliant green liqueurs. In a little alcove, half hidden by flowers, a string band played the waltz song from the "Waltz Dream," and as the buzz of conversation died away a little a girl danced out and sang it, her body swaying to the rhythm—

"Like an enthralling magic it seems,
   Calling and calling, waltz of my dreams.
Joy that is sadness, pain that is bliss,
   Stormy as madnes, soft as a kiss."

The music had its effect on everyone in the room. The women listened with half-closed eyes, leaning closer to their companions. The men ceased smoking, and each one surreptitiously took the hand of the woman he was with. Helen, too, felt the intoxication. Her head swam a little, and a longing for Alick swept over her. She had listened to these waltzes before, but for the first time she realized the inner meaning of them. Nothing else mattered but love. Live in the present—take what the moment offered and let the future alone. She would learn the lesson the music was trying to teach her. If only Alick were with her they could learn it together. She closed her eyes, and a vision of his face as she had seen it—was it only last night?—rose up before her. A feeling of the most voluptuous delight shook her—she could almost feel his lips on hers.

The music died slowly away, the last note quivering through the air like the last faint sigh from the lips of a dying woman. Helen opened her eyes. She felt almost a sense of pain and loss when the burst of conversation replaced the soft strains of music.

"Oysters, madam?" said the prosaic voice of the waiter at her elbow. "Plain or cocktail?"

She started violently. The transition was too sudden. "Oysters? Oh, thank you. Plain, please."

Though Helen had been unconscious of him, a man who was sitting at the opposite table had been staring at her since they had come in. He now leant forward and endeavoured to attract Somerset's attention. He at last succeeded, and Helen, seeing her Uncle's nod of recognition, looked across.

"A neighbour of mine," he explained to Helen in a low voice, "goes to the same church as my wife. I wonder what he wants?" he added, as the man rose from his table and walked leisurely towards them.

"Hulloa, Parsons," he said genially. "I would never have expected to find you here."

"I might say the same for you," replied Parsons, smiling in rather an embarrassed fashion.

Helen looked at the two men with a twinkle in her eyes. Her Uncle with his honest bald head, and the other with a long strand of grey hair brushed across the top of his head and firmly oiled down. She wondered if he were under the delusion that he had really covered up his baldness from the public view. It struck her as rather pathetic, though she could not help smiling as she thought of what he must look like when his hair became unoiled and the long, solitary lock escaped. She could almost see it drooping sadly down over his ear.

"What are you smiling at?" he asked, meeting her laughing eyes. She felt embarrassed, for she could hardly share her amusement with him. "I'm smiling at all this," she answered vaguely. "Life is always amusing, don't you think, even when it is tragic? Though there is not much tragedy here, at least not on the surface," she added thoughtfully.

"Do you like this sort of life?" leaning over the table towards her.

"Not always, but when I am in the mood for it—yes."

"And what sort of mood do you require to be in before you like it?"

"Oh, a sort of don't-care-what-happens mood."

"Are you in that mood to-night? You look as though you were."

"Do I?" asked Helen, smiling happily. "Well, I think perhaps I am."

"Ah!" He stroked his chin thoughtfully. "I'm glad, for that makes me bold enough to ask a favour of you."

Helen looked faintly surprised. She wondered if he were going to beg her to give up this sort of life and to go to Church instead. Perhaps he joined with the worldly throng in the hope of gaining converts.

"I can have a box at the Tivoli whenever I like to claim it," Parsons continued. "Let the three of us go to-night. What do you say, Somerset?"

"I don't think my niece would care ——," he began doubtfully, but Helen interrupted him eagerly.

"Oh, Uncle, please let us go. I would love it. I've never been there."

"That settles it," said Parsons, rising. "We must go. There is no use your making any further objections, Somerset."

They left the restaurant together and hurried to the theatre, which was a little further up the street. Two black-faced comedians, obscene looking creatures with thick painted lips, were on the stage as they came in. One of them looked up at the box and winked, at which humorous by-play the whole house roared. Rather abashed by this attention, Helen pulled her chair further back where she could not be seen. Her Uncle leant forward, his elbows

Q

planted on the edge of the box. He had laughed at the wink, and now followed every sally with intense interest and enjoyment. Helen stared at the stage, willing to be amused, and laughing a little as she got the cues from the others.

"You stole our bath towel," said one man.

"I did not," returned the other. "What do I want a bath towel for?"

"I don't know what you want with a bath towel, but I know you stole ours. When I went into the bathroom this morning it was gone, and I know it was there last year."

Shrieks of laughter from the delighted audience. Never before had they heard such a good joke. They repeated it to each other and explained the meaning to the benighted ones who did not appear to see the point. "He meant he had not had a bath for a year. Ha! Ha! Ha! Very good!"

Gradually Helen's gaiety flagged. She listened to the rest of the turns in a dream. Try as she would she could not keep her attention fixed on the stage. She glanced at her watch. It was nearly ten o'clock. By this time Alick would have arrived in town. To-morrow she would see him again. To-morrow! She smiled a little and moved in her seat. She put her elbow on the arm of the seat and leant her head on her hand. As she did so the sleeve of her soft blouse slipped down, leaving the white, gleaming arm bare. The man sitting next to her gazed at it fascinated. Driven by an impulse stronger than his reason, he grasped her arm just below the elbow. Hardly realizing what had happened, Helen turned round.

"What is it?" she asked, and then, as full realization broke upon her, she tried to draw her arm away. But he held it tightly, and suddenly she was aware of his heavy breathing. She was outraged. He seemed like some vile animal crouched behind her ready to spring. She did not move her arm, disdaining to struggle with him, but a blind fury possessed her. She leant forward and touched her uncle gently on the shoulder.

"Uncle," she said, "your good churchman has taken hold of my arm and will not release it. Do you think he is drunk?"

"What?" spluttered her uncle, turning round. "What's that? What did you say?"

The hand dropped and she could feel the sudden silence as the man beside her held his breath. Immediately her arm was free again, her anger left her, and she tried to shield him and explain away what she had said.

"It's all right, Uncle," she said. "I am sorry I disturbed you. My arm was caught between the two chairs and I could not get it out. However, it is all right now."

"But you said something about a good churchman?"

"Oh, yes, so I did. Mr. Parsons told me that he is a good churchman and takes round the plate. I was surprised."

"Is that all?" grunted her uncle, and returned to the contemplation of the stage again.

When they left the theatre Parsons wore a chastened expression and took leave of them hurriedly.

"Funny chap," remarked her uncle, watching him go. "What was it that really happened in there, Helen? You can't tell me your arm got stuck between two chairs and you could not get it out."

"It was near enough to the truth, anyway," said Helen. "But, Uncle dear, I don't think we will go out with him again."

At home again she found a telegram from Ann saying it had been a false alarm about her mother and that she was returning to town in a day or two. Helen tore up the telegram thoughtfully. She wondered if she wished that Ann had come with her on Sunday. She did not know. She did know that fundamentally she felt the same, though she had lost something she could never regain. She wondered why she did not grieve over it, why she was not overcome with sorrow and repentance. She puzzled over it with frowning brows, but could reach no satisfactory conclusion. The greatest fear in her mind was the thought that she might have cheapened herself—that he might have thought her too easily won. That thought bit at her like corrosive acid. She paced the room restlessly, her pride up in arms and burning fiercely. But her torment did not last long, for a girl, who had rooms opposite Helen's, came in. She brought a large cardboard box which had been left shortly after Helen went out. Helen opened it and gave a cry of delight. It was full of flowers. Purple masses of violets, roses—blood-red, palest pink, and yellow. Daphne, boronia—all the sweet scented flowers that God had ever made seemed to be packed into that box. It needed no card to tell Helen who was the sender. He must have telephoned down to the florist to have them sent to her. She buried her face deep in their fragrant depths. He could not have sent her anything that spoke for him so surely as the flowers did.

CHAPTER II.

ALICK THINKS OF THE FUTURE.

While Helen spent a restless and uneasy day in town Russell, with a clear-cut purpose in his mind, was thinking happily of her and what they would make out of life together.

After she had gone he could not bear to stop alone in the house where she had so lately been, and determined to walk to Launching Place, some few miles further down, and catch the evening train there. He arrived about two o'clock, hot and thirsty, and was welcomed with enthusiasm by a stout and motherly landlady. It was there, seated under a flowering peach tree in the old world garden of the hotel, that he remembered Helen's passionate love of flowers. He went inside and telephoned down to the florist's and ordered a box to be sent to her, then, going outside again, he leant back in his chair and dreamed drowsily through the afternoon.

A light breeze ruffled the branches of the peach tree, and the pink and white petals drifted slowly down. He could hear the drone of the bees busy among the flowers, and the rippling music of the river. A girl's laughter roused him. He looked up and saw two girls punting up stream. They smiled and waved to him, and he watched them out of sight. Close to his feet a magpie chortled angrily at him. He looked rather like a dissipated curate. His sober black and white colouring gave him a grave and parsonic expression, but he walked with a drunken, unsteady lurch, for one of his claws was missing.

Russell lit a cigarette and stared up at the drifting white clouds which half obscured the pale blue sky. His thoughts revolved round Helen. To-morrow, after he had seen her, he would call on her uncle and endeavour to convince him that he was a suitable man for his niece to marry. Then in a week or two, they would be married, and Helen would be his wife. His wife! He laughed aloud with sheer pleasure at the thought of it. After that the whole world lay open to them, and they could roam in it at their own sweet will. What wouldn't he do for her There was not a wish of hers that he would not gratify if he could. He would take her to the South Seas first, through the islands to Java. Then up to Japan. He had not been to Japan, but, ever since reading Lafcadio Hearn, he had made up his mind that some day he would go. "Some day," it had always been, and he had put it off and put it off, for he did not want to go alone. Now the some day had come. He would see Japan for the first time with Helen. They would see it together. Some elusive words floated through his brain and he frowned trying to recall them.

> Clear shine the hills; the rice-fields round
>   Two cranes are circling; sleepy and slow,
> A blue canal the lake's blue bound
>   Breaks at the bamboo bridge; and lo,
> Touched with the sundown's spirit and glow,
>   I see you turn, with flirted fan,
> Against the plum-tree's bloomy snow . . . .
>   I loved you once in old Japan.

Just that picture he would look for, and Helen—Helen seen against a background of glowing colour.

After they left Japan they would travel through Russia, and so to England. She had never seen an English Spring, never seen the South Counties when the delicate hand of Spring gently touches the sleeping earth and it blossoms out with a thousand flowers. They would live in Sussex—Sussex by the Sea, the most tenderly loved of all England's beautiful Counties. He himself had lived in Sussex for a year, and he had fallen under her spell.

> I never get between the pines
>   But I smell the Sussex air,
> Nor I never come on a belt of sand
>   But the old place is there.
> And along the sky the line of the downs
>   So noble and so bare.

He drew in his breath sharply. For the moment he almost tasted on his lips the salt twang of the Sussex air and saw again in the misty distance the blue blueness of the Weald. He could feel the soft spring of the turf beneath his feet. That turf—trodden by Briton, Roman, Saxon, Dane and Norman! What a story it could tell of the mighty history of England—of men and women once full of human vanity and throbbing with vain hopes and desires? Where were they now? Gone where nothing could touch them, where no earthly passion could disturb the calm of their quiet sleep. Often he had stood on Beachy Head and watched the ships pass by, thinking of the gay buccaneers of Queen Elizabeth's time, the gallant adventurers who laid the foundations of their country's glory. He wondered if any of that ancient fire still dwelt in the souls of their descendants. If in himself lay the seeds of great adventure—if he could sacrifice himself for an ideal, no matter what it was.

"Too comfortable," he muttered. "My life has been made too easy."

He was startled by a burst of sardonic laughter. He looked up and saw two kookaburras seated side by side on the bough of a tree. They regarded him gravely and then burst again into laughter. It is not a pleasant sound, this laughter. In the morning it is gay enough, but in the evening when the sun is setting and the gum-trees cast strange and fantastic shadows, the laughter of these birds has a cynical, almost savage, note in it. It seems to mock at the futility of human hopes. Its message is—"The end is nothing. You are nothing—we know—we know!"

It chilled Russell. He was easily influenced and sensitive to impressions. It sounded to him like the laughter of the Three Sisters as they turned the wheel of Fate and crushed his hopes in the turning.

The landlady bustled out with the news that the train was due in about an hour, and would he have dinner before he left? He nodded, and joined the rest of the hotel residents at dinner in the narrow little dining-room, listening abstractedly to the cheerful liar next him who told him strange stories of his adventures on the racecourse and his skill in picking winners.

Just about the time when Helen was opening the box of flowers he had sent her, Russell arrived in town. He was so sure that in a couple of weeks at the latest he would be married to Helen that, meeting Walter on his way from the station, he almost told him the news. However he did not, though there was an unaccustomed buoyancy in his manner that made Walter wonder, but Walter had the gift of silence and never admitted anyone into his thoughts. Sandy had spread abroad his opinion that Russell was in love with Helen, but Walter heard him and held his peace. He was not so sure that Helen was in love with Russell, and that seemed to him the most important part of it, though it did not seem to strike the others that way.

Russell was waiting for Helen when she came out of the office at lunch time. When she caught sight of him, even though she had been expecting to see him, her heart beat violently. It seemed strange meeting him again in the noisy street after parting from him in the soft silence of the mountains. He was eager to talk to her at once, so broke their usual routine, and took her to a cafe in town. There, seated at a little marble-topped table, with a sullen-faced waitress hovering near them, he asked her to marry him. Helen listened, her fingers beating a nervous tattoo on the table. She shook her head when she heard that he wanted to marry her next week.

"Then when will you marry me, Helen?" he asked.

"Can't we wait a little while?" she asked in a low voice. "I—I don't want to be married just yet."

"Why not, dear?" he asked. To him it seemed very simple, but he could not follow the workings of her mind.

She shook her head and avoided her eyes. "I don't know," she said.

He sought for her hand under the table and found it. "You shall marry me when you like, but tell me, dear—look at me—I want to hear from your lips, for now it seems almost a dream—you do love me?"

"Oh, I do." She said it so softly that he scarcely heard it, but the clasp of her hand was sufficient answer, and he was satisfied.

"Have you forgiven me?"

"Forgiven you?" She looked at him with her clear eyes. "I have nothing to forgive."

"For loving you too much?" he whispered.

She flushed to the roots of her hair and rose hur-

riedly to her feet. The morose waitress, seeing her
opportunity and thinking they had occupied the
table long enough, swept the tea things, with a
great clatter, on to her tray.   They walked out together, Russell thinking what a sensitive, highly-
strung creature she was, and how careful he would
have to be with her.

For a time they were perfectly happy, but Russell felt he was in a false position. He could not
understand her reluctance to marry, and time and
time again he made resolutions that he would not
go near her till she had consented, but he could not
keep away from her. Sometimes a doubt would
gnaw at his heart, and he would accuse her of not
loving him.   This she always denied vehemently,
imploring him to believe in her. He would answer
that it was easy enough to prove it by marrying
him.

"Aren't you happy as you are?" she would whisper, and taking her in his arms he would forget
everything.

Once in a moment of madness, he told her the
history of his life. He omitted nothing, encouraged
by the calmness of her attention. He did not find
out until afterwards how ominous was her calmness
and how foolish he had been in his unreserved confidence.

He discovered it the first time she came to his
rooms. It was Sunday afternoon and Lily had gone
out, so they were quite alone. He had shown her
round, pointing out all his treasures, the things he
had picked up in his travels. He noticed that she
did not seem to pay much attention, and that she
was looking round evidently searching for something.

"What is it?" he asked.

"Where's my picture?" she said. "Oh, I know
you bought it."

"Who told you?"

"Sandy, of course. He can't keep anything to
himself."

He laughed. "No, he can't. If you want to be

sure of anything going the whole rounds of the city tell it to Sandy. I didn't want you to know at the time, because I thought you might be annoyed."

"But what have you done with it?" asked Helen impatiently.

"Come in here," he said mysteriously.

He opened the door of another room leading off the little hall, and beckoned to her. She stood on the threshold rather nervously.

"Now do you see it?" he asked. "It's the only picture I want in my room. See—just where it's hung, the morning sun catches it, and your hair seems to burn like fire."

It was indeed the only spot of colour in the room. The walls were lined with white paper, and the varnished floor uncovered except for a strip of matting near the narrow bed.

"You are a strange being," said Helen, looking round with surprise. "Why, this is almost like a monastery cell—not that I have ever seen one—but it's like what I would imagine a monastery cell would be—except for that," she nodded at the picture. "While your other rooms ——"

"This room used to be like the others, but when I got your picture and put it here, the surroundings seemed to take away from it. So I had the walls papered white, and all the furniture taken out, and got these few things. Now you see the result—what I was aiming at—you shine out of the bareness like a precious stone. I can't tell you what joy it is to me to wake up and see you smiling at me, with your lovely hair spread over your shoulders—just as I have seen it. I used to wonder, Helen, if I would ever see it like that."

He bent to kiss her, but Helen ran away from him, back again to the sitting room. He followed her in and flung himself down on the lounge while she amused herself rummaging amongst his books. She made running comments as she took them out and looked at them. It was when she stood in silence, holding a book open at the fly leaf, that he knew she had seen something she did not like.

"What's the matter?" he asked, getting up and coming over to her. She handed the book to him, pretending an elaborate unconcern.

"Something of interest to you," she said cuttingly. "Given to you by one of the many women you have loved. You were evidently very intimate with her, judging by what she has written in it."

He took the book from her, and bit his lip. He would not have had her see the inscription, though for years past he had forgotten it was there.

"It is Swinburne, too, I see," she added, as though that made it a worse offence. "I suppose you have many and many a time quoted me the same things you used to quote to her—learnt from this book, I suppose—the book that she gave you."

He flushed and threw the book on the floor, where it lay, the cover turned back and the pages crushed.

"Helen, you're not fair to me. This happened a long time ago, and I told you about her."

"You didn't tell me you treasured the presents she had given you," she said bitterly.

"I don't treasure them," he replied quietly.

"Then why did you keep that?" she retorted angrily. "Why didn't you throw it away, burn it, do anything with it, when you had finished with her? Why did you leave it here for me to see?"

"I didn't finish with her. We had finished with each other."

"How do you know? How can you possibly tell? You yourself have told me that nothing is certain, least of all love. If she came back you would be just as eager to fall in love with her again as you were with me."

"You will make me believe that women have no sense of justice," he answered, half-bitterly. "I told you all my past life. I told you everything. There is nothing hidden. This affair was—nothing. She amused herself with me, that was all. Neither of us showed in a very noble light and it ended, as all these affairs do, with neither bitterness nor regret on my side or hers; Helen, you must believe that."

"Believe? I don't know what I believe," she answered passionately.

He looked at her in silence, at her flushed, angry cheeks and downcast eyes, then took her by the hand and drew her down beside him on the lounge. She allowed herself to be led, though he could feel it was unwillingly, and that she was still estranged from him.

"Helen!" he whispered. "Helen!" and put his arm around her. She half-sighed and relaxed, and under his hand he could feel the pounding of her heart.

"Poor little heart!" he said gently. "Why do you let it get so angry? Why is it so cruel to me?"

"You are cruel to me."

"Cruel? To you? Ah, no, Helen. That is the anger in your heart still speaking."

She was silent and leant her head against his shoulder, watching the motes moving in the bar of sunlight shining in through the window.

"How am I to believe that you love me?" she said at last.

"Believe? How can I prove it to you? Show me a way and I'll do it. My only desire—my only ambition is to make you my wife, but—but that doesn't seem to be yours."

She sprang to her feet. "Do you know why?" she asked. "Alick, do you know why? I get so angry sometimes, so suspicious. It is because—because I don't quite trust you. You yourself have made me like that. In some ways I trust you absolutely. I know that, even if you ceased to love me, you would marry me if I wished it. It's not that—not that way of trusting, but in other ways. Dear, you've told me too much of your life, too much—that's the trouble. I tell myself that you have loved before and you will again—I can't trust you. I seem to have a grievance against you. Sometimes—Oh! sometimes it is too horrible. I close my eyes and I think—awful things, and I can't get them out of my mind If I had had a lover before you met me, wouldn't you hate it—wouldn't you be jealous of the unknown man? Ah—you would! If only I hadn't known. If only you hadn't told me."

He looked at her in silence for a moment, while bitter thoughts went through his mind. What a fool he had been! If only he had known that she had been nourishing those thoughts in her heart. He could not know. For Helen herself did not realize that it was only a sudden outburst of anger on her part. She was perfectly sincere at the time —she really believed that she had spent sleepless nights worrying over his past, while the truth of the matter was that she had not realized it until she held the book in her hand. Then she was so angry that she did not care what she said.

"Helen," he said, "I'm a man, and I've lived as men do, but I've been a decent enough fellow. What happened in the past is nothing—nothing—how can I make you believe the absolute nothingness of it? You are so young—so young, and you can't understand."

"If only I hadn't seen the book," she muttered.

"What does that matter—you knew!"

"Yes, I knew, but seeing that made it all so plain to me."

"Helen, forget it—forget it—don't let it spoil our day. You don't know how you stab my heart when you are angry with me. You will make me believe that, after all, you don't love me."

That was a spur that never failed to move her. She threw herself down beside him, whispering that she did—she did. He was satisfied, for he was so blinded by his own love that he did not realize the very vehemence of her protestations was an effort to convince herself.

CHAPTER III.

IN THE FITZROY GARDENS.

Helen was deliberately forcing herself not to think of the future. She knew that some day she would have to face the problem, but she shirked it now. She had been borne along on a wave of passion, and the wave receding had left her breathless and a little tired. She found that thinking was useless and unprofitable, for her mind was in a chaotic state. She did not really know what she wanted. She did not want to take the definite step of marrying Russell, and yet she could not bear the thought of parting from him—that caused her infinite pain. She knew that what she was doing could not be right, but she was unable to feel any sense of wrong-doing. The want of it troubled her when she thought about it. She tried to come to an understanding of her own attitude, but failed—she did not seem to have any attitude at all. Her feelings were in a constant state of fluctuation.

"If I were good," she thought, "I would want to be married. But I can't see the difference between being married and not. It doesn't seem to me to matter very much, and yet it does. I wish I were either a very bad woman or a very good one. If I were a bad woman nothing would bother me, and if I were a very good woman I wouldn't think about it. I would just be married, and that would be the end of it. I'm not bad—I know that. I'm good—not really good, I mean—but good enough. It's very confusing. I always thought, when I fell in love, I would know it. I thought it would be something very simple, but it's all so complex that it makes me tired. Of course I love him—I do—I know I do—but I don't want to marry him. At least not just yet. Oh! I don't know! I won't think about it."

It was only when she was alone that she indulged in self-analysis. When she was with him she seemed to lose her capacity for thinking. The touch of his lips still had power to carry her away, but the inevitable re-action followed when she was alone, and she would question herself in vain. She longed for simplicity—she hungered for it—simplicity of thought and life, but how far she seemed to have wandered away from it.

Russell was becoming more and more insistent that she should marry him. She was an enigma, but he honestly thought if only she were married to him the puzzle would solve itself. In the meantime he saw her as often as she would let him. She would not leave the office, though he had begged her to do so, but she preferred to be independent. She said she would not live on his money till she was married to him. When he persisted she got angry and told him that she was not for sale. Deeply hurt, he had dropped the subject.

On Sundays she was free and she always spent that day with him. One Sunday he had been up to see her, and in the evening they wandered outside and up to the Fitzroy Gardens. The Spring had already gone and the breath of Summer was in the air. It was not hot yet, only a gentle, languid warmth. They took their favourite seat under an elm tree out of sight of the path. Here the grass had been allowed to follow its own sweet will and grew nearly a foot in length, though in other parts of the gardens the lawns were trim and neat. The grass was starred with a mass of yellow dandelions, now reluctantly closing their petals as the heat went out of the sun's rays. On a tree near by a thrush poured out his full-throated melody—so joyous, so full of the splendour and passion of life, that it almost made the heart stop beating with the delight of it. When he finished his hymn of joy and flew away to his silent mate, a breathless silence fell over the place. Helen felt the spell of it, and, nestling closer to Alick, smiled up at him. He noticed that her eyes were wet and smiled tenderly at her. He realised how infinitely dear and precious she was to him. Such a young, young thing, he

thought, and felt a twinge of pain at the thought
of his years compared with hers.

They did not speak for a time, but sat hand in
hand like two children, listening to the silence. It
was so calm, so peaceful, so far removed from their
ordinary life, and yet how close! That was more
than half its charm. This silent place in the city.

> How calm it was!—the silence there
>   By such a chain was bound,
> That even the busy woodpecker
>   Made stiller by her sound
> The inviolable quietness;
>   The breath of peace we drew
> With its soft motion made not less
>   The calm that round us grew.

They sat there for half an hour or so, watching
the fading sunlight on the leaves, and the little
bright-eyed squirrel that stared at them unwinking
from one of the trees. He seemed interested in
them, they sat so still, but he disappeared when the
bells of St. Patrick's pealed out. They were not
aggressive like so many church bells, but fitted in
sweetly with the silence, the greenness and the
changing sky.

Helen listened, feeling oddly religious. She
thought how sweet it would be to be good and to
believe. She had a vision of herself and Alick,
kneeling together in an artistic attitude—it must
be artistic—while the light from stained-glass windows fell across them, and high up, a choir sang
beautiful music. Her hand tightened in his and she
wondered if he were seeing the same visions. But
he was not. His thoughts were travelling in another direction, for the bells had aroused him from
the abstraction into which he had fallen.

"Helen," he said at last, breaking the silence
between them. "When are you going to marry me?
There is nothing to prevent you except your own
feelings. Don't you—want to?" He could not disguise his anxiety, for he was beginning to fear that
she did not.

She closed her eyes and leant her head against

his shoulder. She had heard his question, but it had hardly penetrated her consciousness. She wished idly that he would not talk. She was happy, so why couldn't he be content? But Russell could not be content. He hated the position in which he was placed. He felt that he was taking everything from her and giving nothing in return. Helen did not understand his point of view, nor did she make any effort to understand it. His passionate contrition for what he had done completely puzzled her. She thought, as she felt no remorse or contrition, there was no reason at all why he should.

He waited for her answer, but she did not speak. She had already forgotten that he had spoken.

"You don't answer me," he said at last. "Then it is true."

"What is true, foolish one?"

"That you do not want to marry me."

"Why can't you be content with things as they are?" she said slowly, feeling a sense of resentment against him for forcing her thoughts into channels which she wished to avoid.

He put his arm around her and turned her face to his. Her face was grave and unsmiling, but as he looked at her she suddenly smiled and flushed.

"I love to see you like that," he whispered. "With just that expression." He forgot his seriousness of the moment before and kissed her. They sat very still and then he lifted his head with a sigh.

"It's no good, Helen," he said. "I've got to have you. God knows I can't keep away from you, but I don't want you in this secret style. I want to show you to people as my wife."

"Ann told me that you did not believe in marriage," Helen murmured, not moved by his outburst. She always felt a sort of lazy content in his arms and a disinclination to speak.

"I believe I did talk like that," he said, rather ruefully, "but all my convictions have gone overboard. It must be a survival in me of all I used to hate—of what I called the suburban attitude of mind. Now I find that is my own attitude. I want you to belong to me altogether. I want to be sure of you—I suppose that's the truth.''

"But marriage wouldn't make you sure of me,'' said Helen softly, watching the effect of the after glow across the top of the trees.

"Oh, wise young woman,'' he said, half-bitterly. "You are indeed a Daniel come to judgment. That is what I used to say—marriage was the death of love. I firmly believed it—I half-believe it now, and yet I won't be satisfied until I've trapped you, clipped those pretty wings of yours, put a label round you, and exhibit you as my property—mine! Now you see what an absolutely conventional orthodox man I am.''

"Ann would smile if I told her that,'' said Helen lazily, not very interested in the conversation.

"Ann? What has Ann got to do with it?'' he said impatiently. "We weren't discussing her.''

"No. I know that. Still I could not help thinking how amused she would be if she knew how entirely different you are from what she thought you.''

"I'm not interested in Ann,'' he replied moodily.

"Now,'' she said calmly, "you are cross.''

"Helen,'' he asked sternly. "Are you trying to quarrel with me?''

"No.''

"Well, it looks very like it. I try and discuss a serious question with you—a matter affecting my future and yours, and you persist in dragging up some ideas Ann has of me. Women seem to be incapable of following a train of thought to its logical conclusion.''

"I suppose you mean that for me?'' said Helen, drawing away from him and moving to the opposite end of the seat.

He did not reply, but sat with his shoulders hunched up and staring miserably at the ground. Helen looked at him and felt a sense of compunction. She was so fond of him—so very, very fond of him. She felt she would do anything for him, except just what he wanted. She stole up to him and laid her hand on his.

"Dear," she said softly. "Don't be angry with me."

"Angry? Angry with you? How could I be? You—who have given me everything, who have been so generous, so kind, so dear and beautiful. No. I'm not angry with you. I'm angry with myself, with life. Helen, don't you see—can't' you see what a rotten position I am in? Here am I, a man of the world, years older than you—there are you, a young girl, innocent and inexperienced, and I take advantage of you. If any of your friends knew, how could I look them in the face? How could I justify myself—how could I attempt to justify myself? There is no excuse for me."

"They don't know, dear, so why do you worry about it?" murmured Helen.

"But, Helen, don't you understand? It's not them exactly. It's what I feel—I myself. I can't justify myself to myself."

"When you talk like that you make me unhappy."

He rose to his feet abruptly. "Don't let me add that to my other sins," he said. "Let us go for a walk and you can charm this spirit out of me. When I am with you I forget that I have any honor at all."

They strolled off arm in arm, down the avenue of trees whose interlocked branches in summer time, make an archway of light and shade for nearly half a mile.

They quarelled now, very often—bitter, heart-breaking quarrels. It was nearly always Helen's fault. He had developed a quality of almost sublime patience, though he was not naturally a patient man. Often Helen was nervy and on edge, and at these times it would have been better if he had kept away from her. She would meet him with an unsmiling face, looking as though she did not want to see him. These moods of hers frightened him.

He believed that she was unhappy and that it was
his fault. This reduced him to a condition of utmost despair. Always after these quarrels, when
more by looks than by words she reproached him,
she would suffer from a re-action of violent remorse.

One day she had parted from him coldly, so coldly
that she seemed almost like a stranger to him. He
wondered if the lips that looked so cruel now and
said such bitter things, could possibly be the lips
he had kissed. She had left him abruptly and he
watched her walking up the street, feeling as though
the world had come to an end. Almost dazed by
the pain at his heart, he had gone home to spend a
bitter and hopeless afternoon. He believed that all
was over—that she never wished to see him again.

All the afternoon he sat smoking and trying not
to think while Lily crept about outside. She thought
he was ill and made plaintive offers of tea and
brandy, but he waved them aside. He suffered
bitterly, and in the evening when the telephone bell
rang and he heard Helen's voice speaking, he
trembled with the swift re-action of feeling. She
was asking him to come up and see her. In less
than ten minutes, though despising himself for his
weakness, he was knocking at her door. If Helen
was bitter in her quarrels, she was generous in her
reconciliations. His pale face and the suffering in
his eyes stabbed her to the heart. With a low, inarticulate cry she threw her arms around his neck.

"Why don't you hate me?" she cried. "Why
do you come near me? Oh, how I hate myself."

He laughed softly as he held her slender body in
his arms. Was it only this afternoon he had
believed she would never smile at him again?

"Hate yourself if you like, but I can't. You've
got me, Helen. Caught me with those little white
hands of yours and I can't get away, however much
I want to. I ought not to be here. I ought to
leave you now—but I—can't."

"I want you to stay," she whispered. "I want
you to know how much I love you."

His arms tightened around her and he bent to kiss her again but even as he did so a shadow darkened his eyes and he drew back.

"Helen, Helen," he sighed. "You ought to help me—you ought to send me away."

"Do you want to go?" she asked.

"Want to? Helen—you know."

"Then stay."

She believed then that she would never quarrel, with him again, but the reconciliations were nothing, the quarrels were everything, for they were the beginning of the inevitable end.

CHAPTER IV.

THE BEGINNING OF THE END.

The summer wore on, with steely blue skies and a blazing sun. The asphalt melted with the heat and perspiring crowds clustered round the thermometer to see how hot it was. During the day the streets were practically deserted, except by those whom business called out. These people walked with a dejected, limp and slightly ill-used air. Every summer it was the same, but they never got over their first surprise that it was hot.

At night there was a different scene. At night the whole population woke up and poured out from the city and the suburbs in their thousands. They hung on to the trams going to St. Kilda and crowded the trains to Brighton. For miles along the foreshore the beaches were black with people. They swarmed into the sea while the air hung heavy around them, tainted with the smell of burning scrub and trees. Bush fires? What of that! Something to fill up the papers. What had it to do with them? The fires burnt fifty—sixty—a hundred miles away. What did it matter? Into the sea again.

They elbowed each other in the ice-cream saloons and spent money frantically in the search for cooling drinks. "Lemonade, Ginger-ale, Ice-cream!" So it went on. The glasses passing backwards and forwards over the counters and the silver money pouring into the tills from the hands of the willing spenders.

A blaze of light on the left of the Esplanade showed "Luna Park," which was run on "Up-to-date American lines." Inside were still more people, all of them possessed with an insatiable desire for amusement. It seemed to drive them ceaselessly onward like the adulterous souls driven before the fiery blast in the Inferno. And such amusement! To try and walk upward through a revolving barrel. To see oneself elongated or absurdly broadened in a dozen mirrors. To walk in darkness along a narrow passage while the floor broke under the feet. To take shots at a man standing on a swing in the hope of knocking him off into the water below. This was a very popular form of amusement, though probably less popular with the man who had to fall into the water. Still he was paid to do it. If anyone felt a qualm as they saw him disappear under the water, they salved their conscience with that.

All the evening a raucous band played ragtime music, and every hour or so a man and woman would go through some strange convulsions which were popularly supposed to be dancing.

Along the confines of the park ran what was called the "Scenic Railway." The cars, packed with people, crawled slowly upward to a great height, and then shot downwards at a tremendous pace. Everyone feeling the mad exhilaration of the speed, shrieked with joy and clasped each other or anything they could get hold of, as the cars swung violently round the corners. When the ride was over they would emerge, the women, with their hair blown over their ears and their hats off, and eager for more, rush off to join the long queue already waiting their turn.

Everyone seemed to have money to spend, an exhaustless supply of it. So it went on night after night, while the year of 1913 burnt itself out, and 1914 rose red above the horizon.

While in the town people laughed and played heedlessly; in the country men, women, and even children fought silently with the merciless fires that threatened their homes. They gazed with tragic eyes at the pitiless skies, watching for the clouds that foretold the rain. As they watched and hoped, the earth got browner and browner and the grass withered up, while the cattle died in the beds of the dried-up creeks. The farmers, meeting each other, would stand and look up at the sky, then shaking their heads, pass on. There was nothing to say.

But in town nobody knew or cared anything about a drought. They had read something about it in the newspapers, but it had left no impression. They were not hard pushed for water. There was plenty in the Yan Yean Reservoir. The public parks and gardens were as green as they ever were. Only men who knew—men who travelled through the country and saw the land for endless miles stretching out withered and parched, shook their heads gravely and predicted a bad season next year if the rain did not come soon.

The summer was trying Helen severely. She lay with her windows open at night and watched the moon rise over the clouds like a great red balloon. The moonlight streamed through the windows and to her fevered mind it seemed as hot as the sun—hotter, for she could look at the moon and see how red and angry it was, as though it burnt with an inner fire.

In the long, hot nights when she could not sleep, she had leisure to think and understand. Slowly but surely she took the full measure of herself. She had made a mistake. She knew it and could no longer shut her eyes to the fact. There remained only one thing to do and that was to make the best of it. She had taken down the picture of George and put it away. She did not care to look at his honest eyes or to think of the pain she would have to inflict upon him. As for Alick, she supposed the end of it would be that she would marry him. She saw the situation was impossible. Neither of them were happy, and she had not the courage to tell him the truth. She still kept up the fiction that she loved him, trying to fan a warmth that she did not feel. She wondered if he saw through the farce, though she kept a constant guard upon herself. She was gentler with him now, more kind and understanding. As a brother or a friend she wanted him, she liked to be with him, to talk to him, but as a lover he had lost his power over her.

Sometimes she felt that she could not see him, and on these occasions she went out purposely to avoid him. It had happened that, hearing him coming unexpectedly, she had put out the light and stood silently with her hand pressed to her heart to try and still its beating, listening to his knock on the door and then the sound of his slow, listless footsteps as he went away again. She hated herself for doing this, but it seemed that a power stronger than herself drove her to it. She shrank from the lash of her own self-contempt. She knew that she was a coward. Latterly she had become afraid. A possibility that at first she had lightly passed over, now assumed tremendous importance in her mind. She wanted to withdraw before she was irrevocably bound to him, but yet she did not know how to do it. She could not hurt him—she could not. Better, she thought, to live a lie than to tell him the truth.

Whether any of the studio people guessed anything, she did not know. They very seldom mentioned Russell and if they did it was always with a rather self-conscious expression. Helen gathered that they were not quite sure, but were very desirous of giving her to understand that whatever happened it did not matter to them in the least. Walter had had a three-roomed cottage at Brighton lent to him for the summer and here most of them were living for a time. Helen had got into the habit of going down at least once a week. She used to meet Ann in town after she had finished work and both girls would travel down together.

One hot and breathless day she had made an appointment with Ann to meet her and the two of them were going to Brighton. She watched the slow hands tick the minutes away and at the stroke of five she was off. She went home first to cut some sandwiches and get her bathing gown and towel. Just as she was leaving the buildings she remembered that she had not seen anything of Alick for three days. She hesitated. She knew she ought to ring up and see if anything was wrong, but this she did not want to do. If he was in he might want to come with her, and she did not want him to come. She walked off down the street, but her conscience troubled her and at last she turned back. She knew that if she did not ring up she would be uneasy all the evening. When she got to the telephone she found that he was out and left a message for him. Feeling absolutely happy and as though she was released from a sense of oppression, she met Ann. It always gave her a holiday feeling to be with the studio people now. There was no need for a constant guard on herself, when she was with them, to watch her words in case she might hurt them.

It was early when they arived at Brighton and the usual exodus of people from the surrounding suburbs had not yet set in. The boys were already in the water and in ten minutes or so Ann and Helen had joined them. Both Walter and Helen were exceptionally good swimmers and easily outdistanced the others. They swam together with long, steady strokes.

> "O tender-hearted, O perfect lover,
>   Thy lips are bitter, and sweet thine heart."

The lines went through Helen's mind as she felt the caress of the sea on her limbs and the salt spray moisten her lips.

"My lips may be sweet," she thought, " but my heart is bitter—oh bitter! Alick, Alick, why can't I give you what you want? I don't want to be cruel to you. No—I will not think of that now."

She shook back her hair from her forehead and increased her pace.

"See that buoy over there?" she called to Walter. "I'll race you to it."

It was her boast that Walter, good swimmer though he was, could not outstrip her. Swimming against him now she found that the constant practice he had been getting lately had made him a formidable antagonist, and in the effort to keep up with him and the keen physical exertion, she quickly forgot her troubles.

They picnicked on the beach, a gay and irresponsible party. Helen was the gayest of them all. Her laugh rang out the oftenest, and the others hung on her words. She felt exactly as though she had been drinking champagne. It was not that she was particularly happy, but she could not help using her wits to make the others laugh. The sea air had gone to her head a little. When tea was finished they wanted her to walk along the beach with them towards Hampton. But she had become rather tired of them and the pleasure of entertaining them had worn off. She refused to go, saying that she was too tired. Walter said he would stay with her and the others went off. She watched them go, Ann and Sandy walking in front, and the others following a little way behind.

She ran her fingers through her hair, which had been hanging down her back, and finding that it was quite dry, she gathered it together and twisted it round her head. Then she lay back on the sand with her arms supporting her head, staring up at the sky. Walter sat beside her, placidly smoking in silence. He saw no reason for conversation if Helen did not wish to speak.

The beach was now full of people. Every train that thundered into the station brought more to swell the crowd. They did not all come to bathe nor to seek the cooler air. Some came to drink, and some for other reasons.

Two men lurched along the beach. They laughed foolishly together and drank from a black bottle. When they had finished they threw it into the sea. It floated for a while, and then passed, a grotesque and obscene-looking thing, out of sight.

Near Helen lay two people clasped in each other's arms. Though she did not look at them she was angrily conscious of them. She turned her head to look at Walter, but his eyes were fixed on the horizon where the last light of the day was fading from the sky.

She tried to close her ears to the sounds around her, listening to the one sound that went on for ever in a low, resistless monotone. Above the shriek of the engine, the shrill scream of children, and the laughter of the noisy bathers, she heard it—low, steady, passionless. As she listened it seemed to grow in volume until at last it dominated everything else. It terrified her. How many countless tides had risen and fallen on that same beach? How many countless tides would wash the beach when she had gone—she and all these people who laughed so light-heartedly and loved and played out their little hour? With a sudden longing for the sense of human companionship she laid her hand on Walter's arm. His warm fingers closed over it and her terror passed.

"Walter," she said at last. "Have you ever been in love?"

He took the pipe out of his mouth and knocked it out against the heel of his boot.

"In love?" he asked. "No."

"I'm glad," she said. "I always like to think of you as master of yourself. You are so apart from everyone else. You stand so alone. Walter, I want to talk to you."

"I'm listening."

She turned on her side and lay with her face towards him. She could see the white outline of his features and the blackness of his hair, but the expression of his face was hidden from her.

"Walter, I can talk to you as though I were speaking to my own soul. You remember in the 'Story of an African Farm' Lindall says to Waldo —'I like talking to you, Waldo, it's like talking to a spirit,'—that is how I feel with you— as though I were talking to a spirit. You stand away from us all. I suppose it is your art and your singlemindedness of purpose that makes the difference. We are bothering about what we feel, while you, realizing that in the end our personal feelings are absolutely nothing, go straight on."

He did not reply, and she was silent for a time, watching the long line of white surf along the beach and the dark figures of the bathers.

"Walter," she said again, "I am unhappy."

"I know," he said quietly.

"You have guessed how it is between Alick and me?"

"Yes."

"Do the others know?"

"They know he is fond of you, but I think that is all."

"What do you think, Walter?" she asked, "Have I done wrong?"

"No," he replied, "not if it made you happy and made him happy. Nothing could be wrong if it is the means of happiness, but now you are not happy and I saw him yesterday and he—he did not look happy."

"You are fond of him, aren't you, Walter?"

"Yes," he replied. "I am fond of you both."

"Walter, shall I marry him?"

"Do you want to?"

"No."

"Then don't do it."

She sat up and leaning her head on her hand tried to concentrate her mind. It was easy advice to give, but harder to follow. She knew the time had come when she must either marry him or send him away. She felt that she would sooner put a knife through his heart than tell him she did not love him.

"He wants me to marry him, Walter," she said at last. "It is for his happiness."

"But not for yours. You tell him the truth. Don't do him the injustice of marrying him unwillingly. He is too fine a man to want you unless you went to him willingly."

"Would it be wrong to marry him without telling him the truth?"

"Yes. You could not keep up the farce and he would soon find out."

"You believe that?"

"I know it."

"I see," She picked up a handful of sand and let it slip through her fingers. Then she got up. "I—I am going home, Walter," she said, "I am tired. Tell the others."

He also rose to his feet. "Shall I come with you to the station?"

She shook her head. "I would rather go alone. Stay here." She hesitated a moment, then said, "I will think over what you said, Walter. Thank you."

He watched her white-clad figure moving away through the darkness, then, lighting his pipe again, he strolled along the beach back to the house.

CHAPTER V.

ALICK SAYS "GOOD BYE."

Helen did not hear nor see anything of Alick until two days after her conversation with Walter. It was now nearly a week since he had seen her, and she could not imagine what had happened. He had not even replied to the message she had left over the telephone for him, and she was feeling a little hurt. Though she felt that she wanted to avoid him sometimes, it was quite a different thing if he should feel the same towards her. She could not help wondering if he perhaps were getting tired of her.

He came at last one evening about eight o'clock. She had been suffering all day from a sense of extraordinary depression which she was unable to shake off. She had been moody and irritable, inclined to sit staring into vacancy, though when she realized she was doing that, she always pulled herself up sharply. She remembered with terror her father's fits of moody depression and she did not want to fall into the same groove as he. It had been a hot day and when she had finished her work she felt tired and drowsy. She made a languid meal and then lay down on the sofa near the window and tried to sleep. She had gone off into a half-doze, when she heard well-known footsteps coming along the passage. The door was half open, and the footsteps hesitated outside and then walked in. She knew who it was but she did not speak. He stood for a moment peering through the darkness.

"Is anyone here?" he asked softly.

"I am," said a voice from the sofa.

He crossed the room hastily and knelt down at her side. He bent over her and she thought he was going to kiss her. But he only peered into her face and then rose to his feet with a half-smothered sigh.

"Can I switch on the light?"

"Yes, if you wish."

He did so and she lay blinking in the sudden strong light. Then she got up lazily, wondering at the strangeness of his manner.

"What's the matter, Alick? Where have you been all this time? It is nearly a week since you have seen me."

"Have you missed me?" he asked.

"Of course I have." But her tone carried no conviction to him. He looked pale and his eyes were heavy and tired as though he had not been sleeping well.

"Alick," she said again. "What is the matter with you? You look so—strange. Don't stand over there. Come and sit by me and let us talk. I have a lot to say to you."

He shook his head. "I—I can't talk to you when I am near you, and I must talk to you to-night. We must get things straightened out."

"Alick!" She came over to him then, for she saw he was serious and that there was something on his mind. "What is it, dear?"

He looked at her quickly and then moved away, pacing restlessly up and down the room. He paused before the table where George's picture used to stand.

"What have you done with the picture of that clear-eyed boy?" he asked.

She winced, as she always did at any reminder of George. She was trying to forget him and she did not like to be reminded how difficult it was.

"I have put it away," she said at last. "But what has that got to do with you and me?"

"Nothing," he replied, "only—" He spoke slowly and with an apparent effort. "Helen, I am going away. I am going to England at the end of the week."

"Going away—from—me!" She laughed nervously. "I don't believe it. You are teasing me."

"I have already booked my passage."

She looked at him, her straight brows frowning a little.

"But—but I don't understand. Why?"

"Listen, dear. I have been thinking about this for some time, and last week I made up my mind. It seemed to me the only thing to be done. Helen, I have a queer sort of feeling towards you. I love you—passionately. You know that. But mixed up with that passionate feeling, is this—well—almost fatherly feeling towards you. You see I've got to protect you from myself and I can only do that by leaving you. I am doing you no good. I haven't made you happy, and now I'm afraid of harming you even more than I have."

She felt as though her world had tumbled about her ears. She could scarcely grasp the sense of what he was saying.

"Alick, you don't really mean you are going away? Leaving me? You could not be so cruel. I don't believe it."

"Do you think that I have been so blind and so engrossed in my own selfish feelings that I could not spare a thought for you? Do you think I don't know the truth? How could you hope to hide it from me? I love you too much."

Her lips trembled. "If you loved me you could not leave me."

He smiled, a twisted sort of smile. "Ah, dearest, you are wrong. I love you better than myself, that is all. Give me that much grace. I want to give you a chance."

"Alick!" She caught him by the arm and looked up at him, her eyes dark with tears. "Marry me, then, and take me with you. I can't part with you —I can't. I would be so lonely without you."

"Helen, this is serious. For God's sake be frank with me. Tell me the truth, even if you know it will hurt me. You know what marriage means. You know what I am. Remember I would be with you always. Now tell me, do you love me?"

She could not meet his eyes. She knew the truth herself but could not tell it to him.

"Answer me," he urged.

She kissed his hand. "I am so fond of you, isn't that enough?"

"No." He spoke sharply and abruptly and there was an edge of pain in his voice. She felt it, and her cheeks drained of colour. She walked slowly away from him. He watched her with hungry eyes but did not attempt to follow her. Down in the street a tram bell rang noisily. Helen listened to it attentively. Her whole attention was concentrated on that sound. It was the only thing she seemed able to think about. The ticking of the clock, too, was unaccountably loud to-night. She looked at it dully. It was only half-past eight. Only a quarter of an hour since he had come in, yet she seemed to have lived a century.

"Helen!" he said hoarsely, when at last the silence became oppressive.

"Well?" she said listlessly.

"You are blaming me in your heart." He did not ask it as a question, but stated it as a fact.

She looked at him quickly. It was almost an involuntary glance, and he read in her eyes a world of reproach which she could not put into words. He came over to her then, and knelt by her side, taking her hands in his and trying to see her face which she kept averted from him.

"Dearest," he said softly, "you are angry with me. Dear, won't you try and understand how it is I must go away and leave you free, even if it is only for a time. I would have you on any terms, but I know you better than you do yourself, and it would not be fair to you. If you married me now it would be because you were sorry and I don't want that. I must stand off and give you a chance. You may find then that you want me, but as it is, Helen, I don't seem able to hold you. Perhaps you loved me at first. I don't know! But lately you have changed. I feel that there is something in you I cannot touch. Something you hold away from me."

"I have given you all I can."

"That's just it. All you can, but not all that is in you. I have never awakened the inmost you. You have never admitted me into the secrets of your heart."

"I have none."

"Perhaps you were not conscious of your reserve, but it was there and I knew it though I tried to blind myself to it. I have only stood on the outskirts of your life. I have never entered the inmost chamber."

She turned on him fiercely then, a flush of anger dyeing her cheeks.

"Oh, do let us have done with words and phrases. I am tired of them. Why don't you be honest and say you are going because you are tired of me?"

He dropped her hands in discouragement, and rose to his feet.

"You are not trying to understand," he said quietly.

"What is there to understand?" she demanded. "You are going—of your own free will.   That is enough for me."

He raised his hand in a hopeless gesture.

"I am going because I think it is the only decent thing to do.   I have failed with you as I have failed with everything else."

In utter dejection he sat down and covered his eyes with his hand.   The sight of his dejection almost disarmed Helen.   Was he right?   Was she trying not to understand?   Let her be honest with herself.   Her anger against him arose from the fact that he had made his arrangements without consulting her, and that he could speak of going away as if he did not care.

"Alick," she whispered.

He did not raise his head.   Indeed he hardly heard her, so immersed was he in his own gloomy thoughts.   With a sudden revulsion of feeling all her sympathies flew to him.   How she had failed with him over and over again.   He came to her seeking her sympathy and help, trying to do what he believed with all his heart was the only thing possible, and she gave him nothing but frowns and angry words.   She stole over to him, and, sitting on the arm of the chair drew his head on to her breast, caressing his forehead with her soft fingers.

"Dear," she whispered.   "I am so horrid to you. Forgive me, I understand.   I know you want to do what is best for me."

He closed his eyes and sat for a moment quite still.   He tried to believe that the inevitable had not happened and that she was really his.   But his keen, almost feminine sense of intuition told him that now she was only showering sympathy and pity on him.   So might almost a mother have treated her son who came to her sorely stricken.   He took her fingers in his and kissed them, then raised his head and looked at her.

Helen met his eyes pitifully, her heart torn with grief and compassion. No one knew better than she how he loved her, and she knew too well how much she would miss him. She knew that she could not take him into her life as she had done, and then see him go, without a bitter pang. When Alick went, a part of herself, of her life would go with him for ever. She knew that she could never forget him, that as long as breath remained in her body, he would be with her, an unseen ghost, a part of her very life. Therefore she felt very tender towards him, and he saw the tenderness and winced. It was not tenderness alone that he wanted. It was the love that stung and hurt most cruelly even at its height, the love that was both a pleasure and a pain. It was the love that *he* would never find in Helen. He knew it, though he tried to make himself believe that in the future the time might come when she would love him again.

"A year, Helen," he said. "I am giving myself a year. If at the end of a year you find you need me, that I am still first in your thoughts, send for me. You will always know where I am. Walter will tell you, for I will write to him. If I hear from you, darling, I will come back. If I don't hear I will know the truth."

"You will hear from me in a year," she said steadily. "I will want you."

"I am taking a tremendous risk, Helen," he went on. "A year is a long time, and God knows what might happen. You may meet someone else. Men will love you, Helen. Do you know, these last few months you have changed? When I first met you there was a girlish coldness in your face, now there is a warmth and intensity. Your lips got fuller and softer, and your eyes have grown deeper and darker in colour."

"Well," she said with a sigh. "I suppose I have grown up. I was only a girl when you met me."

"Do you regret it?" he asked, looking at her

searchingly. "That's the thing that worries me, Helen. That keeps me awake at night. Have I harmed you?"

Did she regret it? Search her heart as deeply and honestly as she could she was unable to find the answer. Traditions of her grandmothers that still lived in her, the atmosphere of the world she lived in, told her that she should regret. She knew, according to their standards, she had suffered an irreparable harm. Yet she could not feel the sense of harm and loss that she should have felt. If she herself could not feel that she had been wronged, then was she? That was the question. If she were only harmed in the minds of other people, then how could that affect her? It was only the knowledge of her transgression, not the actual fact of it, that would damn her. As it was people liked her and sought her society. If it were known it would not be the fact of the sin, but the knowledge of it, that would affect their attitude towards her.

She did not answer Alick's question, and he continued with a growing sense of bitter anger against himself.

"You were so young. I only thought about you when it was too late. Helen, if you don't regret it now, the time will come when you will—when that time comes you will hate me for what I have done."

"Hate you!" she repeated. "How could I ever hate you? Why, you are part of myself. You remember you used to say to me:—

> For wholly as it was your life
> Can never be again, my dear,
> Can never be again.

It never will—never. I share too many memories with you to forget. It is not your fault that we can't take up our lives together. It's mine. I've failed in this, not you."

"I could have let you alone," he said.

"You can't blame yourself, I know! It was us —let it rest at that."

"I can't. That's the devil of it, Helen. I will

never get away from this feeling of remorse. There's no reparation I can make to you now, except go away. You know in your heart that is what you want, though you are too kind to acknowledge it to me.''

He looked up at the clock. The hands were pointing to half past nine. "It's getting late, Helen, I must go. I—I don't seem able to say good-bye to you.''

She turned deadly pale. "But—but won't I see you again?''

He groaned. "I can't see you again. I can't trust myself. If I meet you again I might not have the strength to leave you.''

"Alick, I can't realize it. I can't! I won't see you again before you leave? It seems impossible—incredible.''

He took her face between his hands and turned it up to the light, looking at her longingly. Some intuition told him he would never see her again.

"You've been beautiful in my life, Helen. All my memories of you are sweet. What a gift of the gods you were! I might have known they would be jealous and take you away again. You will forget me, Helen, not soon perhaps, but that time will come.''

"And you—'' She could hardly speak, "you will forget.''

"Helen, this is true. If I have been honest with no one else, I am honest with you. If I had been ten years younger the memory of you might fade, there might have been other women, but now, Helen, do you realize that I am nearly twenty years older than you? The best of your life is in front of you. The best of my life I am leaving behind—with you.''

He bent to kiss her, but not on the lips. He touched her lightly on the forehead, then, taking up his hat, he turned to the door. She stood for half a second stunned by the abruptness of it, then she flew after him.

"Alick,'' she cried, "you are not going like that.

Alick, my heart is breaking—I can't bear the pain of it.''

His face worked with a spasm of anguish. He tried to open the door, but she clung to his hand as if that were the only thing left to her from the wreck.

"Come back," she sobbed. "Stay with me only for a little while."

"For God's sake let me go, Helen," he muttered. "Help me, darling, I must go. I dare not stay any longer. Oh, Helen, you are tearing my heart out."

She drew a little sobbing breath like a child recovering from a passion of tears, and ceased to plead with him. She looked so childish and yet so beautiful that his heart was wrung with love for her. He caught her in his arms, watching how the blood crept back into her cheeks. It almost seemed as though her former passion for him was revived. But he knew this was only the last flicker.

> Breathe close upon the ashes,
>   It may be flame will leap;
> Unclose the soft close lashes,
>   Lift up the lids, and weep.
> Light love's extinguished ember,
>   Let one tear leave it wet
> For one that you remember
>   And ten that you forget.

It was a bitter thought, but he knew that it was all over, he gathered her up in his arms—how easily he could carry her!—and laid her gently down on the sofa, closing her eyes and kissing the closed lids. Then he went out, without looking back, hurrying as though he would escape from himself.

Helen lay where he had left her. She knew that he was gone, but as yet her stunned brain could not take it in. Her mind was a blank. She thought of foolish things. She counted the number of books in a row on the shelf, over and over again. She watched with intense concentration a fly crawling over the ceiling. She heard people walking along the passage outside. They laughed sometimes. She wondered dully why they laughed, and yet why shouldn't they? She had laughed herself. When was it? Why, only yesterday. She had laughed quite gaily, at something one of the men in the office told her. What was it again? It must have been funny, or why should she have laughed? Oh, if only she could remember what it was. She wanted to laugh. If she could remember it would save her from thinking. She was afraid of her thoughts. If she could only stop them, but they came creeping, creeping back. She must stop them, she must! She got up and moved quickly about the room, but her mind was clear now and she could not get away from them. She could not bear the glaring light and turned it out. Then she was afraid of the darkness, for it seemed to leave her more alone with herself. She ran into her room and threw herself upon the bed, burying her face in the pillow, and all the repressed emotion in her heart broke out in a stifled cry.

"Oh, Alick, Alick—Oh, the pain in my heart. Why has it happened? Why—why—why?"

CHAPTER VI.

GEORGE RETURNS.

For the first few weeks she suffered intensely, then, though she had not forgotten, the first sharpness wore off. Ann and the boys noticed the change in her and though they did not speak about it she felt their sympathy. She suspected that all of them, except Walter, thought Alick had deserted her. However she held up her head and went through with it, and after a time the colour came back to her cheeks and the laughter to her lips. Though she had lived down the worst of it, even yet she could not bear to go to the same places where she had been with him, for memory whispered, "Do you remember?" At first the demands of the past were insistent, but as time passed it faded somewhat and lay dormant, though it was always ready to leap to life again at a chance strain of music or a line of a poem she had read with him. If he had taken something of her, he had left something of himself with her. She found herself using gestures of his and adopting his mannerisms. She would speak like him, say something that she had learnt from him, and even think like him. He had left an indelible impression on her.

Though his influence remained with her, and she missed him, she was yet relieved from a tremendous weight. Her emotions were not in a constant state of turmoil and, though she was not happy, she was contented. She devoted herself now with such an intensity to her work that it awoke protests from the other clerks, all of whom were willing to take as much of her work as possible on their own shoulders.

She was bent over her typewriter one day, her fingers flying over the keys, and intent on a contract she was typing, when the office boy interrupted her.

"There's a chap wants to see you," he said, pointing a grimy thumb over his shoulder in the direction of the outer office.

"Who is it?" asked Helen, without looking up.

"Don't know, Miss."

"Then go and find out."

He went leisurely and whistling softly through his teeth, while Helen went on with her typing. Presently the boy came back.

"He won't give his name," he said grinning, "but he gave me a shilling instead. You had better see him, Miss. He says he knew you well."

Helen dropped her hands into her lap. She felt suddenly afraid. If it should be Alick! A little fear crept into her heart and she began to shake all over. Why had he come back? She did not want to go through it all again, and, if it was he, that was what it would mean.

"Ain't you goin' to see him?" asked the boy, as Helen did not move. "Go on—he's quite a decent sort of chap."

"Bobby," said Helen sternly, "Copy those letters, please, and don't have so much to say."

He thrust his tongue into his cheek, but he obeyed her, indulging in spasmodic contortions of silent laughter.

Helen walked to the outer office, into which strangers were always shown. Before she opened the door she paused a moment, gathering all her strength together. Then she went in. The man in the room had his back to the window and at first she could not see his face. But she knew it was not Alick, for this man was slimmer and of a more boyish build. She stood by the door looking at him seriously. No suspicion as to his identity crossed her mind, but when he moved away from the window towards her, she knew. He was smiling. It was the same smile that had charmed her the first time she had seen him. She knew it so well—that sudden lightening of the face and the extreme sweetness of his expression. She seemed never to have forgotten, yet for a time she had. Now, as she saw him again, the past swept over her. The past they had shared together. She forgot what had come between—what the years had done to her. She remembered their parting, his boyish face looking down at her from the ship; the face so pale, and yet trying to smile. She was the girl he had known, the shy, lonely girl he had helped. All the dear past, that she had never thought about, never dreamt that she remembered so vividly until now, came to her. It gave her eyes a wistful sweetness and her mouth an innocent childishness. She was innocent and a child again as she saw again her boyish lover.

"George!" She could only breathe his name at first, and they kissed each other as innocently as two children—they were children again in the first moment.

"Nelly!" He was ashamed of the tears that same into his eyes. A man should have no truck with women's tears, he thought, but it was the joy of it that shook him and brought the tears he tried to hide. He had dreamt of her so often, just like that, and now his dream had come true. They looked at one another like two young things just awaking to a knowledge of each other, then she laughed.

"Oh, you boy," she said. "I don't believe you ever went away. You left only yesterday it seems now. You have changed though. You have got— let me see you. Yes, you have got older and handsomer. Why, you look like a—like a bronzed god."

"By Jove! You are throwing the compliments about, Nelly. Now it is my turn. Let me see you."

She looked up at him laughing, but under his steady gaze the laughter left her lips. She remembered her secret and a terror lest he should by some chance read it in her face, came over her.

"I am afraid of someone coming," she said hastily, glancing at the door.

"Don't worry about people," said George easily.

"I must," replied Helen. "Do you know that in the other office there are about six young men, and they all know a young man has called to see me? I didn't tell them, but you may be quite sure the office boy has. Now they are all wondering what we are talking about so seriously."

"I suppose I had better go, then," said George reluctantly. "I am going through to Sydney tomorrow night and I can fit in a couple of hours this afternoon with some business I have to do here."

"But, George, aren't you going to stay here?"

"I've got to go to Sydney to fix up a partnership business with another man. We are going in together—mining engineers, you know. I will only be away about six weeks, then I am coming back. When I come back, Nelly—"

"You really must go now, George," said Helen, interrupting him. "We will talk about it afterwards. We can't talk here."

"What time will I call back for you? Five o'clock—very well. I'll be here on the tick." He slapped his pocket. "I've got some money now, Nelly, to spend on you. I used to be so miserably poor."

He came back on the stroke of five, and they went away together. She walked with a light, easy and graceful step. He was three inches taller than Helen and she was a tall girl. His face was bronzed and his features had lost the round, boyish look she remembered. He looked a hard, healthy young man. His blue eyes danced with excitement. He had a tendency to linger in front of the jewellers' shops, to point out to Helen the beauties of a special kind of ring. She tried to manœuvre him away from them, but had to give it up in despair. His will was stronger than hers. He tried, rather clumsily, to find out what kind of stone she liked. He evidently wanted the fact that he intended buying her a ring, to be a dead secret, and he had not the least idea that with every word he said he betrayed himself. When he had thoroughly examined all the shops, he expressed disappointment, and said that he believed there were better shops in Sydney. Helen agreed with this, and he nodded his head mysteriously and said he would wait and see.

"What about dinner, Nelly?" he asked. "Let us go somewhere quiet, and where we can sit and talk as long as we like."

She did not offer to take him home with her. Somehow she shrank from that. She told him she lived in rooms and he took it for granted that it would not be quite the thing for him to go there.

They went up to a little Cafe in Exhibition Street, opposite Her Majesty's Theatre. It was a quiet place, without any pretence of modern style, kept by a Frenchman and his Irish wife. They had their own clientele and did not cater much for outsiders. The room was quite plain, without any gorgeous decorations or bewildering colour schemes. Long mirrors and a few framed advertisements of famous French wines hung on the walls. A white cockatoo walked pleasantly among the diners. He preserved a staid and serious mien, except when he saw a choice morsel of salad disappear which he specially coveted. Then he would allow an expression of extreme disapproval to escape him. When no one

was looking he indulged in wild orgies which the most
reckless of human beings would not dare emulate.
He would drink copiously from the water jug and
then consume cayenne pepper with apparent enjoyment from the little open pots which stood on the
tables.

From her little desk at the door where she took
the money and served out the liqueurs, Madame
beamed amiably on George and Helen as they entered.   She greeted them as though they were old
friends.   Both of them were young enough to feel
flattered at this salutation, and George unconsciously
assumed a very worldly air as he followed the waiter
to a table, though this worldly-wise effect was spoilt
by the ingenuousness of his smile as he turned to
Helen.   It seemed to say—"This is a tremendous
lark, you know.   Aren't we going to have a time!"
There was a joyous air about George as he ordered
the dinner, though he examined the menu with a
grave and serious expression.   The waiter hovered
at his elbow and George looked at him suspiciously.
He suspected the man of a desire to laugh at him
but the waiter's expression was one of grace and
simple benevolence.

"Wine, Sir?" he asked, offering the wine list.

George flushed and looked at Helen, but she shook
her head.

"Bring some water," said George sternly.

"Water, Sir? Certainly, Sir."   He vanished and
almost immediately reappeared again with the water
jug.   He filled both their wine glasses and then retired for a few moments out of hearing.

"I say," said George, looking round to see that
he was out of earshot, "I don't like the waiter.
He's in the way, and he makes me nervous.   There
is one thing I do like about him, though," he added
as an after thought.

"What is that?" asked Helen.

"The way he calls me, 'Sir.'   It makes me feel
big."

They both laughed and smiling into each other's
eyes drank to themselves in clear, cold water.   Two

very sophisticated people at another table looked
across at them.   The woman had tired eyes and a
heavily rouged face, while the man's face showed
that a too long indulgence in the pleasures of the
table and other pleasures, was leaving its mark upon
him.   The woman looked at George and then at her
companion, and her lips tightened a little.

"Those two children are in love with each other,"
she said.   The man grunted and swallowed another
mouthful of food.   The woman still looked wistfully
at them, until at last, with an impatient gesture, she
refilled her wine glass and drank.

George was uneasy until the waiter finally left
them.   He had got it firmly fixed in his mind that
the man was hovering about them with the intention
of overhearing what he had to say to Helen.

"At last!" he said with a sigh of relief, as the
waiter, with a final benevolent glance in their direction, left them alone with their coffee.   "He's gone,
and now we can talk."

He leant back in his chair and fumbled in his
pocket, drawing out a tiny case which he opened and
gave to Helen.

"There," he said triumphantly, "that's for you.
I got it in Broome when I was there.   I happened
to be able to do one of the pearlers a good turn and
he gave me this."

It was a single, magnificent pearl, suspended on a
thin, golden chain, so fine that it looked like a golden
hair.   Helen gave an involuntary cry of delight as
she saw it.   She lifted it out of its hiding place and
it lay on her hand, a sparkling drop.

"It's too big for a ring, you see," he went on,
"and that's the only way I could think of to get it
set.   I wish I could put it on for you but this
crowd might stare if I did.   You put it on, Nell.
I want to see how it looks."

She did as he asked and put it on.   It fitted
tightly round her neck, and the pearl just fell in
the hollow at the base of her throat.   She stared
at it in the glass, unable to keep her eyes away from
it.

"Oh, George, it is beautiful," she said with a sigh of pleasure. "Did you say one of the pearlers gave it to you?"

"Yes," he replied.   "Rather decent of him, wasn't it?"

"But what did you do?" asked Helen. "It must have been something rather big for him to give you a pearl like this."

"It was nothing much," he said, in an off-hand manner.

"I'm sure it was.   You've made me curious now. What was it?"

"I'd rather not tell you," he said awkwardly. "It's rather a sordid tale."

"Well, then what were you doing in it?" she asked.

"Now you've got me," he laughed.   "I suppose I will have to tell you after that.   This chap—the pearler, you know—got mixed up with a half-caste woman there—you understand what I mean?" he asked rather diffidently.

She nodded and smiled a little.   "I think so, George.   It is not very difficult to understand, is it?"

"The woman was married and her husband found out what had happened and he tried to give it to this chap in the neck.   I saw the knife coming down and stopped it.   He got me in the arm, though." He pulled up his sleeve and showed Helen a deep scar just above the wrist.

"You saved his life, no wonder he gave you the pearl," said Helen, shuddering a little as she saw the nasty mark of the wound.   "Why, you might have been killed."

"Would you have cared?" asked George, leaning over the table closer to her.

"George!   I—."   A lump rose in her throat. "Don't speak like that."

"You haven't said much me to me, you know, Nelly.   You didn't even say you were glad to see me."

"You knew I was. You did not tell me that you were glad to see me, but I knew."

"You don't know how glad, Nelly. You don't know what it means just to be sitting here with you, and know I have got through all right. It's a rotten life for a man over there, and if I hadn't had the thought of you in my mind to keep me straight— well, I might never have come back. In some of these little mining towns there's nothing for a man to do except go to the dogs, unless he's got some definite purpose. It's all right during the day, there is work to do. But at night it's a different story. There's nowhere to go but to the hotel, and, if a man starts that over there, it's the beginning of the end for him."

She plucked at the table-cloth with nervous fingers. "Was it really the thought of me that kept you from —all that?"

Well—rather! You were someone I was working for. I had to make good and come back to you. The closer it got to the time when I would see you again the more impatient I became. I thought the last few weeks I spent in the West would never end. Coming over in the boat I nearly went mad with impatience. I wanted to get off the steamer, and help push it along. I walked up and down the deck of that ship until everyone thought I was training for a Marathon race. All the time I was thinking—'You rotten old tub, if you only had my heart in place of your engines we would be there in half an hour.' Then when I saw you," he added simply, "it was worth everything, even the waiting, which was the hardest part of all."

She looked at George and, as she looked, it seemed to her that another stood beside him. It was the ghost of one who came between them, a ghost that she would never be able to forget. She could see them both so plainly. The older man with his eyes a little tired, and the lines deepening about the mouth, and the vivid, eager face of George, with his youth and virility. Both seemed to plead with her, but it was to the younger man that her heart turned. Her youth answered to his. She loved him, and, with the knowledge of that, came a sense of bitter and unavailing regret. Was George the price she had to pay for forsaking the path of the old traditions? She had been let off in one way, but she should have known that she could not escape. The Fates had been spinning their web to catch her, and now, when happiness was within her grasp, it was too late. She could not put out her hand and take it. It meant destroying his happiness, too, and the future that he looked forward to with such confidence. She could not tell him yet. She would wait until he came back from Sydney. That would be time enough to shatter his ideal of her, and show him the painted clay of his idol.

"What are you thinking of, Helen?" he asked, wondering why she was so silent.

"Someone said, 'When half-gods go, the gods arrive.' They might teach us to recognize the half-gods when we see them, don't you think?" she said bitterly.

"Now what exactly do you mean by that?" he asked earnestly, puzzled by her manner.

She laughed a little excitedly. "Don't ask me what I mean, for I don't know. I only said that because I thought it sounded clever."

"No, you didn't," he replied, thoughtfully. "I wonder what you really did mean? Helen, you are different."

"How—different?" she asked, with a little catch of the breath.

"You've changed in some way. Perhaps it is because you are older. When I saw you this afternoon I thought you had not changed a bit, but now I see that you are a woman and— and a beautiful woman."

"George," she spoke very earnest, "tell me the truth. Would you rather come back to find me the girl you left, or as I am now?"

"I always loved you, Nellie," he said simply, "but

I want you as you are now. Any man would. I can't tell you what I think about you. I'm a fool like that. But—well, I've never seen anyone like you.

She flashed him a brilliant smile. "I'm glad you think that. It makes me happy. I was afraid you might think I had deteriorated."

"Deteriorated! What a thing to say!"

"Don't be angry. I said it myself." She pushed back her chair and rose. "Come, we had better be going."

Madame bowed them out with impressive geniality, and they wandered down Exhibition Street and up towards the Treasury Gardens. It was a mild autumn night, and from the lake in the centre of the lawn a bull-frog croaked noisily. They stood for a moment looking down into the dark water and then George, glancing round to see that no one was in sight, drew her to him and kissed her. She forgot everything for a moment, and then her spirit took fright, and she pushed him from her. Would she never forget those other lips? Would they always have a claim on her?

"Don't kiss me like that, George," she said, her breathing a little irregular. "You—you frighten me."

"I could not help it, Nellie," he said in a low voice. "You see I have waited such a long time."

They walked on again in silence, and presently she slipped her arm through his. That much consolation she would allow herself but no more.

"When will you be ready to marry me?" he asked abruptly.

"Marry you?" she faltered, taken by surprise, though she had known that sooner or later that question must come.

"I can marry you now," he went on. "I've got on. I've been exceptionally lucky, I suppose. I've got my life mapped out. Everything always turns out exactly as I want it to."

"Don't be too sure, George," said Helen, in a low voice. "You are tempting Fate."

"I'm not afraid of Fate, Nellie," he replied with a little self-confident laugh.

"I am, George,—horribly afraid. If ever I want anything very much I pretend to myself that it can't possibly happen."

"You silly girl," he said affectionately. "That's not the way. I say to myself 'I want that' and then I try to get it. I always do."

Helen looked round nervously. She half expected to see a malignant face peering at them from the branches of the trees. George had no fears of indignant Fates, specially conspiring to defeat his ends. His purpose was quite clear in his mind. He had come back to marry Helen, and that was what he intended doing.

"About our marriage," he went on. "We'll have a quiet affair, Nellie. We will let the family know when it is over. Auntie may be hurt about it, but we can't help that. I couldn't stand a family wedding. Now the only thing to settle is the date. That's for you to say."

"I'll let you know when you come back from Sydney, George," she said faintly.

"That's settled then," he said, "I'll be back some time in May, and we'll be married as soon after that as possible."

He had spoken in a quick, decided voice, but now he pleaded with her and there was an undercurrent of doubt and wistfulness in his voice.

"Nellie, won't you kiss me?"

She hesitated, and a dozen reasons why she should not went through her mind, but none of them were as strong as her desire to do so. He was going away to-morrow, and when he came back she would not dare to kiss him until she had told him what he had to know.

He stopped and made her look at him. "Won't you?" he asked. He bent his head and she kissed him, a fugitive sort of kiss it was, but he was satisfied.

"I'm glad you did that, Nellie. Do you know for a moment I thought you were not going to?"

She did not reply, but clung to his arm and hid her face against his sleeve. She wished she could find something that would drug her into forgetfulness of the past few months.

CHAPTER VII.

THE THEATRE.

George left the following evening by the express for Sydney. It was early in April when he went and he expected to be back some time in May. This gave Helen from five to six weeks to prepare herself for the ordeal of telling him. She thought of writing to him, but directly she took up her pen she realised the impossibility of taking that way out. She must meet him face to face and tell him. She tried to believe that she would be justified in not telling him. If he did not know he would be happy, but she knew that this was mere sophistry. She would have the knowledge of it in her heart and it would remain a barrier between them and happiness, because she would have something in her heart she did not share with him. She turned now towards, the thought of a life in which love would have no share. She knew that she could never marry Alick. She would never see him again. She knew that George would not want to marry her when he knew. She steeled herself to that thought. She gave herself no loophole for hope. It was inevitable. There only remained one thing to be done. She must tell him and then say good-bye for ever. She saw the justice of it, and she was not going to complain. She had betrayed George, and she would have to see him suffer.

He had been gone about two weeks when something happened which for the time almost swept even George from her mind. It was a pictured face on a theatrical poster which she had seen from a passing tram that awakened her interest and curiosity. The tram had passed too quickly for her to obtain more than a glimpse. But that passing glance was enough. When she reached town she hurried to where the theatrical posters were always displayed. She soon found what she was looking for. It was the head of a woman with half-closed eyes and smiling lips. Helen stood and looked up at it. The face reminded her of someone she knew—she had seen it before. She was sure of that. There was something in the outline of the features that was very familiar to her, almost obscured as the likeness was by the harsh coloring of the poster.

"I know that face!" she said aloud, and her heart beat with a curious sense of excitement and almost foreboding. She told herself that it was absurd, that what she imagined could not be possible, and even as she tried to persuade herself she became more and more excited. She scanned the reading matter eagerly, but it told her nothing except that she was Marguerite Joy from the Coliseum Theatre, London. She bought a paper and turned to the Amusement Columns. This gave her more information. Evidently Marguerite Joy was a bright particular star, for the advertisement screamed her attractions; the salary she was getting, and the stupendous cost of the gowns she wore. She had just finished a successful season in Sydney, and was opening in Melbourne on Saturday. Helen thought rapidly. It was now Friday, and she must go to the theatre to-morrow night. In her excitement she threw the paper away, which was immediately restored to her by an attentive young man who ran after her for two blocks for the purpose. Helen thanked him mechanically, impatient at the loss of time and resumed her hurried flight. She was anxious to catch her uncle before he left the office. It was after five now, but she knew he would be there until nearly six o'clock. She caught him just as he was leaving the building. He looked at her with frank astonishment. She was breathless and strangely excited.

"What has happened?" he asked anxiously.

"Nothing," she replied, panting a little. "Wait a moment until I get my breath."

He looked at his watch rather impatiently. "What is it, Helen?" he asked. "I haven't much time to spare. I have a business dinner on to-night."

"I'll walk down with you and then I won't detain you."

He assented to this, and they went down Collins Street together. He always liked to be seen with his good-looking niece and he unconsciously assumed a little swagger, throwing out his chest and eyeing fiercely any young man who looked at her.

"Now, what is it you want?"

"Are you busy to-morrow night?"

"To-morrow night? Let me see." He thought a moment. "No."

"Well, Uncle dear, will you take me to the Tivoli Theatre? I must go."

"The Tivoli? What do you want to go there for? Why this sudden passion for the Tivoli?"

"Oh, Uncle, please be nice about it, and take me without asking questions," she pleaded. "I want especially to go to-morrow night, and I want to go with you."

"You like going with your old uncle, do you?" he said with a pleased smile.

"Yes, Uncle, I love it. I would sooner go with you than anyone else," she told him, smiling to herself.

His swagger increased. "Very well, my dear, we shall go to-morrow night."

"I had better book the seats to-night then, for we might not be able to get in. I will just have time before they close. Give me the money, and I will let you have the tickets to-morrow."

He gave her a sovereign which she took, forgetting to thank him, and hurried to the booking office. She managed to get two seats right at the side, but in the front row, and she was satisfied that they were as near to the stage as she could get.

On Saturday morning she was so excited that she could hardly keep her mind on her work. The afternoon seemed never-ending. She spent it doing her hair a dozen different ways in the effort to create a unique and startling effect. At the last moment, after she had spent an hour dressing her hair most elaborately, she got disgusted, pulled it down, and re-arranged it in the simplest possible way. Her dress was very plain, but her uncle thought she looked the sweetest thing he had ever seen when he called for her in the evening.

The name of the woman she had come to see blazed in scarlet letters across the front of the theatre. Helen looked up at it as they went in. If what she imagined as a remote possibility were true? What would it mean to her? She did not seem to have any feeling, except excitement, as yet. She must make sure first. Her uncle would know without any shadow of doubt. She had given him no hint as to why she wanted him to come, only told him to be sure and bring his opera glasses with him.

She found, on examining her programme, that the star of the evening would not appear until imme-diately after the interval. She could hardly control her impatience as, with incredible slowness it seemed to her, the first items were gone through. She was not conscious of hearing a word that was spoken or sung on the stage. She could not keep still, and twisted uneasily about, until requested by her uncle, in an agonized voice, to keep still. This she was only able to do by gripping the arms of the seat and holding on tightly. She wanted to move, to be doing some-thing, so as to make the time pass quickly. It was so horribly slow.

With the raising of the curtain after the interval there was a noticeable stir in the audience. There was no need now to tell Helen to keep still. Every pulse in her body, every nerve, even her heart seemed to stop suddenly, waiting for something. The stage was empty for a couple of minutes and then, very slowly and with a languid grace, the actress walked on.

"Now, uncle," said Helen, in a voice of suppressed excitement. "Look at that woman and tell me who she is?"

He put the glasses to his eyes and adjusted them to his sight. Helen tapped her foot impatiently. He seemed so slow fumbling about with them. Then with a muttered ejaculation, he let them fall with a crash to the ground, and rose to his feet, clutching the railing in front of him, and staring as though he could not believe his eyes.

The people round him expressed their disapproval, and up in the gallery a voice called sharply—

"What's the matter with the old gent?"

"He's drunk. Why don't they chuck him out?" complained another.

"No, it's me," said a musical voice from the stage. "I always cause a sensation wherever I go."

There was a shout of laughter, and the audience immediately forgot Somerset's strange behaviour. The hardened theatre-goers expressed their opinion that he had been paid to do it.

Somerset had sat down again. He was trembling slightly, and there was a dazed expression on his face. He looked as though he had received a shock from which he found it difficult to recover.

"Uncle," Helen whispered. "Is it—?"

She left her question unfinished, but he understood. "Yes," he said.

Even though she had expected the answer, and though she had known from the first moment she saw the advertisement who it was, the blood left Helen's lips. She picked up the glasses and tried to look through them, but her hand was shaking so violently that she was unable to hold them. The woman had started to sing, and her dark eyes swept round the house. Helen leant forward and she thought for a moment that the woman on the stage looked at her, and that her eyes tried to convey a message. She could not read the meaning, but she knew it was an appeal. Something told her that she had better go. She suddenly wanted to go. She did not want to stay and listen to that inexpressibly vulgar song, the chorus of which the audience had already learnt.

"Come let us go," she whispered.

They stumbled through the dark aisle and into the
brightly-lit vestibule. Under the strong glare of the
electric light Helen was shocked to see the change in
her uncle's face. He looked drawn and haggard.

"Uncle," she cried, "you look dreadful. Has it
upset you as much as that? I wish now I had told
you what I suspected."

He passed his hand over his forehead, and looked at
her as though he saw her for the first time.

"It's—seeing her again like that," he said in a
broken voice. I did not expect it."

She felt remorseful, and as though she had unconsciously done him an injury. She made him sit
down on one of the red plush covered lounges, anxiously watching till he showed signs of recovery. In
about five minutes the strained look left his face, and
some of the healthy colour returned. She noticed it
with relief for she wanted to know what he intended
doing. As if reading her thoughts he suddenly started
briskly to his feet, and beckoned to the usher standing
near. the door. He took out half-a-crown, also his
card. He wrote quickly on the back of it, and gave
them both to the man.

"Take that to Miss Marguerite Joy when her act is
finished," he said. "I'll wait here for an answer."

The man nodded and opened the door slightly. As
he did so a burst of laughter filtered through.

"She's still on," he said. "Ten minutes or so
yet."

Helen bit her lips and tried to preserve
an outward appearance of calm, but Somerset
made no pretence at hiding his agitation. He
took out a cigar, lit it, and immediately
threw it away again, and walked restlessly up
and down the corridor. The usher threw him a re-
proachful glance when he saw the wasted cigar. He
deplored the wastefulness of these elderly men. At
last, it seemed like hours to the two people waiting, he
opened the door again, beckoned to another man to
take his place and then disappeared. He was back

within five minutes, and Helen felt faint and sick as he came to them.

"Will you come with me?" he said. "Miss Joy was expecting to see you."

They followed him in silence. Through the theatre again and down the narrow dark stairs leading from the circle to the stage floor. They skirted the out-skirts of the stage, walking very softly. It was dark and very dreary. A few men in shirt sleeves sat about on boxes, but there was no other sign of life. Perhaps the notice-boards reading, "SILENCE" and "NO SMOKING" had a deadening effect. Where was the gay and vicious spectacle that fancy paints so lightly as belonging to life behind the scenes? It simply wasn't there. Everyone they met seemed bent on the serious business of life.

They passed some very dilapidated dressing rooms with numbers on them. The usher paused at the door of a slightly larger room than any of the others, and knocked softly. The door was opened by a woman, who, when she saw them, came out into the passage and half-closed the door behind her.

"Mr. Somerset, is it?" she asked. "Oh, that's all right then. Miss Joy did not want to see anyone else to-night and I must make sure."

She stepped back to let them pass, and closed the door after them as they went in. As they entered, Helen closed her eyes for a moment. She could not believe that she was really going to see her mother. She was in some strange fantastic dream, and in a little while she would wake up.

The room was sparsely furnished. There was a small sofa under the window, two shabby easy chairs, and another chair in front of the dressing table. At the back of this table was an enormous mirror lit up at the top and bottom by four electric lights, which blazed into the glass. On the table was a varied assortment of powders, rouges, and grease paints. Thrown carelessly on the chairs, on the floor, were huge masses of flowers. Their perfume mingled strangely with that of the heavily-scented powders.

Nailed up on the walls was a haphazard collection
of photographs.   For years past everyone who had
occupied this room had put up a photograph before
leaving.   They stared down from the wall now.
Some in tights, some dressed as clowns, some as harle-
quins, columbines.   Men dressed as women, women
dressed as men.   They were a motley company.   They
smiled, grimaced and postured.   Some of them were
old now, forgotten by a world that very easily forgets.
Others had been dust for ten—twenty years, and
their foolish songs and gestures silenced for ever.

As they entered the woman who was seated at the
dressing table, turned her head.   Her eyes flew to
Helen first and then she looked at Somerset.   The
three of them were silent.   Then she rose.

"Yes, it's Jimmy," she said, and Helen heard the
same musical voice she had heard from the stage.
"Dear old Jimmy!   And not a bit changed either,
excepting for the baldness and the—what shall we say
—extra stoutness."

She laughed a little, but though she spoke to him
her eyes were on Helen.   He took her hand and
kissed it humbly, and she touch him lightly on the
head as he bent over it.

"You haven't forgotten me, then?   It's been a
long time, Jimmy."

"Yes," he said brokenly.   "A very long time."

He dropped her hand and turned to Helen.

"You know who this is?"

"Yes," she said slowly.   "I know."

Helen looked up at her.   She was still beautiful
though her face showed the ravages of time.   She
looked as though she had lived intensely.   Helen
could not believe yet that this woman was really her
mother.   The unfamiliarity of her surroundings depressed her, and the careless luxuriance of her mother's
appearance intimidated her.   She did not know
what to do or say.   Her uncle looked pained.   He
had expected the moment of meeting between mother
and daughter to be an emotional and touching scene.
Their quietness disappointed him.   He remembered

Helen's outburst against her mother previously, and he wondered if she were feeling like that now.

"Helen," he said anxiously, "haven't you anything to say to your mother?"

Before Helen could answer, her mother had interposed. "Don't bother her now, Jim. She has not got used to the idea of me yet. Remember I am still a stranger."

She took the flowers off one of the chairs and motioned to him to sit down. Then she sat down herself on the sofa. She smiled at Helen, and Helen came over and sat down beside her. When she did so her mother put her arm around her.

Helen could feel the warm strong pressure of her arm, and she found that she liked it. For a little while Helen sat very erect and then she gradually relaxed until at last her head lay against her mother's breast. She kept it there for the resting place was so warm and soft. Under her ear, it seemed, she could hear the beating of her mother's heart. How loud it was—almost like the steady beating of a drum. So it had done its work from the hour of birth, and so it would do its work until the hour came when it ceased for ever. She wondered if her father had ever lain like this and listened to the beating of that heart.

Her mother looked down at her and gently touched her hair. Then she looked up at Somerset.

"Well, Jimmy, you forestalled me. I only came across from Sydney to-day, and on Monday I intended coming to see you. Is the office still at the same place?"

"Yes. I kept it on just the same after Arthur gave it up. You know that he is—dead?" he asked with an effort.

She nodded carelessly. "I heard by chance a year ago. I came then as soon as I could. Jimmy, I'm so tired, so dreadfully tired of everything. I think I've been tired for years. I wanted a rest, but I could not rest over there. I had to keep on with what I was doing. I was so tangled up, I couldn't get free."

"What are you going to do?" he asked.

"When this season is over I'm going to stop here. I want my—." She looked at Helen and smiled faintly. "She's like me, Jimmy, and not very like her father. I'm glad of that."

"Margaret, remember he is dead, and that you—you hurt him."

"I know that, but I can't forget that he hurt me also. Tell me—I don't suppose he forgave me?"

He shook his head gravely. "I don't know," he replied. "I did not see him for years before his death. He cut himself off from all of us. In fact, I did not even know where he was living."

She sighed and seemed to droop a little as though she were disappointed.

"I'm sorry he did not forgive me," she said, "but still I didn't expect it. He was hard and bitter. I don't think he would ever have forgiven an injury to him." She gave a little bitter laugh. "Jimmy, do you remember how I loved him once, when we were first married? What a child I was, what an infant, what a fool!" She spoke with passionate contempt. "He could have done anything with me if he had liked. I remember your wife used to think it was positively indecent the way I loved him. Well, she was right, perhaps. It did not last long, and so—it happened."

He was looking at her miserably, and as she saw how unhappy she was making him, she stopped.

"I'm sorry, Jim. We won't talk about it any more. Let it go at that."

She bent down and kissed Helen on the cheek. "You're coming home with me to-night," she said.

Helen stirred and raised her head quickly. "To-night?" she repeated. "Do you really want me to come to-night?"

"Why, of course. You did not think I was going to let you go away, now that I have found you. You must come to my hotel."

Somerset got up quickly. "Margaret," he said, "there is something I must ask you. I don't like doing it, but you understand I feel a responsibility towards this girl."

Her face hardened slightly. "Well, what is it?" she said sharply.

"I must ask you this question, Margaret. It's my duty."

"A lot of unpleasant and often impertinent questions are asked in the name of duty. However, I give you absolution before you start, just because you are dear old Jimmy, who used to be so fond of me. But I will allow questions from no one else."

He flushed a little. "I still am fond of you. What I want to' ask you is this—are you—." He hesitated again, and then made another effort. "I can't allow you to take Helen with you unless you are alone."

She laughed mockingly. "Remember my daughter is listening to you."

He looked at Helen moodily. "She knows!"

"Does she?" She put her finger under Helen's chin and raised her face to hers. "Arthur told her, I suppose. Well, I expected that. He swore he would and he was always a man of his word. However, James, you need not be alarmed. You may safely leave Helen in my care. I would not have suggested taking her with me, if, as you so tactfully put it, I had not been alone."

"That's all right then," he muttered. "But you understand, I hope. I had to make sure."

"Of course I understand, you silly old boy. I will take Helen with me to-night and we will arrange about the future afterwards. Now you must be going, I'm afraid. I want to finish dressing and it is late. Just put your head out in the passage and give my maid a call. She will be somewhere about."

He did as she asked, and then came back to take his leave of her. She put her arms on his shoulder and smiled into his eyes.

"You have forgiven me, I know."

"I never had anything to forgive," he said, thickly.

"Even if you had, you would forgive." She kissed him suddenly, and went with him to the door. Helen watched him go, and realized that he had quite forgotten her existence.

CHAPTER VIII.

HELEN'S MOTHER.

After her uncle had gone, Helen sat very still and silent watching her mother dress. When they had come in she had still been in the dress she had worn on the stage, with her white gleaming shoulders and arms bare. Helen could see her reflection in the mirror and the sober-faced woman who tended her so deftly. Helen experienced that strange sense of unreality. She felt almost as though she were not there—someone else had taken her place, and she herself was standing off, watching. And Helen watched with a curious, impersonal detachment. She had not yet adjusted herself to what had happened. She knew the woman she was looking at and who smiled at her in the glass was really her mother. There could be no doubt about that. Even she could see the strange likeness that existed between them. But she could not feel it. She remembered how, as a girl, she had longed to see her mother. The castles in the air she had built, the pictures she had formed. Now that the time she used to dream of had really come, she could not feel anything at all. Nothing, except that they were strangers, and that love does not spring up at a moment's notice. It must have something to feed on, something tangible to cling to. For years Helen had had nothing but a picture and a bundle of old love-letters which she was afraid to read.

"Ready, little daughter?" asked her mother, laying a hand on her shoulder.

She gathered up some of the flowers lying about, and told the maid to bring the rest with her. Then they went out through the long, dark passages to the stage door. Here, contrary to all romantic stories, no eager young men gathered round the door to strew with flowers the path of the stage favorite. There was merely an extremely dirty doorkeeper with an unshaven face, who wished them a surly good-night. A taxi was waiting outside for them. They got in and were driven quickly away.

By this time Helen had given up any will of her own. She was just accepting things as they came without question. She made no attempt to speak, but leant back in her corner and stared out at the pageant of life that passed before her like figures seen in a moving picture show.

The theatres and the picture theatres were just out, and the streets were full of a multitude of people who hurried and jostled each other in their desire to catch the last trains. The trams moved slowly through the streets, clanging their bells impatiently, the gripmen muttering imprecations. Motor cars and cabs manoeuvred among the crowd. Near the station the man selling hot pies raised his raucous voice. The fire burnt under the boiler and sent a red glare across the footpath. Three boys had bought pies and were standing round the cart eating them, the gravy trickling down between their fingers. The newspaper boys were still crying out the contents of the evening papers. Some of them sold another paper whose shocking headlines disclosed a world of shameful sin and horror. The hotels were just closing, and the last few stragglers staggered into the street. In the quieter and darker parts of the town, furtive-eyed women watched for their prey.

As they passed up the Collins Street hill away from the light and movement, Helen turned her head and looked at her mother. She found that her eyes were fixed on her. Helen smiled faintly and timidly. At her smile her mother leant forward and took her hand in hers.

"I was looking at you," she said. "You looked so —grave. What a silent child you are."

Helen's hand trembled. "It is because I cannot believe that this is happening. I seem to be in a dream. Are you really my mother?"

"I suppose it is hard for you to believe," said her mother wistfully. "It is my fault. I could not wonder if you hate me. I have always feared facing you, my child."

"Oh, don't!" said Helen, tremulously. "Don't!" She saw that her mother's eyes were wet. She kissed her mother very softly and lightly on the cheek.

The taxi stopped in front of the hotel and a liveried porter sprang to open the door. Helen could not help noticing that as they went through the lounge her mother seemed to change. She was conscious that people were looking at her, and she was deliberately acting for their benefit. She became the woman Helen had seen for a few minutes on the stage. The woman who had smiled down at her from the advertisement poster. She held the roses she carried to her face and smiled over them. The men in the room sprang to their feet and bowed, while the women stared. She smiled graciously at them again, and passed slowly through the room, followed by Helen, whose bright eyes saw everything. The whispered comments of the women, the bold stare of some of the men, and their efforts to attract her mother's attention to themselves. She could not help admiring her mother's *sang froid*—the smile that included everybody and favoured none.

They entered a large, luxuriously-furnished room, showing all the evidences of hasty travel. Trunks of all sizes stood about the floor, some of them still corded and thickly plastered with the labels of railway stations and hotels in all parts of the world. Others were open and the contents scattered carelessly about. As they stood looking at the confusion the maid came hurriedly in and began to gather the things together. Margaret Somerset stopped her.

"Leave them for to-night," she said. "You must be tired. You had better go to bed."

"Very well, madame. Is there nothing I can do for you before I go?"

"No, not to-night." The maid turned away, but as she got to the door, Margaret Somerset called her back again.

"By the way, Alice, this is my daughter."

The woman looked at Helen gravely, and then smiled. "I guessed that," she said. "I am glad you are with your mother again, miss." With a bow that included them both she silently disappeared.

Margaret turned to Helen. "I have had her with me for years," she said. "She has been a very good friend to me."

"She seems fond of you," said Helen rather awkwardly.

"And when are you going to get fond of me," asked her mother suddenly.

"Me?" faltered Helen, taken by surprise. "I—"

"I can't expect it yet, I know, but soon, my child, soon. I want you to love me. I came back just to see you. Come, talk to me. Tell me all you have been doing since you were taken away from me."

She sank down amongst the cushions of the big divan, and drew Helen down beside her, putting her arm round her shoulders.

"Lean against me," she said softly, "like you did before. When you laid your head on my breast, so simply and naturally, it was just as though you had been born again. I felt you were again my little child, the child you were before—Oh, well!" she interrupted herself with a sigh. "We won't talk about that. Tell me everything that has happened to you. You are the only thing in the whole world that I love."

Helen's heart stirred within her. A little spark of love had flamed into life. She raised her eyes and looked into her mother's face, and as she looked it seemed to her that she saw her now for the first time. The mouth was soft and tender, and the dark eyes looked lovingly into hers. On a sudden impulse Helen threw her arms round her neck and kissed her.

"I love you," she said. "Oh! I am so glad you are my mother."

Margaret Somerset listened to the story of her daughter's Odyssey with a white, strained face. She did not speak or interrupt her, only when Helen told her how she came home and found the body of her dead father, her hand tightened on Helen's arm.

"That's all, Mother," said Helen, when she had finished, "and so you see me. Why! what's the matter?"

For Margaret Somerset had risen quickly and had thrown herself down by the side of the bed, her face buried in her hands. Helen followed her, infinitely distressed.

"Don't cry, Mother," she said. "It's horrible to see you cry. I am sorry I told you now. Really there is no reason why you should be unhappy about me. My life has been interesting. I wouldn't have had it different. Really, I wouldn't."

Margaret raised her head and looked at Helen, trying to smile through her tears. "It's remorse, my dear," she said with a little laugh. "Your mother is feeling remorseful. That's the first time for many long years. I'm such a stranger to the feeling that I hardly recognised it." She rose to her feet again. "Well, it is no use weeping over what is past and gone. You shall come to me and I will look after you now. I don't want you to do any work again."

"But, Mother," protested Helen. "I want to work. I can't live on you."

"Nonsense, my dear. I have plenty of money for both of us."

This was not in the least what Helen wanted, but she soon found that it was no use protesting. If her mother wanted to do anything, she did it, and no arguments that Helen could raise had the slightest effect on her. She took Helen on a wild shopping expedition, when to Helen's inexperienced mind she seemed to spend hundreds of pounds on clothes both for herself and Helen. When the things came home, her mother insisted that she should try everything on. Remonstrances were of no avail. Her mother and the maid spent a perfectly happy afternoon, and Helen a very uneasy one. She did not like being treated as a doll. She looked at herself ruefully in the glass after they had dressed her in what the maid described as the "gem of the lot."

"Is it really me?" she asked doubtfully. "I don't think I like myself."

"You ungrateful girl," said her mother. She looked at her critically. "How do you think she looks, Alice?" she asked.

"Like your daughter, madame," replied the woman.

Margaret smiled swiftly. She always responded to flattery.

"You are pretty, Helen," she said, "but not as pretty as your mother was when she was a girl. Oh, take them off," she added with a sudden change of tone. "I'm tired."

"Not as tired as I am," said Helen quickly, for she saw her mother was suffering from a reaction of feeling. "You wicked woman, you keep me standing for hours and hours trying on silly dresses, and then you say that you are tired. What about me? How tired must I be feeling?"

Margaret had thrown herself into a chair before the mirror and was staring at herself with gloomy eyes. She was subject to these fits of despondency, when the sight of herself moved her to abject despair. Helen had soon learnt to know and dread these moods. Her mother would mourn over what she called the wreck of her life if she discovered or fancied she had discovered a faint line in her face.

"Of course, I make up all right," she said, looking at herself closely, "but I can't stand the strong light, not like you, Helen."

"Oh, Mother," said Helen, "you are naughty. You know you are." She sat on the edge of the table and shut the mirror away from her sight. "You are beautiful, you know that quite well, you naughty thing. You only want to hear me say so. Doesn't she, Alice? Everybody raves about you, and who does that for me? Why, nobody. Who do the people come here to see? Me? No, certainly not! They would not come over the road to see me. I walk along in the reflected glory of my mother. Do you know what people say to me? 'Oh, is Marguerite Joy your mother? How charming! Isn't she perfectly sweet? Do you think you could get her autograph for me?' Nobody ever wants my autograph, but they use me as a medium for getting yours." She took her by the hands. "Come along, little Mother. You must lie down and have a rest, or the gods will be calling in vain for you to-night."

Helen never went to the front of the house while her mother was on the stage. Though neither spoke about it to the other, they nevertheless understood one another. Helen knew that her mother did not wish that she should see her again on the stage, and Helen herself shrank from doing so. She usually went down to the theatre with her and waited behind until she came off. It was in this way that she became familiar with the lives of the careless, good-natured people of the stage. Many wonderful histories were confided to her keeping, and, though she suspected that some of them were not strictly true, they were none the less entertaining for that. Every dancer she met was a potential Genèè or Pavlova. Every singer a Melba or Caruso. Every comedian another Harry Lauder or George Robey.

Strange and varied was the philosophy of life she heard. They soon discovered that she liked to listen while they talked, for Helen loved them all for the almost childlike simplicity of their hearts. Dreadful stories of suffering and disillusion were told to her casually, for pain and disillusion are soon forgotten in the hurried life of the stage.

In spite of all the jealousy that existed there was yet a kind of freemasonry that bound them together. If another professional was in want he would never appeal in vain to any of his fellows. Their last coin would be gladly shared. Their money was hardly earnt and easily spent. In many cases the greater part of it went for other things than their own needs. Their careless generosity knew no bounds. They asked no inconvenient questions. It was enough that one of the "pros," one of themselves, was in need of their help. They had a code of morals of their own, and the highest virtue of all was to stand by one another.

Margaret Somerset's season was drawing to a close. She had taken a flat overlooking Collins Street and she was living there until she had made up her mind what she intended doing. One day she told Helen they were going to England, the next that they would stay in Melbourne. Helen had given up trying to make any plans for she knew now that, even if her mother approved of them, the chances were that in an hour or so she would have changed her mind.

Helen had given up her own rooms. She had only kept the things she valued and given the furniture away to Ann, who had at last achieved her independence of the boarding-house. Many of Helen's books her mother recognised, and she had looked with a sigh and a smile at her own picture. Helen had told her how she had found it amongst her father's things, and this seemed to please her. After a great deal of thought and with great diffidence, Helen had brought out the bundle of letters she had found. She gave them to her mother, telling her what they were. Margaret took the bundle, looking at it curiously.

"My letters," she said. "How strange." She fingered it thoughtfully. "I wonder," she said slowly. "Shall I open them? I have almost forgotten what they are."

She hesitated, and then with a decisive gesture, tore away the paper in which they were wrapped. She opened one out very slowly, while Helen walked to the other side of the room. She felt that she did not want to look at her mother while she read the words she had written so long ago. There was silence for a moment or so, and then she heard her mother give a stifled cry. Helen turned quickly round. The letters were lying scattered over the floor except for one which her mother held tightly clasped in her hand.

"What a horrible thing dead love is," she said in a low voice. She seemed to be talking to herself. "Am I really the woman who wrote these? Oh, how horrible!" She shuddered violently. "Take them away."

Helen knelt down and gathered the letters together. She unclasped the one in her mother's hand and she let it go without protest. A fire burnt in the grate for the days were turning cold. Helen dropped the letters one by one into the fire, watching them crumble into black ashes. She glanced over her shoulder at her mother, and found that she was watching attentively what she was doing. As soon as the last one had caught the flame, flared up for a moment, and then died away, Margaret Somerset got up and left the room.

With her head leaning on her hand Helen stared into the red heart of the fire. A procession of events passed before her. All the people she had ever known smiled to her, beckoned, or passed her by with averted eyes. There were four people who stood out from the others—four people who had affected her life most, Her father, her mother, Alick and George. George! He was never distant from her thoughts for long. He was always at the back of her mind, even when she was thinking of other things. Now that the first excitement of her mother's return had evaporated and she had plenty of time on her hands, her mind dwelt with a dreadful persistence on the words she had to say to him. Many people came to the flat in the afternoons to see her mother, and Helen, while talking to them, would forget. Then suddenly, perhaps in the middle of a sentence, she would remember. Immediately her smile would become forced and strained, and her attention begin to wander. The people round her seemed like the merest shadows of a dream. The sword of Damocles was hanging over her head. Already the writing was on the wall. She felt that she, too, would be weighed in the balance and found wanting.

A coal dropped noisily into the fender, and roused

her from her thoughts. The afternoon light was waning, and dark shadows were creeping into the room. Alice came in briskly, switching on the lights as she did so. She brought some letters just come by the last post. One of them was from George. Helen opened it quickly. He would be back in a week's time. She felt that the sword had already fallen.

CHAPTER IX.

HELEN PAYS THE PRICE.

The autumn days, with their soft tones of red, yellow and brown, had gone. Winter had set in with torrential rains and bitterly cold winds. Helen chafed at the enforced inaction. Only by walking could she ease the restlessness of spirit that possessed her. From her window she watched the passers-by running for the shelter of the nearest verandah, the overflowing gutters, the rain dripping from the bare branches of the trees. It looked inexpressibly dreary, but not half so dreary and forlorn as Helen felt.

The night before George's arrival, she was particularly restless. It had been raining heavily all day, but in the evening it cleared up and a pale moon shone fitfully through the watery clouds. Helen prepared to go out. Her mother did not like her to wander at night by herself, but she was at the theatre, so Helen could go without question. She hurried out into the street, buttoning her thick fur coat close to her neck. She had been alarmed at the price of it when her mother bought it for her, and privately thought it was waste of money, but now she appreciated it. A south wind whipping up from the sea brought the tears to her eyes, but she bent her head to it, and nestled her chin down into the depths of the warm, soft fur. She walked quickly through town, across the bridge and along the river path. It was quite deserted save for one man who passed her going towards town. His hands were thrust into his pockets and his eyes were fixed on the ground. He was muttering to himself. Helen felt that he was unhappy. She wanted to stretch out her hand and touch him, telling him that she too was unhappy, and that they belonged to the same community of despair. But convention was too strong for her. She could not follow the impulse of her heart. He passed her without seeing her.

She walked to the end of the long avenue, and then turned back again. She opened her coat at the neck, for the quick walk had made her hot, and let it swing open, lifting her face to the wind. The exercise had done her good, and by the time she reached town again, her cheeks were glowing and her eyes sparkling. She hoped to get home before her mother, and so save the necessity of explanations.

She had almost reached their door when she noticed a woman standing half-hidden by one of the trees that line the pavement. Helen stopped suddenly. The woman had looked at her as she passed. It was only the glance of a second and then she had looked with a certain hungry expression in her eyes at a man who was walking down the street. Helen took two or three steps forward and then she paused again. She felt her warm fur coat, and thought of the luxurious room she was going back to. Then she turned and looked again at the woman.

She wore a skirt and a white silk blouse, open at the throat, and her bare arms showed red through the thin silk. She held her hands to her breast, clasping them together as though seeking warmth. Her face was heavily rouged, the lips painted a bright scarlet in a ghastly travesty of beauty. Under the paint her cheeks were thin and haggard, yet she seemed young. Though the eyelashes and eyebrows were blackened, youth looked out of the clear blue eyes.

Helen might have gone on but there was something terribly tragic in the way in which the girl held her hands to her breast. She looked so cold—so utterly defenceless against the bitter wind. So Helen went back.

The girl stared at her. She did not seem pleased to see her. She was not used to women speaking to her in the street, and she could not understand it.

"What do you want?" she asked hoarsely.

"Will—will you come and have a cup of coffee with me?" asked Helen timidly.

"Look here," said the girl suspiciously, "what's your game? You needn't try the converting line with me, because it won't act."

"Oh, no," replied Helen hastily, to reassure her. "Why should I want to do that? I only want you to come and have something warm to drink. You look so cold."

The girl burst into a hoarse laugh. "You're a queer sort. Can't afford it, my dear. I haven't the time. Time's money to me, you know."

"I will give you money," said Helen eagerly. She opened her purse and looked in. She had two sovereigns and some silver. She drew out the sovereigns and offered them to the girl rather diffidently. "That is all I have. I hope it is enough?"

The girl burst again into her hoarse laugh. "More than I can earn, my dear." She took them hastily, evidently afraid that Helen might change her mind, and tied them up securely in the corner of a very dirty handkerchief.

"You are a queer one," she repeated, giving Helen a sidelong glance of the greatest astonishment. "What are you after, anyway? You can't be one of the Bible-banging sort, for they're not too keen on giving money away."

"I'm after nothing," replied Helen. "I only want to talk to you. Come with me."

"Have it your own way, of course," said the girl, following her obediently. "You've paid for it."

They went into a small café, and as the girl seemed to be hungry, Helen ordered coffee and toast, and everything else that she seemed to take a fancy to. A haughty waitress with a superior manner served them. She looked at Helen's companion with immeasurable scorn.

"If she looks at me like that again," said the girl audibly, as the waitress left them, "I'll hit her in the eye."

"Oh, no; you mustn't do that," said Helen hastily. "You see, she doesn't understand.'

"I'll make her understand," muttered the girl, attacking her toast with zest. "I've met her kind before, and I've seen them come to a sticky end."

Helen watched the girl with reflective eyes. She thought of herself, of her own life, and then of this girl. Wherein lay the difference? What Fate was it that ruled their lives so differently? What kind of Fate could it be that allowed her to walk the pleasant paths of life, and condemned this girl to stand shivering in the street. A woman at the back of them laughed. Helen looked round with a frown. She found that everyone in the room was staring at them. She looked at them with bitter scorn. She hated them for their smug complacency. She felt neither love, liking, or even pity for the girl she was with, but she preferred her to the smug suburban women with their intolerable air of conscious virtue. She turned her back on them, and faced her companion squarely so that she was almost hidden from sight.

The girl was too interested in her supper to notice anything else. While Helen was consumed with indignation, she went on quietly with her coffee and toast, and when she had finished that, licked her fingers clean, and started with unabated vigor on some cream-cakes that she had ordered.

Helen could not help smiling as a sudden thought struck her. "Do you know?" she asked, leaning forward, "that a very great man once said you were one of the saviours of the world?"

The girl paused with the cream-cake half way to her mouth and gazed at Helen in the blankest amazement.

"Go on," she said at last, placing her teeth firmly in the soft, squashy cake, "I'm no bally saviour. Not for me, thank you."

"I suppose there is nothing in being one of the saviours of the world unless you can feel it yourself?"

"Eh?" said the girl, her mouth open a little.

"There is another thing, too. Why should you be chosen to save the world? What have you done that you should occupy that exalted position? Why should you be the saviour of me, for instance, and those other women," she nodded round the room, "who since you came in have looked at you so insolently? If you are indeed the saviour of the world, we should put a statue to you, make a saint of you, fall down and worship you. There should be no end to the honors we should shower upon you."

"Look here," said the girl, leaning forward confidentially, "do you know what's the matter with you? You're a bit balmy, touched you know." She tapped her forehead significantly.

Helen laughed. "No, I'm not," she said. "I'm angry, that's all. I can't get over the monstrous unfairness of life, the matchless hypocrisy of people. Why should you have to walk the streets shivering with cold, while I go about in a fur coat? I'm no better than you. These women are no better than you. We all sell ourselves for something, only you are more honest about it.

She paused, shrugged her shoulders, and rose from the table. "You have finished, I think," she added quietly. "We had better be going."

"I hope you will go straight home," she said abruptly when they got outside. "Good-bye."

She hurried off, leaving the girl staring after her in perplexity. She looked uncertainly up and down the street, and then sloughed off in the opposite direction.

George came the next day about three o'clock. He knew where to find her for Helen had written to him and told him of her meeting with her mother. It was Wednesday and her mother was at a matinee performance, so Helen was alone. He came in with quick, decided steps, eager to see her and sure of his welcome. His cheeks were ruddy through the tan. He looked as though he had just come from a long ride on horse-back, instead of a train journey of over six hundred miles. Helen rose when he entered and stood with one hand resting on the table. She was very pale, and that was the first thing George noticed.

"Why, Nelly," he said, coming towards her with outstretched hands. "You look ill. What have you been doing to yourself. You want me to look after you, that's evident."

He put his arm around her waist and, stooping, kissed her cheek. She did not raise her eyes or move, but stood quite rigid in his embrace.

"What is it, dear?" he asked. "Aren't you well? Tell me."

She did not reply, but her lips twitched a little. A line was going through and through her mind. "Canst thou minister to a mind diseased?" She wished she could forget it. The repetition worried her, and she wanted to listen to George.

"Nelly dear," he said reproachfully, "this is a nice way to greet me! Haven't you anything to say? Wait a moment though —" his face broke into a beaming smile. "I've got something to show you."

"No, George," said Helen suddenly, drawing herself away from him. "Don't show it to me, not yet until —"

"Until what?" asked George. He paused with his hand in his pocket, waiting for her to finish the sentence.

"Until I tell you something."

"What is it?" he asked anxiously. "I say, you don't mean to tell me your mother doesn't want me to marry you?"

"I haven't told her anything about you, because— well, I had to see you first."

She sat down in a chair by the fire and pointed to one opposite.

"Sit there," she said, "there where I can see you."

He obeyed, though with an air of humoring her.

He was quite satisfied to wait until she had finished and then—he thought of what he had in his pocket for her, and his eyes smiled. Helen watched him for a few moments before she spoke again. He was sitting in a straight-backed chair, his legs crossed, and his strong, brown hands lightly resting on the arms. There had been a cushion on the chair but he had thrown it aside. With a little pang she remembered how George had always disdained cushions. He said they were not manly. He had kept so many of his boyish traits.

He looked across at her and smiled. ''Well, what's the great secret? Hurry up or I'll come over, lift you out of that chair and smother you with kisses. You know you owe me a lot of them.''

''How gladly I would pay all I owe you, if it were in my power,'' she said in a low voice, ''but—but—'' She hesitated, and then added with a passion of feeling in her voice. ''George, you must believe I love you. Whatever happens you must believe that. No, don't you get up.'' For he had risen. ''Stay where you are. I haven't nearly finished yet.''

There was a little frown between his brows as he sat down again. He was puzzled by her manner.

''Look here, Nelly,'' he said. ''What's up?''

''George, take your mind back to the time you went away. I was only a girl and so inexperienced —how could I know whether I really loved you or not. I missed you at first. I know I was unhappy —Oh! for quite a long time. Then the memory of you began to fade. You seemed to have passed out of my life altogether. Of course, I knew you had not, but it seemed like that.''

''I wrote to you,'' he interrupted.

''You wrote—yes! But somehow your letters never brought you to me—they seemed such dead things. I used to read them and think you did not care.''

''But you knew, Nelly. You must have known how I felt. Anyway, what's the use of going through all this? You say you love me. You know I love you. That is all that matters."

"Oh George, if it only were. If I could believe that love was the only thing that mattered. But it isn't. I've got to be honest with you. Not because I particularly want to, but because I can't help myself."

She leant forward, her chin resting on her hand, the firelight playing on her features, and sparkling in her red-gold hair. "Listen, last year I was so happy, so perfectly happy. Life seemed so full of possibilities, so—so adventurous. If you had only come back last year! But you did not. Instead of you I met someone else—someone who—who loved me." She said the last words very softly.

He bit his lip nervously. "But you love me," he said.

"If you will only believe that!" Her lips were pale, and as she raised her hand to brush aside a curl of hair that had fallen across her eyes, her hand trembled. "I don't know now whether I fell in love with him, or what it was possessed me, but George, that man was—"

She stopped and looked at him piteously, begging him mutely to help her. He met her eyes steadily and she could not read his thoughts.

"Go on," he said, very quietly.

She shrank back in her chair, so that he could not see her face. "I can't go on," she whispered. "I can't say it. I thought I could, but I can't. Not to you, George. But—you can guess."

He came and stood over her. It seemed to her that he towered above her. He took her hands in his and held them so tightly that she winced with the pain.

"What was he to you? Tell me."

She did not answer him, and he repeated again. "Tell me. I insist!"

Helen rose to her feet. She looked at him unflinchingly. "Very well, then. He was my lover."

He stared into her eyes. His face looked grim

and hard. Then he laughed, but it was not a pleasant sound. "And you say you love me. Lies —lies, all lies. Why don't you go to your lover?"

He flung her hands from him and walked to the window, standing with his back to her. "Where is this man?" he asked at last, without looking round.

"He has gone away."

He turned quickly at that. "Did he desert you?"

"No. He went because I would not marry him."

"But—Good God! I don't understand."

"George, I can't explain. It's no use asking me. It just happened, and there seemed no reason why I should not drift with the tide. I know you can't understand—how could I expect you to to? But there is one thing you must believe. That man has gone out of my life for ever. I know how utterly false I must sound to you, but it is there, in my heart the strongest and best feeling I have, my love for you. Won't you believe that?"

He sat down and buried his face in his hands. "How can I believe you?" he muttered. "You are asking too much."

She stood looking at him tenderly, and then laid her hand very lightly on his bent head.

"George," she said softly, "before you came I was like a ship without a rudder, or a reed blown about in the wind. I did not know myself, or my own heart. I did not know what I wanted, except that I was seeking happiness. That seemed the greatest thing in the world. Then the rainbow bubble came along and I grasped it. It burst, and I knew there was nothing in it. But I had followed it such a long way, George, and it had looked so beautiful in the distance, that at first I would not let myself believe I had grasped nothing. Then you came back, George, and I saw all my follies and mistakes, and I could distinguish the true from the false. Look at me, George."

He raised a haggard face to hers.

"It was me you loved, George, me with all my

faults, though you did not know how great they were. If I could wipe the slate clean I would do it, but for your sake, only for yours. What I am now, I am, and you must accept it. If your love is greater than your pride, this will not be the end, and you will come back. If not—if you can't forgive, I will understand. I will belong to no other man but you. Whatever happens I am yours."

"Why didn't you wait?" he asked bitterly. "Was that too much to ask?"

"You think that I am spoilt for you," she said, "but, George, I'm not. I can love you better because of what—what went before."

He pressed his hands to his forehead with a gesture of pain. "I can't think," he muttered. "My mind is confused. I must get away. I must think it all out."

He rose and went blindly to the door, fumbling with the handle.

He leant his forehead against the panel of the door, seeking its coolness for his hot head, and a half-sob broke from his lips. The sound stabbed Helen to the heart.

"George," she said faintly. "Oh—George!"

He turned and took her fiercely in his arms, kissing her roughly. Then with an inarticulate exclamation he pushed her from him and went swiftly from the room. She could hear his footsteps echoing on the landing and the sharp peal of the bell as he rang for the lift. What little things people have to do at great crises—life was full of anticlimaxes, she thought bitterly.

She went to the piano and began turning the music over idly. If she did not do something she knew she would break down and her mother would soon be home. The door behind her opened again. She turned quickly. It was only her mother. She came in, bringing with her a bunch of purple violets. Their sweet perfume floated through the room.

"These are for you, Helen," she said. "One of your admirers at the theatre sent them."

Helen took them mechanically. She looked into their purple depths. She laid them down, for they were just the colour of George's eyes. She could see him looking at her again with that dreadful hurt expression.

"By the way," continued her mother, "who was that extremely rude young man I met in the vestibule downstairs. He brushed by me as though he was not aware of my existence. Alice told me he had been up to see you."

Helen started violently, turning to the piano again. She ran her fingers over the keys.

"That," she said in a muffled voice, "was a young man who could not stand the truth."

"You talk in enigmas, my child," said her mother lightly. She put her arm around Helen's neck.

"There is something troubling you. What is it?" she said softly.

"Nothing," answered Helen. "At least—," she kissed the white, scented hand, "nothing that you can help."

CHAPTER X

LOVE AND WAR.

Margaret Somerset had been ill. She said she had left the stage never to return; though knowing her mother, Helen doubted this. The doctor said she was suffering from a nervous breakdown, and for days Helen and the maid, Alice, nursed her between them. It was a painful time for Helen, for she felt that unwillingly she was spying on her mother. She would mutter in her sleep, and utter little sobbing cries that cut Helen to the heart. She spoke of people whom Helen had never heard of and sometimes, though not often, Helen heard her father's name.

As she got better she became quiet, and seemed content to lie with closed eyes. Through the long afternoons Helen sat by the bedside and watched her, listening to the slow ticking of the clock and the sounds that came from the building—the clicking of the lift as it rose from one floor to another; a strange voice heard; a vagrant laugh. Sometimes as she listened, waiting for she knew not what, the silence of the room frightened her. It was so still and yet it seemed alive—alive with all their thoughts.

She looked at her mother and she knew then what made her afraid. It was the aloneness of them all, the terrible aloofness of the spirit. Her mother lay with closed eyes, the heavy plait of hair hanging over her shoulder and her face turned away from the window. She seemed to be asleep, and yet Helen knew she was not. She was thinking. Helen could feel her thoughts, but she could not read them. She wondered at the closed mystery of her mother's life. All the memories she must carry in her heart, and that she could share with no one. She was alone.

Helen looked at Alice then. She was sitting at the other side of the room. Her hands were folded in her

338

lap, her eyes staring into vacancy. What was she thinking of? Her thoughts, too, filled the room. What was it that held her in thrall? What was that secret empire over which she alone had command? Her time belonged to her employers, but they had no power over her thoughts. They were hers alone.

"Strangers," Helen thought, "that is what we are, all strangers from one another. Those we love are strangers from us, even the one we love best. George and I, we too are strangers. I cannot help him nor he help me. What we have to suffer we must suffer alone. No one can help us."

She seemed to move through a terrible world—a world where everyone walked alone. There was George, she saw him afar off and he had to fight his battle alone. There was her mother with all her history wrapped up in her heart, her secret thoughts unknown. There was Alick too. She could think of him now without pain and without regret, but she could not help him. He had to walk alone.

Her mother moved restlessly and sighed. Helen bent forward and saw what was troubling her. A shaft of sunlight had fallen across her face. Helen remembered how she hated the strong light. She motioned to Alice and the blind was pulled down.

When she was better they went away for a time. She had been seized with a desire for perfect peace. She wanted to go somewhere where they would be quite cut off from the world, nothing else would satisfy her. Helen appealed to her uncle and he suggested that they should go to the Grampians. Once on a never-to-be-forgotten holiday he and some friends had spent a month wandering over these mountains. They had taken a tent and a store of food and for a month they had lived without seeing anyone, for the mountains are almost inaccessible to the ordinary tourist. He made all arrangements and a few days later they arrived. They stayed at an apple orchard on the slope of one of the mountains. Above them rose the dark serried masses of the mountains, below them lay the fertile plains of Western Victoria.   Here they lived for four weeks seeing neither letters nor newspapers.   Helen could almost have believed that they had died and were in another world so remote they seemed from everything that made up their ordinary life.   They left with regret, though both were secretly longing to get back to town. When they got back early in August it was to find that the whole world had burst into flame.

Then Helen knew that she would see George again. It might only be to say good-bye, but he would come. She knew it!   All through the terrible days that followed she waited.   The little flame of hope in her heart never flickered or died out, though the slow days passed and he did not come.   But she believed she would see him again, believed it as earnestly as though he himself had whispered across space to her. And one night in late October he did come.

She was sitting on the little balcony overlooking Collins Street, watching, as she loved to do, the light fade slowly from the sky, when suddenly she heard a voice she knew.   It came from the room that opened off the balcony.   She started to her feet and leant forward listening, her hand pressed to her breast. She heard her mother's voice and then his voice. They were talking together, but she could not hear what they were saying.   Then there was silence, but she still stood waiting.   The thing had happened that she knew would happen.

He stood outlined against the light, his figure blocking up the doorway.   When she saw him she could not speak, and her limbs trembled.   She faltered and would have fallen, but he dashed forward and caught her in his arms.   As he kissed her, she knew that he had forgiven.

"You are going then?" she said at last, raising her head and touching with her fingers the uniform he wore.

"Yes," he replied.   "We sail next week."

"Next week?" she sighed.   "So soon!"

"Yes, so soon.   And to think I've wasted five

months.   Nearly five months it is since I saw you, but it took me all that time to get my bearings."

"But you have come back," she whispered.   "That makes up for everything."

"I had to come, Nelly," he said simply.   "I could not stay away."

She sat down on the cane lounge, and he sat beside her.   She took his hand in hers and, as he spoke, stroked it softly with her fingers, laying his palm against her own.

"That day," he went on, "you remember?   When I left you—it seems years ago now—I hardly knew what I was doing.   I felt you had cheated me and I tried to believe I hated you.   Hated you!" he laughed softly, "as though I could hate you, but how hard I tried to believe it.   All the time I went about my work I had this feeling in me like an ugly wound that was hurting.   I could not forget it, it was always there.   Then Nelly I—" he hesitated, but only for a moment.   "I will tell you everything and we can start off square.   I went after other women.   I had some sort of feeling that I was revenging myself on you, and that I could forget you.   But it wouldn't act.   That's the sort of fellow I am, Nelly."

For reply she lifted his hand to her cheek, then kissed it softly.

"Then war broke out, and after that I seemed to change.   For the last few weeks I've been marching and thinking, thinking and marching, and at last I got it all clear.   I thought of what you said to me—'If your love is greater than your pride you will come back?'   That made me wonder whether it was my pride alone that was hurt.   If you loved me now, I thought, wasn't that the greatest thing.   One night I was on sentry-duty and—and you seemed to be very close to me, and I thought what a little time any of us have.   Such a little, little time to love and be happy, and I was wasting it, throwing it away.   Then I had to come back, for I knew that if we loved each other nothing else matters.   Nothing outside can affect us if we believe in one another."

"The greatest things in the world are love and truth and honor," said Helen. "We have found those three and we can face anything else. I love you. I don't know why. It's just there, and I can't help it. I would be happy anywhere with you. I don't seem to want to lead the ordinary civilised life with you. I would like to tramp the roads with you, our whole furniture slung over our backs. Or I remember something better. There's a dirty little ketch down at one of the docks. I used to see her there. I know she smells of tar and oil and fish. We'll take her and spend our lives sailing up and down the Bay."

"I believe you mean it," he said tenderly.

"I do, I do. Any sort of a life with you would make me happy, George. Even if it was only a hovel in a back street."

"It's your spirit I love," he said. "It's so brave. You're different from other women. When I come back we will be happy." He held her close in his arms, and he felt the sudden tremor that shook her. "What is it?" he asked.

"You are going away," she said slowly. "I had—forgotten."

"You would not have me stay behind?"

"No," she replied. "But—." She rose abruptly and went to the side of the balcony. She had forgotten that he was going, and she wanted to hide her sudden terror from him. He followed her and stood silently beside her, laying his hand over hers as it rested on the railing. He did not tell her, but for the time he too had almost forgotten that he had to go.

As she felt the touch of his hand Helen turned to him. "George," she said passionately. "Why is it? This war I mean. What is the meaning of it? Why has it come?"

"God knows," he answered. A silence fell between them, and then he added. "There is only one thing I know. A man has got to go."

"A man has got to go," she repeated slowly.

He put his arm around her and she leant her head

against his shoulder.   "I wouldn't say this to any-one but you, Nelly.   A fellow feels a fool if he talks patriotic stuff, but—well, I'm glad we belong to Britain."

"So am I," she said.

A girl's laugh floated up from the street below. People were strolling arm in arm, they laughed and whispered to one another.   The great buildings of the city rose black against the sky.   The electric lights blazed along the streets. At the big hotel across the road dinner was still on.   The two listeners could hear faint sounds of laughter, and then a band began to play.   Life flowed on the same as ever. Unafraid, they lived and laughed and loved.   Some-one who passed below carried a bunch of boronia.   Its sweetness filled the air and lingered long after the passer-by had vanished.

"George," said Helen.   "We have dreamt it all. There is no war.   See, everything is unchanged."

"A dream," repeated George.   "Look there."

She saw what he was pointing at.   A platoon of soldiers that marched steadily down the hill.

THE END.

VIRAGO MODERN CLASSICS

The first Virago Modern Classic, *Frost in May* by Antonia White, was published in 1978. It launched a list dedicated to the celebration of women writers and to the rediscovery and reprinting of their works. Its aim was, and is, to demonstrate the existence of a female tradition in fiction which is both enriching and enjoyable. The Leavisite notion of the 'Great Tradition', and the narrow, academic definition of a 'classic', has meant the neglect of a large number of interesting secondary works of fiction. In calling the series 'Modern Classics' we do not necessarily mean 'great' — although this is often the case. Published with new critical and biographical introductions, books are chosen for many reasons: sometimes for their importance in literary history; sometimes because they illuminate particular aspects of womens' lives, both personal and public. They may be classics of comedy or storytelling; their interest can be historical, feminist, political or literary.

Initially the Virago Modern Classics concentrated on English novels and short stories published in the early decades of this century. As the series has grown it has broadened to include works of fiction from different centuries, different countries, cultures and literary traditions. In 1984 the Victorian Classics were launched; there are separate lists of Irish, Scottish, European, American, Australian and other English speaking countries; there are books written by Black women, by Catholic and Jewish women, and a few relevant novels by men. There is, too, a companion series of Non-Fiction Classics constituting biography, autobiography, travel, journalism, essays, poetry, letters and diaries.

By the end of 1986 over 250 titles will have been published in these two series, many of which have been suggested by our readers.